The DEMON of DAKAR

Also by Kjell Eriksson

The Princess of Burundi

The Cruel Stars of the Night

The DEMON of DAKAR

Kjell Eriksson

Translated from the Swedish
by Ebba Segerberg

MINOTAUR BOOKS ■ NEW YORK

This is a work of fiction. All of the characters, organizations, and events portrayed in this novel are either products of the author's imagination or are used fictitiously.

A THOMAS DUNNE BOOK FOR MINOTAUR BOOKS.
An imprint of St. Martin's Publishing Group.

www.thomasdunnebooks.com
www.minotaurbooks.com

The Library of Congress has catalogued the hardcover edition as follows:

Eriksson, Kjell, 1953–
The demon of Dakar / Kjell Eriksson ; translated from the Swedish by Ebba Segerberg.—1st U.S. ed.
"First published in Sweden under the title Mannen från bergen by Ordfront" —T.p. verso.
p. cm.
ISBN-13: 978-0-312-36669-8
ISBN-10: 0-312-36669-8
1. Lindell, Ann (Fictitious character)—Fiction. 2. Women detectives—Sweden—Fiction. I. Title.
PT9876.15.R5155 D46 2008
839.73'8—dc22

2008003270

ISBN-13: 978-0-312-36670-4 (pbk.)
ISBN-10: 0-312-36670-1 (pbk.)

First published in Sweden as *Mannen från bergen* by Ordfront

First Minotaur Books Paperback Edition: July 2009

10 9 8 7 6 5 4 3 2 1

The DEMON of DAKAR

One

The clouds slid lazily down behind the mountain on the other side of the valley. The slender, bone-white streaks of mist that crept through the pass in the east, often during the late afternoon or early evening, ran together and formed white veils, sometimes intensely silver-colored, that were illuminated by the sun sinking behind the mountain peaks. The trees along the ridge stood out like soldiers in a shiny column that stretched farther than Manuel Alavez could imagine.

The clouds had been out in the world, down to the coast of Oaxaca to gather nourishment and moisture. Sometimes, for a change, they went north, to taste the zsaltiness of the Caribbean.

When they returned, the sides of the mountains were still damp and steaming, a hot breath exuding from the thick vegetation. The people and the mules that were only marginally larger than their loads inched their way down the paths toward the village, where the dogs greeted them with tired barks and the smoke rose from the brick-shingled rooftops burnished by the sun, shimmering in warm red tones.

The clouds shifted indolently closer to the mountain. Manuel imagined that they and the mountain exchanged fluids and then told each other what had happened during the day. Not that the mountains had more to report than some idle gossip from the village, but the clouds let themselves be satisfied with that. They craved a little everyday chatter after having sailed forth across a restless continent, marked by despair and hard work.

La vida es un ratito, life is a brief moment, his mother would say and display an almost toothless mouth in a little grin that both underscored and diminished her words.

Later he reformulated her expression to *La vida es una ratita,* life is a little rat, a little rodent.

Manuel, his mother, and his two brothers would look at the mountains from the terrace where they dried the coffee beans. From this vantage point they could look out over the sixty houses in the village.

A village among many, remote from everyone except themselves, about an hour away from the nearest larger road that would bring them to Talea and from there, after a five-hour bus trip, to Oaxaca.

The coffee was packed in some harbor, no one knew which one, and shipped to *el norte* or Europe. When the buyers loaded the sacks and shipped them away, the villagers lost control. They knew their coffee tasted good, and that the price would increase tenfold, perhaps twentyfold, before they found their consumer.

Manuel leaned against the cool airplane window, staring out into the crystal-clear Atlantic night, exhausted by the long trip from the mountains to Oaxaca and another seven-hour bus trip to the capital and then a half-day of waiting at the airport. It was the first time he was flying. The worry that he had felt had transformed into an amazement that he was now at eleven thousand meters.

A cabin attendant came by and offered coffee, but he said no. The coffee he had received earlier did not taste good. He watched the attendant as she served the passengers on the other side of the aisle. She reminded him of Gabriella, the woman he was going to marry. It was high time, his mother said. In her eyes he was old. It felt as if he had to marry her now. They had met several years ago, during his time in California, and they had kept in touch through letters. He had called a couple of times. She had waited for him, and this now felt to Manuel like a millstone. He did not have the heart to deny her what she had expected and been waiting for for so long: marriage. He loved her of course, at least he told himself he did, but he felt a growing anxiety about binding himself forever.

He fell asleep between two continents and immediately Angel appeared to him. They were out on a *milpa* where they were growing corn, beans, and squash. It was just before the corn harvest. His brother had stretched himself out in the shadow of a tree. He was in good spirits and laughing in that way that only he could, a clucking sound that appeared to come from his rounded belly. Angel was chubby and had been called *el Gordito* in his childhood.

Angel was telling him about Alfreda from Santa Maria de Yaviche, the neighboring village. They had met in February, during the fiesta, and Angel was describing her face and hair in great detail. He always took great care with the details.

Manuel stood up, unsettled by Angel's frivolous tone. The young woman was only seventeen.

"Make sure you don't lead her astray," Manuel said.

"She's the one leading me astray," Angel chuckled. "She is the one who makes me tremble."

"We have to get back," Manuel said.

"Soon," Angel said. "I'm not done yet."

Manuel couldn't help but smile. Angel could be a writer, he is so good at storytelling, he thought, and sat down again.

A couple of wild rabbits were tumbling about on the other side of the field. They jumped around carefree, curious, and playful, unaware of the hawk sailing in the sky.

"You are also a *conéju,* but life is not all play," Manuel said, regretting the words as he said them.

He was the oldest of the three brothers and all too often adopted the role of the responsible one, the one who had to scold and set them straight. Angel and their middle brother, Patricio, were always ready to laugh and dream up childish pranks. They fell in love as often and as quickly as frogs. They feared nothing and Manuel envied their optimism and frivolity.

Angel followed his brother's gaze, sighted the predatory bird that was slowly plummeting through the layers of air, raised his arms as if he were holding a rifle, aimed, and shot.

"Bang," he said, and looked laughingly at Manuel.

The latter smiled and lowered his head toward the ground. He knew the hawk would soon drop into a steep dive and he did not want to see if it was successful in its hunt.

"I missed, but the hawk has to live too," Angel said, as if he had read his brother's thoughts. "There are plenty of rabbits."

Manuel was suddenly irritated that Angel was speaking Spanish, but did not have time to correct him before he suddenly awakened, straightened, and glanced at the woman in the seat next to him. She was sleeping. Apparently he had not disturbed her when he startled.

Patricio was down there somewhere. Ever since Manuel had been informed of Patricio's fate he had alternated between anger, sorrow, and grief. The first letter consisted of three sentences: I live. I have been caught. I have been sentenced to eight years in prison.

The next letter was somewhat more detailed, factual and dry, but behind the words Manuel sensed hopelessness and desperation, feelings that came to dominate the subsequent letters.

Manuel could not imagine Patricio behind bars. He who had loved the open fields and always fixed his gaze as far away in the distance as possible. There was a stamina in Patricio that had always amazed Manuel and Angel. He was always prepared to take several more steps to see what was concealed behind the next curve, hill, or street corner.

Physically, he was the strongest of the brothers, roughly one hundred and eighty centimeters and therefore taller than most of the villagers. His height and posture, coupled with his eyes, had given him the reputation as a sensible man worth listening a little extra to. If Angel was the chatterbox who did not like to expend extra effort, then Patricio could be described as agile and taciturn, thoughtful in his speech, and restrained in his actions. Their laughter was really the only thing they shared.

Manuel had gleaned from his brother's letter that prisons in Sweden were completely different from those in Mexico, and he tried to make a great deal of the fact that they were allowed TVs in their cells, and that they could study. But what would he study? Patricio had never liked books. He was a person who had lived his life studying others and nature. He went about his work reluctantly, regardless of whether it was sowing, weeding, or harvesting. He wielded the machete as if it were an enemy in his hands. Despite his strength, his blows were often weak and without concentration.

"If you think I am going to remain a pathetic *campesino,* then you are mistaken," he repeated when Manuel reminded him that they had a tradition to uphold.

"I do not want to sit in the mountains like a *ranchero,* eating beans and tortillas, come down to the village once a week and drink myself silly on *aguardiente* and just get poorer and poorer. Can't you see that we are being cheated?"

Could he handle eight years of jail? Manuel feared for his brother's life and health. To Patricio, being locked up was essentially a death sentence. When Manuel wrote to say that he was coming to Sweden, his brother had immediately replied that he did not want any visitors. But Manuel did not care. He had to find out what had happened, how everything had evolved, how and why Angel had died, and how Patricio could have been stupid enough to get involved in something as dirty as drug smuggling.

As the plane descended through the clouds, banked, and went in for the landing, Manuel's thoughts returned to the mountains, his mother, and the coffee beans. How beautiful the beans were! When they had dried and lay in open, bulging jute sacks, wedged into every nook and cranny in the house, even next to their sleeping quarters, they invited his caress, and Manuel would slip his hand down into the strangely unscented beans and feel pure happiness filter through his fingers.

La vida es una ratita, he mumbled, making the sign of the cross and watching the foreign country spread out below him.

✦

Two

Slobodan Andersson laughed heartily. His face split into a wide grin that revealed his tobacco-stained teeth. They resembled wooden pegs that had been filed down into needle-sharp weapons.

Slobodan Andersson laughed often and as yappily as a little dog, yet he was not what one would call a happy sort.

His enemies, and they had grown in number over the years, would talk disparagingly of "the lying poodle." Slobodan did not appear to take offense. He would lift one leg and yap a little extra whenever someone reminded him of this nickname.

"The poodle," he would say, "is related to the wolf."

It was not only his face that was wide. All of him had swelled up over the past two decades, and he had an increasingly difficult task of maintaining the pace that had brought him both admiration and fear as a pub owner. What he had lost over the years in physical mobility he made up for in experience and a growing ruthlessness. He left people behind often perplexed and at times crushed, and he did this with an indifference that was not mitigated by any amount of laughter or backslapping.

His life's story, which barflies in the city loved to tell and embroider with amazing additions, was full of obscurities, and Slobodan liked to support this with a mixture of unusually detailed and drastic anecdotes from roughly thirty years in the business, alternated with vague statements that were left open to interpretation.

What one knew for certain was that he had a Serbian mother and a Swedish father, but no one knew if they still lived, and if so, where. Slobodan Andersson was silent on this point. He would talk about his childhood in Skåne, how, as a fifteen-year-old, he began working at a well-known restaurant in central Malmö. He refused to utter its name, simply referring to it as "the joint." He had spent his first three months there scrubbing and scouring. According to Slobodan, the head chef—"the German swine"—was a sadist. Others said that Slobodan, who advanced to sous chef, had stuck a fish knife in the head chef's stomach. When asked about this, he laughed his poodle laugh and held his stomach. Opinion was divided on how this was supposed to be interpreted.

After various excursions to Copenhagen and Spain, Slobodan sailed into Uppsala's culinary world and surprised everyone by opening two restaurants at the same time: Lido and Pigalle. Tasteless names, many thought, and the food received a similar evaluation. What the two watering holes also had in common was their expensive interiors. Lido was outfitted with a zinc bar counter eleven meters long, into which the customers were encouraged to engrave their orders with specially supplied screwdrivers. The screwdrivers were subsequently removed in connection with a brawl.

Pigalle was a dark hole of a place with an unsuccessful mixture of orientalism, incense, and dark drapes—and Mediterranean flair with fishing nets in the ceiling, shells, and a stuffed swordfish that brought to mind vacations in Majorca in the late sixties.

Both restaurants folded after barely a year. Slobodan Andersson salvaged the interiors, driving some things to the Hovgården dump but retaining that which might be worth something, and opened Genghis Khan, a restaurant with more potential from the outset. Genghis Khan did not gain a reputation for any culinary sensations. Instead it developed into a popular hangout, and now one started to perceive Slobodan's talent for uniting a hip bar feel with an atmosphere that bordered on chummy. He often tended the bar himself, was generous and ruthless at the same time, knew how to choose favorites among his customers, those who were loyal and drew others in.

Genghis Khan went to its grave with a bang, or rather with fire and smoke, for in the end there was a fire in the kitchen. New kitchen equipment was purchased, but then there were three burglaries in a row and failed payments.

Slobodan left Uppsala. There were rumors that he had gone to Southeast Asia, others said the Caribbean or Africa. There was a rumor that he had sent a postcard to the federal tax enforcement agency. After a year, he returned, suntanned, with a somewhat reduced circumference and his head buzzing with new projects.

Suddenly there was money again, a lot of money. He tossed a couple hundred thousand in the direction of his creditors and shortly thereafter Alhambra opened its doors. It was the end of the nineties, and since then his restaurant empire had only grown.

Alhambra was located in an older building in the middle of town, a stone's throw from the main square, Stortorget. The entrance was extravagantly appointed with custom marble on the stairs and hand-hammered copper doors engraved with the owner's initials and the restaurant's name in silver-colored looping letters.

Once inside, the impression became more muted. The suggestions for the interior from the chef, Oskar Hammer, were dismissed with a poodle laugh.

"Too cool," Slobodan said, and stroked his emerging bald spot as he evaluated the sketches that Hammer had commissioned.

"There should be razzle-dazzle, bling, lots of gold."

And so it was. Many decided that the effect was so consistently pursued that it achieved a measure of style. The gold and magenta walls were profusely covered in sconces and blurry prints in wide, white frames. The prints all displayed motifs from Greek mythology.

"The name of the restaurant is, after all, Alhambra," Slobodan said, when Hammer raised objections.

The tables in the dining room were set in a rococo style with heavy silver-plated dinnerware and candelabras, procured by Armas, who had been Slobodan's trusted assistant through the years.

Now Slobodan's empire stood at the threshold of yet another venture. This time he turned to a new continent for inspiration. The restaurant was christened Dakar, and from the start, it worked. The walls were decorated with photographs from West Africa, some of them enlarged to nearly a square meter, depicting images from markets, daily life in the village, and sporting events.

The photographer was a Senegalese man from the southern regions of the country who had traveled around taking pictures for many years.

Slobodan wanted to lay it on thick. He was going to invest in the "gilded package," as he put it. The goal was to convince diners to overlook the restaurants Svensson's Guldkant and Wermlandskällaren in favor of Dakar.

"That old bolshevik," he said disdainfully about the owner of the fish restaurant where the bourgeois Uppsala establishment liked to lunch. "I'm going to make sure the ladies sashay on over here. I'm going to get so many stars that the world press will line up outside. My menus will be printed in schoolbooks as examples of the complete kitchen."

There was no limit to Slobodan's visions and conviction that he would take Uppsala and the world by storm.

"I need chefs!" he exclaimed at the first meeting with Hammer and Armas.

"What you need is money," Hammer said.

Slobodan turned sharply to him and the chef awaited the invectives that usually followed objections of this sort, but the restauranteur's steely gaze was this time replaced with a grin.

"That's been taken care of," he said.

✦

Three

"On my way," Johnny Kvarnheden mumbled, and turned up the volume on the car stereo. The late-evening sun was bathing in Lake Vättern. Visingö looked like a towering warship, steering south, and the ferry to Gränna resembled a beetle on a floor of gold.

There was something cinematic about his flight, as if someone had directed his melancholia, set the lights, and added the music. He was conscious of this cinematic effect and was steered, allowed himself to be steered, caught in the classic scene: a lone man leaving his old life behind, on his way to something unknown.

A telephone call was all it had taken, a split second of deliberation in order for him to make up his mind, pack his few possessions—too few, and in too much of a hurry—and set out on the road.

He wished that his road trip could last forever, that the contents of the gas tank, his hunger, and his bladder were his only constraints. That the trip could be the focus, that he could fly down the highway unconnected to everything except the friction between his tires and the asphalt.

If there had been a camera, he would have turned it on the road, toward the black of the asphalt, the traces of traffic, and the grooves from the teeth of the snow-clearing trucks, not at his face or the landscape that flickered past. The sound track would not be Madeleine Peyroux's voice from the CD player, but the rhythmic thumping from the roadway. The stiffness of his shoulders and the cramplike grip of his hands on the steering wheel would be the voice that spoke to the viewer.

He kept his disappointment and grief at bay, but also his hopes and dreams. He thought about descriptions of food, plates of one prepared dish after another. The fact that he was a chef saved him for the moment.

He was worthless as a lover, couldn't even get it up anymore, and was just as worthless as a partner. This had slowly but surely become clear to him, and this insight had struck him with full force yesterday evening when Sofie described his attempts as "pathetic."

"You aren't living," she said, in a sudden burst of volubility, "and your so-called attentions toward our relationship are ridiculous. It is nauseating. You don't know how to love."

He reached out and touched her, pressed his body against her, and felt desire for the first time in months. Repulsed, she shook him off.

"NAUSEATING," HE SAID OUT LOUD. "What kind of a word is that?"

He passed Linköping and Norrköping. Then he thundered on into Sörmland with an accelerating desperation that made him drive much too fast. The direction no longer worked. He turned the volume up higher, playing the same album over and over again.

As he approached Stockholm he tried to think of his new job. Dakar sounded good, like a solid B. He didn't know more about the restaurant than what he had learned on the Internet the night before. The menu looked all right on paper, but there was something about the presentation that was jarring, as if it was aspiring to be high class but couldn't quite manage to live up to its own superlatives. There was no lack of self-confidence. The writer had simply put in too much.

It was his sister in Uppsala who had told him about the job and he had called the owner. The latter had quickly jotted down his references and called back half an hour later to say he had gotten the job. It was as if he sensed Johnny's situation.

He didn't know more about the city than that it had a university. His sister hadn't told him very much, but that had not been necessary. He was going to . . . yes, what? Cook, of course, but what else?

✦

Four

"Imagine being able to sail."

Eva Willman smiled to herself. The newspaper article about the holiday paradise in the West Indies was accompanied by a photograph of a yacht. It was at half sail and waves were breaking against the bow. A pennant fluttered at the top of the mast. There was a man dressed in blue shorts, a white tank top, and a blue cap standing in the stern. He looked relaxed, especially for someone with the responsibility for such a big boat. Eva sensed that he was the one who was steering. His gaze was directed up at the billowing sails. She thought she could see a smile on his face.

"I wouldn't even be able to afford the cap," she went on and pointed.

Helen leaned over and looked quickly at the page before she sank back into the sofa and continued to file her nails.

"I get sea sick," she said.

"But just think what freedom," Eva said and read on.

The article was about the island cluster of Aruba, Bonaire, and Curaçao.

They were described as paradise islands, an el Dorado for snorklers and divers. A place where you could leave your troubles behind.

"The Antilles," she muttered. "Think of how many places there are."

"Sailing isn't my thing," Helen said.

For a while Eva studied the map of the string of islands north of Venezuela. She followed the coastline and read the foreign place names. The rasping sound of the nail file was getting on her nerves.

"I would like to see the fish, those tropical kinds in all the colors of the rainbow."

She glanced at the digital clock on the VCR before she continued to browse.

"Maybe I should enroll in a class," she said suddenly. "Learn to sail, I mean. It's probably not that hard."

"Do you know anyone with a sailboat?"

"No," Eva said, "but you can always get to know someone."

She stared unseeing at the next story. It was about a school in southern Sweden that had burned down.

"Maybe I'll meet some hottie with a boat. It has to be a sailboat, not anything with an engine."

"And who would that be?"

"A nice, handsome guy. A good man."

"One who would want a middle-aged bag with two kids? Dream on."

The words struck Eva with unexpected force.

"Well, what about you?" she said aggressively.

The nail file stopped in the air. Eva kept flipping through the magazine. She felt Helen's gaze. She knew exactly how her friend looked: one corner of her mouth turned down, a vertical wrinkle in her forehead, and the birthmark between her eyebrows like the period in an exclamation point.

Helen was adept at looking displeased, as if someone was always trying to put one over on her. Which was true. Her man was constantly unfaithful to her.

"What do you mean?"

"Nothing in particular," Eva said, and shot a quick look at her friend.

"What the hell has gotten into you today? I can't help the fact that you feel dumped."

"I haven't been dumped! I've been laid off after eleven long fucking years."

Eva pushed the magazine away and got to her feet. It wasn't the first time that Helen was using the word *dumped.* Eva hated it. She was thirty-four years old and far from washed up.

"I'm going to get myself a new job," she said.

"Good luck," Helen said, and resumed her filing.

Eva left the living room and walked out into the kitchen, hastily shuffling together the papers from the unemployment agency and pushing them in among the cookbooks in the kitchen. Patrik would be home soon.

The rhythmic filing could be heard all the way out in the kitchen. Eva ended up standing in front of the cabinet where the box of O'boy was. The most routine duties became important, every movement, such as taking out milk and chocolate powder, became significant. She stretched out her hand. The white line on her wrist where her watch had been was a reminder of the passage of time. She moved guardedly as if she were a stranger in her own kitchen, while the seconds, minutes, and hours marched on relentlessly. Her hand was warm but the cabinet handle cool. Her arm was tanned and covered in tiny liver spots that had grown more numerous over the past few years.

Eva opened the cabinet. The filing had stopped and the only thing she could hear was the rustle of Helen turning the pages of a magazine.

There was sugar, flour, oats, popcorn, coffee, and other dry goods on the shelves. She sized up each package as if it were the first time she was looking at it.

Her paralysis was only broken when Patrik suddenly opened the front door. Eva quickly took out the powdered chocolate mix, then opened the refrigerator door and took out some milk. Barely two liters left. The cucumber was almost gone, the cheese an ancient monument, the eggs, okay, and enough yogurt, she summed up.

"Hello!" she yelled, surprised at how happy she sounded, but only the sound of his feet on the hallway floor made her smile.

Behind his shuffling movements and somewhat grumpy demeanor there was a capacity for observation that never ceased to amaze her. He was becoming wiser and more mature. When she pointed this out he became dismissive, and when she praised him he appeared completely bewildered, as if he did not want to admit to having been thoughtful or kind.

He walked into the kitchen and sat down. Eva set the table in silence.

"Who is here?"

"Helen. She wanted to borrow the iron."

"Doesn't she own one?"

"It's broken."

Patrik sighed and poured out some milk. Eva watched him. His pants were starting to get worn. When he claimed that they were supposed to look like that, she laughed heartily. When worn clothes became trendy, the poor man had the advantage for once.

"I have a job for you," Patrik said suddenly.

He was making his fourth sandwich.

"What?"

Patrik looked at her and Eva thought she saw concern in his eyes.

"Simon's mom was talking about it. Her brother is moving to Uppsala, for a new job."

He took a sip of the O'boy chocolate milk.

"What does that have to do with me?"

"They need a waitriss. He's a chef."

"Waitress, not waitriss."

"But chef is right."

"I'm going to work as a waitress? What else did she say? Did she talk about me?"

A new sigh from Patrik.

"What did she say?"

"You'll have to talk to her yourself."

He stood up with a sandwich in his hand.

"I'm going to the movies tonight."

"Do you have money?"

He shuffled off to his room without answering, and closed the door behind him. Eva looked at the clock on the wall. Simon's mother, she thought, and started to clear the table, but stopped. Hugo would be home from school soon.

Helen came into the kitchen and sat down at the table.

"Where's Patrik?"

Eva didn't bother to answer. Helen knew very well where he was. Fury boiled up in Eva at the sight of her friend.

"You think I put you down, yes, I know it," Helen said, with unexpected loudness. "You dream of sailboats and nice, wonderful men, but have you thought of something?"

Eva stared at her.

"That you never do anything about it. Get it? It's only talk."

"I've got a job," Eva said.

"What?"

"Waitress."

"Where?"

"I don't know," Eva said.

Helen looked at her and Eva thought she saw the flicker of a smile on her lips.

When Helen had left, Eva poured out the last of the coffee and sank down on a chair. Not to be taken seriously, she thought, that was the worst. Or rather, that others didn't have any faith in one's abilities. Helen had tried to hide her taunting smile, she knew her friendship with Eva could not withstand everything, but the split-second insight that in the future, her friend would spitefully remind her about the waitress job made Eva rage inside. Helen would probably ask about it in passing, about how did that turn out, because . . . yes, what? Only in order to feel superior? To take her frustrations out on Eva when she ought to put her own life in order? Helen had not worked since she stopped running her home day care several years ago.

She drank some of the coffee. She could hear music from Patrik's room. Eva wished that he had stayed in the kitchen and told her a little more about what Simon's mother had said. But she sensed there was probably not much more.

Am I worthless? This question came to Eva Willman as she was pulling out a new trash can liner from under the sink. At the bottom of the plastic container there was a decomposing banana peel and a sticky, foul-smelling mass, in whose brown gooey center new life appeared to be flourishing. She took out the new liner, at the same time pulling out the trash can and placing it on the counter. Then she ended up sitting in a crouch, staring into the hole under the sink that the drain pipes disappeared into.

She was about to call out to Patrik, have him come out into the kitchen and show him how disgusting everything became if one did not take care of something as basic as the trash, but why should she bother? She came off as enough of a nag already.

How many times a week did she take out the garbage? How many times did she reach in under the sink, press down the contents, pull up the bag, and tie it?

The sharp smell penetrated her nostrils. This is my smell, she thought, and this is my terrain, drain pipes and a collection of packets of hygiene products and brushes. She reached for the sponge that was tucked in between the pipes and had the urge to bite into it, chew it into green-yellow pieces and savor the taste of cleaning and dishwashing and chores that were threatening to overwhelm her.

There was a splashing sound from inside the pipes. That was probably the upstairs neighbor, a newly arrived Bosnian woman doing the dishes. The sound reminded Eva that she was not alone in the building.

She visualized the apartments as boxes arranged one on top of the other. Five entrances, four stories, and three apartments on each level. Sixty apartments. She knew the names of ten or so renters, nodded in recognition to some fifty people, and did not associate with any of them.

Her legs ached and she sank down on the floor, leaned against the kitchen cabinets, resting there with her elbows on her knees and gently stroking her forehead with the tips of her fingers. Why was she sitting there, nailed to her own kitchen floor as if an invisible hand was pressing her down?

Sometimes she entertained the idea of getting up, taking Hugo and Patrik and walking around to all sixty apartments, ringing the doorbell and saying . . . What should she say? Would they even open up, as suspicious as everyone had become since the shooting incident down at the school? No one had been hurt, of course, but the sound of the shots had rung out over the entire area.

The woman one floor up had just stepped off the bus with her two children when it happened. She had recognized the sound of gunfire and had picked up the youngest and held the other by the hand and had run straight into the forest, through wilted grass and brush and into the shielding cover of the trees. She had run into the woods as people have always done in uncertain times and was only discovered under a spruce the next morning by an orienteering team from the UIF sport club who were setting up signs. Luckily, it had been a warm night.

It had been in the papers. They had written about the woman's background. The building complex had its own celebrity.

Would she open the door if Eva rang the bell? Or Pär, the single man who went by on his bike every morning with a pained expression on his face but who greeted Eva with a smile when they bumped into each other outside. Would he open his door?

Eva had talked to him before. He would often sit on the bench by the little play area and watch his five-year-old son build an endless series of sand castles. Sometimes the son was gone and Eva guessed he was with his mother. Pär was from the north. That was the only thing she knew about him.

The woman above her came from the south. She had mentioned Tuzla, but also a village that Eva could no longer remember the name of.

They had all gathered in a building with fifty-seven other families. Eva imagined them all walking from various directions, leaving behind them lives, relatives, and friends, in order to end up in a rental apartment building on the outskirts of Uppsala.

An area at the outskirts of the city where the cries of the tawny owl could be heard from the forest.

Earlier she had not thought about her surroundings so much. It was only after her divorce from Jörgen that she felt that she had the room to think. While they were still living together, it was as if he took all her time, used up all the oxygen around her, filling the space with his volubility and his thundering laugh. There were those who felt that he was sick, that his incessant talking was a manic fixation on the threat of silence, but Eva knew better. It was an inherited characteristic; his father and grandfather had been the same.

It was possible that he suffered from an overinflated self-confidence. The problem was that he seemed to nourish this self-confidence by turning to his surroundings, preying on Eva like a predatory digger wasp in order to strengthen himself.

Sometimes she pitied him, but only sometimes, and more rarely lately. As they sat in the lawyer's office discussing the divorce, she felt only fatigue and great scorn. Jörgen was going on as usual, as if he did not understand that they were there to discuss the custody arrangements for the children.

The lawyer interrupted his stream of words by asking if he could really afford to stay in the highly mortgaged condominium. That halted his speech and he gave Eva a terrified look, as if seeking the answer to a question he had never posed. Eva understood that it was not the financial aspect that frightened him, but the sudden realization that he would have to live alone from now on.

Since then, this anxiety did not seem to want to leave him. It did not make him quiet, quite the opposite, but for Eva, Jörgen's tentative questions about her well-being and tiptoeing into areas that they had not previously touched on were indications that he was not really mature, not conscious of what it meant to share one's life with another person, that their marriage had simply been an extension of Jörgen's life with his single mother. She, the bitch, as Eva called her in private, really had only one close friend, and that was her son.

Now the thoughtfulness and questions came too late. Eva was never tempted to grab one of the hooks he tossed out that they should perhaps try again. She maintained her distance and was mostly exaggeratedly formal. She knew that it hurt him, but in an obscure way it gave her a sense of satisfaction. It was a primitive revenge, but she could not be bothered with his sad monologues, where self-pity always lurked behind his account of how difficult life was.

Jörgen came and picked up Patrik and Hugo every other weekend and Eva put up a wall held together with indifference and suspicion toward his incessant drivel, glad to have escaped but careful not to become mean or ironic. He complained that he and the boys did not have a good relationship, but when Eva suggested that the boys should spend longer periods of time with him, he backed off.

Nowadays she had all the time in the world. The only schedule she had to observe were the appointments at the employment agency, and her only duty was to care for her two children, make sure that they got off to school, and went to bed at a somewhat reasonable hour.

Sometimes she was grateful for the fact that she had been laid off. It was as if the process of making herself free had started with her divorce, and that the freedom had now taken a new and higher form. It was a frustrating feeling, this remarkable mixture of anger at not being needed and the joy of being free to do as she pleased.

She formed the impression that it was more expensive to be unemployed. And yet she cut down on everything. She had stopped smoking about a month ago and calculated that she had already saved four hundred kronor. Where had they gone? she asked, but the answer was immediate. Fitting Hugo for instep supports had cost over a thousand kronor.

Her freedom may have increased, with all the hours alone with her thoughts, but her self-esteem was at rock bottom. She felt that she was different, or rather that everyone around her saw with different eyes. She was at the disposal of potential employers. The problem was that no one was disposed to employ her. Could they see it on her, did unemployment leave physical marks? Was there something in her posture that made the girls at the ICA supermarket only a little older than Patrik, or the bus driver when she climbed onto the bus in the middle of the day, regard her as a second-class citizen? She did not want to believe this, but the feeling of being worthless had eaten into her.

And now Helen, who appeared to be growing at Eva's expense. It was as if she unconsciously saw the possibility of diminishing Eva as a way to take revenge for her own shortcomings and her submission to a man she should have left many years ago.

Eva had shrunk, been pressed back against the kitchen cabinets and the drain pipes under an increasingly shining countertop. Everything in the apartment was cleaned, picked up, dusted, everything was in its place, only that she was no longer needed. Wrong, she thought. I am needed. They had talked about that at work, how important they were, not least for the old people who patiently waited their turn in line, thumbing letters and forms. Someone decided that the post office should be reduced and that the number of customer chairs should be cut. One day there were carpenters there, putting up a wall. That was how it started. And the old people had to stand.

Then came the reduced hours. Everything became crowded, the tone cranky, complaints increased, and the clerks had to deal more often with the customers' frustrations. One day lists appeared in the waiting area where the customers could sign protests of the worsening service and the closing of more post office locations. Many letters to the editor appeared in *Upsala Nya Tidning,* but nothing helped, and even Eva's post office was eventually closed down. That was now nine months ago.

God, how she had looked for jobs! She had spent the first couple of weeks running around to stores, calling the county and the city, getting in touch with friends and even asking Jörgen if he couldn't get her something at the sanitation company where he worked.

But there was nothing to get. During the summer she had worked for a few weeks in Eldercare Services, and thereafter at a supermarket, filling in for someone on disability, but the employee had miraculously arisen from his sickbed and returned to work.

Thereafter, nothing.

✦

Five

This was how Manuel imagined a prison: a gray wall and barbed wire that ran the perimeter of a high fence. He had also imagined a manned guard post where he would have to present the reason for his visit, but there was only a gigantic door with a smaller door carved into it.

He approached the building hesitantly, glancing up and to the side. He felt observed by cameras that were most likely maintaining surveillance of the entire area. Suddenly he heard the squeak of a loudspeaker.

He could not see a microphone so he spoke straight out into the air, explained the reason for his visit in English, and the door unlocked with a click. He was in.

"Do you speak Swedish?"

Manuel stared back without comprehension at the young man behind the counter. He resembled Xavier back in the village, dark hair in a ponytail and kind eyes.

"English?"

Manuel nodded and a shiver ran down his back. The man looked more closely at him and explained that in order to be cleared to visit anyone, Manuel would have to produce a certificate from his homeland declaring that he was not a felon. One could not simply turn up on a whim and expect immediate entry to the prison.

Manuel explained that he had written to his brother and that the latter had spoken with the prison management and then written back to say that everything was in order.

"You are Patricio's brother?"

Manuel nodded and was grateful for the fact that someone knew his brother's name. Patricio was not simply a number, a prisoner among hundreds.

"This is no regular tourist attraction," the man said behind the desk, in an apparent attempt to reassure him, and then explained the rules of the institution as he sized up Manuel.

There was nothing unfriendly in his manner, quite the opposite. Manuel thought he seemed decent, and some of the tension eased, but he still felt the sweat running down his back.

Soon he would see Patricio. It gave him a feeling of unreality—after so many nights of questions and concerns over his brother, and so many conjectures about the other country, the prison country, and what it actually looked like—to finally be here.

When he parked the rental car outside the prison his courage had almost failed him. He imagined that he would also be apprehended. He knew so little about Sweden. Perhaps he would be viewed as an accomplice?

"You will have to lock up your valuables," the man said and pointed to a row of green-painted lockers. Manuel chose locker number ten, his lucky number, and locked up his wallet and passport. The prison guard asked for Manuel's bag.

"Your brother is studying Swedish," the guard warden said, and emptied his bag of its contents. "It is going pretty well. He is behaving well. If everyone was like Patricio, there would be no problems.

"*No problemas,*" he said and smiled. "Are those presents?"

Manuel nodded. That his brother was studying Swedish came as complete surprise. It felt wrong, somehow.

"What is this?"

"That is a vase," Manuel said, "from our mother."

"Patricio cannot receive it right away. We will have to check it."

Manuel nodded but secretly wondered why a ceramic object had to be checked so carefully.

"If you only knew how many vases we receive that can work equally well as pipes for smoking hashish," the guard said, as if he had read Manuel's thoughts.

Seemingly out of nowhere, a dog appeared in the corridor outside the small waiting room.

Manuel got out of the chair.

"Hello, Charlie," the guard said. "How are you doing?"

The dog made a small whine and wagged its tail. Manuel took a step back and stared at the Labrador that had now stuck its head through the metal detector in the door and appeared to be looking at Manuel with professional interest.

"Are you afraid of dogs?" the dog handler asked.

Manuel nodded.

"Don't you have dogs in Mexico?"

"Police dogs are not nice," Manuel said.

"This is not a police dog. This is Charlie. We have to let him sniff you."

"Why?"

The dog handler came farther into the room and studied Manuel.

"*Drogas,*" he said, grinning.

"*No tengo drogas,*" Manuel burst out. Frozen with dread, he watched the Labrador draw closer.

The dog sniffed at his shoes and pant legs. Manuel shook and sweat broke out on his forehead. He remembered the demonstration in Oaxaca where a handful of German shepherds had gone to attack and plunged madly into the crowd.

"You seem clean," the dog handler said and called on Charlie, who had now lost all interest in Manuel.

Manuel was brought to a visitation room, where the only furniture consisted of a cot with a red plastic cover and a pair of chairs. There was a sink in the corner. He sat down and waited. The sun was shining in through the iron bars of the window. There was a hint of blue sky above the wall and barbed wire.

The door opened and Patricio was standing there. In the background, he could see the man with the ponytail. He smiled over Patricio's shoulder and nodded at Manuel.

The brothers stared at each other across the room. Patricio's hair was cut short, almost a buzz cut, just as Manuel had expected, but otherwise he looked different. He had gained weight and there was an expression of sorrowful pessimism around his mouth that reminded Manuel of their father. Patricio had aged. The green shirt was tight around his stomach, the blue pants were too short, and the slippers looked completely foreign.

"Everyone sends their greetings" was the first thing Manuel said.

Patricio immediately burst into tears and was not able to talk for several minutes. Manuel braced himself. He wanted to have the strength of a big brother and somewhere he also had the anger that his brother was crying over a situation that he had brought on himself.

But he embraced Patricio, patted him on the back, and Patricio inhaled deeply at his brother's shoulder, as if to draw in something of the scent of his homeland. Manuel noticed that Patricio's ears had become somewhat wrinkled.

They sat down on the cot. Manuel looked around.

"Are they recording this?"

"I doubt it," Patricio said.

"How are you?"

"I am fine. But what are you doing here?"

"Have you forgotten your family?" His anger made Manuel stand up, but Patricio did not react. "Mama only talks about you and Angel. The neighbors say she is going crazy."

A bird flew past the barred window. Manuel stopped talking and looked at his brother.

"How do they treat you?"

"They are nice," Patricio said.

Nice, Manuel thought. What a word to use about people who work in a prison. Now that he had the possibility of satisfying his curiosity, all of his interest in Patricio's prison life disappeared. Manuel did not want to hear what he did, how he passed the time.

"What happened to Angel?"

Manuel had not intended to ask about his brother immediately, but the words tumbled out of his mouth before he realized how much it must hurt for Patricio to talk about what had happened. In the letters home he had time and again returned to his own guilt, that he was partly responsible for Angel's death.

Patricio told him the story with a stranger's voice. The time in prison had not only changed him physically. Perhaps it was the joy of being reunited or the pleasure of speaking Zapotec that made him so open and talkative?

Most likely, Angel had been shadowed all the way from Spain to Germany. He had called Patricio, who was still in San Sebastián, from somewhere in France. They had decided not to contact each other, but Angel had been distraught and told him he was being followed. He wanted to return to San Sebastián, but Patricio had convinced him to continue on to Frankfurt as arranged.

He wanted to throw away the package, but Patricio had urged him to calm down. If he got rid of the cocaine he would end up with big problems.

"How did he die?"

"I think he was trying to escape the police. He ran over some tracks and . . . the train came."

"Angelito," Manuel sighed. He could see his brother in his mind, running, stumbling on. If it had been Patricio with his long legs it would perhaps have been fine, but Angel was not built for running.

"They sent eleven thousand pesos," Manuel said.

Patricio looked at him and repeated the sum to himself under his breath. His lips formed "eleven thousand pesos" as if it were a spell.

"Is it the fat one who is behind all this?"

Patricio nodded. Manuel saw that he was ashamed, he remembered that day in the village so well. How the tall one, who called himself Armas, climbed into a large van together with a fat white man. What Manuel could remember best was how much the fat one had been sweating.

"Where is he?"

Patricio glanced around the room.

"Do you have a pen?"

Patricio tore off a piece of the wrapping paper that had encased the small ceramic vase from their mother, wrote a few lines, and pushed the note over to Manuel.

"Restaurante Dakar Ciudad Uppsala," it said.

Manuel looked at his brother. A restaurant.

"The fat one and the tall one?" he asked.

"Yes," his brother said. "They promised me ten thousand dollars, even if I got caught. They would make sure Mama got the money."

When he mentioned their mother, Manuel lowered his gaze.

"Ten thousand dollars," he repeated quietly, as if to test the amount of money, and he immediately translated it into pesos: one hundred and ten thousand.

"That is over seven thousand hours of work," he said and tried to calculate how many years that represented.

"How did you get caught?"

"At the airport. They had a dog."

"You haven't told the police anything?"

Patricio shook his head.

"Why not? You would get out sooner."

Up to this point they had not mentioned Patricio's severe sentence.

"I don't think it works like that here," he said sadly.

"It works like that everywhere," Manuel said vehemently. He was becoming more and more upset by his brother's passive attitude.

"Not in Sweden."

Manuel tried a different approach.

"Maybe they would give you a better, bigger cell and better food?"

His brother smiled, but still looked sad.

"I have never eaten as well in my life as I do here," he said, but Manuel did not believe him.

"I go to the chapel as often as I can. There is a priest who comes here. We pray together. It is a remarkable church," he added, then stopped abruptly.

"What do you mean?"

"Here there are all religions. We are over two hundred inmates and everyone prays to his own God. It doesn't bother me. I usually talk to an Iranian in the chapel. He has lived in the USA. There is a clock on the wall, and it comes from Jerusalem, and when I look at it I think about the suffering of Christ and that my problems are nothing compared to what God's son had to go through. Being in the chapel makes me calm."

Manuel stared at his brother. He had never talked so much about religion before.

"But what about the money?" he asked, in order to change the topic. "You can do a lot with ten thousand."

"You don't know how it works," Patricio said. "The greenbacks would do me no good in here. It is better if they send the money home. How are things back there?"

"They're fine," Manuel said.

Patricio studied him in silence.

"I will never see the village again," he said. "I will die in here."

Manuel stood up quickly. What could he say to prevent his brother from sinking more deeply into a depression? In his letters he had talked about taking his life, that only his faith prevented him from doing so. As Manuel looked at Patricio, at his altered gaze and posture, he sensed that the day when his faith weakened, when doubt crept into his brother's body, yes, then he would also waste away, perhaps end his life.

Manuel believed his brother's words were an unconscious way of preparing him, and perhaps himself, for such a development.

"Of course the money could help you," he resumed.

"To buy drugs, or what?"

"No, I didn't say that!"

"Tell me one thing . . ."

"Patricio, you are twenty-five years old and . . ."

"Twenty-six. It was my birthday yesterday."

Manuel fell silent before his brother's gaze.

"Patricio, Patricio, my brother," Manuel mumbled when he was back in the parking lot, next to his rental car. He could not make himself leave. He stared at the building, trying to imagine how his brother was escorted through endless corridors back to his cell and how the massive oak door was shut behind him.

It was as if his brother did not exist, he was hidden behind walls of concrete, forgotten by everyone except the guards and Manuel.

Patricio had changed, and his despondence had shocked Manuel. He did not seem to want to do anything to improve his situation. Manuel did not for one moment believe the talk of how he was fine. Ten thousand dollars could improve his living conditions, Manuel was sure of that. That was how it worked in Mexico, and human beings were alike all over the world, but Patricio had not done anything to try to recover the money.

Manuel looked at the piece of paper on which Patricio had written the name of the restaurant. He unlocked the car door, took a map out of the glove compartment, and located Uppsala almost immediately. The city lay about an hour's drive from the prison.

Manuel held the map spread out against the roof of the car and again looked up at the prison walls and the gate that kept Patricio locked inside. He suddenly understood why Patricio did not try to claim his fortune. He was ashamed and he wanted to punish himself. He could be living better, even shortening his sentence, but he was denying himself these possibilities. Filled with guilt and shame, he wanted to rot away in his cell.

Manuel studied the map and tried to memorize the names of the places along the way to Uppsala: Rimbo, Finsta, Gottröra, and Knivsta. It was as if the mapped-out terrain on the page spoke to him; the green and yellow irregular fields formed patterns that he tried to convert into images. He looked around. The trees that surrounded the institution were swaying in the wind, bowing down and straightening their backs. So similar to how it was back home and yet so foreign.

He had been in Sweden nine hours. He had traveled with only one goal: to check up on his brother. He had gone into debt in order to get the money for the ticket, had assured his mother that he would be careful and not do anything illegal. Was it illegal to persuade the drug dealers, the fat one and the tall one, to pay Patricio the ten thousand dollars that they had promised?

If Patricio didn't want it, then it certainly would provide Maria with security in her old age. She would never again have to worry about money. It was the thought of this that convinced him.

He folded up the map, got in the car, and drove slowly out of the parking lot.

✦

Six

The sign flashed "Dakar" with three stars, alternating in green and red. Eva Willman leaned her bicycle against the wall, although a sign expressly forbade this.

She had asked Patrik to look up Dakar online. He had received ten of thousands of hits. Dakar was the capital of the West African country of Senegal. Together, they had looked it up in the atlas and Eva felt as if she was embarking on a trip.

Patrik sat leaned over the kitchen table, tracing his index finger across the open pages.

"Timbuktu," he said suddenly.

The multicolored nations, the straight lines that indicated borders, and the blue ones that followed the laws of nature, meandering across the map, joined up with other arteries and lead to the sea in a finely branched network of threads. Patrik smiled to himself.

The pale sunlight fell in through the window. The light and shade in his young face formed a continent of hope. There was absolute silence in the kitchen. Eva wanted to caress Patrik's blond hair and downy face, but she let her hand rest on the back of the chair.

"Dakar is by the sea," Patrik said and looked at her with an expression that was difficult to interpret. There is nothing to the west before America, only water."

Now Eva was standing in front of a Dakar that was far from the sea. The closest you could come to the Atlantic around here was the Fyris river, a body of water that rarely evoked any dreams, a line that divided the city. It reminded Eva of her grandfather. He had been a construction worker his whole life, a communist, and an alcoholic—a life-threatening combination, especially for her grandmother who became the target of her husband's frustration and hate. Only in her sixties did she manage to leave him.

In protest, Eva's father had voted for the conservatives and had continued to do so from sheer habit, long after his ruddy father had shuffled off this mortal coil.

Eva's inheritance was twofold, consisting in part of a hatred toward pretention and hypocrisy, against those in power, and in part a belief in the role of personal responsibility for one's own well-being. She had always had difficulties reconciling herself with the collective, with those who spoke for the many but who did not always live as they preached. She had seen enough of that at the post office.

Her grandmother had worked as a waitress at the well-known hotel and restaurant Gillet in her youth, an experience that she constantly mentioned. It was not so much the tired feet and fresh-mouthed customers that she remembered, but more the feeling of having a job and therefore value. When she married, her husband forbade her to continue working. He was jealous, convinced that the men would soil her with their gazes.

Now Eva was standing in front of Dakar. She had called her grandmother, who lived in an assisted-living unit, and told her that she was applying for a job at a restaurant.

"I can teach you a thing or two," the old woman chuckled.

It had taken Eva half a day to gather enough courage to call Dakar.

She had spoken with a man named Måns, but the person she was going to meet was the boss himself, Slobodan Andersson.

"He can be a bit tricky," Måns said and Eva thought she could hear him smile. "Ignore his laughter, look him straight in the eye, don't look down even if he insults you."

"What do you mean, insults me? I'm applying for a job."

"You'll see what I mean," Måns said.

She stood for a while with her hand on the door handle before she took a deep breath, stepped into the restaurant, and was greeted by the smell of cigars and beer. She could hear a faint buzzing sound and Eva assumed it was a drill. She continued on farther into the room, full of tense anticipation for what she would see, and aware of her own breathing. She couldn't seem pantingly eager.

A carpenter was putting up shelves behind the bar. A fat man was standing behind the counter, nonchalantly leaning against it, observing the work. He had apparently not heard her come in. He said something that Eva did not catch. It must be him, she thought, looking at his beefy face and the hand that rested on the counter.

She coughed and the man turned his head and waved toward an armchair. Eva sat down. He made a good-natured impression standing there, as he smiled and nodded from time to time as if to assure everyone that everything looked good. When the last screw was in place, he turned to Eva.

"One can never have enough shelves, don't you think?"

"That's true," Eva said, and recalled Måns's words about looking him in the eye.

"I am Slobodan Andersson and this is Armas, the shelf master," said the fat man and nodded at the carpenter.

The latter stepped out of the shadows and glanced briefly at her. He was considerably taller than Slobodan Andersson, with a completely bald pate and a face as expressionless as a statue.

"So, my little postmistress, you would like a job?"

Eva nodded.

"They don't grow on trees," he went on. "What makes you think

Dakar won't go under if you start working here? Are you so damn good at dishing up food?"

"That's all I do these days," Eva replied.

"Is that so?"

"I have two teenage boys at home."

He nodded and smiled.

"Are they well behaved?"

"Yes, they are."

"I hate hooligans. What are their names?"

"Patrik and Hugo."

"Good," Slobodan said. "Now, stand up."

Eva rose hesitantly to her feet.

"Why don't you take a stroll between the tables."

"If you think you can direct me like a robot, you are wrong," Eva said and made an effort to keep her gaze steady. His look was difficult to take, nonchalant and taunting, as if he was playing with her. "But certainly, I can take a little walk."

She sauntered around the tables, taking in the giant photographic prints on the walls, then returned. Slobodan was watching her with an attentive expression, as if she was a shoplifter.

"Nice pictures," she said.

Slobodan gave Armas a look and let out a sigh. Eva recalled the job interview at her last employer. There had been forms and endless conversations, introductions and courses.

"There you have the heart," Slobodan said suddenly and pointed into the inner regions of the restaurant. "The kitchen! You out here are only slaves under the kitchen. Nothing but errand boys or errand girls, if you so will. Are you a red stocking?"

"I don't know what you mean."

"Women's talk, you know."

"Well, I am a woman, and I certainly do talk."

Slobodan studied her pensively. Armas, who had not said anything thus far, coughed and nodded to Slobodan before receding into the shadows. Slobodan stared after him and then smiled at Eva.

"When can you start?"

"Today," Eva said quickly, without a second's hesitation.

She ran her hands quickly down her legs.

"And the hooligans?"

"They'll manage."

"You'll have to fix your hair. Armas, call Elizabeth!"

Eva swallowed and unconsciously touched her head.

She biked back through the city streets like a madwoman. The sun was shining from a clear sky and the traffic signals appeared synchronized to give her all green lights.

Above all she longed for Patrik and Hugo. The night before they had talked about the waitress job, or rather, Eva had talked about it while her sons had silently evaluated her chances at around zero. Finally she was the bearer of good news.

The only downside were the hours. She was going to work the lunch shift twice a week, as well as an evening shift three times a week and every other weekend. The salary, eighty-five kronor an hour to start, was worse than she had been expecting, but she accepted it without protest. Slobodan had implied that it could perhaps improve after a while. How much the tips added, she did not ask, but Slobodan had explained that everyone shared alike. That meant the entire kitchen crew, including those lowest on the rung, the assistant chefs and the apprentices from the Ekeby School.

Tiredness hit her at the Ultuna commons and she stepped off her bicycle. A combine harvester was moving across the field, leaving golden brown stalks of straw in its wake. Through the dust billowing across the broad header that was devouring the stalks and grain heads, she caught sight of the driver. Eva waved, and he waved back, smiling. A feeling of solidarity with the harvest worker gripped her. The wheat that the chefs and bakers would turn to food, and that Eva would serve at the table, was being harvested right here and now.

A bus swept past on the road. Soon she would be sitting on it on her way to and from her work.

"A job!" she cried, and she pedaled past Kuggebro.

When she came home, Patrik was sitting at the kitchen table eating a sandwich. Hugo was at the computer.

"He's been sitting there for two hours," Patrik complained.

"I'm doing my homework!" Hugo yelled.

"You're kidding me," his brother muttered.

"Come here, Hugo," Eva said and sat down at the table. He immediately appeared in the doorway, leaning up against the doorpost, prepared to do battle for computer time.

"I got the job," Eva said.

Patrick gave her a quick look, before he cut another slice of bread.

"Then we get to eat at a restaurant every day," Hugo burst out.

It took a long time before the boys went to bed. They wanted to know everything about Drakar and Eva felt that she wanted to promise them something, so they could get a more immediate advance on the lottery win she had scored. That was how she felt: an incredible and unexpected triumph. No one had expected her to get a real job, least of all Helen. The first thing Eva was going to do tomorrow morning was call her.

The clock in the living room sounded twelve times. She should have called her parents in Ekshärad, but it was too late now. Perhaps she should wait a couple of days until she had started at Dakar and grown into her work.

As she was pulling the bedspread from her bed, she decided she would shower and change the sheets, despite the late hour.

Afterward she carefully applied her citrus-scented lotion. She looked at her body in the bathroom mirror and the feeling of being chosen was mixed with the longing to have someone to share the happiness with. The boys were pleased, of course. Hugo had already had time to count up everything she should buy, while Patrik had mostly been silent. Eva sensed that his pleasure lay more in the knowledge that they now had a mother who had a real job.

But sharing this joy with her sons was a controlled joy, one where she constantly had to apply a realistic view: the job at Dakar did not mean she was embarking on a dizzying career track. It was just a job, and not an especially well-paid one at that. Not a lottery win or a ticket to the easy life.

She longed to share her sense of optimism with a man. It was that simple. The lotion was intoxicating with its scent and smoothness, but in its way it was a wasted effort, and she felt guilty that she was throwing money away for no reason.

She went to bed with an excitement in her body that reminded her of an infatuation.

✦

Seven

Slobodan Andersson's office was tucked behind Alhambra's kitchen. Only he and Armas were allowed in there. The two of them had been in business together since they had met at a strip club in Copenhagen twenty years before. Armas had been sitting in the very front and with his formidable size had almost taken up two seats at the tiny table. Slobodan had joined him. Not because he wanted the company, but because he wanted to sit close to the stage.

The strippers were mediocre and apparently bored, because they moved with so little energy and creativity that many of the customers stopped watching. Slobodan sighed.

"It's a disappointment every time," he said, but Armas stared back at him without appearing to concur and simply shrugged.

Slobodan stretched out his hand and introduced himself. After a second's hesitation, Armas grasped his hand and muttered a name that Slobodan did not catch.

That was the beginning of their many years of working together.

Now they were sitting on either side of the desk. Armas was silent, while Slobodan was talking a mile a minute. He unfolded a map and placed his chubby finger on a town by the northern border of Spain.

"This is where it will take place," he said.

Armas already knew this. In fact, he already knew everything about the upcoming operation.

"You take the car down there. I will write out a list of restaurants that you will visit. Above all, this one north of Guernica. Drive around for at least a week, talk to chefs and collect ideas. But not some damn *bacalao*—I'm so damn tired of cod. But buy as much cheese as you want. You know what I like. If they check you out in customs, then go ahead and act a little nervous about the cheese. And wine, but only Basque varieties, so the customs officials feel proud. Make yourself out to be an idiot when it comes to food. Offer to pay taxes or whatever the hell else, tell them your boss will strangle you if you don't come back with a good piece of Cabrales."

Armas nodded and looked at his boss: the sweaty face, the wrinkled suit—one sleeve of which was soiled with a large grease stain—and the plump fingers that continuously fiddled with papers on the desk. Slobodan looked worn out. There were no wrinkles in the shiny round face, but the area around his eyes was growing darker, as if they were sinking more and more deeply into their sockets. The dark, combed-back hair was getting increasingly thin and new gray hairs appeared every day.

"Do you get it?"

"I get it."

"Jorge e-mailed me the other day."

Armas looked astonished.

"E-mailed? Has he lost his mind?"

"I deleted everything," Slobodan said, irritated.

Armas snorted.

"You will meet Jorge outside the aquarium in San Sebastián. Not far from there, on the pier, there is a restaurant. You will see exactly which one it is. They had decked the place out with a lot of flags and knick-knacks. Eat there. I know one of the waiters. He's called 'Mini.' "

"Is he involved?"

"No, not directly, but he stays informed. He knows exactly what happens in the city, if the police are up to anything."

Armas didn't like it. He didn't like Jorge and definitely not a new

Spanish idiot. It was typical of Slobodan to improvise like this at the last minute.

"I know what you think," Slobodan said, "but a little local backup is always good."

"Why can't Jorge go up to Frankfurt, like last time?"

"I don't trust him. You know what happened to the other one. Mexicans are so damn clumsy. They stink scofflaw to the high heavens. And the German cops are smarter than the Spaniards."

"If they are so clumsy, why—"

"You know why!"

Armas snorted again. He knew how everything had started and it had gone well. Angel's demise was something that couldn't be helped. He only had himself to blame. There was nothing that could tie Angel to Sweden and definitely not to either Slobodan or Armas.

It had been worse with the next idiot, the one who was picked up by Swedish customs and was now sitting in jail. For half a year, during the questioning and the trial, they had lived in a state of terror, but had finally realized that Patricio had not said a single word about his employers. He had remained silent throughout the entire process and the sentence had surely been more severe because of it.

Slobodan tossed a folder onto the desk.

"Here is the list of restaurants," he said.

He was intending to repeat all of his warnings and orders about what Armas should do in Spain and how he should treat the restaurant personnel, authorities, customs, police, or whoever he bumped into, but then realized this would only worsen the Armenian's mood.

Armas eyed the list. He had nothing against the prospect of eating well for a week. Perhaps he could even pick something up that could be of use to them at Alhambra or Dakar.

What troubled him was the prospect of Mini. Armas did not like unknown cards. The fact that he had managed to survive, and without spending a single day in jail, was entirely due to his policy of never relying on unknown cards. Mini was just such an untested quantity, even if Slobodan had vouched for him.

Jorge he had met in Campeche, Mexico, and had judged him to be significantly more reliable than Angel. That damn Indian had only had one thing in his head, and that was women. That could only lead to one thing: Hell. Armas put great pride in never starting a relationship that lasted more than a couple of days, perhaps a week. The record was held by a French woman he had met in Venezuela. They had been together for three weeks before she disappeared without a trace.

For a while, he kept to whores. They were professionals, like himself, but he grew tired of them. According to Armas, women made you lose your focus, and he was completely convinced that this was the reason Angel had failed. There must have been a woman involved. He had never trusted the Mexican. He talked too much about broads.

There was only one thing that spoke in his favor. He didn't squeal. They did not have any details beyond the sparse information in the German papers. The only thing they really knew was that he had thrown himself in front of a train at the Frankfurt Central Station when he had realized that he was surrounded by German police and would soon be apprehended.

That was well done. Both Slobodan and Armas thought so. Slobodan had even anonymously sent a thousand dollars to his family. A negligible amount in the context, but a fortune for Angel's family.

He closed the folder.

"You," he said. "Do me a favor and stay away from e-mail. Even if you delete everything, there is always something left."

"There is?"

Armas shook his head. Sometimes Slobodan seemed like a complete idiot and amateur.

"Sure, the cops can dig out old messages. It takes them five minutes."

"Okay, I'll get rid of it," Slobodan said and gestured to the computer. "Buy a new one before you leave, since you understand these things."

Armas gave one of his rare smiles. Slobodan chuckled. Suddenly Armas realized why he had been able to stand this fat slob for so many years.

The telephone rang. Slobodan answered.

"No, not in here. We'll do it in the kitchen," he said and hung up.

"It is Gonzo," Slobodan explained. "He's in the bar. He wants to talk."

Armas shook his head.

"We are done talking," he said.

It was Armas who had fired him, and when Slobodan had asked why, Armas had not provided a real answer. He didn't like it, but he trusted Armas's judgment.

"We can at least hear what he wants," Slobodan said and heaved himself up out of the chair.

Armas gave him a look, and this look was something Slobodan would later recall. What had it meant? It was not the usual trace of arrogance and irritation in the habitually so expressionless face, but something else. Was it fear? Slobodan did not think so, neither then nor later. Perhaps Armas felt as if Slobodan was rejecting his assessment that Gonzo had to go?

That had always been Armas's weak point. He could take much, but the few times that Slobodan criticized him, he became hurt, grew silent and withdrawn. It was an almost frightening reaction, coming from him. Slobodan liked it much better when he got angry.

"He probably wants to talk nonsense like always," Slobodan said.

They took Gonzo out to the kitchen. Armas sat down in a chair. Gonzo did not look as confident as usual. In fact, he seemed to have shrunk.

"Well, what do you want, Mr. Gonzo?"

"It's not fair," the waiter said, glancing quickly at Armas.

"That is finished," Slobodan said. "It is not anything to talk about."

"He's firing me only because he . . ."

"Shut up!" Armas yelled.

Gonzo momentarily lost his balance, as if the gust of air from Armas had hit him square in the chest.

"One more fucking word out of you and you know what happens!"

Armas had stood up and looked even taller than usual.

"You'd better be going," Slobodan said and put his hand on Gonzo's shoulder, pushing the door open and leading him out of the kitchen.

When the swinging doors had come to a complete standstill, Slobodan turned.

"What was all that about?"

"He is a little shit," Armas said.

"Can that be a problem?"

"Yes, but only for himself," Armas said and Slobodan heard him try to adopt a slightly lighter tone.

What had Gonzo done to upset Armas so much? Good waiters did not grow on trees, and the Dakar was understaffed. Now they had to take on an untrained waitress. All they needed was for Tessie to get sick for a day or two and service would collapse. Armas knew all this and had fired Gonzo anyway.

The reason must be personal. If it had been anything to do with the job, if Gonzo had cheated with the tips or swiped a bottle of hard liquor, Slobodan would have heard about it.

Slobodan had the question on the tip of his tongue but held it back, afraid of hurting his partner.

✦

Eight

The party at the far end of the restaurant was singing so loudly they could hear it all the way in the kitchen. Johnny smiled to himself, leaning with the torch over a crème brûlée so that Pirjo would have time to pee.

"It is the medicine," she said apologetically.

Johnny wondered what kind of medication an eighteen-year-old girl needed, but had not asked, only waved encouragingly.

It had been a full-speed start. The day after Johnny had met Slobodan for the first time, and the other chefs Feo and Donald, he found himself in the kitchen at Dakar, with his knives wrapped in a kitchen towel, full of anticipation but also a little tense about a new workplace and new routines.

He would help out, above all with the cold food and desserts, the presentation and general kitchen organization.

Feo was the one who seemed the most open and talkative. Almost as soon as they met, he had started talking about the woman he had met in Algarve, how he had served her, fallen in love, saved up money, and traveled to Sweden for better or for worse, stepped off at Arlanda with a note in his wallet with her name on it and the city where she had said she lived.

With the help of a friendly man outside the railway station in Uppsala he had located the woman's name in the telephone directory.

"Now I am very happy," he said and Johnny saw that he really meant it.

"It will be a boy!" Feo laughed as he chopped celery. "I promise you!"

He radiated joy, and not only because he was going to be a father. He performed his work in the kitchen with a degree of accuracy that testified to a deep-seated sense of personal satisfaction. Many times that day Johnny found himself staring at his colleague.

Feo's joie de vivre also found expression in his body movements, which could have been a disaster in such a narrow space, where his long legs and windmill arms always appeared to be in motion. But like a professional dancer, he was coordinated and in complete control.

He had brought his love of fish and shellfish from Portugal. The most wonderful sauces were magically transfigured by his fish broth.

Donald, who was the head chef, was much more restrained. He had wished Johnny welcome but not said much else. He always worked at the meat stove and disliked, not to say hated, Slobodan Andersson.

"The lying poodle is a miscreant, a spectacularly failed combination of Skåne and Belgrade," he said when Johnny asked how Dakar's management worked.

"Slobodan is a pig, but a good pig," Feo objected. "He is perhaps not . . . what do you say about dogs that do their business inside?"

"House-broken," Johnny suggested.

"Exactly. Slobban is perhaps not house-broken, but he makes things happen."

As he talked he put a couple of pieces of halibut into the frying pan. Donald stood frozen at the stove. A fillet was sizzling in the pan. Tessie requested another order of halibut. Donald nodded, and Feo laughed.

"Yes, please, another halibut. Hello there, Tessie!" he yelled out after Tessie, who left as quickly as she came in. Donald shot him a sharp look.

Johnny smiled to himself. He thought that he would enjoy working in Dakar's kitchen. He had not thought about Sofia in Jönköping for several hours.

"How long has Tessie been working here?" he asked Feo.

"She started at about the same time as me. She is from New York."

"Long Island," Donald added.

Feo grinned.

"She is never in love, that is her biggest problem," he continued. "She needs a man."

Pirjo returned from the bathroom. Tessie came in with two new orders.

"Two anglerfish," Donald said.

"Loud and clear," Feo replied.

Johnny helped Pirjo. Gonzo came in from the dining room, went without a word to the dirty dishes, and started loading up the dishwasher.

It was his last week. Everyone had heard how he and Armas, in connection with opening up after the summer break, had screamed at each other in the changing room. Armas had emerged with a satisfied expression, as if he had killed a rat.

Gonzo came out after five minutes but did not go out into the dining room. It was only after Armas came in and told him that Gonzo went out to do his job. Everyone was amazed that he had not left immediately. He also didn't try to engage his coworkers' support in the conflict, only muttering to himself.

No one asked him what it was all about, but Tessie had mentioned something about Gonzo trying to pressure Armas, that he had information that could hurt Armas. It was gossip of the kind that Feo and Donald thought laughable—what could little Gonzo know that could possibly harm the powerful Armas?

A woman came into the kitchen a little after nine. Donald glared at her but said nothing.

"The bathroom is to the right in the corridor," Feo said.

Sometimes customers went through the wrong door.

"I'm supposed to start working here," the woman said.

"You are the new one! Wonderful! We need many beautiful women here, isn't that right, Johnny?"

Feo closed the door of the warming cabinet and wiped his hands on the cloth he had tied at his waist.

"Welcome. I am Feo."

"Thank you. I'm starting tomorrow and I'm more than a little nervous. I've never waitressed before."

"Typical Slobodan," Donald muttered.

"That is Donald. He is nice, I promise. Johnny talks funny and he is also new. You will have to start a club, don't you think? What is your name?"

"Eva Willman."

"Of course I will," Feo exclaimed in an attempt at a pun, and Donald stared at him.

"Your anglerfish," he said and Feo threw himself over the stove.

Johnny introduced himself and shook hands.

"You are the brother of Simon's mother, aren't you?"

Johnny nodded.

"It was through her . . ."

He returned to the dessert but snuck glances at the new waitress while Feo enthusiastically talked about Dakar. She was around Johnny's own age. His sister Bitte had told him that Eva was divorced with two teenage boys. Johnny studied her from behind. He had noticed that he had started staring at women, not to check them out but to find faults and defects, as if his time with Sofia had perverted his sight.

She had rejected him too many times, and when she later approached him, he was unable to make love. Their cooling relationship had made him limp. It was not only the physical change, more fundamental was that his view of women had changed. He was as interested in women as before, but now he felt disdain, or even sometimes hatred had stolen in, like a malignant virus.

A woman's laughter in the street, the hint of a beautiful curve in a woman's body, or a woman's voice now left Johnny largely indifferent. If any feelings made themselves known then it was simply disdain, a cold dismissiveness. Where he had earlier thought he saw genuine joy, desirable beauty, and promising optimism, he now increasingly saw hypocrisy and falseness.

Women had become a foreign and antagonistic group.

The feeling of being rejected was not pleasant, and he was not happy with the change, it was nothing he had wished for. In moments of clarity he questioned his perception, tried to get some insight into what it was that had perverted him. Was it simply the disastrous relationship with Sofia? Was there something in himself that had nurtured these feelings?

Sofia had rejected him, and not only in bed. He felt that she had also shut him out of the different parts of her life, as if he was not worthy of accompanying her.

"You are so immature," she would say, and he would feel as if he were a child caught doing something wrong.

He became more and more disgusted with himself, as if he had allowed himself to become a victim, and one day he did what Sofia had perhaps wanted for a long time. He packed up his few possessions and left.

Now he stared at the waitress who was laughing together with Feo. Johnny heard the Portuguese tell her about the expected baby, how happy he was and what a fantastic woman he lived with, and he saw how Eva lit up.

Donald sighed, making a little extra noise when he carelessly tossed the pan into the sink.

"Fix the pan," he told Pirjo, who obeyed him immediately and started scrubbing it under the faucet.

Her face was flushed from the heat in the kitchen. She cast a brief glance at Johnny, pushed some stray hairs off her forehead, and turned her body as if she wanted to hide from the world.

You think I'm nothing but an old man, Johnny thought, and wished he could show his disdain for all little girls who thought they were hotshots in the kitchen.

Tessie appeared in the window again. After a period of calm, the pressure was once again mounting in the dining room. It was as if waves of customers were washing in over Dakar.

Johnny sensed that Gonzo was not being much help. He was not going to put in much effort this last week.

"One veal," Tessie said, but Donald did not answer.

"Did you get it or do you want it in writing?" Tessie said with such aggression in her tone that even Donald looked up.

Then he turned his back to her, nabbed a piece of meat, and threw it in the pan.

"Deep down she's nice," Feo said. "All Americans think everyone hates them."

"Why do you say that?" Eva asked. She had placed herself in the doorway.

"They're bombing the hell out of everyone," Feo said.

"They should bomb this place," Donald said.

"Then you would die," Feo said.

"I *am* dead."

Donald smiled unexpectedly at Johnny and leaned nearsightedly over a plate. He painstakingly arranged a few leaves in a salad, then straightened his back and regarded the arrangement before bending down again for a final adjustment.

Tessie turned up again.

"Sweet love," Donald said in English, and pushed over a plate.

The waitress stared at him, but the hint of a smile swept across her for the moment rather tense features before she left.

"Just think what a little diplomacy can achieve," Donald said, and Johnny was forced to revise his opinion of him. There would be many times that he would get to experience how Donald awakened from a basically catatonic state and started to engage in wry and lightly ironic banter.

The new waitress hung around and watched them attentively in their work. It was as if Feo's introduction and jocular patter had done her good, because she looked relaxed. Johnny could see that she, like most visitors in a restaurant kitchen, was careful not to get in the way. The kitchen in Dakar was narrow. Three chefs and an apprentice were crowded into the space of several square meters.

At his last restaurant in Jönköping, where Johnny had worked for about a year, the dining room had swelled out into a veritable sea while the chefs worked with the claustrophobic feeling of being in the cabin of a submarine.

The work required a choreography of quick but well-thought out movements and an intuitive ability to sense where one's coworkers were and where they were likely to move in the next moment.

"Behind you," came from Feo, who was between the fish stove and the window, and with a smile he slipped past Donald, who in turn was making a sudden excursion with the meat thermometer.

Pirjo was sent out to fetch more filets. Donald watched her brushing the meat, while he prepared two Cornish game hens.

The temperature rose. Feo, who was preparing a sauce for the salmon, was bright red in the face. Pirjo returned to the desserts. Donald poked the poultry breasts with his index finger and then lifted them onto the plates that had been prepared for them. He drizzled the morel sauce over them, corrected the potato-and-duck liver terrine, and rang the bell. Tessie appeared and took the plates away.

Dozens of pots and pans were cooking at once. Steam rose lazily from the fish broth, pans sizzled, an open flame suddenly appeared on the stove and the plates that Pirjo supplied clattered.

Feo looked up and gave Johnny a quick glance as if to say: now you understand why we are grateful that you came.

Johnny, as yet untrained in the particular routines and the others' patterns of movement, tried to keep the pace and see to the priorities.

A sudden break in the flow of orders created a few minutes of breathing room. Everyone straightened their backs. Feo drank a little water and Donald slipped off to the hand sink.

"You smoke too much," Feo called out.

Donald did not reply, but the cloud of smoke from the sink area showed the lack of impact of his coworker's views. Johnny was surprised that a kitchen chef would take a smoke break. He had never experienced this before, but he did not comment on it.

It was completely quiet in the kitchen. Pirjo was resting against the counter, examining her cuticles with a dreamy expression. Feo was standing at the sink provided for their personal use, looking at his face in the mirror while he thoroughly dried his hands with a paper towel.

Eva lingered in the doorway. She had not said anything in a while. She knows us, Johnny thought, and it struck him that she reminded him a little of his sister. A somewhat reserved manner, often with a cool smile on her lips, a smile that could come across as superior but that in his sister's case expressed a desire for mutual understanding. Johnny was often irritated by Bitte's tentative personality, her somewhat lazy appearance and her tendency to submit to others.

If Eva was the same, it would be hard for her. You had to be able to take what you needed in this business. If you didn't stand up for your rights, you would be taken advantage of.

"How much are they paying you?" Johnny asked.

Eva looked around the kitchen. Feo was studying her in the mirror. Donald, who had returned from his smoke break, let out a snort.

"Not very much, but it's supposed to increase later," Eva said.

"That's what they always say," Donald muttered.

"It's a job," Eva said and tried to catch his gaze.

"A job," Feo repeated.

Johnny knew that his question had broken a silent agreement not to publicly discuss their remuneration, especially not with someone who was newly hired. At that point one was expected to hold one's tongue and only slowly develop a clearer picture of all the constructions and agreements in the business. One had to make the mark before one gained the right to ask such questions, and that could take half a year, perhaps longer.

"At least we share the tips equally," Eva said.

Johnny hoped she would not ask how much that yielded, and he thought she understood the look he gave her, because she swallowed her next comment and laughed as if she didn't want to be pulled into a game in which she only guessed at the rules.

"See you tomorrow," she said and glided out the door, returning almost immediately.

"There's a famous cop out there," she said.

Donald froze in the middle of his movements. Feo turned around.

"Who is it?" they asked at the same time.

"Her name is Lindell," Eva said. "She has a kid at the day care next to the school where my youngest is."

"What is she doing here?"

"Having dinner, of course. What did you think?"

Feo shrugged and chuckled. Donald stared sourly after the waitress.

"What the hell is up with her?" he asked.

"I wonder what the cop is doing here," Feo said.

"You heard her," Johnny said, "she's having dinner."

"I don't believe in cops," Feo said.

"What the hell is up with her?" Donald repeated. "Gonzo isn't the greatest, but at least he doesn't gab so damn much."

Feo peered out through the window.

"Cops don't just come here and eat," he said. "She's probably investigating something."

"Is that a problem?" Johnny asked. "Are you working under the table?"

For a moment, Feo looked upset and he shot Johnny an angry look, but then he resumed his carefree demeanor.

"No, but I am from Portugal," he said.

Johnny waited for an explanation but it never appeared, and he simply shrugged.

Pirjo, who had hardly said one word all evening, laughed. A dry, joyless laugh that made even Donald look up.

"I am from Finland," she said.

"I am from Småland," Johnny said.

"Tessie is from the USA," Pirjo said.

"Gonzo is from Gonzoland," Feo added.

Everyone's gaze was directed at Donald. It was as if a great seriousness had gripped the staff of Dakar, as if someone had entered the kitchen in order to deliver some grave news.

The meat chef turned a fillet in the pan and then looked around, allowing his gaze to travel from Johnny, on to Pirjo, and finally landing on

Feo with a contemplative smile, stroking his chin with one hand while the other reached for a frying pan, seemingly of its own accord.

"I was born in Kerala," he said after a couple of trembling seconds of absolute silence, turning his back to the others and pulling down yet another pan from the rack above the stove. He held it outstretched above his head for a moment, as if it were a torch.

"Kerala," he repeated.

Feo burst into a thunderous laughter but stopped as suddenly.

"Where is that?" Pirjo asked.

"To the East," Donald said.

"So is Lempälä," she said.

"And we are all gathered here," Johnny said. "In Dakar's kitchen."

For a few moments he experienced a feeling of expansion, despite the limited space of the kitchen. He was suddenly very happy that he had left Jönköping and Sofia. It was as if life had taken a little hop, and not simply straight up in order to land in the same spot, but Johnny now knew that the move to Uppsala meant a forward movement. He studied Feo, who was leaning over a plate of anglerfish, and then let his gaze wander over to the head chef. Donald really was a complicated person. Johnny could not yet decide when he was joking and when he was serious.

His face looked as if it had been carved out of marble, with heavy cheeks and a meaty nose above the deeply set eyes. Eyes that appeared to regard the kitchen as the only possible refuge, but also a prison for the dreams he painstakingly concealed behind a dismissive facade.

Donald had worked in perhaps fifteen different kitchens in his thirty years as a chef. Johnny had met many of these cooking nomads. If they could maintain some semblance of balance between the late work shifts, the subsequent late nights, alcohol, and an attempt at a social life, then their professional skill could flower and become a security in any stormy and stressful kitchen, a rock for many a restaurant owner.

Maybe Donald was this kind of man, he would find out in time. He watched over the plates that left Dakar's kitchen like a hawk, and they were a series of perfection.

"This and nothing else," he said and showed Johnny how the veal should look.

"Nothing else," he repeated and polished away a spot that was quite invisible to Johnny.

He nodded, studied the plate, and, realizing that there was nothing to alter, tried to memorize the arrangement.

Donald left the kitchen at ten o'clock. Pirjo also went home after Johnny promised to handle the cleaning up. He put things away, rinsed and scrubbed the floor while Feo made a rapid inventory check and called in orders to suppliers' answering machines.

Afterward they each sat down with a beer. Feo smoked a cigarette, only one, in silence, with obvious pleasure.

"You go home," Johnny said. "I'll take out the garbage."

Feo shook his head.

"This is the best time," he said and smiled at Johnny. "Let's drink some coffee and have a calva. We have to celebrate your start here."

"How come you speak such good Swedish?"

"Practice," Feo said. "I talk with my wife all the time and she corrects me. Our place is like a language course. It is the only way to become a person, to understand the words. Should I go around like a *svartskalle* and understand nothing?"

"One thing," Johnny said. "Where does Donald come from? He said Kerala, but that's in India."

"His father was a missionary," Feo answered. "Donald lived in India for fifteen years. You should taste his bean dishes and lamb cooked in yogurt. He could open an Indian restaurant."

He stood up, left the kitchen, and returned with espresso and calvados on a platter.

"Slobodan's treat," he said.

They drank their coffee in silence. Johnny experienced the fatigue in his body as a pleasant mutedness. Voices and laughter could be heard from the dining room and the bar while the kitchen rested in stillness. The best time, Johnny thought, and stared into the shimmer of the calvados for a long time before he tasted it.

The spirits exploded in his mouth and he jerked forward as if he had received a violent blow to his back, but he managed to put the glass down before he ran over to the sink.

Feo watched him but said nothing. Johnny remained leaning over the sink. He spit, and did everything he could to quell his impulse to retch.

"Damn," he said, when his body had calmed down, "it must have gone down the wrong way."

"Have a little water," Feo said.

After exchanging a few words with Måns in the bar, Feo and Johnny said their good-byes in the alley outside Dakar's kitchen entrance. The Portuguese unlocked his bicycle and rolled away. Johnny stood and watched his new colleague as he left.

He should have known better than to have a strong drink like that. It had started about a year ago, the nausea and heaving and a diffuse ache in his abdomen. An ache that sometimes turned into a stabbing pain. Beer was all right and sometimes also white wine, even if the enjoyment of having a glass was now diminished since he feared the nausea and pain. At first, Sofia had urged him to go to a doctor, but then it was as if she had lost interest in his well-being and she stopped commenting on his contorted expressions.

What had Feo thought? Did he sense that Johnny's claim that the drink had gone down the wrong way had been a lie? Feo had not said anything, but his eyes revealed that he had not completely bought the explanation.

Johnny walked home. He did not mind that it was a long way, perhaps two kilometers. He actually appreciated the mild and restful evening, the occasional person he encountered did not bother him, and he thought that his new city reminded him of a foreign country. It was a feeling he would carry with him for a long time, that he was a guest, a stranger who did not have any duties to the town and its inhabitants.

If anyone talked to him, posed a question, or sought his opinion, he could excuse himself with the fact that he was new, a temporary visitor, and in this way avoid all responsibility.

It was Sofia, connected to his dream of a life with meaning, who haunted him. He knew that his self-imposed outsider status was a defense. He lived as if in quarantine. Working as a cook at Dakar was the only thing that made him human, a social creature. He did not seek the company of others, their warmth or acceptance. He could just as well have been wandering in an uninhabited land. It was as if he had taken a job that was offered out of habit. Lacking all will, he had allowed himself to be influenced by his sister and moved to Uppsala.

There had been a time when he had loved his work, but his goal of becoming a great chef had started to fade. Now he saw it as his only possibility to survive, nothing more. It gave him a salary and the illusion that he had a task. The passion was gone, and deep inside he was terrified. At least thirty more years in the business and the disdain for food magazines, enthusiastic guests, and curious aquaintances, their constant chatter about newly discovered dishes, exhausted him, made him increasingly embittered. His former friends had no idea what it was like: the constant pressure to turn out beautiful presentations of delicious food, while life itself was distasteful and anything but beautiful.

When did the whole thing start, this process of decomposition as life crumbled away? Or rather, rotted, as there was nothing life-affirming about the process, no healthy microorganisms that diligently and naturally went about their business. This was oxygen-poor putrefaction, the stinking decay of unblemished blood and flesh, that was wreaking havoc inside Johnny.

He observed this change with fear but also fascination, because it was with the misanthropy of a masochist that he presided over his own deterioration as a human being. He wanted, and did not want, to sink to the bottom and from thence spread his inhuman venom, spiked with self-disgust and an increasing animosity, to the people around him who still appeared to nurture hope.

When he arrived at the apartment, a one-bedroom flat by Klockarängen, he lit a candle. Candles belonged to winter, the dark season, but as he was unpacking his things he had found a candle, which he placed on the old teak coffee table.

The candle gave off the slightly sweet scent of vanilla. He sat for a while in the sofa, made of a plasticky artificial leather, and stared at the fluttering flame before he got up with a sigh, blew it out, and went to bed.

He fell asleep and slept heavily and without dreaming for ten hours, but was awakened by a nightmare when it was already late morning. He sat up with a start. The morning sun shone in through the provisionally erected curtains.

✦

Nine

Eva Willman took out two apples and put them on either side of the kitchen table. It created an appealing picture, full of promise, as if Patrik and Hugo's future rested on the fact that each morning there were two gleaming red apples at their places.

Even though it was only six-thirty she wanted to wake them up, get in those extra few minutes and tell them about Dakar. When they were young, they always woke up early, and they had some time together before Eva had to leave for work and the children to their school or child care programs, but now breakfast usually consisted of some sleepy comments, a few whining complaints, and a couple of sandwiches consumed in haste.

She looked at the apples, red, thick-skinned, with stickers declaring their land of origin: New Zealand. Someone sends fruit from the other side of the globe, she thought, and pictured an orchard in a foreign land. There were people there, dressed in khaki shorts and T-shirts with logos on the front. They drove small vehicles with carts on the back. From time to time they stopped, reached for an apple, and applied a tiny sticker. Eva imagined that they had a Patrik and a Hugo in their thoughts as they carefully laid the apples in a basket.

She made coffee and waited for the children to wake up. Today things would start in earnest. She couldn't help feeling it in her stomach. She was going to shadow Tessie, who was teaching her.

One thing that worried her was pronouncing the names of the dishes correctly. Anglerfish and duck breast were no problem, but the menu consisted of so much more. Then there were the wines with all those foreign names. Eva had brought home both the menu and the wine list and practiced the pronunciation, had even asked Patrik and Hugo for help.

And even if she had basically mastered the pronunciation then the question remained about what it meant. She had no idea what "confit" and *concassé* were, or if "Gevrey Chambertin" was a red or white wine.

She hoped that Tessie would have patience and that the guests would not get irritated or make fun of her.

Eva had decided she would try not to talk too much. If she adopted a calm attitude and did not chatter on, the guests could get the impression that she was skilled and reliable. She couldn't screw up this job. Whatever it took, she was going to become a knowledgeable and quick-witted waitress, someone Slobodan Andersson could rely on.

This was not only a job, it was her entry to another life. That was how she felt. She was going to enter new areas, meet people other than the same old in Sävja and in the ICA store in Vilan, and become more interesting herself. She did not know anyone who worked at a restaurant, there were not many among her few acquaintances who were in the habit of going out to eat. Now she would be able to talk about something beyond the usual.

Suddenly she was frightened. What if it didn't work out?

"Hugo!" she cried out. "It's time!"

There was no sense in calling Patrik, he had to be shaken awake in the mornings.

✦

Ten

A piece of whale carcass that had washed ashore—that was how Haver had described the body, and Ann Lindell understood why as she studied the photographs that were arranged in a row on the table.

The feeling of revulsion was mixed with equal parts tingling anticipation.

"Do you believe me when I say that all investigators love a murder?" Ottosson had asked her many years ago. Back then she had dismissed his statement as absurd, now she was prepared to admit he was right.

Even the fact that she was given a reason to walk up to the wall map gave meaning to her life, and she studied it with the resolute concentration of a general, following the course of the Fyris river, memorizing new names and wondering if she had ever been to the Sunnersta hole, the old hillside gravel pit that had become a ski slope.

Her gaze traveled from the ridge to the river and located Lugnet. In the river, in the reeds, lay a human body that in Ola Haver's eyes had been transformed to a lump of flesh.

The body had been discovered by two boys who had been throwing rocks at the wild ducks that lived in the reeds. One of the boys, eleven years of age, had stayed by the body while his friend had run across a paddock and up to the road in order to flag down a car.

When Haver later asked the eleven-year-old why he had remained behind, if he hadn't found it creepy, the boy had replied that he didn't want the birds pecking at the man.

Even though Lindell had lived in Uppsala for many years, she had never taken the road between Nåntuna and Flottsund. Fredriksson had said that it was a beautiful road, especially in spring. He liked to watch the birds that gathered along the Fyris river. In April, the northern lapwings held a great conference on the open fields by the Flottsund bridge.

"Then I know it's spring," Fredriksson said. He had two interests: birds and harness racing.

Ottosson even had a literary reference. He claimed that the Swedish writer Göran Tunström had written a novel that was partly set in this area, and that the book was worth reading. Ottosson offered to bring it in if anyone was interested, but no one responded.

Lindell let them talk without interrupting. Instead, she focused on her own tension, increasing her enjoyment.

"Could it be a boating accident?" Ottosson threw out, while he examined the police photographs. "Perhaps he fell overboard?"

He was leaning over the images.

"With his throat cut?"

"Yes, an outboard motor," Ottosson said, and turned his head to give her a look that said: agree with me, let it be a tragic accident.

It took several seconds before Lindell understood what he meant.

"In his underwear and nothing else?" she said.

"No, of course not," Ottosson muttered.

"Who is he?"

"He doesn't really look Swedish," Fredriksson said.

"What do you mean, Swedish?"

"Not born in Sweden, I mean," Fredriksson said, his eyes twinkling at Lindell.

Lindell sighed, but it was more an expression of sympathy with Ottosson than exasperation. The spring had been catastrophic. Perhaps not from a weather perspective, which did not mean much to her, but professionally. Boring routine matters one after the other, with eruptions of youth violence in Gränby and Sävja, and a hooligan armed with a knife who had wreaked havoc in the downtown area for a few weeks, assaulting nighttime wanderers on their way home from the bars. He had been seized without drama, and by accident. It had turned out to be a mentally deranged individual who had been returned to the clinic from which he had come.

Summer had not been much better. She had spent her vacation at home, except for a weeklong visit to her parents in Ödeshög and a long weekend in a loaned summer cottage. That was the best of her four weeks off. Erik discovered insects, and together they immersed themselves in the lives of ants, beetles, and spiders. For him it was a new world while for her it was sheer antiphobia therapy.

She realized that he was starting to develop new needs, that he was becoming more active, curious, and engaged in the world around him, but also more demanding. It was no longer enough for him to have a piece of paper and some crayons or Legos. He wanted Ann to be engaged, overwhelming her with questions and thoughts. Sometimes she was not equal to these demands, grew tired, wanted most of all to stretch out on the sand by the small forest lake, read or simply ruminate with her gaze fixed on the pair of ospreys sailing over the water. She could not hand Erik over to someone else. It was only the two of them.

In the evenings after he fell asleep, she sat down with a bottle of wine in a rusty hammock with ripped cushions, slowly swaying back and forth, thinking about her life. Normally she resisted these thoughts, but it was as if this setting, the isolation in the cottage, and the complete contrast to her daily life forced her to reflect. Perhaps also Erik's new needs meant that her future looked more uncertain than before. During those unusually sunny days in the cottage she saw her lone responsibility for his development in stark relief. He would start school within a few years and she could only imagine what that would involve. Thereafter he would shortly become a teenager and she would be approaching fifty.

She read the first page of the medical examiner's report of the autopsy. The man had bled to death after suffering a knife wound of eleven centimeters across his throat. He was dead before he hit the water. His age was estimated at between forty and fifty, he was one hundred and eighty-six centimeters tall and weighed ninety-two kilograms, was in good physical condition and without any distinguishing physical characteristics, except for what Lindell took to be the remains of a tattoo on his upper right arm. A patch of skin about five centimeters in diameter had been removed from the arm. What remained was a small dark line of about half a centimeter, which was what made her think there had once been an entire tattoo. There were two possible explanations to the flaying: to make the identification of the victim more difficult, or else the tattoo could have a direct link to the murderer.

Lindell picked up the close-ups of the upper arm area.

"What should we think?" Fredriksson said. "Was he murdered here or did he float here on the current?"

"We have people on both sides of the river who are looking into it," Lindell said, "but they haven't found anything so far."

"But how likely is it that a corpse can float down along the river without someone seeing it?"

"I don't know, Allan," Lindell said.

She stared at the photograph.

"Can't you check with TattooJack or whatever their names are. There must be tattoo experts."

"This isn't much to show them," Fredriksson said.

She pushed the photograph across the table without making eye contact.

"Check it anyway," Lindell said.

"Sure, babe," Fredriksson said.

Lindell gave him a long look. Sammy shot her an amused glance but kept his mouth closed.

"Anyone reported missing?"

"*Nada,*" Sammy Nilsson said. "I've checked the records six months back. But I've put a notice on the Web. We'll see what that brings."

If only the dead could speak, Lindell thought and smiled.

"I don't think he was a regular working stiff," Sammy said.

"You're thinking of his hands?"

Sammy nodded.

"One of his thumbnails was black and blue," Lindell said.

"Which can happen to the manager of a golf course," Ottosson said.

"What about his teeth?" Lindell asked.

"Good overall, according to the medical examiner, but some poorly executed dental work in his youth. Perhaps done overseas."

Lindell nodded.

"We'll have to hope for evidence recovered along the riverbank," she said after a moment's silence, and then got up from the table.

"Is anyone hungry?" she asked, but did not wait for an answer. Instead, she whisked out of the room, after first snatching her pad of paper.

"Why almost naked?" she said under her breath, while she took the elevator to the foyer of the new police station building. Though it had been inaugerated last fall, Lindell had not really grown accustomed to it yet. In spite of everything, she missed their old quarters. Of course, everything here was much airier and more functional, but something was missing. No one else had expressed any longing for Salagatan, so Lindell had kept her nostalgic musings to herself.

She continued to ply herself with questions during the rapid walk downtown. She followed Svartbäcksgatan along the river. Like in the area of Lugnet, where the corpse had been discovered, the wild ducks were chattering at the water's edge and terns were screeching up above.

The removed tattoo was important, that much was clear. If the victim had lived in Uppsala and was reported missing within the next day or two, and the identity could be determined, relatives and friends questioned, then it should not prove difficult to find out what the tattoo had looked like and perhaps where and by whom it had been done.

Then the act of taking the trouble of removing it would be undermined. In addition, the maneuver would turn out to be a way of putting the tattoo in focus, giving it a gravity that it would otherwise not have possessed. In other words, in Lindell's view, it was an irrational act.

She glanced at her watch. None of the restaurants that she passed had appealed to her and now she was suddenly pressed for time. In the pedestrian zone she instead bought a "Kurt," which was what one of her colleagues for some reason called a thick hot dog on a bun. She washed it down with a Festis fruit drink.

As she stood in the street with people walking by, entertained by what she at first took to be a performance troupe but that turned out to be a group of devotees of the evangelical church Livets Ord, her thoughts about the removed tattoo returned and she became increasingly convinced that its removal was largely a symbolic act.

She listened for a while to the heavenly choir and thereafter to a short testimonial by a member of the congregation. He was talking about Jesus, who else? He looked happy, almost ecstatic, as he triumphantly related how he had become a whole person through his Lord, Jesus Christ.

"I lived in poverty . . . !" he shouted.

"What do you make now?" someone in the audience shouted back.

The speaker was momentarily thrown off-kilter, but then resumed his preaching.

Lindell headed back to the station. Walking had become her way of trying to improve her condition. At her last checkup, the doctor had pronounced her fitness level terrible.

This had the result that she often ate lunch on her own. None of her colleagues had any desire to rush around town at her speed.

Back at her office, sweaty and barely full, she again rifled through the reports pertaining to the murder. What shall I call him for the moment? she wondered and picked a new notepad off the shelf.

"Jack" she wrote spontaneously on the first page. It was a pad of graph paper but this did not distract her. She immediately started to write out her thoughts on the significance of the tattoo. So far it was the only thing she could write about. All other facts were stated in the autopsy report. In time they would also receive the forensic findings.

Lindell produced half a page of notes in her, for her colleagues, illegible handwriting. Despite this meager start she felt pleased, optimistic even. Perhaps it was the warmth of late summer, perhaps it was simply the joy of feeling so strong, that the relationship with Charles Morgansson, the newcomer in the unit, that had ended in the spring was now definitely behind her, without pain. No doubts, no hard feelings, nothing unresolved between them, at least not from her side.

They had met last fall and very carefully embarked on a relationship. Charles was a very sweet person, she said to those who asked, but too meek for Lindell's taste. It took several months before they made love, and then it was not particularly passionate or even pleasurable. It was as if he apologized every time he initiated anything, and that wasn't often. Ann realized very early that he had problems. For a while she even suspected that he wasn't attracted to women, but she eventually concluded that it was his previous relationship in Umeå that still troubled him. Something had gone wrong. Perhaps that was the main reason he had moved to Uppsala, even though he claimed that his involvement in a traffic accident was the cause. Lindell didn't really want to know. She did not want to play therapist.

Their brief and underwhelming liaison was a closed chapter, an experience that strangely enough had strengthened her confidence. Görel, her friend and Erik's loyal babysitter, had tried to console her but Ann had dismissed her attempts.

"If anyone needs consoling, it's Charlie," Ann said and Görel had told her she was merciless, but laughed.

She had followed their whole story and was pleased deep down that it was over.

"You don't need a loser," she said.

"Agreed," Ann said, "I need . . ."

She could not bring herself to complete the sentence, because immediately an image of Edvard appeared. Edvard, her old love, gone from her life forever.

Görel realized that she was upset and guessed at the cause. She put an arm around Ann but was sensible enough not to make one of her sassy comments.

Lindell called Erik's day care and told Gunilla that she would be picking him up half an hour, or even a whole hour, later. The preschool teacher said that it was all right, but Lindell picked up a note of criticism in her gruff voice. The problem of parents not respecting the agree-upon dropoff and pickup times was something that came up at every parent-teacher meeting.

Lindell ended the call with the same feeling she always had: that she did not take good enough care of her son. He received everything he needed, and in fact enjoyed day care, but the feeling of inadequacy plagued her. To be both a police officer and a single mother was not an easy combination, but she sensed this was probably true for any single working parent. There was simply no good solution to the problem. All she could do was make the best of it. Lindell never worked on the weekends and very rarely worked evenings.

Ottosson, her immediate supervisor, was understanding and did everything in his power to make things easier for her. Without his support it would have been much harder, perhaps impossible, to continue in her current position.

On several occasions, Ottosson had talked to her about the superintendent training course, but she had always rejected his suggestions. On top of which, the course was located in Stockholm. And why should she set her sights on courses anyway? She was happy where she was and had no desire to ascend the career ladder.

After making a few more calls, she went to the lunchroom. Berglund was sitting with one elbow on his knee and his forehead cradled in his hand, as if he were nursing a headache. He was listening to Haver, who was telling him about his plans for his winter vacation. Lindell had time to hear that Haver was planning to travel to northern Italy with his wife, Rebecka, and their two daughters.

"The alps are nice," Berglund said, mostly in order to have something to say.

Lindell saw that his thoughts were elsewhere and when she sat down he took the opportunity to change the subject.

"Ann, do you remember Konrad Rosenberg?"

Lindell took a slurp of her coffee, reflected, and then nodded.

"Was he the one . . . it was something about fraud, credit cards, and drugs?"

"Exactly," Berglund said. "His name turned up in the investigation about the burglaries I'm working on. Not because I think he had anything to do with it, but, well, it turned up. Do you remember that he got a few years and went through detox?"

Lindell nodded and suddenly felt a sense of satisfaction at recalling something that happened many years ago, as well as a great joy that Berglund had thought to ask her in particular. It was like a verification that she meant something, that the two of them had a shared past.

Berglund was perhaps the colleague she was closest to. She felt secure with his calm temperament and loyalty. He was also a wise man, thoughtful, rarely judgmental, and free of pretension and desire for his own gain. He was an Uppsala native. In his youth he had been an active sportsman and had played both soccer and bandy. Later he had taken up orienteering and sat on the board of the club. Through his sport, his engagement in HSB, the housing cooperative, and his membership in the Mission church—something Lindell had found out about only recently and that surprised her, but also not—he had a number of threads connecting him with society. He functioned as a human seismograph that perceived the tremors in the city.

The only area that was closed to him was the Uppsala of the youth, students and immigrants. There he felt lost and admitted it freely.

"He has been clean for a number of years," Berglund said, "but now it seems he is on the move again. One of the informants—'Sture with the hat'—I questioned about the burglaries named Rosenberg, though only in passing. When I asked further it turned out that Rosenberg is suddenly in the money, as Sture put it."

"I've met Sture, he was a real talker," Haver inserted, "he only wanted to shine, appear interesting."

"Like so many others," Lindell said.

"It's possible," Berglund said.

"Maybe it was a way of getting around the subject of the burglaries, or else he doesn't know a thing but still wanted to seem helpful and have something to give you," Haver went on.

Berglund made a gesture to show that it was possible, but Lindell saw he had a different opinion.

"He recently bought a brand-new Mercedes," Berglund said. "I talked to a friend at the Philipson car dealership and, according to him, Rosenberg went straight for the luxury models."

"Did he pay in cash?"

"Without bargaining."

"Have you talked to the drug squad?" Lindell asked.

"No, it's all a bit thin," Berglund admitted.

Haver snickered.

Leave already for Italy with your Rebecka, Lindell thought impatiently, with a vague sense of envy.

"But if you hear anything," Berglund said in closing on the topic of Konrad Rosenberg, and then asked how things were going with the river murder.

"We're proceeding in the usual way," Lindell said, "but there's nothing so far. He's not in our records, at any rate. We've checked the prints."

"Maybe he's Russian?" Haver suggested.

"It's possible. What I'm wondering about the most, and I guess it's the only thing we have to speculate about right now, is the tattoo that was removed. I think it's some kind of symbolic act."

"That seems insane," Berglund said, and Lindell knew her colleague had quickly arrived at the same conclusion as she had, the amatuerishness in bringing attention to the tattoo.

"Maybe a red herring," Lindell said. "I don't know."

She took her coffee cup and returned to her office. The tattoo on the murdered man's arm, plus the fact that he was basically naked, was a mystery. Maybe these details were connected? Had the murderer undressed him in order to check for tattoos? Ann Lindell had seen almost everything but was nonetheless confounded, the ritualistic aspect of the flaying being unexpectedly frightening. She was more and more convinced that this had not been an ordinary act of punishment in the criminal world, something many of her collagues had intimated.

She wrote her thoughts down on her notepad, well aware of the fact that it was basically useless work, as her thoughts were in no way original. Her notes functioned more as a kind of therapy for the mind of a bewildered policewoman.

✦

Eleven

Ann received a shock when she arrived home, dragging a tired and whining Erik, who immediately threw himself down on the floor in the hall and refused to take off his coat and shoes. She didn't care, allowing him to sit there and stew, and simply went mechanically to the kitchen and got some crackers that she slipped into his hand.

The letter was lying on the doormat. A white rectangle against a green background. She thought it looked like a painting. She hesitated before picking it up. She recognized his handwriting. How could she forget it? His childish cursive, the sprawling style like that of a twelve-year-old. How many letters had she received from him? Perhaps one, and then a couple of postcards.

She stared at the letter with a feeling of paralysis mixed with anger. Why is he writing? Now? About what? She tried to understand, find reasons for Edvard to take the trouble. He was no letter writer, and in view of his vacillating character he had had endless opportunity to change his mind, even before he put the letter in its envelope and affixed the stamp. Ann could picture him in her mind, hesitant, his tongue poised to seal it. Thereafter, when he was on his way to the mailbox on the island or in to Öregrund, he could have left it on the table, said to himself that there was no hurry, or left it, unconsciously or consciously, in the car. Then, above all, the postbox, what agonies he must have suffered. And at last, the terror once the letter had been posted and he returned to the house on the island.

She bent down and picked it up. Erik had eaten up the crackers and was screaming for more. With the letter in her hand she pulled off his outerwear, stood him on his feet, dragged him into the kitchen, poured out some juice, and took out some chocolate-covered crackers.

There was nothing she didn't feel terrified about in the context of a letter from Edvard. There were evenings with half-drunk bottles of wine, warm nights and sticky sheets, mornings with a stiff body and a paralyzing feeling of meaninglessness, days at work, in front of the window facing east across the flat landscape, with the pointed spire of the Vaksala church as marker of the direction of her thoughts.

It was all this, all these hours, that were Edvard. Then to get a letter, so unlikely, so unfairly unnecessary, for what good could come of this? The most innocent greeting would mean a taunt. Some kind of apology equally so, but what did he have to apologize for? She was the one who had caused the breech. That he had later met a woman on his unexpected Thailand trip was something she had sniffed out but had not confirmed. That was a long time after they had broken up, so he could not be blamed for it. She herself had become pregnant by another man, which was far worse.

A thought that perhaps he had moved made her take a second look at the envelope, but there was nothing to indicate the sender's address.

Why send a letter when he could just as easily have called? Was the content such that he could not bear to give it over the phone? Was it an invitation to his wedding? That was the kind of event one chose to send out formal notices about. No, he would not be so cruel.

Erik had finished his chocolate and begged for more. Ann tore off a piece of paper towel and wiped his hands and mouth.

"I'll give you a little more, but that's all," she said and felt a pang of guilt. It was Erik who was her life, the one she loved and longed for. What did a silly letter mean?

For a moment she considered throwing it out, but it was such a painful thought that she immediately dismissed it.

She tore open the envelope. Inside was a full-size sheet of paper. The text consisted of only a few lines:

Dear Ann,

I hope you are well. I just wanted to tell you that Viola has broken her hip and is at the Akademiska Hospital. It happened in the hen house. She is in the orthopedic wing, 70E. I'm working mostly. She would be grateful to have a visitor.

Regards, Edvard

Ann read it again. So typical of Edvard. Short sentences, a jumble of hen houses and hospitals. No personal information other than that he was working. As if that was new. Nothing about how he was or what he was thinking.

She read it a third time. Perhaps Viola was in bad shape? She was over ninety years old, after all. That must be it, Ann thought, otherwise he would not have written. He thinks she is going to die and knows I would not forgive him if he had not told me. Perhaps Viola asked him to write? Perhaps the idea had been hers alone?

After Edvard left his family many years ago he had lived in Viola's house in Gräsö. It was an old archipelago homestead from the 1800s, and Edvard rented the whole upstairs. He had eventually acclimatized to the island, found a job with a builder, and regarded himself as a permanent Gräsö inhabitant. For Viola it was both a security and a comfort to have Edvard as a tenant. She lacked family, and after he had lived there for a couple of years she decided that it was Edvard who would be her heir.

At first Viola had seen Ann as a threat, someone who would perhaps convince Edvard to move away. But in time the old woman had accepted her, seemingly against her will and gruffly, as was her manner. She had perhaps hoped that Edvard and Ann would become a couple on Gräsö.

Viola herself had had an unhappy love affair in her youth—Victor, an old childhood friend of the same age. At some point Viola had let slip that she once, seventy years ago, had hoped that they would marry. But nothing came of it. Victor went to sea, was away from the island for a few years, came back and took over his parents' farm. They still saw each other. Victor came by almost every day. Ann saw them as the world's most devoted noncohabiting couple.

Perhaps it was there, in the old peoples' unconsummated life together, the material source for why Viola had let Ann come close. She saw that however intimate Ann and Edvard were, they didn't manage to make it.

Ann didn't know anything about what it meant to break a hip, but imagined that for an old person it could mark the beginning of the end. Perhaps Viola sensed this and wished to see Ann one last time?

Candy and juice had perked Erik up and he crawled down from the chair. Ann watched him as he disappeared into his room. He was largely independent now and she thanked the gods for it.

Of course she had to visit the old woman. She wanted to go to the hospital immediately, but she couldn't take Erik. Ann also didn't want Viola to meet him, since he was the reason why Ann and Edvard had broken up.

She decided she would go there tomorrow directly after the morning meeting at work. She would spend the evening with her speculations. She read the letter one more time and wished she could have seen Edvard when he wrote it.

✦

Twelve

Lorenzo Wader ordered a Staropramen, then took the beer to the room beyond the bar, lit a cigarillo, and leaned back in an armchair. The little man would arrive in ten minutes.

Lorenzo did not trust him, why should he? A little rat spreading gossip. But he was a useful rat. Lorenzo smiled to himself and gave a couple of the other hotel guests a nod as they walked past on their way into the bar. They had exchanged a few words the day before and the men had told him they were attending a seismology conference with participants from around the world. Lorenzo had pacified their curiosity by telling them that he was a businessman who was looking for new markets and contacts, which was true. He wanted to expand.

At the agreed-upon time the rat slunk in through the entrance, gave the receptionist a worried look, caught sight of Lorenzo Wader, and steered a course toward him.

Lorenzo put down his cigarillo and stood up.

"On time," he said simply and stretched out his hand.

They sat down. Olaf González shot a glance at the beer but gave no indication of an intention to order one for himself.

"Well," Lorenzo said, "what's new?"

"Armas is on his way to Spain," González said.

The high pitch of his voice was accentuated by the slight Norwegian accent.

"He is going by car."

It was clear that he had more to say, but Lorenzo did not help him along. Instead he sat quietly, sucking on the revived cigarillo, and reached for his beer.

"I have been fired," Olaf González said, and this was followed by the whole story of how unfairly he had been treated.

Lorenzo Wader understood that his story also contained a veiled critique of himself, or at least an expectation of his support.

"I'm sorry to hear that," Lorenzo said, "but I am sure it will turn out for the best." He wanted to keep the rat in a good mood, without promising too much.

"I gave him the package and the next day he came down to Dakar. He was furious. I thought he was going to kill me."

"But you only lost your job," Lorenzo said. "Why? Do you have any dirty laundry?"

"What do you mean 'dirty laundry'?"

"Does Armas know anything about you that is not so flattering?" Lorenzo explained.

González stared at him. How stupid you are, Lorenzo thought.

"How did you know?"

Lorenzo sighed.

"Would you like a beer?"

The waiter looked insulted, unexpectedly shook his head, and Lorenzo perceived a small movement.

"Stay seated," he said and González sank back into the chair. "You have done a good job," he went on, "and the bullet hit its mark, that is the important thing. This is the good news, much more important than the unfortunate fact that you lost your shitty job at a shitty restaurant. This is how you must see it. It is called perspective."

Lorenzo studied the man on the other side of the table. He knew too little about González, but on the other hand he knew the type and trusted his first impression. González was for sale, and right now he was in a spot. Lorenzo knew that his prospects of getting another job in this town were limited. This was to Lorenzo's advantage, even though he would have preferred to keep him positioned at Dakar.

He could finish him off, but González was still useful. He knew the town and the restaurant business.

"What do you want with Armas anyway?" González asked.

Lorenzo winced at this word choice, but he answered with a smile.

"Nothing bad," he said.

"I don't believe you," González said with unexpected vehemence.

"Why spend so much time on him if this isn't something big? I'm not that stupid."

"I never said you were. Why did I contact you? I am so tired of shady types and barflies with an inflated sense of their own importance. I wanted to have an experienced contact here. Someone who could introduce me around town."

Not a single word revealed Lorenzo Wader's real purpose, that of establishing himself in Uppsala. One of Lorenzo's runners had gotten in touch with González a few weeks ago and had asked him to give Armas a package. The payment for his troubles had been two thousand kronor, enough to indicate that this was not your usual mail delivery.

When González had accepted, Lorenzo got in touch with him directly. The transaction was completed and the money changed hands.

The next step was already planned, and in this González had no role to play, but even so Lorenzo decided to keep him in a good mood. He could be useful in the future.

"Olaf, it is partly my fault that you have become unemployed," Lorenzo said, "and this is regrettable, but of course you shall remain untainted. There will be other jobs."

Olaf González could not repress a smile.

"Call me Gonzo," he said.

✦

Thirteen

Two days at Dakar and Eva was completely exhausted. Her arms and legs ached, but above all it was the stress of trying to perform that drained her. She was supposed to respond both to her clients' wishes and to Tessie's orders, because orders were what she gave. Without reservation, without a smile, except for a wry expression now and again that Eva interpreted as critical oversight. With her stress level, Eva also had trouble understanding Tessie's rapid commands in broken Swedish.

But all in all, Eva felt she was managing all right. Feo was the one who gave her constant encouragement. His thin face shone with kindness across the counter where the chefs placed their finished plates.

"Take it easy, take it easy," he repeated. "It'll be fine."

Eva smiled at him and couldn't help laughing when he made faces at Tessie.

"America is great but not the greatest," he whispered, "for that is love."

Already on the first day he complimented her on her hair.

"Your hair is as beautiful as silk."

Even Donald chuckled. He glanced briefly at Eva across Feo's shoulder and shook his head.

But it was true that Slobodan's hairdresser had done wonders. Patrik and Hugo had stared in amazement at her when she came back from the salon.

"What have you done?" Patrik asked.

"Wow!" Hugo burst out. "You look like someone on TV."

When Helen looked in she ended up standing in the doorway.

"Well, I do declare, you're certainly primped. Now all you need are the bunny ears."

Not a word about it looking nice, just small snorts and the toss of her head.

That evening Eva stood in front of the mirror for a long time and tried to get used to her reflection. She wasn't sure what to think, but in the end she decided to like her new appearance. Helen's attitude had made her unsure of herself. As Eva stood in front of the mirror, she decided that in future she was going to limit her interaction with Helen. Bunny ears, indeed!

Eva had been allowed to go home at eight-thirty, when the worst of the rush was over. Hugo was home, sitting in front of the TV. She sat down for a while and rested her legs, stroking her son's head and telling him what she had done during the day, but the knowledge that she should do a couple of loads of laundry made her restless.

"Where is Patrik?" she asked and stood up.

"He was going to see Zero and then down to the old Post Office."

The latter was an old post office that had been converted into a community cafe for young people. It was the local parish that ran it. It offered snacks and pool tables, from time to time a lecture on some topic. After a slow start it had become a popular hangout for teenagers in Bergsbrunna and Sävja.

Eva thought it was good that something was being done for the young people in the area, but she did not approve of Patrik hanging out with Zero. Zero, whose family came from the Kurdish part of Turkey, was famous in the area for his hot temper. He often became involved in disputes and sometimes fights. The police had caught him a couple of times but it had never gone any further.

Zero's father was disappeared. He had returned to Turkey for his mother's funeral but was immediately arrested. That was six months ago. A cousin had called and told them that they believed the father had been brought to a military prison, but no one knew anything for sure.

To all intents and purposes, Zero had stopped attending school. Admittedly he did turn up from time to time, but that was mostly to have a bite in the cafeteria and to provoke conflict. Eva thought that deep down the teachers were probably happy not to have to deal with the unpredictable boy. She had heard the teacher everyone called "Gecko" complain that no one could control Zero and get close to him.

"It's not that he's stupid," the teacher said, "but he's so completely asocial that he's hard to take."

That Patrik had started hanging out with Zero was a bad sign. What was there about that boy that Patrik found tempting? It could not be anything other than the lure of excitement, perhaps music or computer games.

Eva returned to the living room and stared at the television screen.

"What is this?"

"A series," Hugo said.

"But what is it about?"

"It's a gang that's going to revenge themselves on the other gang, with traps and stuff. Outsmart the others. Then they get points."

"Oh, that sounds exciting."

"It's really bad," Hugo answered.

"What are Zero and Patrik up to?"

"How should I know?"

"What interests does he have, that Zero?"

Hugo looked up in surprise.

"Are you joking? Zero has no interests. He doesn't know what the word means."

"Well, music then."

Hugo sighed.

"Since his dad disappeared he only listens to Arab pop."

"I thought he was from Turkey."

"It's the same thing," Hugo said.

"You should turn off the TV if it's bad," Eva said. "Don't you have any homework?"

"The math teacher is sick. It's great."

"Don't you have a sub?"

Hugo shook his head.

Eva returned to the bathroom and put in a load of wool delicates. With regard to her neighbors it was actually too late, but a wool cycle did not take long. She would have to do the rest the next day.

She wondered if she should call Patrik, but decided to wait until ten o'clock.

By a quarter to eleven. Patrik had still not come home. His cell phone went to voice mail and Eva recorded a message. At eleven she called again but the result was the same, just voice mail.

Hugo had reluctantly gone to bed.

Eva sat in the kitchen and checked the time on the wall clock at regular intervals. He usually called when he was going to be late. She stood up and walked to the window. In the building across the courtyard most of the windows were dark. In Helen's place, on the first floor of building seven, the light was on. She was probably sitting up knitting. Perhaps she was waiting for her husband. Sometimes he worked nights, or at least claimed to.

She leaned her forehead against the windowpane. If only he would come home soon, she thought, and glanced at the clock again.

She did not know exactly where Zero lived and she did not have his telephone number. She had seen Zero's mother at a meeting at the school, but from what Eva could tell she did not speak Swedish.

It struck her that maybe Hugo had Zero's cell phone number and she gently tiptoed up to the door of his room.

"What is it?" Hugo called out immediately.

"I thought maybe you had Zero's cell phone number," Eva said and tried to sound as normal as possible.

"I've already called," Hugo mumbled. "There's no answer."

The first thing Eva saw was the blood. As if the rest of Patrik did not exist. It was when he closed the door behind him that all of him appeared.

"What have you done?"

The question that all parents in all times and cultures ask their children. Thrown out with an anger that conceals the first gnawing anxiety and even finally the fears of the worst.

"I fell," Patrik said.

"Fell?! Your whole head is bleeding."

She saw that he had made an attempt to wipe away the worst of it, but even so his forehead and one cheek were covered. At the hairline he had lumps of clotted blood and his lower lip was swollen.

For a moment they stared at each other. Patrik had that expression in his eyes from a long time ago, before he imperceptibly and then all the more clearly changed into someone else. Eva assumed it was the teenager's way of developing, distancing himself in order to find himself, but she still missed the old connection and closeness.

Now it was there again for a few seconds and Eva realized she had to tread carefully.

"I'll put on some tea," she said.

Patrik took off his jacket, which was covered in blood, and held it indecisively in his hand.

"I'll take care of it later," Eva said. "Drop it on the floor."

A jacket, she thought, bought for a couple hundred kronor—what does it matter? Her whole body trembled at the sight of him. At that moment the door to Hugo's room opened.

"What is it?"

Eva knew he must not have slept a wink.

"It's okay," she said. "Go back to bed."

Hugo looked bewildered and a little frightened at his brother.

"No, I take that back, you can have tea with us."

While the water was heating up, Eva wiped Patrik's face clean. The wounds were not so large: one three-centimeter cut at the hairline, a scratch across his right eye, and a swollen lip.

She wondered if the cut at his hairline needed stiches, but decided in the end that it didn't. It would heal fine and a small scar, concealed by his bangs, wouldn't matter.

Patrik winced every time she dabbed at the cut with disinfecting solution. He smelled of sweat. His hair was sticky and his face pale.

Hugo had put out mugs. At the center of the table on a small plate were three tea bags, all with different flavors. Now he was standing at the window in his robe, looking out.

"Do you think he's coming here?" Hugo asked.

"Who?"

"Zero."

"I don't think so, and we don't know what's happened. Are you afraid of him?"

Hugo shook his head while Patrik sat at the kitchen table.

Eva poured out the water.

"Tell us about it," she said.

✦

Fourteen

Manuel's grandfather had been a *bracero,* one of those who traveled around the United States in the 1940s in order to fill the gaps left by the men who had been called up to war. Most of them had done well for themselves, returning from Idaho and Washington with colored shirts, leather shoes, and cash.

This created an impression that life in the United States was easy, that one could quickly amass a fortune there. Many followed the pioneers. Manuel's father was one of these. He returned, thin and worked to the bone after three long years, and with a gaze that alternated between an expression of desperation and optimism. Two years later he died. One day his carotid artery burst and he was dead within minutes.

In 1998, two days before he turned twenty-two, Manuel made his first trip.

It was easy to be impressed by the land in the north. What Manuel noticed first were all the cars, then he saw how he, as a Mexican, was not regarded as fully human. He worked for a year, saved four hundred dollars, and returned to the village.

Patricio worked out that if all three brothers worked for two years in the fields to the north, they would be able to rebuild the house and buy a mule, and so they set off together.

Those who went to the border rivers had three to choose from: Rio Grande, Rio Colorado, and Rio Tijuana, all different, but out of whose waters thousands upon thousands of men, women, and children crawled.

Manuel, who had heard of people drowning, chose the highway. The first time he crossed the border near San Ysidro, south of San Diego, and everything was simple. He understood that the terrifying descriptions of all the Mexicans who had died in their attempts to cross over—people spoke of numbers in the thousands—were exaggerated, perhaps these were rumors spread by the Border Patrol or the vigilantes, volunteers who helped to patrol the border.

But four years later it was significantly worse. A wall, that did not appear to have an end, had been erected. There was something absurd and frightening about this construction that cut through the desert landscape.

Angel and Patricio stood silently by his side. A few other men from Veracruz, whom they had met in Lechería and had joined up with, laughed in exhaustion and nervousness. Angel, who was severely run-down, glanced at Manuel. Patricio stared east.

"I guess we just have to walk," he said.

"Walk?" Angel repeated.

He had been suffering. He had misplaced his cap and the sun had beaten down on him relentlessly. He scratched his forehead and large strips of skin came off.

"We can cross over by Tecate," one of the men from Veracruz said, and pointed east. "This wall can't go on forever."

Patricio had already started to walk. They arrived late in the evening. The men from Veracruz, who had the experience of several border crossings, led the group to a dried up riverbed and across a godforsaken stony slope where only cacti were able to survive. Signs that warned them they were approaching the border made them shrink reflexively. The only thing to be heard was the sound of feet stumbling over rocks. Suddenly the light from a mobile watchtower was turned on and caught the men in a circular dip in the landscape.

In the distance they heard the frantic barking of dogs. The brothers ran, tripping their way across the stony ground. Angel fell and was helped up by Patricio. Manuel urged them on. He had read about dogs and the new ammunition that the border patrols were armed with. The bullets that tore your body apart.

Two of the group were driven into a ravine. One of them tried to climb up the steep cliff but lost his footing and fell when he was only a meter from the top. Manuel saw the shadowy figure fall and disappear from view and heard the scream that ended abruptly.

Perhaps the patrol unit was satisfied with two Mexicans in their net, for the brothers and four others managed to get across the border, reach highway 94E, and thereafter set their sights on Dulzura. They were in California. Angel laughed and suggested they rest for the night, while Patricio wanted to push on. If he had been allowed to set the pace they would have made it to Oregon before sunrise.

Their father had worked in Orange County, and this was also the brothers' destination. It was no better or worse than anywhere else. They picked fruit and planted new fruit trees that would in the future be harvested by new generations of young men from Mexico and Central America.

Manuel realized, once they had reached a broccoli farmer where they would build an irrigation system, how many of his fellow citizens had come north. The farmer, who was the best one they had encountered, would come by in the evenings, sit outside their barrack, open a few beers, and talk.

"Half a million a year, at least," Roger Hamilton said and smiled. "There are twenty-three million people in this country with Mexican heritage."

He held out a beer to Manuel, who took a swig and tried to imagine this amount of people, unsure of what he was expected to say.

"It is because of your own government," the farmer continued. "They do not want to keep you."

Manuel had heard similar arguments at home. In the headquarters of the farmer organization in Oaxaca they had discussed NAFTA, the free-trade agreement between Mexico and the United States. For Manuel, and most others in the room, it was too big. He did not understand the implications of NAFTA. Not until cheap surplus corn from Alabama and Georgia started to flood the country.

The villages shrank and everything old broke up. Who wanted to celebrate when the village was being drained of youngsters? For many young men, the move north was a kind of rite of passage. Manuel thought that was one of the reasons why Angel and Patricio were so insistent that Manuel bring them along to California. They wanted to become men.

The broccoli farmer would also bring them food. "To save you the trouble," he said and smiled. He smiled often. He also smiled the last time they saw him. That was when he had tricked the brothers out of their remaining salary, over five thousand dollars, and then given them up to the police who picked them up outside the barracks.

During the trip back, in a specially constructed van, they sat without speaking. They got off in Tijuana. During the trip Manuel had decided that they would never again leave Mexico in order to work in the north.

"Only one in a hundred has any success," Manuel objected when, after only a month or so, Patricio and Angel started to talk about returning to the United States.

"But not everyone is tricked," Angel said.

"Most of us remain wetbacks, despised by everyone. Many of us get sick. Look at your hands!"

Angel had broken out in a rash of large boils that burst and became infected and Manuel was convinced that the cause was the pesticides they had used in the field.

Manuel stood his ground, but could not stop his brothers from going down to Oaxaca several days later. What should he have done? Struck them down and bind them to the plow?

Angel and Patricio had been tempted by the *bhni guí'a,* "the man from the mountains," an old term that the brothers did not want to admit to knowing, but one that was familiar to all Zapotecs. He was the one who came down from the mountains above the village, dressed in western fashion, shining shoes, and swinging a cane with a silver handle. He offered money and took your soul.

This man carried no cane but he did have a bundle of green dollar bills. He was large, almost bald, introduced himself as Armas, and spoke Spanish.

Angel and Patricio kept to the background, letting Manuel do the talking. In part because he was the eldest, in part because he knew English well, and during their time in California he was the one who had managed the negotiations in the fields outside Anaheim. But this time Manuel immediately turned away. There was something about the man that he did not like. Instead, Angel stepped forward.

The following day, when the village celebrated Saint Gertrudis, the three brothers sat in front of the church and discussed the matter. Manuel rejected it outright—no good could come from that man's promises.

"But it is not a job," Angel said. "All you have to do is fly to Spain with a package."

"What do you think is in that package?" Manuel asked.

"You heard him. It is business papers that cannot be sent by mail," Angel replied.

Manuel looked sadly at him.

"I would not have believed you were so stupid," he said and shook his head. "He is lying to us, don't you understand?"

Patricio had not entered the discussion until this point, but Manuel could see in his eyes that even he was tempted by the offer.

"With that money we can buy our own coffee mill, and we can clear more land for plants," he said.

"Perhaps buy a car," Angel picked up the thread and kept fantasizing. "Then we can transport goods to and from the village and make more money."

That time, on the bench in front of the church, Manuel did not take the matter so seriously. He was only worried about his brothers' naïveté, the fact that they allowed themselves to be pulled in and dream about future riches.

The young Ernesto, their closest neighbor, was preparing for the fireworks. The Alavez brothers watched him pick up the bull-shaped disguise, swing it onto his back, and set off running around the plaza in front of the church. The first bang was deafening and was followed by spurts of fire and whining missiles that enveloped everything in a sharp smell of gunpowder.

Angel jumped up and took the disguise from Ernesto. Manuel

laughed at his brother's wobbling stomach as he attacked the flocks of small boys who ran away.

Manuel started thinking about their father. He had loved the fiesta, sometimes getting a bit too drunk but always in a good mood. He had not been a particularly good *campesino*. It was his dreams that mostly got in the way. He paused in his work and you could not do that as a small-time Mexican farmer. Nonetheless he had a good reputation in the village. He was considerate and he was the one who had the initiative for the coffee cooperative, and in this way he did his share to help propel the village out of the worst of its poverty.

Now Manuel was standing next to a new river, one that was much gentler than the one he was used to. He had, after studying the map, understood that it was the same river as the one he had camped next to before. But this time he found himself upstream from the city and he was happy about that. He would not have enjoyed bathing in the same water he had dumped Armas into.

He had gone to the tourist information center to get a map. Or was it fate that had led him there? When he stepped out onto the sidewalk, Armas was there, as if transported by a higher authority. He was tucking a yellow envelope under his suit jacket and spotted Manuel as he looked both ways before crossing the street.

Armas recognized him immediately. Manuel walked up to "the quiet one" as Angel had called him. The lie came to him in a moment's inspiration.

"I have come in Angel's place," Manuel said, and not even then had he imagined what was about to happen.

He smiled tentatively, as if he was speaking to a gringo who was maybe going to give him a day's or a week's worth of work.

Armas looked around. It made Manuel momentarily unsure that he understood English and he repeated the sentence in Spanish.

"Where?" Armas asked.

"My tent," Manuel said, and he saw Patricio's face before him.

He wasn't even sure if the water next to his tent could really be called a river. It was mostly reeds. He was amazed that so few people came to the water. There was the man with the fishing rod, but no one else.

He very much liked the grass in this foreign country. It smelled good, was soft against his skin and reminded him of a special kind of grass that they sometimes found in the mountains above his village. Otherwise the grass there was mostly stiff and sharp.

He was lying on his back with his hands under his head, staring up at the sky. Time and again his thoughts turned to Armas, how he had staggered only to collapse in front of Manuel's feet, his hands pressed against his throat. There was something mesmerizing about the way the blood pumped out between his fingers, in fine red ribbons that were strangely free but also condemned outside their path of circulation and the heart that propelled them.

As he thought about Armas, an image of Miguel came to him. Miguel, his neighbor and childhood friend, who almost always laughed, conceived children like a hamster, and burned for the village, for the Zapotecs and autonomy.

When Miguel was shot to death outside his home there was no beauty. His death was ugly and tattered. Seven bullets tore apart an already dirty and broken body, marked by harsh circumstances and hard work.

Miguel's blood was dark, almost black, and his limbs were desperately tensed, as if all of him was screaming. One hand rested against the house wall. In the window above his hand, whose fingers appeared to be fumbling for something, one could see his three children.

The villagers stood in a semicircle around the dead man and found that there was no justice in his death, no beauty. Who would have been able to say that Miguel was an attractive corpse? His dead body was as repellant as the life he had been forced to lead.

Miguel's death was expected. The extinguishing of his life was fated.

One who lives in a mountain village in Oaxaca, is *campesino* and Zapotec, and does not settle for what this means is put on the list. Behind the roar of life and Miguel's laughter, there was always Death peeking out with his grinning mask. It was as if the flies were drawn to Miguel. The flies of death.

Armas's end was different. He was a fine corpse. Manuel had at first not realized that the strong body with its smooth skin and well-manicured hands were without life. It was only when the first fly landed on Amras that Manuel fully grasped that the man was in fact dead.

Armas had attacked him, had wanted to kill him. Manuel should have understood the full extent of Patricio's words that a man like Armas never had good thoughts. For him there was no dilemma, nor any difficulties, in killing another person. It was only a question of opportunity and purpose. The purpose of Manuel dying now appeared self-evident in hindsight. Manuel despised his own ignorance. He was the oldest of the brothers but not an ounce smarter.

Armas spoke Spanish with an element of haughtiness in his voice and Manuel had wanted to ask if he spoke his own language with the same carelessness. But now he understood that Armas was careless with life itself. He neither feared God nor any living man.

Now he was dead by Manuel's hand. But he still felt the threat that Armas's physical presence had radiated. What amazed Manuel in hindsight was the doubleness in Armas: one second his hands were clenched and his movements were like a vigilant animal, the next moment he could speak in carefree terms about women.

Manuel wondered if there had been a woman in Armas's life. He tried to imagine her sorrow but he could only visualize a laughing woman. So it was, he said to himself, that relief followed Armas's death. It was an act that pleased God, if one interpreted God's will in terms of wishing for peoples' happiness. Armas had been a misfortune.

His gaze had been cold, with small lifeless eyes and pupils as dark as soot. He looked like a reptile, but his body spoke another language and that had at first confused Manuel. Armas moved in a supple way, not to say elegant, although he was so large. As long as they had still been in the city he had been reserved, holding Manuel at arm's length with his eyes, but as soon as they reached the river and parked their cars, he placed his arm around Manuel's shoulders and asked him if he was cold.

"It must be hard for a Mexican," he said, as if he wanted to warm Manuel, but he let go of Manuel's shoulders.

If he only knew how cold it could be, Manuel thought. Thousands of thoughts and impressions swarmed like angry bees in his head. Should I demand the money that Patricio spoke of? Why does he laugh when his eyes say something different? What really happened to Angel?

But it was Armas who overwhelmed Manuel with questions, when and how he had come to Sweden, if he had met any Swedes, yes, perhaps even made some friends.

"Swedes love Latinos," he said. "You could start a dance class tomorrow and get a lot of women to shake their asses."

He spoke well of Mexico, that he would like to return and that Manuel could be his Mexican friend. Had Armas really believed that Manuel was going to take up his brothers' business? He implied as much. Dropped hints of riches. Manuel was amazed. One dead, and one in prison, and the man dared to talk about dollars.

When they reached the tent—it took about ten minutes because Armas stopped constantly—he praised Manuel on its placement and how well Manuel had arranged everything.

"How did you recognize me?" Manuel asked abruptly. "We only saw each other for a short time and that was a long time ago."

"You are like your brothers," Armas said, "and I have a good memory for faces. I know which ones are important to remember. I work with people and it . . ."

Then he stopped suddenly, in the middle of a sentence, and looked at Manuel.

"Are you angry?"

Manuel nodded, but could not say anything. Nothing of what he had thought the last few months came to his lips.

"Have you visited your brother?"

"Yes, once."

"And he told you a lot of nonsense, of course?"

"He talked about money," Manuel said and cursed himself. As if money was what was important.

"So he is still hungry for money," Armas said with a smile, and now he suddenly switched to English.

"I think you should be happy he is alive," he said cryptically.

"What do you mean?"

"Many unpleasant things happen in prison, people are stressed."

Manuel stared at him, tried to understand.

"Some are racists and don't like Latinos coming here with AIDS and drugs."

"AIDS? Is Patricio sick?"

Armas laughed.

"I think you should go home to the mountains," he said. "Today."

Suddenly Manuel understood. He was a threat. Patricio was a threat. As long as they lived they could squeal. He drew back from Armas, who followed.

"I'm staying," Manuel said. "I will look after my brother."

Armas leaned over him.

"If I tell you to go home, then that is what you should do. That will be best for you and your brother."

"And for you and the fat one?"

"For everyone," Armas said and smiled.

"I want justice," Manuel said.

Armas stuck his hand into his pocket and pulled out a gun. It looked like a toy in his hand.

"Are you going to kill me?"

In a way, Manuel was not surprised. In his mind, he saw Miguel lying in front of his house. Miguel's death smelled of herbs. In his fall he had crushed a plant, a rue bitterwort. It helped a headache, but no plant in the world would get Miguel back on his feet again.

Manuel turned around.

"Then you will have to shoot me in the back," he said, while he put his hand in his pocket and took out the stiletto that clicked open with a metallic sound. Manuel threw himself forward and to the side, raised his arm and slashed. The cut was perfect. Armas fired his pistol at the same time. The whole thing was over in seconds.

Later, as he was pulling the heavy body down to the river, Armas's shirt ripped and revealed a bare shoulder and upper arm. Manuel immediately recognized the tattoo and an intense rage grew. How could this murderer and drug smuggler have gotten the idea of having a feathered snake tattooed on his white skin? It was an insult, and in his rage Manuel kicked the lifeless body. Quetzalcóatl meant something that neither Armas nor any other gringo could understand. He took out the stiletto again and with a quick flick of his knife sliced the tattoo away.

Manuel went through the events again and again and discovered to his surprise that there was a bizarre feeling of distance in the deadly conflict by the river. He had never been to a theater, only had a performance described to him, but it was in this way that he imagined a drama, that he and Armas were actors in a play.

The beautiful nature around him, the clearing framed with the green of the trees, roses with pale red rosehips, brush at whose feet there were dark green leaves and in the distance the cackling of sea birds from the reeds, this is what the scene had looked like for a drama of life and death.

The roles had been simple, likewise the dramaturgy: one man prepared to kill and the other forced to do so. They needed no directions, life itself provided the dialogue and action.

It was a drama that Manuel could see from the outside, as if he was no longer an actor but forced to be a passive viewer, one in the audience. And from that position he could see the archetypal in what had happened, frightening and full of anguish, as a drama without artifice.

The feeling of unreality, that he had cut the throat of another human being and dumped him into the water as if he was a bag of trash, had grown stronger afterward. Armas was no longer real. His death had nothing to do with Manuel.

✦

Fifteen

It sometimes happened that Ann Lindell woke up beautiful. It happened at varying intervals, more often in spring and summer, so that she was both surprised, as if someone had unexpectedly complimented her, and also struck by a familiar happiness, as on a fine summer morning when one goes outside and steps into the sun.

She stretched out in bed as if to identify her limbs, and really feel that all the parts of her body belonged together. That it was she, Ann, who lay there, half awake, half lingering in sleep, still brushing the dream that was perhaps the source of her well-being.

The warmth under the covers did her good. She almost always slept nude, in contact with her body. Sometimes she kept her panties on, with a mixed feeling of intimacy and need for protection. She did not know how she should describe the feeling, but didn't care. That was simply how it was, and that was enough.

She stroked her stomach and breasts in a weightless state of rest.

Erik would wake up soon, probably in a good mood, as he usually was in the mornings.

Ottosson laughed when he caught sight of Lindell, she on her way in, he on his way out of the elevator.

"Look at you," he said.

"If you like," she replied, and smiled.

He turned and before the elevator doors slid shut he explained that he would be back in five minutes.

It took ten minutes before Ottosson joined them. The others who were investigating the murder of "Jack" were already in place.

"I'm sorry," Ottosson said, "but the elevator was on strike."

What little in the way of reports was available was quickly processed.

The murder victim was still unidentified. His fingerprints were not registered. Investigators from the drug, surveillance, and economic crimes units had checked the photographs without recognizing him.

"Jack" had been dead when he hit the water, there had been no difficulty in determining this. Despite the cut left by the removal of the tattoo, there were no wounds on the body other than the slit throat.

"But that's enough," Haver added.

After the meeting, Lindell went into Ottosson's office and told him about Viola. She could have run out without telling him, but after last year's mistake of setting off on an individual investigation, an adventure that almost cost her life, she was eager to keep Ottosson informed, even if a visit to the hospital was not normally associated with any danger.

"Of course you have to go see her," Ottosson said.

To find a parking space close to entrance 70 at the Akademiska Hospital turned out to be a challenge. Ann lost patience in the end, parked her car at the corner of a construction site, tossed her police identification on the dashboard, and walked away, ignoring the protests from a couple of carpenters.

Viola had a private room. Her face was turned to the window and she had apparently not heard Ann open the door. Ann was unable to determine if she was sleeping or not.

The old woman looked more frail than usual. Her slender arms rested on the blanket. Her hair, which Viola mostly kept under a cap when she was on the island, was chalk white and in need of combing. She was completely still, but then Ann saw her bony fingers moving, pulling threads on the blanket. The thin tendons on the back of her hand, which was covered in brown age spots, tensed and relaxed with a regularity that convinced Ann that Viola was awake.

What was the old woman thinking about? Ann turned on her heels and left the room, the door shut with a sigh and she hurried along the corridor toward the exit.

A nurse was standing outside the nurses' station. Ann walked over to her and introduced herself.

"I know who you are," the nurse said. "I worked in the intensive care unit last year."

"Oh, I see," Ann replied sheepishly, suddenly ashamed as she always was when she was reminded of that event. "I wanted to visit Viola but I think she's sleeping and I don't want to disturb her. Can you tell her I was here?"

The nurse looked at her before nodding.

"Of course I can, but I'm sure Viola would appreciate it if you—"

"I don't want to wake her," Ann repeated more forcefully. "I'm in a hurry," she added in a gentler voice and felt even more embarrassed.

"Are you related?"

"No, not at all. How is she?"

"She is . . ." the nurse searched for the right word, "a real bitch. No, I was only joking! She is quite brusque, if you know what I mean, but a wonderful old lady. There's no screw loose in her head. She was telling me how the first thing she will do when she goes home is slaughter the hens."

"Viola has said that for as long as I've known her. But wish her all the best," Ann said.

The nurse looked as if she was going to say something, but only nodded, gave a professional smile, and then walked into the office area.

Ann started walking toward the elevators, but turned almost immediately.

"One more thing, does she have any visitors?"

"Yes, her son has been here a few times, I think he is her son. And an older man."

"I'll come back another time," Ann said.

"You do that. She rarely sleeps during the day, so you were unlucky."

Lindell returned to the police station, poured herself a cup of coffee in the lunchroom, and leafed through an issue of *Upsala Nya Tidning.* The murder was a large item on the front page. There was a picture of the river that, if it weren't for its connection to a murder, could have been lifted from a county tourist publication. The picture had been snapped in the evening. The sun had disappeared behind the Sunnersta ridge and the remaining light cast a dreamy glow onto the meadow, the lead-gray water and the light golden brown stalks of the reeds.

Lindell had experienced this so many times before, how the apparent idyll concealed a streak of unexpected eruptions of violence and grief. The landscape itself was innocent, it was only a stage for human failings, a backdrop against which people acted in all their foulness.

From her professional perspective, Lindell felt that it was worse to investigate a crime in the countryside where nature, in its inconceivable diversity, concealed man. She often thought about the last homicide case when two farmers had been murdered in their homes. It was as if nature was tripping up her thoughts. How could something so horrible happen here? There was not only a crime victim to contend with, it was as if the whole area had been raped. The crime, to deprive someone of his life, appeared even more monstrous against the backdrop of a peaceful forest.

A murder in an apartment, by contrast, appeared more natural. No one was surprised that someone killed someone else in a kitchen filled with the items that people accumulated. It was rather the opposite: how could it be that more people didn't fall victim to violence? A pool of blood in the street surprised no one. A pool of blood on a mossy bed in the woods seemed to fly in the face of reason.

"The philosopher Lindell in action!"

She turned around. Ottosson was standing there with a coffee mug in his hand. She had not heard him enter. She smiled but did not like being interrupted in her thoughts. If it had been anyone other than Ottosson she would have registered her dissatisfaction.

As it was, she told him what she had been thinking. Ottosson refilled his mug and sat down.

"You are right," he said when she had finished, "but you're also wrong. A kitchen, a little refuge, even if it is dingy and small, stands for security. Or it should. To have a roof over your head, warmth, and food on the table are the preconditions for becoming someone else, if you know what I mean. We are always striving for . . ."

He trailed off, as if he couldn't manage to finish his train of thought, or as if he did not himself fully understand, or was unable to formulate, what he meant.

"Man is a strange creature," Ottosson resumed, and employed a worn cliché that only expressed their usual frustration.

"Hasn't anyone called in?" Lindell asked.

Normally the phone at the station would ring off the hook after a murder had been committed. Spontaneous tips that in most cases did not lead to anything.

"No, nothing that gives us an identity," Ottosson said. "I thought for a while that he did not come from Uppsala, that someone transported him here in order to dump him in the river."

"But why there?" Lindell asked and then realized the ridiculousness of her question. Many times there was no rationality to a killer's actions.

Ottosson shrugged.

"Perhaps our rounds in the city will give us something," he said.

They had made copies of the murder victim's photograph and detectives from the violence and intelligence units were looking up individuals who would perhaps recognize him. It was the usual roundup of drug users and petty thieves. Sometimes they were willing to drop a little information in the hopes that it made them look good or for the simple reason that a murder was a disturbance to their own business and they wanted a quick resolution.

The investigative team in the violent crimes division had discussed possible motives as a matter of routine. These were freewheeling speculations that perhaps did not yield much, especially since they did not know the victim's identity, but that nonetheless set the machinery of their brains in motion. One tossed-out idea gave way to another that was rejected that led to a third possible explanation that was taken seriously. Everything mixed, became layered, was judged more or less believable. Together this resulted in a concoction of loose assumptions, out of which one could finally perhaps distill a motive and a perpetrator.

"It is the tattoo, or rather, its removal, that is the key," Lindell said.

Ottosson agreed.

"Why does one get a tattoo?"

"To show one's affiliation," Lindell said. "A brotherhood."

"It used to be a mark of class," Ottosson said. "Only workers used to get tattoos. Now little girls have tattoos everywhere."

"It functions as a kind of marking. You choose a design that says something about yourself or the life you lead, or with the direction you feel life should take."

"Or it's just a fun thing you do when you're drunk," Ottosson added.

"He doesn't look the type."

"Perhaps in his youth?"

Lindell shook her head.

"I can't say why, but this guy is no common . . . alcoholic who likes to get loaded in Nyhavn."

"But in his youth," Ottosson insisted. "Perhaps he went to sea?"

"He did end up in the water finally," Lindell said.

"And almost naked to boot."

"I think that was done in order to humiliate him," Lindell said. "Why would you otherwise take the trouble to remove his clothes?"

"Two possibilities," Ottosson said, "either the clothes say something about the victim or else he was only wearing his underpants when he was killed."

"A betrayed man who finds them naked in the bedroom and kills the lover?"

"Or a homosexual."

Ottosson had trouble with the word *bög,* which was slang for "gay." Lindell already knew this. He claimed it was denigrating, even though many homosexuals used the word themselves.

Lindell looked at the picture in the paper. She didn't bother with the text. She had enough of an idea what it said.

"Going door to door in the area may still give us something. There were some houses in the area where no one answered yesterday."

"Fredriksson and Riis are out there right now, but the victim may just as well have been thrown in from the other side of the river and floated across," Ottosson said. "It's not very wide. Or else he was dumped farther upstream."

"It would be strange if no one had seen anything. After all, it takes awhile to carry a body from the road across the meadow and into the river."

"I think he was thrown in higher up," Ottosson said.

They continued to speculate before Lindell got up from the table.

"I went to the hospital," she said suddenly.

"How was she?"

"She was sleeping."

Ottosson nodded.

"Have you talked to—"

"No," Lindell said.

✦

Sixteen

She was riding her bike into the wind. Eva regretted not having taken the bus, even though this way she was saving money and improving her fitness, maybe even losing a few pounds.

Her thoughts kept coming back to last night. Patrik would end up in trouble if he kept associating with Zero. She had not managed to get more out of him except that they had had a fight.

"Some idiots from Gränby," he had said, but denied knowing them and he would not tell her what the fight had been about, more than that it was about "stuff." Stuff could apparently refer to just about anything and it frightened Eva. Boys have always had fights, she told herself, but given what had happened in recent years, stuff could lead to a bad end, even to death. She remembered a shooting in Gränby several years earlier all too well. The accused, a teenager, was freed after the main witness had changed his story.

Patrik had denied that anyone from that gang had been involved in last night's skirmish.

"It was some other idiots," he said.

"Friends of Zero?"

"No, they were Swedes."

"But you are a Swede and apparently friends with him."

"That's not the same thing."

Eva couldn't quite imagine what these adolescents' lives looked like, how their loyalties worked, or even what the words they used meant. And now her main task, along with the work at Dakar, was to raise two teenagers, and that in an environment she had trouble understanding.

Patrik had promised to stay out of trouble and try to reduce his interactions with Zero, without causing the latter to feel betrayed.

"He would go crazy in that case," Patrik said.

He had given her two promises, and Eva knew that both of them would be hard to keep.

The county was constructing little areas with park benches and flower beds up and down East Ågatan. It was being spiffed up and made more accessible. Perhaps they were hoping to achieve a more continental look in the inner city, where Uppsala residents and tourists alike could stroll under the chestnut trees and where lindens grew right next to the river.

Eva paused, in part because she was feeling hot and did not want to arrive at Dakar dripping with perspiration, in part because she wanted a chance to watch the workers. A couple of men were laying stones, roughly hewn rectangular pieces that were mortared together into a wall or bench if one so desired. The men had the aid of a backhoe, in whose claw the stones were directed into place. They adjusted the stones with metal tools. It looked astonishingly easy even though they were handling such weights. The machine was doing its part, of course, but Eva thought she could read a great satisfaction in their work in the men's faces. One of them put his hand on a set stone, almost like he was petting it, as if to say, "Here you are now and it looks good," before it was the next block's turn.

Eva was struck by the durability of their work. Around the city there was stone in the paved streets, on the front of buildings, in bridges and ornamental structures in parks. No human force could shift these stones. Once a worker patted them into place they were set, testifying to his work.

She compared this to her own job, waitressing at Dakar. This left no visible traces more than for the moment, that was simply how it was, just like her earlier work at the post office. "The woman at the counter," that was what she had been for many years, but God forbid she leave her place for a quick bathroom break or to sign a form in one of the inner regions of the office. Then there were immediate complaints.

The men coaxed a new block into place. The driver swung the backhoe to the side, allowing it to rest on the pile of stones. Perhaps they were going to take a break. One of the workers gave her a quick, curious look.

"It's turning out well," she said and climbed back onto the bike.

The man nodded and took a few steps closer to her, putting one foot up on the block he had just set.

"Time for me to go to work," she said.

"I was just going to offer you a cup of coffee," the man said and Eva couldn't tell if he was serious or not.

"Are you taking a break right now?"

"No, we're done for the day."

Two of the man's fellow workers were waiting in the background.

"Where do you work?"

"At a restaurant. It's called Dakar."

"Then you will have to be the one to invite me," the man said and laughed. "See you!"

He gave her a mischievous look before he joined his colleagues and left for the work trailer.

She ended up standing around for a little while longer before biking the rest of the way.

A heated discussion was under way in Dakar's kitchen. Feo's aggravated voice and Donald's interruptions could be heard out all the way into the dressing room.

When Eva stepped into the kitchen the two chefs abruptly stopped and stared at her.

"Don't let me interrupt," she said.

Donald turned his back on her, grabbed a pot from the rack but changed his mind, put it back, and walked out to the bar instead. They heard how he took out a bottle of soda or mineral water. Donald never drank anything stronger than this on the job.

"We were talking about the union. They want to come here."

Eva nodded.

"Anything in particular?"

"No, they have some campaign. I'm in the union now, but not Donald. He calls them parasites."

"I don't know that I've ever found them so helpful, but I still think it's important to join."

"Exactly! Suddenly it happens."

Donald returned.

"Have you formed a club now?"

"Yes, you are treasurer," Feo said.

This, her third evening, involved the most work so far. A party of sixteen had come thundering in at six o'clock. They had been playing golf all day and now demanded drinks and food. Eva recognized one of them, a classmate from the Eriksberg school, but he did not recognize her, or else he didn't want to acknowledge it.

"I hate golfers," Tessie said.

After the party, which had not been booked in advance and created a great deal of work in the bar and kitchen, there were dinner guests in a steady stream until nine o'clock. Luckily Johnny was working as well and so they were three chefs and one apprentice.

Tessie demonstrated the extent of her professional capabilities. Eva quickly realized that the other waiter, Gonzo, did not maintain a particularly stunning pace. After having being fired he mainly walked around muttering about the "fascists," Slobodan and Armas. It was even worse after Slobodan turned up at eight o'clock to have a glass of grappa. Then Gonzo seemed to move in slow motion.

It was Tessie, assisted by Eva, who managed to maintain the level of service and Eva's respect for her increased even more.

At half past nine things calmed down. The last desserts were going out, the party of golfers had disbanded after lounging in the bar for an hour, the rest of the dinner guests were gradually paying and leaving. Eva sat down. Donald had started scrubbing down the meat stove; Feo, who was putting finishing touches on the last desserts, offered Eva an ice cream, which she declined, while Johnny started to cover things in plastic wrap, clear things away, and put them into cold storage.

Måns, the bartender, looked in.

"There's a phone call for you, Eva. You can take it in here," he said rapidly, and left again.

Eva looked around, bewildered. Feo pointed to the wall where the telephone was mounted. The kids, she thought, and an image of Patrik's bleeding face appeared in her mind.

She listened without saying more than "yes," "no," and "of course," then she replaced the receiver.

"I have to go home," she said. "I have to stop now."

"Has something happened?"

She shook her head, but changed her tack as quickly.

"It was the police," she said.

"The police?" Feo asked.

"And to think I'm on a bike," she sobbed. "Can someone call me a cab?"

"I can take you," Johnny said, immediately untying his apron. "I took the car today. The rest of you can manage, can't you?"

Donald nodded.

A patrol car was parked outside the front of the building, and a group of teenagers had assembled in the yard. Eva recognized many of them. A few were classmates of either Hugo or Patrik.

Johnny accompanied Eva into the apartment. She had not said a single word during the drive to explain what had happened. Johnny suffered with her and the silent anxiety that drove her to lean forward in her seat with one hand on the dashboard.

There were two police officers in the kitchen, one female and one male. Two unfamiliar and frightening people in her kitchen, two gigantic figures who took up the entire room, that was how Eva perceived them and they gave her a feeling of terror.

There is no security, she thought. Everything breaks down, the joy of the past week with a new job, a new hairstyle, and a new life. All of that had been brushed aside.

"What has happened? Where is Patrik?"

She stared at Hugo who was sitting wedged in between the wall and one of the officers.

"Come here!"

Hugo got up and stood behind her.

"We're looking for Patrik. We have received a report of an assault and we have reason to believe he was involved."

It was the female officer who was speaking.

"Assault? You think Patrik assaulted someone?"

"Wouldn't you like to sit down?"

Eva shook her head, suddenly infuriated by the fact that these two were occupying her home, her kitchen. This was a place for Eva, Patrik, and Hugo and no one else!

"Was it necessary to drive a police car up to the front of the building?" Johnny asked.

"Who are you? Are you Patrik's father?"

"I'm a colleague of Eva's," Johnny said. "I gave her a ride here."

"Perhaps you could leave us now."

"He stays," Eva said.

"Okay," the male officer said. "We know that a man was assaulted in this area last night. This evening someone was stabbed. We have reason to believe it is the same man. He is being treated at a hospital for his injuries. He is in fairly bad shape."

He looked fixedly at Eva while he spoke.

"We believe that Patrik had a part in this. There are a couple of witnesses who say he was there, at least last night. Do you know where your son is?"

"No, I've just come from work."

"So you have no idea of where your son may have been last night or where he is right now?"

"What is your name?"

"I introduced myself before but I can do so again. I am Harry Andersson, and my colleague is Barbro Liljendahl."

"Do you have any children?"

He nodded.

"How old are they?"

"That's not relevant to the matter at hand."

"Do you know exactly what they are doing right now?"

"That isn't relevant in this context."

"Don't come here, you little shit, and tell me how I should raise my children."

"I understand that you are upset, and naturally we are not here to criticize you, but you have to understand that it is our duty to follow up on anything that can have a bearing on an assault case. Especially when there is a knife involved."

"Patrik doesn't own a knife."

"Tell us about last night," Barbro Liljendahl urged.

Eva felt Hugo's arms around her middle.

"Hugo came home and went to bed around ten o'clock. I sat up and waited for Patrik who was supposed to be home by ten-thirty at the latest, but I fell asleep on the couch. I was really tired. When I woke up in the middle of the night, Patrik was home. He was sleeping in his room. Then I went to bed too."

"So you don't know when Patrik came home?"

"I was completely exhausted. I've just started a new job."

"When did you fall asleep?"

Eva shrugged.

Barbro Liljendahl jotted something down in her notebook.

"We have tried to call Patrik on his cell phone—we got the number from his brother—but he doesn't answer. Don't you have any idea where he might be?"

"No, but isn't it better if you go out and look for him rather than sitting here?" Eva asked.

"It's helpful for us to know where to look," Harry Andersson said.

"Hugo," Eva turned around and pushed the boy into the hallway, "I think it's best you went to bed."

He dutifully followed her into the bedroom. Eva closed the door behind her.

"What have you said?"

"That I was sleeping."

He was close to tears.

"Good, stay here, you can play a video game or something. We'll talk more after the cops leave. Do you have any idea where Patrik is?"

Hugo shook his head.

"Is he with Zero?"

"I don't think so."

She hugged Hugo, returned to the kitchen, took out a glass and let the water run until it became cold. Then she took four long sips and racked her brains for where Patrik could be.

The two police officers were sitting behind her back. Johnny was standing in the doorway to the hall.

"I don't know where he is," she said finally, putting the glass down so loudly that Harry Andersson jumped.

"As soon as he gets home, we would like you to call this number," Barbro Liljendahl said and handed her a card.

Eva laid the card on the kitchen counter without looking at it.

"Of course," she said.

When the police had left, Eva turned to Johnny.

"Thanks for your help," she said and sank down onto a chair in the hall.

"It was nothing. What are you going to do?"

"I thought maybe you could stay here for a little while. Is that all right? Just so Hugo doesn't have to be alone. I'm going to look for Patrik."

Johnny nodded and pulled off his coat.

"I want to come with you," Hugo said. He was standing in the door to his room.

"It's better if you stay here, in case Patrik calls. You can try to call Ahmed, Giorgio, Anton, Emil, and . . ."

"Mossa," Hugo finished.

"Good. Mossa too. But don't say anything about the police. If they ask, just say you want to reach Patrik. If Patrik calls tell him to call me on my cell phone, okay?"

Eva did not like the narrow walking paths that connected the various areas of the neighborhood. Some stretches cut through dense forest and were poorly lit. This late at night there were not usually many people out, perhaps a couple of teenagers or the occasional dog owner.

She walked at a brisk clip in the direction of the school and saw a patrol car in the distance. Naturally they were going around, snooping. But if they thought they could find Patrik they were naive. He was smart enough to stay away. The Sävja jungle drums did their work and he would surely know they were looking for him.

The first wave of anxiety was beginning to give way to anger. What was he doing out in the first place? He had promised to stay home. But she should have known better. Patrik was a restless soul who hated staying in. Sometimes she could tempt him with watching a video, otherwise he left as soon as dinner was over.

And now she would have an even harder time keeping tabs on him. Several times a week, and every other weekend she had to work. She stopped at an intersection. Should I stop working at Dakar? Is it right to be gone so much? She turned to the right and came to an area that was even more deserted.

The darkness was oppressive where the streetlamps were even more spaced out. She heard rustling in the fallen leaves, a blackbird flew up and disappeared into the tree canopy.

She ran around for an hour, to the school, toward the southern part of the area and back, swung down to the grocery store and turned back again. During this time she called Patrik's cell phone a few times and once back to Hugo at home.

She encountered ten or so other people, of whom four were dog owners and three were teenage girls. Eva knew one of them from preschool. That was ten years ago, but you could tell it was the same girl. She nodded to

Eva, who slowed down a bit, not sure if she should ask if they had seen Patrik, but decided not to and continued on quickly to the old post office.

She heard the girls laughing behind her. They probably knew that the police were out. Tomorrow all of Sävja and half of Bergsbrunna would know.

She stopped under a streetlight. Was there any sense in running around like this? She was convinced Hugo was calling around to all the friends.

Patrik was wanted by the police, he was most likely aware of it by now and God only knew what the child was going to do.

She ran the last part home. The assembly of young people in the yard had dispersed. The light was still on in Helen's apartment. Darkness descended over the area. A tawny owl started to make its call.

Her cell phone rang at that moment.

"Hi, it's me."

"Where are you?"

"That doesn't matter."

"What have you done?"

"Nothing. It's just the cops who—"

"Tell me about the assault!"

She could hear Patrik's breaths.

"Are you okay?"

"Sure. What did the cops say?"

"You are the one who should tell me what's happened," Eva said. "They talked about a man who had been stabbed."

"It was Zero."

"Zero was the one who did this? Were you there?"

"I have to stop now. I'll be home later."

"You come straight home. Now."

"I think the cops are keeping an eye on the building."

Eva looked around. There was nothing that indicated that the police were present, but Eva realized they would hardly park in the middle of the yard.

"I want to see you. Think about Hugo, he's also worried."

Patrik was quiet and Eva knew he was thinking it over.

"The community gardens, go there."

"How will I—?"

"I'll see you when you come."

Patrik hung up. Eva stood frozen for a while, then she called Hugo.

✦

Seventeen

The bar at Alhambra was the place that Slobodan Andersson liked best. Dakar was okay, he dropped by there every evening at eight o'clock to have a grappa, but it was at Alhambra that everything had started, really gotten going. Here he had planned and discussed things with Armas. Slobodan recalled how the tight anxiety mingled with the triumphant feeling of doing exactly the right thing, how they laid out the plans and went through the details again and again. Armas had a feeling for the small details, those that could mean the difference between catastrophe and success. He never left anything to chance. In a few words he steered Slobodan where he wanted. Slobodan was sometimes struck by the suspicion that he was inferior to Armas and knew that he more than once had Armas to thank for his successes.

Strangely enough Slobodan was worried. That did not happen often. Perhaps it was Armas's comment about the computer, that the police could easily retrieve even those messages that had been deleted. Slobodan wondered for a long time if this could be true, but by now the machine had been taken apart and discarded, and Armas had purchased a new laptop and installed it before he left for Spain.

Slobodan sat at the short end of the bar, smoked a cigarette, and observed those who came and went, greeting old customers with a nod or a brief handshake, exchanging a few words but not embarking on more extensive conversations.

Alhambra was doing well. He registered every transaction that Jonas and Frances made with the cash register, not the sums but the sound of the fingers on the buttons and the click when the cash drawer popped out.

He recalled how, at the start of his restaurant career, he had stared at the figures every evening, counted and figured, compared and planned, wished. Now he no longer had to be so concerned; still, he kept a daily check on how the business was doing. He trusted his staff. He was the one who had hired them, and to question their competency and honor was to dismiss his own judgment. In the case of Gonzo at Dakar he had been wrong, but now that mistake had been corrected. Despite Armas's protests he had allowed Gonzo to work a couple more weeks and take out all of his remaining pay, even his vacation compensation. Anything beyond this would be ridiculous. Thereafter a kick in the ass.

The post office gal seemed perky and alert. Tessie had praised her. Slobodan had increased Tessie's salary by three kronor an hour for the extra work she was taking on. If the post office gal kept at it he would raise her salary as well. Then Dakar would have a solid service team that could be supplemented with extras.

Slobodan's mood improved and he waved Jonas over.

"Get me a grappa and offer Lorenzo Wader, or whatever the hell his name is, a cognac."

Jonas sent a snifter sliding across the counter. Lorenzo looked up with surprise, glanced at Slobodan, raised the glass and smiled. Slobodan nodded, but without returning the smile. Lorenzo was a new acquaintance. Slobodan believed he was in the illegal gambling business. Perhaps he was checking out the scene in Uppsala in preparations for a foray into this market. Not that Slobodan had anything against this. It would very likely be good for business.

Slobodan had the impression that Armas and Lorenzo knew each other from before, or at least that Armas had heard of this well-dressed crook—for a crook he undoubtedly was, Slobodan was sure of it. But Armas denied having ever laid eyes on Lorenzo before.

Slobodan turned his body slightly so he could study Lorenzo more closely. It was difficult to pinpoint his age. Between forty-five and fifty, but he could also be ten years older. A well-dressed scoundrel with money and a certain measure of style, Slobodan decided. He had never heard Lorenzo raise his voice, had actually never heard him speak, and that was a testament to his style, in Slobodan's opinion. He hated loudmouths, who allowed their voices to dominate a room. Lorenzo was a man who comported himself without fuss. He had dined here a few times, but mostly spent his time in the bar, always started with a Staropramen, thereafter ordered a double espresso and a cognac and smoked a cigar.

He always arrived alone but was often joined by a man Slobodan assumed was a subordinate. The man, barely thirty and very pale, always listened attentively to Lorenzo, but rarely offered his own comments. He always drank rum and Coke, which according to Slobodan was the most unimaginative drink that could be served, often excused himself to go to the men's room and often remained at the bar for a while after Lorenzo left. Then he relaxed, ordered another rum and Coke, and savored a cigarette or two.

Lorenzo twisted his neck and met Slobodan's gaze, nodded and smiled. Slobodan slipped off his bar stool and walked over to Lorenzo, who pulled out a chair and made a gesture of invitation.

"Thank you," he said and gave Slobodan a new smile.

Slobodan nodded and scrutinized his guest a little further. Lorenzo had dark brown eyes and a small white scar between his eyebrows. His hands were unusually small and gave Slobodan the impression that Lorenzo had them manicured regularly. He gave an almost feminine impression, smiled in a relaxed manner, and there were no questions in his eyes, no anxiety, only a touch of mischief and mockery.

"Is everything to your satisfaction?"

"It feels like home," Lorenzo answered.

Slobodan stretched his hand across the table and introduced himself. After the eyes, he judged people most by their handshake. Lorenzo's was quick but a little too dainty for Slobodan's taste. His hand was cold.

"I haven't seen Armas in a while."

"Do you know him?"

"How does one define 'know'?" Lorenzo said and his smile started to wear on Slobodan. "We had a little contact many years ago."

Slobodan waited.

"In my younger days," Lorenzo said after tasting his cognac, and something in his face revealed that he felt it was much too long ago.

"He is away right now," Slobodan said.

"Vacation?"

"Among other things."

"Armas is mulitfaceted," Lorenzo said.

Slobodan didn't like it. He scoured his memory for when they had discussed the new guest and certainly he had made a comment about Lorenzo, but he could not recall that Armas had said anything about Lorenzo being an old acquaintance. Why would he lie about a thing like that?

"How do you like Uppsala?"

"A nice city," Lorenzo said. "A good size, manageable. Good for the soul. A little calmer, but nonetheless open to possibilities."

He spoke in short sentences, with an imperceptible accent that Slobodan believed to be Spanish. Lorenzo leaned back and his gaze lingered on Frances as she walked by with a tray.

"A beautiful woman," he said and Slobodan had the impression that he included the waitress in his assessment of Uppsala. But Frances was anything but manageable, definitely not calm and open to possibilities.

"Her husband has run away," Slobodan said. "No one knows where he is and Frances is walking around like a loose hand grenade."

Slobodan wanted to get Lorenzo started, get him to talk, but the information about Frances's husband did not alter Lorenzo's relaxed posture and did not appear to whet his curiosity.

"I am sure he will turn up," he simply said, but continued to watch Frances, as if weighing his chances.

Slobodan waved his hand and Jonas, who had learned to interpret the least little gesture of his boss, immediately poured a small glass of beer that he brought to the table.

"I have lived in this town for a long time," Slobodan said.

"Yes?"

"If you should need any assistance, I mean."

"And what would that be?"

Slobodan was beginning to hate the pleasantly smiling Lorenzo and his superior attitude.

"You tell me," Slobodan said and smiled sardonically.

He took a gulp of beer, stood up from the table with an excuse about unfinished paperwork, and left Lorenzo.

The brief conversation with Lorenzo had irritated Slobodan. Above all it was the patronizing tone that bore witness to an unusual degree of arrogance. Slobodan was accustomed to being treated with a great deal more respect.

It had also unsettled him. It was news to him that Lorenzo knew Armas from before, and it was not a good thing. Armas was his and Slobodan felt something that could be characterized as jealousy. In addition, Lorenzo was much too cocky. Slobodan had encountered this attitude many times and had never had any problems breaking the most brazen and obstinate fellow. But this man had an authority that not only testified to self-confidence but also about an ability to create problems.

Slobodan thought about Armas. If only everything worked out on this trip to Basque. He was taking a risk in sending Armas, but there was no alternative this time. If anything went wrong and the transport failed he would lose a great deal of money and possibly lose his best friend and partner. It was in the pot and Armas knew it. Even so, he had not protested. Even he knew how much this meant.

Slobodan had decided that they would thereafter take it easy for half a year, maybe even a year. One thing he had learned and that was not to try to bite off too much. One had to think big, but only in one's own league. Then one could, if everything went well, eventually qualify for a higher league.

He checked the time. If he knew Armas, then he was already in southern Sweden.

Slobodan smiled to himself as he came to think of his time in Malmö and the "German swine." The memory had bothered him for a long time, how he had been bullied and humiliated, but now he could think back on the whole episode with greater calm. The German had been made to pay. It did him good to think of it.

✦

Eighteen

The darkness unsettled her. She tripped on roots that stuck up, a branch whipped her in the face and she stumbled. Since she had called Hugo and told him that Patrik was all right, a fear had taken root in her that he was injured or that he had injured someone else. But surely Patrik wouldn't fight with a knife? It was an impossible thought, that her Patrik would deliberately stab someone.

She ran straight there—or what she thought the best way was, since her fear had confused her. She felt as if she was too late.

When she finally arrived at the community gardening area, the last ounce of courage left her and she started to cry. Suddenly she thought of Jörgen, Patrik and Hugo's father, and about how unfair life was.

A shadow dislodged itself from the dark. Patrik came toward her. How big he has become, she thought.

"Hi Mom," he said, and she started to cry again.

"It's okay," he said.

"What is happening? I have to know! Why do you do this? Now when everything . . ."

"Everything is fine, Mom. It's only that the police have their own ideas about stuff."

Patrik told her what had happened the last two days and Eva was amazed at how calm he was, how clearly and methodically he proceeded from event to event.

When he finished his story she was struck by how unreal everything was, that they were standing in a community garden in the middle of the night, with the smell of earth and with the occasional mosquito buzzing around their heads, talking about violence and a world she couldn't imagine.

Is this my Patrik, she thought. Is this our life? Our neighborhood?

"Shouldn't you tell this to the police?"

"What the hell do you think?"

Eva bounced at the hardness in his voice.

"But if you—"

"They won't believe me, you know that. And Zero will go crazy, and so will his brother."

"But drugs, it seems so—Have you done it?"

Patrik shook his head.

"I don't want to lose control," he said.

Eva believed him instinctively. It would be so unlike Patrik. He wanted to have control, as he said. He hated the unexpected.

"Let's go home," she said, suddenly steady and grateful that he was fine.

To her surprise, Patrik did not protest. He just stood up without a word and started to walk. She watched his silhouette.

That is my boy, she thought again and again. That is my boy.

When they got home Hugo and Johnny were sitting at the computer playing games. Patrik walked straight to his room and closed the door behind him.

"Thanks for staying," Eva said.

"We've been having a good time," Johnny said. "Isn't that right, Hugo?"

The boy nodded while he concentrated on the game.

"Would you like anything before going home?"

Johnny shook his head. Despite the late hour he did not feel tired. In fact, he felt the opposite. The trip to Eva's had livened him up. His own apartment held no attraction for him, but he realized he should get up and leave them in peace.

"We've had a good time," he repeated. "Did you find out what had happened?"

"Not really," Eva said. "We'll see tomorrow. I think Patrik has to spend some time alone and think it out."

"Are you going to the police?"

"I'll probably call them tomorrow. We'll see."

Eva sat down on Hugo's bed.

"You should get some rest," Johnny said.

Johnny drove home with mixed feelings. Other peoples' problems were nothing he needed and now he had fallen into one. He didn't want to be pulled in and Eva had not made any further attempt to do so. He was grateful for that. He would not have had the energy to stay all night and comfort her.

At the same time he felt uplifted. He had done something for another human being who clearly trusted him. Eva had hugged him before he left. He laughed out loud in the car.

On the last stretch before home he thought about her. How brave of her to raise two teenagers on her own in this world.

✦

Nineteen

Konrad Rosenberg was one of five sons of the infamous Karl-Åke Rosenberg, the drilling and blasting expert, of whom more or less believable stories still circulated on construction sites. Karl-Åke had set off his last load of explosives in Forsmark in 1979 and died shortly thereafter, more or less on the spot, from a heart attack, so shot through with dust and drill residue that he was indistinguishable from the rock. It was said that the body had to be cleaned with a high-pressure hose.

With every son that Elisa Rosenberg bore, it was as if there was not quite enough material. The firstborn, Bertil, was a giant like his father, but thereafter the sons were more and more feeble. Konrad was the youngest, one hundred and fifty-seven centimeters tall, equipped with a sunken chest and shoulders that stuck out like hangers. In elementary school the other kids played the harp on his ribs and his shoe size was only thirty-eight.

What he lacked in physique and ability, he made up for in a neverwavering optimism and a self-confidence that unfortunately often led him astray.

At the age of seventeen he embarked on a drug addiction, and one year later he was charged by the Uppsala courts with burglary and the assault of a civil servant. He was found guilty of the burglary but the second accusation was dismissed by the court. It was regarded as unlikely that Konrad had the capacity to offer any significant resistance.

That was the first in a long series of sentences. Most of them concerned drugs and crimes related to his drug habit, primarily fraud. He was a scoundrel, well known to the police and people in the blocks around the central station.

During his last prison term Konrad had participated in an ambitious program to kick his drug habit, and when he was released he had against all expectations kicked his drug dependence and was provided with a small apartment in Tunabackar, on the same street where he had grown up.

Konrad Rosenberg was forty-six years old when he was granted early retirement. He used to sit on Torbjörn Square, down a beer or two, and converse with other lushes or other retirees who were happy to have someone to talk to. Many of them had been acquainted with Konrad's father and loved to tell the usual stories about legendary explosions.

Sometimes he used the shuttle service to go downtown, shoplift in a couple of stores, selling the goods quickly below market value and returning home with a green bag of alcohol.

Life was simple for Konrad. He was still optimistically cheerful and was generally regarded as a little slow but harmless, since he had never committed any violent crimes.

One day, things looked up for Konrad Rosenberg. He appeared, in new clothes, at a bank branch on Torbjörn Square, where he opened an account and deposited fifty-six thousand kronor. The clerk, who recognized him from the park benches, could not conceal his surprise.

"It is an inheritance," Konrad explained somberly.

"My condolences," the clerk said.

"It is all right," Konrad said. "It's just a distant aunt who popped off."

After that, smaller amounts flowed into the account, a couple of thousand from time to time, on a few occasions a five-digit amount. A couple of years after the initial deposit, the sum had grown fivefold.

The bank clerk reminded Konrad of the possibility of a more favorable retirement savings account option that, once he had received an explanatory overview, Konrad politely declined.

"The devil only knows how long one has to live. One could kick the bucket at any moment."

One day he parked a Mercedes on the street, circled the car a few times, opened and locked the doors with a remote control system, unlocked the door, sat down in the car, only to step out again immediately, lock it, walk some distance away and turn around and regard this miracle, before he finally ducked in through the front doors of the building.

Konrad Rosenberg, as "Sture with the hat" had put it to Berglund, was in the money.

But fortune is a curse. From his relatively problem-free existence on the square, Konrad had now been plunged into a whirlwind of new acquaintances who, like the male butterfly that can detect a female at one kilometer's distance, appeared to be drawn to the smell of money that emanated from him.

At first he was flattered, liked to buy rounds for his new friends and was seen more often in public. Then suddenly everything ground to a halt. Konrad Rosenberg became sullen and unwilling to play along. No more small loans, no restaurant meals, visitors were turned away at the door.

When spring came, he was again on the park bench in the square. The bank account, which had almost been emptied, was again being filled at a steady and secure rate.

It was the summerhouse that was the source of Konrad Rosenberg's unexpected advancement.

In the sixties, the explosions expert Rosenberg had bought a piece of land from a local farmer about ten kilometers east of the town. On the stony property, which he spent the first summer blowing to bits, he built a large cottage of sixty square meters. In addition to a main room, where he and Elisa slept, it included a kitchen and two sleeping alcoves where the sons made do as best they could.

After Karl-Åke died, it only took a few weeks for Elisa to pass away. Konrad was in jail and could not really look out for his interests, but was happy with the money he received. The rest of the brothers sold the apartment in the city, as well as all the furnishings, and divided the money among themselves. Bertil made off with the summerhouse, but after an attack of guilty conscience, offered it for his little brother Konrad's use.

Konrad had lived there during difficult times in his life, but had never really felt at home there. It was too far from the city, but it breathed of childhood. Not that the latter had been unhappy in any way and perhaps this was what created the discomfort. The house reminded Konrad dimly of the fact that there were alternatives to the life he had chosen to live.

The neighbors were hardworking, decent types, and Konrad felt their scorn. He had renovated the house, had it repainted, replaced the woodwork, and had a new tin roof put on, but none of this helped. The neighbors continued to remain distant. What they did not know was that the summerhouse was the foundation of his renaissance. It was remote enough that it functioned as a repackaging center and did not figure on the police radar of hot spots. Konrad himself played no part in the planning of this but was nonetheless smart enough to realize the relative value of this modest house. He thought it was a lucky break that he had been recruited, but the fact was that it was the summerhouse that was of interest. Konrad was only part of the bargain.

He carted the tube of cooking gas, the container of water, and the suitcase up to the house, unlocked the door, and was greeted by its characteristic smell: a mixture of gas, mold, and childhood. He grinned, without being aware that he was doing so.

After installing the tube and putting the old one on the veranda, Konrad boiled water and made a cup of instant coffee, which he drank in measured sips while he wondered when the next delivery would take place. It irritated him that he was kept in the dark. He felt more important than this and did not want to be regarded simply as a mere delivery boy. Next time he was going to speak his mind.

"What the hell am I sitting here for?" he burst out, in an attack of clear-headedness.

He pushed the cup away so that the coffee spilled out and formed a triangle-shaped stain on the wax tablecloth. He pulled his finger through the liquid and suddenly felt a strong urge to sleep with a woman. Just to sleep. Without fuss, to be able to sleep with a warm woman by his side.

"Well, what do you know, Dad," he said out loud, and the resolve in his voice surprised him.

He looked around the cottage, allowing his gaze to wander from the old woodstove over the hastily made bed, to the dresser where a few decorative items bore witness to the Rosenberg family's former life.

He shook his head as if to get rid of his discomfort, stood up, unsure of why he felt so uncomfortable.

The fortune he now possessed normally gave him a rush. He had never been so successful, and especially with such minimal effort. He felt more respectable and thought he was treated with more respect than before, not only at the bank but everywhere. He almost felt as if he had a real job.

But now he packed the goods into small tidy packets with a feeling of sadness.

When the bag was filled he left the house, carefully locking it, and drove back into town. A young boy was trying to hitch a ride in Bärby.

"Get your own car," Konrad muttered, and stepped on the gas.

✦

Twenty

"I know who he is."

Her colleague, Thommy Lissvall, who Lindell only knew in passing, could not conceal a triumphant smile.

"Great," Lindell said, flipping open her notebook.

"He is not a celebrity by any means but naturally I know him. It is strange that no one has identified him before now."

"In that case, what have you been doing for the past three days?"

"I was at a workshop," Lissvall said.

He looked at Lindell.

"A good one," he added.

A Dalarna accent, she thought. Why do they have to be so damned long-winded?

"All right, maybe you could kindly bring yourself to reveal who he is?"

"He has been in this town for a long time, but as I said—"

"What restaurant?"

Lissvall was thrown off for a second, blinked, and smiled at Haver who was sitting at the far end of the table.

Lindell had taken a chance. The city unit, which Lissvall belonged to, worked with restaurant-related crimes.

"Several," Lissvall said.

"Slobodan Andersson's imperium, in other words," Haver said suddenly, with unexpected loudness. "Because I can't imagine it is Svensson's?"

"A name," Lindell said. She was thoroughly sick of the guessing game.

"Armas."

"And more?"

"I don't know what his last name is," Lissvall was forced to admit, "but it is no doubt a mouthful. I've never heard anything except Armas."

"And he worked for Slobodan?"

"Yes."

Lindell shot Haver a quick look.

"I was at Dakar with Beatrice recently," she said.

Lissvall chuckled.

"Thank you very much," Lindell said firmly, and stood up. "I take it you have no further information."

"I guess not," he said and got up from the table.

"What an idiot," Lindell said when he had left the room.

"What do we do?" Haver asked.

Lindell examined her notes. She had written "Armas" in capital letters. She was relieved, grateful that the murder victim was from Uppsala. It would have been boring with a dumped Stockholmer.

"We go out to dinner," she said lightly.

Slobodan Andersson's apartment was located in a one-hundred-year-old building just east of the railroad. It was within walking distance of the police station. The morning had been clear and chilly, but now, with the time approaching ten o'clock in the morning, the sunshine was warm. Lindell couldn't help pausing for a few seconds and closing her eyes. She lapped up the sun and thought about her visit to Dakar. Had Armas been there that evening? Lindell could not recall any member of the staff except the waitress.

Haver, who had pushed on, stopped, turned around, and looked at Lindell.

"Come on," he said.

Lindell laughed. Haver couldn't help but smile.

"You find it invigorating with murder, don't you?"

"Maybe," Lindell said and tried to imitate Lissvall's dialect, but failed miserably.

"No, not really," she resumed. "But I do find it invigorating to do some good."

They discussed how they should proceed in their conversation with Slobodan Andersson. They considered bringing someone from the city unit, but finally rejected the idea. Lindell had awakened the restaurant owner with her call. It was difficult to determine if it was the circumstances that made him appear confused. He had asked what the call was in regards to but Lindell had only said she wanted to talk.

"Can't it wait until this afternoon?"

"No, I don't think so," Lindell said.

After getting the door code from Slobodan Andersson and informing Ottosson of their plans, they immediately left the station.

Slobodan Andersson received them in a lime-yellow robe. The apartment, which consisted of five rooms with high ceilings, deep windowsills, and ornate moldings, was newly renovated. Lindell could still smell the paint. Andersson asked them to sit down and offered them coffee, which they declined.

Lindell sat down while Haver remained standing by the window.

"Well, how can I be of service to the police?"

No trace of the earlier confusion remained.

Lindell studied the restaurant owner. She thought she had seen him before. Maybe at Dakar? On the other hand, he had the kind of appearance that stood out. He was ample, Lindell decided, summing up her impression, not to say fat.

Lindell estimated his age at around fifty. On his left hand he had a gold band on his ring finger and around his throat he had a gold chain with an amulet. He gave off a waft of perfume or aftershave.

"You have an employee by the name of Armas, don't you?"

For a moment, Lindell thought she saw a shift in Slobodan Andersson's expression that revealed surprise, perhaps even concern, but he answered in a steady voice.

"Yes, that's right. Armas has been in my employ for, well, for many years now. He is my right hand, as they say," Slobodan said and looked down at his own hands.

"Do you know where he is?"

In the corner of her eye, Lindell saw Haver move a couple of meters and look with curiosity into the next room.

"Yes, I know exactly where he is. He is on his way to the north of

Spain to meet with a few of my professional contacts. As you know, Basque cuisine is exquisite. Armas usually travels around and gathers some ideas, brings home recipies, tips on good wine, everything that a restaurant owner needs. Perhaps come home with a good cheese."

"When did he leave?"

"A few days ago. He is driving down. Has anything happened? Has he had a car accident?"

"No, it is more serious than that, I'm afraid," Lindell said. "I'm sorry to have to tell you, but Armas is dead."

Slobodan Andersson pushed back in the sofa and stared at her without comprehension.

"It is not possible," he said finally.

"We haven't made a definitive identification yet, but there is every indication that it is him. Does he have a family?"

Slobodan shook his head.

"No relatives?"

"No, it is him and me," Slobodan said in a low voice.

"Do you think you could come in and identify your friend? As you can understand we have to be sure."

Are they a couple? Lindell wondered. That would be revealed in time. She took out a photograph of the dead man. It was a picture that partly spared the viewer since the image was cropped under the chin. Slobodan glanced at it and nodded.

"How did he die?"

"His life was taken," Lindell said.

"What do you mean?"

"He was murdered."

Slobodan stood up abruptly, walked over to the window, and ended up standing there. They heard a train go by. She exchanged a quick look with Haver.

A minute went by, perhaps two. The clanging bell of the railway crossing was the only thing they heard. A new train was approaching.

"Where?" Slobodan asked through clenched teeth.

"We don't know precisely," Haver said, now speaking for the first time. "You may have read in the newspaper about—"

"I don't read newspapers!"

The clanging had stopped.

"Who?"

"We don't know that either. We were hoping you might be able to help us," Lindell said.

It turned out that Armas's apartment was in the same building. Slobodan had spare keys and Lindell called Ottosson, who arranged for a technician to come by. After twenty minutes the doorbell rang. Lindell gave Haver a look, and he went to open the door. Lindell walked away so she was not visible from the front door. She heard Haver exchange a few words with Charles Morgansson.

An hour later Lindell left Slobodan Andersson's apartment in the latter's company in order to bring him down to the morgue to make an identification of the body, while Haver went to Armas's apartment. In this way she could avoid seeing Charles.

"The tattoo" was the first thing Ottosson said when Ann Lindell came into his office.

Lindell laughed and sat down across from him.

"Slobodan thought it was a sea horse or some other kind of animal, and that fits with the part that is left. I thought it looked like a foot. He didn't know when Armas got the tattoo. Armas had always had it, according to Slobodan."

"Did you tell him it had been removed?"

"No, I simply asked what it was."

"Let's have a cup of coffee," Ottosson said. "I bought cheese sandwiches and some doughnuts."

He looked pleased. Lindell sensed that he, like herself, was happy that the identity had been established and that the victim came from Uppsala. This aided the investigation considerably.

While they drank their coffee, Lindell reviewed the most important aspects of the case for Ottosson. The two men had parted at around four o'clock. Armas was going to sleep for a couple of hours before starting his drive down to Spain. According to Slobodan he preferred to drive at night. He owned a blue BMW X5 of last year's model. Armas was going to be gone for two weeks. Slobodan characterized the whole thing as a combined vacation and business trip.

"But to drive all the way down to Spain?" Ottosson said.

"Armas had a fear of flying."

Ottosson nodded. Lindell knew Ottosson shared this fear.

Slobodan could not see any motives to the killing. Armas was a loner, someone who basically had no circle of friends, had no association with anyone, as far as Slobodan knew, and he had trouble imagining that Armas had some secret life.

"He lived at and for the restaurants," Lindell summed up.

"A model citizen," Ottosson said. "What about money?"

"Slobodan thought he had at most two or three thousand in cash. He may have gone down to the Forex money exchange to get some Euros. We'll have to check that. Fredriksson has made sure the cards have been blocked. We'll retrieve information about account activity."

Lindell checked the time.

"Day care?"

"No problem," Lindell said. "Görel is picking up today."

"The car?"

"It shouldn't be hard to find. I don't think the apartment is where the murder took place. It looked completely normal, an exemplary state of order, according to Haver."

"Too clean?"

"No, but I think Armas was a bit of a neatfreak."

"Should we talk to the city unit?"

"Yes, but not with the guy from Dalarna, Lisskog or whatever his name is."

"Lissvall," Ottosson said, smiling. "He was in the fraud unit for a while, but they got sick of him."

Lindell looked like she had already repressed all thoughts of her colleague and resumed her review. When she was done they discussed the future investigation and what should be prioritized.

Fredriksson would coordinate the background investigation. The details of Armas's life had to be fleshed out and Slobodan himself had to be closely examined.

Berglund and Beatrice would handle the questioning of the restaurant employees.

"Done! We'll nab him by Tuesday of next week," Ottosson said confidently.

Lindell nodded.

"Thanks for the doughnuts. That was thoughtful of you."

Ottosson became embarrassed as usual when he received praise.

✦

Twenty-One

It was only when Eva Willman woke up the following morning, abruptly, as if she had been startled by a bad dream, that she realized the enormity of what had transpired these past two days.

She suddenly imagined her son as a criminal, a juvenile delinquent who would soon grow up and gradually be pulled down into a morass of criminality and drug abuse.

"No!" she sobbed, sinking back into the bed, pulling the blankets more tightly around her and glancing at the time. Half past five.

There were no guarantees in life, no insurance that would keep you from harm. That had been clear to her for a long time, but now it was as if reality, that which was written about in the papers and spoken about on television, came rushing toward her. Every person makes their own decisions, however crazy they may seem, however unlikely they may appear to others.

What decisions had Patrik made? She did not know. She thought she knew what was going on, but now realized with a newly won and overwhelming certainty that her influence was limited. Perhaps she had reached him last night during their brief conversation in the community garden, but for how long?

Who decides over us? she thought. Suddenly life appeared so incomplete and unpredictable. Her marriage to Jörgen, two children in rapid succession, then divorce, her job at the post office, then being laid off, her happiness at finding a new job, but for how long? And now this with Patrik. Up till now he had never so much as hurt a fly and always stayed out of trouble. Of course he and Hugo fought, but that never lasted. In middle school he often complained that others were getting into trouble. He couldn't stand the sight of blood, and even a blood test was a challenge for him. Now he had come home bleeding and was suspected of assault on top of it.

She got up and fetched the newspaper, quickly leafing through it to see if there was anything about yesterday's events. On the fourth page there was a short article. "A new violent attack in Sävja" was the title.

"A forty-two-year-old man was stabbed yesterday in the Sävja residential area, in south Uppsala. This is the most recent of a series of violent conflicts that have attracted attention in this area. As recently as last week ago a young woman was assaulted and in January a bus came under gunfire. The man, who lives in Uppsala, was visiting Sävja when he was attacked without provocation by some young men. According to the police, the man attempted to escape his attackers but was overcome in the vicinity of Stordammen school, where he was stabbed in the abdomen and received many kicks. His condition is described as serious but not life-threatening."

That was all. Eva imagined the newspaper had received the information so late that they had not had the opportunity to include more. Most likely, tomorrow's paper would include more details.

She read the article again. "Some young men." Patrik was not a man, he was still a boy, a teenager who only two or three years ago had gone sledding and read comic books.

She had an urge to move away from the area. Settle somewhere else with her sons where there were no "violent conflicts that attracted attention." But where would that be? Did those places even exist?

From her kitchen window she could see how her neighbors were coming to life, some were eating breakfast while watching morning TV, others were already on their way to work. She saw Helen's man half-running toward the parking lot. He was late as usual.

Again she was struck by how isolated this block was, how the inhabitants were divided from one another by invisible walls. Even though they were neighbors they were strangers to one another. The suffering of one did not affect the other. People who had lived perhaps ten years on the same level had never set foot in one anothers' apartments. They knew their neighbors' names, but it could just as well be a number, an assigned code. Those who lived on level seven could be called 7:1, 7:2, 7:3, and so on.

She herself would be 14:6–1, Patrik 14:6–2, and Hugo 14:6–3. It would be simpler, at least for the authorities. They could inscribe the numbers on their foreheads.

She smiled at her crazy ideas while she set the table for breakfast.

They had once all joined together. That was when the housing association wanted to remove part of the playground and build a room to house the garbage. Then they had all assembled in the neighborhood and decided to protest. Helen had been the most active, going around with lists and putting up flyers in all the stairwells. You could say what you wanted about Helen, but she was not shy. She ended up in the newspaper. The clipping was still on her refrigerator door.

Eva stood in the window but was irritated by her limited view. She only saw a courtyard, a few buildings, and in the background an arm of the forest, or really just a few fir trees. People want to see far, she thought, because then you gain a perspective on your situation and you can discover things beyond yourself. She recalled a visit to Flatåsen in the deep northern forests of Värmland among her grandfather's relatives, how he had brought her up on a hilltop—her grandfather called it a mountain—from which point they could look out over miles of forests and lakes. For once her grandfather had been quiet. He pointed out villages and swathes of forests where he had worked as a lumberjack in his youth.

Eva, who was in her early teens, had never before seen such large land areas at one time. They lingered up there for a long time. It was her dearest memory of her grandfather, the otherwise so gruff and at times alcoholic communist who in his bitterness no longer trusted anyone and no longer held anything to be of value.

"Everything nowadays is cat shit," he would mutter in front of the television.

Her head was spinning with thoughts. Her usual morning effectiveness was gone and it had taken her half an hour to put out the dishes, brew some coffee, and empty the dishwasher.

She thought she was on to something important. Maybe she should talk to Johnny at Dakar, or even Feo—someone outside her immediate neighborhood. Helen would just start ranting about this or that kid.

Just then the telephone rang. She picked up at once, convinced it was the police.

"Hi, I saw that you were up."

It was Helen, she must have noticed Eva in the window. Eva pulled the kitchen door shut and sat down at the table.

"I heard about it yesterday. It's just like the cops to blame it on Patrik. It would be better for them to go angling around the others."

Eva had no trouble imagining what Helen meant by "the others." She stuck the received under her chin, took out a mug, and poured out some coffee.

"They just wanted to talk to him," Eva said.

"Nonsense. They make up their minds and spread a lot of lies. You should hear what they told Monica last night."

But Eva did not want to.

"What is Patrik saying?"

"We haven't really talked," Eva said and started to cry.

"I'm coming over," Helen said.

"No, don't. Maybe later. I have to talk to the boys first."

They ended the phone call and Eva sat with her hands wrapped around the coffee mug. It had the words *the world's best mom* on it.

✦

Twenty-Two

For the first time since his months in Malmö as a sixteen-year-old under the thumb of the "German swine," Slobodan experienced great anxiety.

The physical sensation itself was unpleasant, it radiated out from a point level with his navel. He was even more disturbed when he discovered what the discomfort actually consisted of: pure and unadulterated terror.

This was a feeling that, ever since he had tamed the Malmö restauranteur, he reserved for others. That was the time he had discovered the power of terror. The freshly sharpened fillet knife stuck into the man's abdomen, only two or three centimeters deep but enough for the blood to start trickling down onto the tile floor and bring fear to the German's eyes.

The knowledge that he was on his own from now on drove him beside himself. There was only one Armas, who was now lying naked in a refrigerated storage facility. And Slobodan was powerless. When he realized that the police were searching Armas's apartment he immediately started thinking of a counterstrike, but to his surprise he could not think of one. He was in the hands of the police.

He was not particularly concerned that the police was going to find any evidence of their activities in the apartment. Armas was smarter than that. But despite his well-developed concern for security and care, there was a risk. A telephone number hastily scribbled down on a newspaper, a name in an address book, or something else that could point the police in a certain direction.

Slobodan thought intensely about whether he had any incriminating material in his own apartment or at the restaurants, but could not think of anything. He realized that the police were not going to overlook any areas in their search for Armas's killer. Even he himself would be examined. He had gathered as much from the female police officer's questions.

He immediately started to work his way through his phone book, flipping through the notes he had made, searched all his desk drawers. Then he stood there for a long time, sweating and staring into space, scouring his mind for anything that could threaten his freedom.

At Dakar or Alhambra there was less of a danger, for there Armas had been in charge. Slobodan knew no one who was as careful as Armas. Now he had fallen victim to someone. To seize him was an almost inhuman assignment, but someone had outsmarted him.

He thought about the last thing they had done together, updating the computer. Had Armas sensed that something was afoot? Did he feel threatened? Hadn't he said something about "gaps" that needed to be filled? Had he meant Rosenberg? Armas had long been irritated over Rosenberg's indulgent lifestyle. Admittedly he had improved since Armas had worked him over, but Slobodan knew that if he could choose they would cut out Rosenberg.

"His kind only understand one language," Armas had said.

Insecurity came creeping. Perhaps Armas had concealed something from him? Slobodan rejected the idea. Armas had been his friend, his only friend. They were incapable of betraying each other.

What was it Lorenzo had said of Armas? "Multifaceted." They knew each other from their youth. "Youth," what kind of nonsense was that? It was a foreign word when it came to Armas. He had never talked about his youth or childhood. Slobodan's impression was that Armas had never been young. And was this Lorenzo likely to know things about Armas that he himself didn't know? Multifaceted? What the hell did that mean?

Slobodan paced around the apartment. Circles of sweat appeared under his arms. The pain in his chest, that had come and gone over the past year, grew into a pressure that made him draw deeply for a breath.

Suddenly the phone rang. It is Armas, he thought for a second. Not many people called Slobodan at home: Armas, Oskar Hammer, occasionally Donald at Dakar, and then a couple of others.

He let it ring. Against his will he had a grappa. He forced himself to down the stinging liquid in an attempt to regain his focus.

"This is not fair," he muttered, and it was not Armas's fate that he was thinking of, but the failed delivery in San Sebastián. It was lost, he realized, there was no plan B. And it would be completely insane to think of an alternative at this point.

He turned on the laptop, eyed the e-mails that remained, and decided to erase all of them. A great deal of information would be lost—he did not know how he would be able to save the innocuous files—but his anxiety about what might be concealed in the inner regions of the computer made it into a threat.

After finishing his grappa he called a cab and left the apartment with his computer bag.

Once he was out in the fresh air he felt better. The knot in his stomach died away and he watched with satisfaction as a taxi pulled up, almost somewhat astonished that everything worked as before.

He ordered the driver to take him to the dump in Libro. He had been out there with Armas before and thrown away old papers and garbage from the restaurants. He asked the taxi to wait, made sure no one was watching, banged the laptop into the side of the container a few times before he wedged it in between an old filing cabinet and a mess of metal scraps.

He exhaled and stood stock still. Out of the corner of his eye he saw an attendant approaching. If you complain about something I'll kill you, he thought, but the man only looked indifferently at him with weary eyes.

Slobodan returned to the cab with the empty computer bag and asked to be dropped off at Alhambra. While he sank back into the seat, exhausted, he wondered if he should call Rosenberg but decided to hold off. That's what Armas would have done, he thought, and realized suddenly with great sadness how much he was going to miss him.

✦

Twenty-Three

Eva and Patrik were waiting in the reception area at the police station. Patrik sat down while Eva looked around. On the wall opposite the reception desk there was a piece of art that depicted a man's gigantic head. Eva thought it was grotesque and she wondered what they had been thinking when they hung such a frightening piece to welcome their visitors.

She looked at her watch. Barbro Liljendahl had said eleven and it was now ten past. She walked over to Patrik who had slouched on the chair.

"I bet she'll be coming out soon," Eva said.

Patrik did not look at her and didn't say anything. He stared dully straight ahead. How can one be so calm? she wondered.

Barbro Liljendahl turned up at a quarter past eleven. She excused herself, but Eva was struck by the suspicion that she had deliberately let them wait.

She had always disliked women police officers. Women and uniforms did not go together. She had recently seen a report on TV about American soldiers in Iraq and there had been two women in the group. One of them was called Stacey. She spoke with utter confidence about their "mission" to clean up a little village outside Tikrit. She described the assignment as if it were like killing mice or other vermin, as if they were dispatched by a pest-control company. Her self-assured face glowed under the disproportionally large helmet. She chewed gum and in her eyes there was no doubt, only a discomfiting degree of certainty.

Eva and Patrik were led into a narrow room. Liljendahl took her place behind the desk, which was bare except for a folder and five paper clips laid out in a straight line, and asked them to sit down across from her. Eva considered remaining on her feet but saw the childishness of such a reaction.

Barbro Liljendahl opened the folder, but changed her mind and quickly shut it again, looking at Patrik for a moment before turning to Eva.

"Thank you for coming in," she said and Eva gave her an almost imperceptible nod.

"This is an unfortunate situation," she continued. "I hope for your forbearance with any difficulties this may cause."

Eva thought of the patrol car outside the building and all the kids who had gathered around.

"As you know, we have a report of an assault from the night before last. Three witnesses claim to have seen a man assaulted by a group of young people, they are not sure of the exact number. There may have been three, perhaps four. The accounts diverge at this point. This assault was never reported; the victim was able to leave the scene on his own and when we arrived everything was calm."

She leaned forward and directed her attention at Patrik.

"Have you heard about this incident?"

Patrik shook his head.

"There must have been talk in the neighborhood. No one you knew was involved?"

"No," Patrik managed to get out.

His voice was hoarse and he shot Eva a quick look before staring down at the floor again.

"And then last night. Then it was more serious. A man, but we no longer believe the victim was the same man as the night before, was stabbed with what we believe was a knife. He was cut in the stomach and also sustained injuries to his neck and right arm. He lost a lot of blood."

The silence in the room grew thick for a few seconds before the policewoman continued.

"He will survive, but we regard this as an attempted murder."

Patrik lifted his head and looked at Barbro Liljendahl.

"And what does this have to do with me?"

The policewoman inadvertently sighed and Eva felt a sting of guilt.

"We're not saying that you were involved, but you may know something that is of interest."

Patrik shook his head.

"It does not have to come out that the information came from you."

In your dreams, Eva thought. Patrik did not say anything.

"Where did you receive those injuries to your face?"

The swollen lip had more or less receded and the cut on his forehead was difficult to spot under his bangs.

"I fell," Patrik said. "Skateboarding."

Eva knew he was lying but could not bring herself to say anything. You bitch, she thought, what do you know about us?

"How long ago was that?"

"A couple of days ago."

Liljendahl nodded.

"Your brother," she said after a moment's silence. "Do you think—?"

"What does he have to do with this?"

Eva stared at the five paper clips in order not to throw herself over the policewoman in an attack of uncontrolled rage.

"Why do you have to get Hugo involved in this," she got out.

"I thought he may also have some information, something he may have seen or heard."

She is threatening me, the damn sow, Eva thought. She wants to rip my family apart. Eva suddenly thought of Jörgen and that made her even angrier. That idiot should be here right now, taking responsibility. But it wouldn't make any difference anyway. He would just want to be accommodating and talk too much.

"Why didn't you ask him to come in as well, then?" Eva asked and saw the discomfort in the woman's face.

"There is no reason to get upset," she said.

"There isn't? But why—" Eva said. The uncomfortable feeling of hiding behind a lie caught up with her fury and silenced her abruptly. She blushed and stared down into her lap.

Barbro Liljendahl opened the folder with a sigh. Eva observed her while she eyed through the uppermost page of a bunch of papers. Different-colored paper clips were attached to some of the pages. Eva feared the folder for what it might contain. It was as if it held all that could determine her, Patrik, and Hugo's fate.

This is my day off, she thought suddenly and her anger flared up again.

"You know someone by the name of Zero, don't you?"

Patrik nodded.

"We have had our eye on him for a while. As you know he is a bit . . . restless."

"We played soccer together," Patrik volunteered. "Before. He was . . ."

"Yes, what?"

"Nothing."

Barbro Liljendahl gazed at him for a while before she went on.

"We think he is involved in drugs. Do you know anything about that?

"Cocaine and Ecstasy," she added after a long period of ominous silence.

Eva turned and glared at her son.

"Did you know about this?" she asked sharply.

Patrik shook his head.

"You're lying!" Eva screamed.

Patrik looked up. His expression betrayed fear and astonishment. Eva rarely raised her voice.

"I don't know anything," he said quietly. But Eva could see by his face that he would soon begin to talk.

"Perhaps you should leave us for a while," Barbro Liljendahl said, and at first Eva thought the policewoman meant Patrik, then she realized this was directed at her.

She looked at Patrik, who nodded faintly. Eva stood up, full of contradictory feelings, and left the room without a word.

✦

Twenty-Four

On another floor of the station, the brain squad, as Ottosson called the unit, was assembled. The group consisted of Ann Lindell, almost forty years old, who after a series of publicized cases was perhaps the most well known among the police officers in the room; Ola Haver, same age, a doubter, sometimes happily married to Rebecka, at other times paralyzed by indecision as to how best to organize his life;

Berglund, whose first name had been forgotten long ago, the veteran whom everyone privately admired for his wisdom; Allan Fredriksson, the gambler and birdwatcher, a skilled investigator who remained somewhat too disorganized to be truly top-notch; Beatrice Andersson, perhaps the most eminent psychologist among them, hard as flint, according to the male chauvinists in the building; and then Ottosson, the boss, who was referred to as "Liljeholmen"—as in the candle manufacturer—by someone on the drug squad because he liked to make things cozy by lighting candles.

Ottosson poured the coffee and Beatrice heaped *mazarin* cakes on a plate. Lindell chuckled.

"You are too much, Otto," she said.

Ottosson patted his stomach.

"A little sugar never hurt anyone," he said.

Berglund leaned over and nabbed one of the frosted marzipan cakes.

"Should we begin?" Fredriksson said, for once the person who initiated the discussion.

"Sure, sure," Ottosson said. "Jump right in. Why don't you go first, Allan, and tell us about the apartment."

"Almost clinically clean, you could say. There were three sets of fingerprints. Apart from Armas's own prints, there were some from Slobodan and a third person. Slobodan's prints were located in a variety of places, in the bathroom, kitchen, and a marble windowsill. The unknown set of prints was found on a videocassette lying on top of the television."

"What was the tape?"

"Porn," Allan said.

"So Armas was watching porn with a lady friend?" Ottosson asked.

"I think it was a man," Allan replied. "It was a homo flick."

Lindell smiled to herself. She could hear exactly how disgusting Allan thought it was.

"I'll be damned," Haver said. "So Armas—"

"If you'll let me finish, we can delve into speculation later," Fredriksson interrupted. "Apart from this, the place was, as I said, clean. Nothing out of the ordinary, nothing hidden. No weapons, cash, papers, or anything like that. I examined an address book and it contained nothing sensational from what I can tell. Some thirty names, most of them with connections to the restaurant world. The examination has not been completed yet, but I don't expect we'll find anything remarkable there."

Fredriksson turned a page in his notebook before he went on.

"Regarding videotapes: there were about a hundred. Schönell is checking them out right now. It's conceivable that there is a private tape among them. He will probably be done by tonight. Unfortunately he broke a tooth last night and had to go to the dentist. He was probably dreaming—"

"Okay," Ottosson said, "the gay thread is the only aspect of interest we have from the apartment, if I understood you correctly, Allan?"

Fredriksson nodded.

"Berglund?"

"We have conducted initial sessions of questioning with most of the staff at Dakar and Alhambra, altogether seventeen people. Half a dozen are missing. Someone is traveling, another at a funeral, a third we have been unable to reach, and a fourth is actually in the midst of another investigation, but I think it's a coincidence. Her name is Eva Willman and her teenage son may be involved in the stabbing of an old client of ours. It happened in Sävja recently. Barbro Liljendahl is leading that one."

"Look into it," Ottosson said, and Berglund gave him a long look before resuming.

"It's the usual crowd, some who have worked in the restaurant business for a long time, others are more temporary, especially among the waitstaff. If we increase this to look at employees from the past few years that adds another ten, fifteen people. If we can rely on the medical examiner's report and assume that Armas died early or late afternoon, then most of these people have alibis. They were working. The rest are being checked on."

Berglund accounted for the additional information that the questioning had yielded. Everyone was naturally shocked. None of the staff could provide a self-evident motive for the slaying.

"What did they say about his character, the kind of person he was?" Lindell asked.

"Quiet. Did not make a lot of noise, but from what I gathered he wielded a lot of power. One of the bartenders at Alhambra said he always got nervous when Armas was around. He kept an eye on things, but rarely said anything. It was Slobodan Andersson who stood for the talking."

"Did he drink?"

"He was basically a teetotaler," Berglund said.

"Anything about his sexual preferences?" Haver asked.

Berglund shook his head.

"No one could give the name of any girlfriend. But if he was known to be gay that would probably have come out."

"Can you watch gay porn without being gay?" Beatrice tossed out. The rest of them look at each other and Haver burst out laughing.

"Out with it, boys," Beatrice said.

"No," Haver decided, "I have trouble believing that. What do you say, Allan?"

"You would know better than I," Fredriksson said, making a face.

"A quiet man, 'hard as a rock,' as one of the chefs put it, rarely had a drink, 'dutiful' said another, not friends with anyone except Slobodan," Berglund recited.

"Closet homosexual," Haver added.

"You like that gay stuff, don't you?" Allan Fredriksson said.

"That's my thing," Haver smiled broadly at his colleague.

"There is a guy," Berglund picked up again, "his name is Olaf González, but apparently goes by Gonzo."

"What the hell kind of name is that?" Fredriksson asked.

"Norwegian mother, Spanish father," said Berglund, who hated to be interrupted. "He has worked at Dakar for a couple of years, but was apparently fired a couple of weeks ago. According to the others there was a conflict between him and Armas that led to his termination. No one knew what it was about. According to González himself, he quit saying he was sick of the fascist Slobodan, but had nothing negative to say about Armas."

"We'll have to check with Slobodan," Ottosson said, "but it seems a bit much to slit someone's throat because they gave you the boot."

"We don't know what was behind it," Berglund said.

"Black earnings?" Beatrice suggested.

"I've checked with the restaurant unit and according to them Slobodan has been an exemplary citizen the past few years."

"The tattoo," Lindell prompted.

"There was actually only one person who had seen it and he could not describe it exactly. He thought it was some kind of animal."

"Had Armas made any comment about it?"

"The guy didn't asked him, just saw it by accident when Armas changed his T-shirt once."

"Damn mysterious," Ottosson said.

The discussion continued for another half an hour. Was Slobodan a possible suspect or coconspirator to the murder? Lindell did not think so. His reaction when she and Ola Haver delivered the news spoke against this. She had had the impression that Slobodan and Armas really were good friends and that Slobodan's shock and grief was genuine.

Could it be as simple as a robbery-assault? Lindell wondered. According to Slobodan, Armas always wore a gold watch and a gold band on the ring finger of his left hand. He could have been observed when he changed his money, followed, and then killed. She presented this theory but dismissed it herself the next moment. The removal of the tattoo spoke against this.

"Do we have any leads from Forex?" Ottosson asked.

"He has been recorded on the security tape. The time is sixteen fifty-six," Lindell said, "and we know that he changed five thousand kronor to euros."

"Men have been killed for less," Fredriksson said.

"How do we proceed?" Ottosson asked, and sighed hugely.

"I'll take on Slobodan," Lindell said. "Berglund continues talking to the staff. Ola, follow up on this gay lead and if you have time, help Berglund produce a summary report for the interviews. Allan can continue his digging with Lugn from the restaurant unit. I spoke with him this morning and we have a green light."

"What about me?" Beatrice said.

"You can reconstruct Armas's life," Lindell said.

"Okay, but I can't give him his life back."

"Write his biography," Lindell said and smiled. "That's enough."

As if on a given signal, the brain squad stood up from the table and left the room. All that remained were six coffee mugs, six plates, and the crumbled remains of a few *mazarin* cakes.

✦

Twenty-Five

Manuel Alavez studied the people who walked by. Some of them hurried, walking with deliberate steps, looking around hastily as they passed the parking lot, speeding by like projectiles with shoulders pulled up and their gazes directed far into the distance, as if they were target-seeking missiles, programmed for a single purpose.

Others sauntered, conversed with their partners, slowed down, uttered exclamations and laughed, perhaps put a hand on the partner's arm, only to continue aimlessly on their way. They paused, cheerfully allowed cars to pass, as if they had all the time in the world.

It is like the *zócolon,* the square in Oaxaca, he thought, this mixture of people. The expressions are the same, but do the Swedes feel in the same way? Do they get happy about the same things. Does love strike them with equal force, and what does their pain look like?

Sometimes they imagined, the villagers on their benches, that the white men were a foreign race, that, although they were equipped with arms and legs, they had eyes that perceived without seeing and mouths that talked constantly but with words that did not touch the reality that the villagers knew.

From the parking lot Manuel had an unobstructed view of Slobodan Andersson's building. Manuel was not sure exactly why he was sitting here spying on him. Ten thousand dollars could be a good enough reason, even though Patricio did not seem particularly interested. His indifference at his fate had surprised and perplexed Manuel. He couldn't take seriously the comment that money would not be able to alter his conditions in prison. Surely money had the same power here as in the rest of the world?

And if Patricio was not personally invested then there was Maria, but Manuel assumed that it was his brother's guilty conscience that was bothering him. He did not want any blood money.

They had sent them eleven thousand as compensation for Angel's death. Eleven thousand pesos. That was worth half a coffee harvest for the Alavez family. Half a year's work was what Angel's life was worth in the fat man's eyes.

Did Manuel want to see the fat man dead? He searched his soul during the idle hours in the car. Armas had died by his hand, but would he be able to slay Slobodan Andersson in cold blood?

No, he did not think so. That would not give him Angel back and it would not help Patricio. The only thing that could improve his situation was money and that was what Manuel wanted to lay his hands on. But what if the fat man refused?

In order to clear his head, he turned on the car radio, but then turned it off immediately. He didn't like the music, and he didn't understand the language.

Will the world be a better place if Slobodan dies? This was a question he had asked himself many times but had not been able to bring himself to answer.

He turned the radio back on again. Now an American melody that he recognized from California was playing and he let it stay on.

He had become a murderer but he regretted nothing. It was only in his dreams that he felt anguish.

Then he saw the fat man step out his front door and walk with short, hurried footsteps to a taxi, and get into it. Manuel started the car and followed.

He spread out the map in the passenger seat in order to follow the taxi's route. It was driving north. Manuel was impressed and amazed at how disciplined the Swedes conducted themselves in traffic. The most remarkable thing was that they stopped for pedestrians. Manuel had been close to running over a couple of teenagers crossing the street right as he was driving by. He honked aggressively, scared and angry, but soon realized that this was the way traffic functioned. The slow ones had the right of way.

It was a short ride. Slobodan stepped out of the taxi in front of a three-story building. Manuel parked behind a van. Slobodan walked to the nearest door. As soon as he had walked in, Manuel ran up to it, stopped the door before it closed, and slid inside. He heard Slobodan panting in the stairwell and Manuel ran up to a landing with quiet steps, stopped, listened, and continued.

Suddenly the fat man stopped. Manuel heard his heavy breaths. He peered up the stairs and saw Slobodan's hand on the railing. He was almost at the top now. Then he walked on. Manuel followed. Within himself he felt the hatred grow, how the muscles in his body tensed and how the sweat started to bead on his face. Despite his resolution not to hurt Slobodan Andersson, his bitterness rose up at the man who had devastated his family. Why should he be allowed to live when Angel had been forced to die for his greed?

Manuel knew he was the more supple and quick. He had lost the knife but could, if he wanted, kill Slobodan with his bare hands. He had the strength and the fury of the righteous. He made the sign of the cross and tiptoed on without a sound.

Slobodan came to a stop on the highest landing. Manuel counted the steps, six, plus as many again in the next section. Perhaps six, seven rapid steps in all. The whole thing could be over in a couple of seconds.

Suddenly there was the sound of a doorbell. Manuel instinctively crouched down. It was the door on the right. After ten, fifteen seconds a door opened and a man said something, then fell silent. A brief, whispered conversation in the foreign language ensued before the door closed and Slobodan and the other started to walk down the stairs. By then Manuel was already down at the front door. He continued down into the basement, where a door blocked his passage. The men came closer. Manuel pressed himself up against the door, and hoped for dear life that they did not have a reason to go to the basement. He counted the steps. Slobodan's breaths and the other man's high-pitched voice were now very close.

Manuel caught sight of them as they opened the front door and left.

He is a small man, Manuel thought and smiled to himself, short like a Mexican. They stepped into a Mercedes, with the short man behind the wheel.

The trip went beyond the city limits. Manuel had trouble orienting himself at first but recognized the roundabout at the southern edge of the city where he had come in on his way from Arlanda.

Slobodan and the "Swedish Mexican" went three-quarters of the way around the roundabout and Manuel followed the distance of a car's length.

A great calm descended over him. How simple everything was.

Then the Mercedes turned onto a gravel road, crossed some railway tracks, and continued up to a small cottage at the edge of the forest. The car pulled up to it and stopped, the men stepped out, while Manuel continued on for a while longer before he braked.

Shortly after a curve, Manuel found a small road that he turned onto, parking the car in a copse of trees and bushes. It was not ideal, but he did not want to go too far away and lose contact with the two men. It was possible they were only stopping briefly at the cottage.

The wheat growing on the other side of the clump of trees was at its peak. Manuel tore off a stalk and chewed on the kernels while he followed the edge of the field toward the forest. He was partly hidden by the bushes and boulders on his way to the cottage, but tried as best he could to keep an eye on the Mercedes. He arrived at a road that consisted of two wheel tracks with grass in the middle. To the right there was a field and to the left a row of houses. He walked to the left in order to circle past the row of houses and approach the cottage from the forest. Then, after a hundred meters or so, he left the trail and plunged into the woods.

Concealed by the vegetation, he broke into a run. After several minutes he ended up thirty or so meters behind the cottage. The car was visible between the branches. Manuel hid behind a tree and the scent of the sticky sap transported him to the path to his family's *cafetal*, their coffee plantation.

He exhaled and scouted out the road up to the cottage: a shed, a couple of big trees surrounded by a thicket of flowering bushes, and thereafter an open area of about five meters that he had to cross unseen. There was a window behind the house but he could not detect any movement inside it.

Manuel ran up to the shed, waited a couple of seconds, rushed doubled over toward the thicket, and then continued, half-crawling, half-running toward the cottage.

He pressed himself against the wall and his sweating body deposited a few drops on the sticky paneling. He listened and thought he heard the men talking.

He carefully peered in through the window. Slobodan sat with his back toward the window. The other man leaned against the opposite side of the wall and stared intently at Slobodan, who was talking and gesturing with both hands. Manuel recognized the gestures. He was in the process of convincing the man of something. The short man made an objection, his waving something away, but immediately received a rebuttal.

This went on for several minutes. Why did they come here? Manuel asked himself. If they were just going to talk surely they could have done so in town.

The answer came after a little while. The short man bent over, lifted the lid of a storage bench, and took out a sport bag that he placed on the table in front of Slobodan. The latter unzipped the bag and put his hand in. The short man looked displeased.

Manuel sensed what the bag must contain. He decided to leave his vulnerable position immediately. He looked up at the neighboring house that could be glimpsed between the trees. He could be discovered at any moment. All that had to happen was for the neighbor to step out on his terrace.

But he had uncovered another piece of the puzzle. He knew about the cottage, what the short man looked like and where he lived. Everything had gone better than planned. He retreated into the concealing curtain of the forest, sat down with his back against a tree, and waited.

Like his people, he was good at this. It felt as if they had been waiting for five hundred years. *Zapotecos, mixes, mixtes, triguis,* and all the other people in Oaxaca, Chiapas, Guerrero, yes, everywhere in the land that was called Mexico. They all waited. Standing like severed trees, captured by the storm and cracked, whittled away by the weather and wind, seasoned and hardened. Nothing to be reckoned with, without value, without an ability to reproduce itself. But in the stony barrenness of the terrain, in the green valleys and on the wind-whipped plains of the high country there were seeds, in whose center all the old ways were preserved in code.

That was his conviction. His hope.

Then he heard a car start and through the trees he saw the Mercedes with the two men bouncing along the dirt road with a cloud of dust whirling up behind them.

Once again, Manuel made his way up to the cottage. He could hear nothing from the neighbor, perhaps they were not home. He felt more secure now and sneaked over to the shed, unhooking the door that was not locked. In the dim light within he could make out a lawn mower, a few old garden chairs, and a work counter with various tools. He picked up a crowbar and a container of gasoline and left the shed with a newfound feeling of power.

He chose the window on the corner that was out of the neighbor's line of sight. After about a minute he had it open, and he crawled into the cottage.

A faint smell of sweat still lingered in the main room. A few dirty rag rugs were rolled into sausages on the floor, as if ashamed of their pale fronds. The furniture was simple and worn. A single painting hung on the wall. It depicted an alpine landscape. The exaggeratedly pointed mountaintops were dusted with a grayish cap that was supposed to represent snow, and in the valley below there was a log cabin that was supposed to function as the romantic center of the composition, but only looked like a deserted ghost house whose inhabitants had long ago abandoned the area.

The dusty isolation depressed Manuel but he also found it natural.

They were isolated men, Slobodan, Armas, and the short one. Men who came down from the mountains with a single purpose: to make money. It struck him that they were doing violence to the very idea of a human being. They lived alone, loved no one but themselves, and hardly that. No, they were unable to love, perverted by greed, surrounded only by betrayal and joyless successes.

Without women, Manuel continued his train of thought, how could a man live without a woman?

How could one live without closeness to the soil? Without a faith in God? He made the sign of the cross and sat down on a chair.

Now he, Manuel Alavez, had assumed the role of God. No, he was only a tool. These isolated men only did evil. The world would be better if they were done away with. This was not only a matter of personal revenge, about Angel and Patricio. He was staining himself with the blood of others. He was sacrificing his own soul. So it was, he would suffer all the torments of Hell, but it was for a good cause.

Calmed by his conclusions, he lifted the bag from the bench and carefully lowered it out the window, found some matches on a shelf in the kitchen, and poured gasoline over all the furnishings.

✦

Twenty-Six

The paralysis did not ease up until Eva sat down at the kitchen table. The phone rang and she was sure it was Helen, who had very likely seen her and Patrik come home. But Eva did not pick up, she didn't want to hear her friend's busybody comments or have to listen to her good advice.

Patrik immediately went to his room. She knew he wanted to be alone. The relief he had shown after speaking with Barbro Liljendahl was obvious. He had been almost exhilarated on the bus on the way home, but this state also did battle with the feeling of an unexpected and shoddy betrayal that made him fall silent and stare out the bus window with a penetrating, searching gaze, as if he was trying to look into the future.

And the future for Patrik consisted of the next day, the next week, perhaps a month, at most the end of the semester. He measured everything against the present, Zero and the others' immediate reactions, and therefore his action had been heroic. Eva imagined that he now regretted having spoken so freely with the police, and she understood intuitively that she had to give him time.

She was proud of him. This was her dominant feeling. Fear and anger had fallen away and made room for gratitude at her son's maturity, which bore traces of a child's forthrightness and a wish to be understood and forgiven. He was not yet hardened, encapsulated by his own and the gang's distorted image of the world.

Barbro Liljendahl had skillfully tread the razor-sharp edge, showing him trust and respect, but also applying pressure when he threatened to slide away. She had won his confidence, otherwise he would never have allowed Eva to leave the room.

Eva looked at the time. In an hour Hugo would be home. She was hungry, but couldn't bear to think of eating.

The phone rang again and this time Eva picked up.

"How did it go?"

Eva pulled the kitchen door shut, amazed by her own feeling of gratitude that Helen had called. She was the only one Eva could talk to, because in spite of her occasional impertinence she was the only one who cared.

"It went well," she said and summed up what Patrik had told her on the way home.

"You mean they're trying to get our kids to do drugs? Here in Sävja?"

"Are you surprised?"

"No, perhaps not exactly, but . . . I'm coming over!"

Helen hung up on Eva and several minutes later she was sitting in the kitchen.

"Ingemar is at some construction meeting," Helen said. "You know how he is and God knows when he'll be home. I wrote a note to the kids. Maybe we should have pizza together?"

Eva nodded and looked at her friend and knew what was coming. It was the garbage shed all over again.

"We have to do something," Helen fumed, and now she was hard to stop. She flooded over with indignation at the teachers, the county, the police, and any conceivable authority. Even the church and the local parish received a tongue-lashing.

But she didn't stop there, for that wouldn't be like Helen. Eva listened and nodded, inserting a comment from time to time, but basically Helen spoke without ceasing until the phone rang.

"That's probably Emil," she said.

Helen had two children. Emil, who was the same age as Hugo, and Therese, who was eighteen and in her final year at the Ekeby school. She was rarely home, preferring to spend the night with her boyfriend in Eriksberg.

It was Emil who was calling and he was hungry, just like Hugo, who came home just as Helen hung up the phone.

Patrik did not want to eat pizza, and Helen sensed why. Then someone had to go down to the pizzeria, and that would most likely be Patrik, who with his moped normally took on the task of delivering the pizza, and it was very likely that he would bump into friends in the process.

"Can't we have spagetti?" he said.

"I have ground beef," Helen said. "I'll call Emil and tell him to bring it with him."

After dinner the three boys retreated to Hugo's room.

Helen put the dishes in the dishwasher while Eva made coffee. They sat down in the living room.

"Should we have a . . . ?"

"I think we should," Helen said.

After Eva had poured out the liqueur, Helen picked up where she had left off.

"What do we know about cocaine? Nothing. Hard alcohol we know something about, don't we? But drugs, nothing. Emil said something about hashish being harmless, or perhaps it was marijuana, he had heard someone at school say that. Do you understand? I lectured him for a whole evening but in the end I didn't know what to say. If he had said that vodka is harmless then I would have had a leg to stand on, you know how Emil's grandfather is, but what did I know about marijuana?"

"Schools should teach them about it," Eva said.

Helen snorted.

"Are you kidding? They just have free periods and a lot of programs that don't amount to anything. No, I think we have to do something ourselves. I should post flyers and hold a meeting, don't you think?"

"The garbage room," Eva grinned.

"Yes. Should we really just sit on our butts and watch these drug pushers destroy our children? Heavens, we should break their necks, line them up against a wall. There isn't punishment enough for the likes of them."

It was past ten before Helen and Emil went home. She had called her husband, but he didn't answer, not at home or on his cell phone.

Eva saw how Helen tried to conceal her pain. There was no concern any longer, just a tired certainty that he was being unfaithful.

"Throw him out," Eva said, regretting the words as soon as she said them.

Helen winced. Never before had Eva expressed herself so directly. Helen said nothing, called Emil's name, and they went out into the mild late-summer evening.

Eva watched them from the kitchen window. Helen walked with long strides while Emil shuffled across the yard.

"Throw him out," Eva repeated quietly to herself.

✦

Twenty-Seven

Three days after Armas's murder, Valdemar Husman called the police information line. He had found a note on his door in Lugnet urging him to contact the police.

He was immediately connected to Lindell. There were several others to choose from, but Gunnel Brodd in the call center and Ann Lindell knew each other well. They were both from the same region, Lindell from Ödeshög and Gunnel Brodd from Linköping. Sometimes they socialized. Like Lindell, Gunnel was a single mother, so they both belonged to a sisterhood that spanned both a longing for as well as the desire to circumvent the need for men.

"It's about the murder, isn't it?"

"I see," Lindell said noncommittally, and her thoughts went to Viola in Gräsö. The man had a similar dialect.

"There was a note on the door when I got home, I imagine it has to do with the murder."

"I see, in that case I understand, you live in the area. Yes, we wanted to get in touch with everyone who may have seen or heard anything."

"Well, I don't know," the man said. "I have been away. I left the day before the murder. To my brother in Fagervik. I stay there when I service my clients."

Valdemar Husman was a blacksmith with roots in northern Uppland who had moved to Uppsala a year ago.

"For love," he said with a bittersweet chuckle.

He immersed himself in a discussion of how difficult it was to build up a new clientele. Lindell sensed he might have been more positive if his "love" had worked out better.

But he had been able to retain his clients in his former area and so three or four times a year he would "do the rounds" and spend the night at his brother's house.

"Did you notice anything unusual before you traveled to north Uppland?" Lindell said, jumping into his tirade, sensing that there was something here.

"Some devil camped out below my house, but now when I went down there and checked, he was gone."

After they finished the conversation, Lindell went to see Ola Haver, who was sitting in his office, busy consolidating all the alibis for the employees at Dakar and Alhambra.

"I'm glad you came by," he said as she sat down across from him.

"You are driving up to Lugnet," Lindell informed him.

She would have liked to do it herself but had decided to pay another visit to the hospital. She didn't really want to, but knew that if she hesitated any longer she would never get around to it. Maybe they would send Viola home first.

She told him what Valdemar Husman had seen. It could turn out to be nothing more than a harmless tourist who wanted to avoid the camping fee, some teenagers taking advantage of the last warm spell of summer, or perhaps an infatuated couple seeking privacy, but this lead had to be followed up. It was actually the only thing so far of any substance.

"Take Morgansson or one of the other technicians with you."

Haver looked up at the mention of Morgansson's name, but Lindell pretended not to notice his gaze, continuing on without an outward sign. Morgansson was a completed chapter.

"Husman is at home. Get in touch with him and pick a time," she said, completely unnecessarily in order to conceal her irritation.

This time she was not going to hesitate, she was going to march straight into Viola's room and wake her up if need be.

But Ann Lindell never got that far. When the elevator door slid open in the 70 building of the Akademiska Hospital, Barbro Liljendahl walked out.

She had been to visit Olle Sidström, the man who had been stabbed in Sävja, and conducted follow-up questioning. He was not suspected of anything, or rather, Barbro Liljendahl could easily suspect him of a million crimes, but this time he happened to be the victim.

She looked quizzically at Ann Lindell.

"Are you also going to talk to Sidström?"

She couldn't help but feel a sting of irritation.

"No," Lindell explained, equally surprised to bump into someone from work, "I'm here to see a good friend. I had a couple of minutes to spare."

Liljendahl nodded and then looked doubtfully at Lindell.

"I was thinking of something," she said. "Sidström was stabbed and you have a stabbing homicide, don't you? It was done with a knife, wasn't it?"

Lindell nodded and understood where she was going with this.

"Could there be a connection?" Liljendahl continued.

Lindell hesitated for a split second.

"Do you have time? We could have a quick cup of coffee and talk about it."

They sat down in a corner of the cafeteria on the ground level. Two tables away there was an older couple, the man wearing hospital clothing and the woman palpably concerned that he drink all his juice.

"You need liquids," she said.

The man shook his head but picked up the glass and took a sip.

Both policewomen observed the couple for a while before they quietly began to talk.

Liljendahl told her about her case, how Sidström had been assaulted, without prior provocation, according to him. He had been in Sävja to take a look around, as he put it, because he was thinking of moving there. He was currently living in Svartbäcken.

He had only a diffuse memory of the events. He could not give a description or age of the person who stabbed him, he could also not recall if it had been one or more persons involved. This was not unheard of in these circumstances, but Liljendahl did not believe him.

"I think he knows the perp and does not want to reveal his identity," she said. "He lies constantly and has done so his entire life. His list of priors is three pages long. Mostly drug-related offenses but even assault and exhortation. A little shit.

"On the other hand we have witnesses, primarily a couple who were barbecuing on their patio about fifty meters away, who saw three, perhaps four young men attack him. They appeared to have been involved in a loud discussion before the knife came out, but Sidström denies this."

"Any suspects?"

"We have a very likely suspect, a young guy who goes by the name of Zero. He's laying low but will probably turn up soon. His mother, and above all his brothers, are insanely angry. They have mobilized the entire clan in order to find him.

"They are Turkish or Kurdish," she added when she saw Lindell's expression.

"Do you have any reason to suspect that Sidström was in Sävja with criminal intent?" Lindell asked, and was struck by the officious tone of her own words.

"Drugs," Liljendahl said simply. "Most likely cocaine. I don't know if you've heard, but this town is swimming in cocaine. In the past, cocaine was a trendy drug that did not appear on the street. It gives a similar kick to an amphetamine but is more expensive. The usual drug users choose amphetamines. But now the tide appears to have turned. I think the supply has increased and driven down the price."

"How much does it cost?" Lindell asked.

"A gram goes for around eight hundred kronor. That is enough for ten doses. Amphetamines cost around two hundred."

"Isn't cocaine what they chew in South Africa?"

"Yes, the leaves, but that's mostly to be able to bear the work and the cold. Haven't you seen those pictures of Bolivian miners?"

Lindell hadn't, but she nodded anyway.

"And you believe there's a possible connection with the homicide?"

"Knife and knife," Liljendahl said.

Lindell sipped her coffee. The doughnut she had bought lay untouched. It probably wouldn't taste as good as Ottosson's. Of course, she thought, there was something to what her colleague was saying. Knives were not exactly unusual, but two incidents so close in time, perhaps . . .

"I have a list," Liljendahl said, pulling a folder out of her bag, locating a piece of paper and handing it to Lindell.

She's good, Lindell thought, and ran here eyes down the list of names of Sidström's old acquaintances. Lindell recognized many of the names, but there was one name in particular that caught her attention.

"Can you make a copy and toss it up to me later?"

"No problem," Liljendahl said, with a tweak of satisfaction around her mouth.

Ann's resolve to go see Viola had deteriorated after the discussion with Barbro Liljendahl. Again she stood at the elevator but this time she was considerably more irresolute. What will I do if Edvard is there, she thought, and the very idea made her back up a few steps and allow a group of hospital staff to pass. The elevator left without her.

She despised herself. This was about Viola and nothing else. She could ask at the desk if Viola had any visitors. She pressed the elevator call button for the third time and this time the doors opened at once.

Viola was sitting in a wheelchair by the window. Ann coughed but the old woman did not move. The silver white hair stood on end. Her right hand was tapping lightly on the armrest. This was the same old Viola, restless, eager to get away, Ann thought.

"Hi Viola," she said and the old woman turned her head and stared at Lindell without displaying in gesture or expression that she recognized her visitor. Lindell took several steps into the room.

"It's me, Ann."

"Do you think I'm blind?" Viola said. "No, you think I'm completely senile."

For a second or two Ann was incapable of replying, her hand went up to her face as if to ward off Viola's searching gaze. She masked her gesture by pulling back a few strands of hair.

"Dear me, you poor thing," Viola said softly, and they were the most tender words that Ann had ever heard her say.

"I heard that you had taken a fall," Ann said, fighting to keep the tears back. If only she were my mother, was a thought that came flying, and it made her feel guilty.

"Things are as they are," Viola said. "The damned chicken coop tripped me up."

"Are you in pain?"

Viola shook her head.

"When will you get to go home?"

"They say next week, but there's so much talk here you don't know what to make of it all."

Ann pulled out a chair and sat down beside her.

"How is everything with Victor?"

"As usual, a bit frail in the winter but he perks up when the sun comes."

Ann didn't know what else to ask about. As in the beginning of their relationship, Ann felt self-conscious and awkward.

"And you?" Viola said.

"I'm doing well, thanks. Working and busy. Right now we have an unpleasant murder case."

"You have always been involved in unpleasantries. And the boy?"

"Erik is fine. He's at day care."

Ann swallowed. Go on, she thought, looking at Viola's face, ask me.

"Edvard was up here yesterday," Viola said. "He had an errand to run."

Lindell nodded.

"He is working with Gottfrid as usual. They are working so hard, you wouldn't believe it."

The note of pride in her voice was unmistakable. She studied Ann with amusement. The old woman hasn't changed a bit, she thought. She is a miracle.

"That's wonderful," Ann said.

"Yes, but of course it's far too much," Viola said grumpily, and in this way annulled her earlier contentment.

This was typical of her. Nothing was allowed to remain really good. On the other hand things were certainly allowed to be thoroughly awful. She had no difficulties with that.

"I've never spent this long in Uppsala. I usually make do with the town," Viola said, and Ann gathered she was referring to Öregrund. "During my entire life I've been to Uppsala perhaps twenty or so times, but never for this long."

She fell silent and looked out the window.

"They are building so much," she said, and took on a look of satisfaction. Ann sensed that she was thinking of Edvard.

What joy she had received from Edvard. She must have thanked her lucky stars countless times for that evening when Edvard had come knocking and asked if he could rent a room.

"It's time for me to leave," Ann said. "Are you sleeping well?"

Viola chuckled.

"That was a question," she said. "Go on, get out here and catch some thieves."

Ann put her chair back and walked to the door, turning when she was halfway. The old woman was looking at her. Ann quickly went back, leaned down, and gave her a clumsy hug. Then she left without saying anything else and without turning back.

She felt that it was the last time she would see Viola. "Go on, get out here and catch some thieves." At the start of their friendship Viola had openly expressed her disapproval over the fact that Ann was a police officer. She said it was not a suitable occupation for a woman. Now Ann interpreted her last comment as a sign of approval. Perhaps it was her way of saying that she liked Ann despite everything, despite what she had done, in betraying and hurting Viola's adored Edvard. Ann had always had a feeling, which admittedly had grown weaker with time, of inferiority to the old woman. It was not only her awe-inspiring age, her stubborn strength, and independence that inspired this feeling, but also the fact that she had lived and continued to live a life outside society.

In some obscure way this both appealed to and frightened Ann. It was probably her guilty conscience playing tricks. She had left Ödeshög and her parents, sick of the duck pond that her home town was in her eyes, and bored by her parents, whose only goal in life appeared to be keeping the spirea hedge in top form.

She was about twenty years old when she left Östergötland for the Police Academy. Contact with her parents had been sporadic since then. At the end of June, when she had gone down there for a week, she had started to miss Uppsala after only one night.

Ann Lindell was upset but did not know how to sort out her thoughts, much less draw any conclusions and formulate goals. There was too much at stake, her own life, Erik's, work, Edvard, her parents—everything had been brought to the surface by her visit to the hospital.

She decided to push these thoughts aside. She had techniques for this. Right now the solution had the name of Berglund.

Berglund had gone home! Lindell listened astonished to Ottosson's account of Berglund coming down with a migraine.

"That's never happened before, has it?"

"No," Ottosson replied. "I can't remember the last time Berglund was sick. Some time in the eighties, I think."

"What did he say?"

"Nothing. I was the one who sent him home and he didn't protest. He was as pale as a corpse. Allan gave him a ride."

"Oh," Lindell said, in a defeated voice.

"Was there anything in particular?"

"I was going to check on something, a name that turned up."

Lindell told him how Berglund had mentioned in passing a crook who had recently come into money and how the same name had now turned up in connection with the case in Sävja.

"Rosenberg," Ottosson said. "Yes, he's a jewel of a guy. I knew his father. He was part of the gang at the Weather Vane, an old beer hall on Salagatan. They tore it down about six months after I started patrolling. There was another joint on Salagatan, Cafe 31, there was an old lady by the name of Anna who . . . she lived, if I remember correctly, almost at the top of Ymergatan, you know, on the same street as Little John, you know, grew up. There was a Konsum grocery store there that had damned good fresh buns, fifteen öre a piece or if— It's almost a pity that places like the Weather Vane fold, because— The stores were packed so tightly back then. There was a Konsum store on Väderkvarnsgatan as well, and then a Haages Livs grocery on Torkelsgatan, up by Törnlundsplan there was also something, what was their name? . . . Brodd or something like that, and then Ekdahls at the corner of Ymergatan and St. Göransgatan, and then the milk-and-bread store in Tripolis. You see! All within five minutes' walk from one another."

Ottosson lost himself in revery. Lindell had to laugh.

"I should have known," she said.

"But I don't associate Rosenberg with violence and definitely not with big business," Ottosson resumed.

"Maybe it's worth checking into anyway," Lindell said and told him about Liljendahl's observation that a knife was involved in both cases.

"Well," Ottosson said, "I think that's pushing it. We have a lot of conflicts where knives are involved."

"I'm still going to have someone check up on Rosenberg. In any case, it would be amusing to find out what has made him so conspicuously rich. Have you heard anything about Haver's excursion to the camping spot by the river?"

"He called and wanted you to call him back."

"I had my phone turned off at the hospital. What did he say?"

"That the camper may have been our man."

Lindell hurried to her office and dialed Haver's number.

He sounded pleased, almost excited, and he had good reason to be. They had most likely located the scene of the crime, a small clearing perhaps some twenty square meters concealed behind a thicket and a large mound of rubble, not visible from the road, perhaps four hundred meters north of the place the body was found, and some one hundred meters from the river.

The technicians had almost immediately isolated samples from the ground of what they believed to be blood, and also traces of what most likely was urine.

Apparently one or more persons had occupied the site for several days. A rectangle of flattened grass suggested the presence of a tent. The surrounding area was trampled, there were broken twigs and the remains of a fire. A veritable feast for the forensic team.

Valdemar Husman, who had alerted the police, had nothing to say about the person or persons who might have been camping. He had only noticed something peeking out of the vegetation, and had assumed it was a tent. He explained that he had not approached it further so as not to appear curious, and not to get "dragged into anything."

"What did he mean by that?" Lindell asked.

"I don't know," Haver answered. "He didn't say."

"I mean, did he have a suspicion that something illegal was going on? Did he hear or see anything that appeared suspicious?"

"Neither. He simply didn't want to get involved."

"A little more curiosity wouldn't hurt," Lindell said. "Will you be there for a while?"

"I don't know, I don't have much to do here. Morgansson and the rest are the ones who are busy. They're thinking of erecting a tarp over the site in case it rains."

"Okay, but can we hope for a little DNA?"

"Looks like it."

"Then the question is, what was Armas doing there? Did he go willingly or was he forced?"

"I'll let you figure that one out," Haver said.

After she hung up, Ann Lindell sat absolutely still and stared into space.

"Who camps out?" she muttered.

Tourists or young people seemed most likely.

The site was private and probably chosen with care.

"Okay, you come to this city for murky business," she said out loud. "You are careful not to be seen in a hotel or even at a public campsite. Instead, you camp in the forest, but you are so clumsy you leave a corpse and numerous traces behind."

She shook her head. Something didn't make sense.

She went over to Ottosson and recounted what Haver had told her, and added her own thoughts.

"Maybe the perp couldn't afford to stay in a hotel," Ottosson said.

"What kind of murderer is that?" Lindell exclaimed.

"Most people don't stay in hotels," Ottosson said with a grin.

The rest of the day was spent reviewing the material that had been collected. This had to be done, but above all Lindell felt a need to be alone. More and more she suffered an almost claustrophobic feeling in her dealings with people, whether at work, in meetings at Erik's day care, or in situations where the room was small and the number of people large.

There were reports from questionings, an initial overview of Slobodan Andersson's business dealings, and the autopsy report.

Armas's personal history was still missing. Slobodan Andersson had contributed a part, but much of his early life was still unknown.

Lindell heard Ola Haver return, and could hear him and Fredriksson chatting in the corridor. Her thoughts went to Berglund. She decided to wait until the following day. If he didn't come in to work she would call him at home.

✦

Twenty-Eight

The call was received at two twenty-two in the afternoon. The firefighting unit at the Viktoria fire station, just east of the city, arrived on the scene seven minutes later, but at that point there was not much more to do other than keeping the fire from spreading into the adjacent areas.

The closest neighbor, who had discovered the fire when he returned from a mushroom-picking trip in the forest, had hauled his garden hose over, which did not reach more than halfway. If he pinched the nozzle, however, he was able to drizzle water onto the shed.

The firefighters thanked him for his efforts but then asked him to move out of the way.

"Do you know if there are people inside?" the fire chief asked him.

"I don't think so," the neighbor said.

The cottage, which had been constructed with sugar crates, burned down in about twenty minutes. The shed was saved but a shower of sparks lit a few fires at the edge of the woods. These were quickly extinguished.

"Just as well that piece of shit burns down," the neighbor said and gathered up his hose, "but it's lucky it didn't explode. I think they have kerosene in there."

The fire chief reacted immediately by ordering all onlookers to stand at least one hundred meters back. He physically shoved the neighbor away and did not let him collect his hose.

"How fucking stupid can you be?" he said to his coworker.

The patrol unit, which had arrived ten minutes after the firefighters, went around methodically questioning the onlookers who were gathered in a group on the road. No one turned out to have any useful information to contribute that could explain how the fire had started. No one had seen or heard anything. People rarely came out to the cottage. No one was sure who owned it.

"It must be one of the dynamiter's sons," an older man said. "The Rosenbergs, there are quite a number of them. Try Åke, I think he's the oldest."

"Have you seen him here lately?" the police officer asked.

"He came out when the chimney sweep was here, but that was at least a year ago. We exchanged a few words. He's in the explosives business, just like his father."

The fire chief walked up and took the police officer aside.

"It's arson," he said.

"Are you sure?"

"Fairly. The house isn't wired so it can't be electric. And we saw a ten-liter container in there. We haven't checked it carefully yet because it has to cool down first. Apparently there's a kerosene tank in there. That's what the neighbor thought. But the container was the first thing we saw. It was located in full view on the metal plate in front of the woodstove.

"Could it be someone who simply wanted to start a fire in a hurry?"

"That wouldn't surprise me," the chief said, "but why start a fire in this weather?"

"To put on a pot of coffee?"

"According to the neighbor they cooked on a kerosene stove."

The officer nodded.

"I'll call forensics," he said. "Are you sure no one was left in there?"

"I can't say for sure, but I don't think so."

Åke Rosenberg was contacted. He was in the middle of a blasting job in Mehedeby in north Uppland. He confirmed that he was the one who owned the cottage but said he had not been there since the spring.

"I come out twice a year to rake leaves and do basic maintenance."

"Does anyone else have access to the cottage?"

"No," Åke Rosenberg lied. "It must be some young devil who did it. I'll come by tomorrow when I get back to town."

As soon as they finished, he called his brother Konrad. Åke was angry, but also pleased. The cottage was insured and now he was spared the task of pulling it down—something he had been planning to do for years. He had toyed with the idea of building a house and moving out there.

"When were you there last?" he asked Konrad.

"Where?"

Konrad sensed that something was up and had a deep fear of his brother.

"Answer the question!"

"It must have been awhile," Konrad said.

"It's burned down. According to the cops only soot is left. I thought you might have set it on fire. It wouldn't have surprised me in any case."

Konrad Rosenberg sank down on the hall floor. A fortune up in smoke.

"I said nothing to the cops about you spending time there. I thought that was best. One never knows what you get up to with your drinking buddies. So keep your mouth shut, otherwise there can be problems with the insurance company."

"Sure," Konrad said faintly and hung up.

It took him an hour to work up enough courage to call Slobodan Andersson.

✦

Twenty-Nine

What is happening? Slobodan Andersson wondered. First Armas and now this.

Never before had anyone treated Slobodan Andersson in this way, but now he was too alarmed to be really angry. This development put Armas's death in a new light. It had not been a robbery-related killing, an accident that he died. And how could anyone know about the cottage?

Konrad Rosenberg assured him he had said nothing and Slobodan was inclined to believe him. Even if Rosenberg was a zero he was smart enough not to reveal the source of his wealth.

Could it have been a coincidence that the house burned down only an hour or so after he and Rosenberg had been there? And now the cop was coming to see him. Did they suspect anything. Did they see a connection between the murder and the fire?

Slobodan walked to his window and looked out. On the other side of the railway there was group of schoolchildren on bikes with a teacher in the lead. An older man was walking his dog and a couple of women turned the corner toward the center of town. Long rows of cars were parked in the parking lot below his window. Everything appeared normal and yet it wasn't. Someone, or more than one, was out to get him.

Suddenly it struck him that there were only three people who had known about the cottage: Rosenberg, Armas, and himself. Had Armas revealed the hiding place to anyone?

The thought was so inconceivable that he immediately dismissed it, but the very fact that it had appeared depressed him even further. After pouring himself a large cognac, he found himself back at the window, staring at the cars and the passersby.

Had someone followed him and Rosenberg to the cottage? He took a swallow of cognac. There were too many questions. Take it easy, he told himself, take the questions one by one, that's what Armas would have done. Grief for his friend burned in his chest like acid. The taste of cognac in his mouth made him nauseated, but even so he returned to the wet bar and refilled his glass. The doorbell rang at the same moment that he raised the snifter to his lips, making him jump, spilling some cognac on his shirt. Then he remembered about the female officer.

"I'm coming!" he yelled automatically, as if he had been caught red-handed. He looked out the window to the parking lot. It would not have surprised him if it had been full of blue-and-white patrol cars.

Ann Lindell was alone. That soothed his nerves somewhat. At the last visit he had been irritated by the other officer's presence, how he sneakily moved around beyond Slobodan's field of vision.

Now he had control. He placed her in the white sofa that was expensive and contemporary but in which it was completely impossible to sit comfortably and at ease.

She smiled, but not particularly warmly, and, without any small talk, started to ask him if he had thought of anything new on top of what he had already told them.

He shook his head. "Say as little as possible" went through his head, and the idea reassured him. They know nothing, they are fumbling in the dark and trying to get more information from me.

"We think we know where Armas died," Lindell said. "Was murdered," she added.

He waited for more, but it didn't come. Instead she posed a new question.

"Could Armas have been involved in things that were unknown to you?"

"Excuse me, but I don't remember your first name," Slobodan said.

"Ann, Ann Lindell."

He nodded.

"Could this have been the case?"

"Excuse me?"

Lindell repeated the question and Slobodan read from her expression that he could not drive her too far.

"No," he said firmly. "I knew Armas as well as myself. He was a friend, like a brother to me."

Lindell sat quietly for a moment. Slobodan glanced down at his chest. The cognac stain bothered him.

"Even brothers can let you down," she said, but did not proceed to develop this thought, simply continuing with her somewhat haphazard line of questioning. "I was thinking of the tattoo. Isn't it strange that you, if you were as close as you say, did not know what it represented? You must have seen it on numerous occasions. Weren't you curious?"

"Armas was my friend, not my partner or someone I snuggled with. He was reserved but unquestionably loyal."

"So you didn't snuggle?"

"What do you mean?"

"Did Armas meet women?"

Slobodan stared at her for a few seconds before answering.

"It happened, but seldom."

"You mentioned last time that there was a woman in his life."

"That was more than ten years ago. She disappeared."

"Could Armas have been interested in men?"

Slobodan burst into laughter. "My apologies, but this is too funny. You can count yourself lucky that Armas is not here to hear you."

"We found some pornographic materials in his apartment that leads us to believe this," Lindell said and met his gaze.

"Armas was not gay, whatever you have cooked up," Slobodan asserted with a steadiness in his voice that surprised him. "I don't want you to sully his memory, suggest a lot of nonsense that hasn't got the least to do with his death."

"Would it bother you if this were the case, if Armas was attracted to other men?"

"What do you mean, 'other men'?"

"Would it?"

"That is the lowest! That is a pure insult. Should—"

"I have no homophobia," Lindell interrupted calmly.

The exchange went on for several minutes. Slobodan thought longingly of another cognac. This ape, who insolently enough had kicked off her shoes and pulled her legs up under her, was egging him on like no one had done in decades. But he knew he couldn't strike back.

"In reality, you have nothing," he said abruptly, with a fitting blend of contempt and exasperation.

"On the contrary, we have a great deal," Lindell said. "We know that Armas amassed a, perhaps not a fortune exactly, but at least a significant amount of money."

"How much?" Slobodan let out.

Lindell smiled.

"Perhaps the two of you were not close enough that he cared to discuss it," she said.

Slobodan did not answer. Instead he stood up, walked over to the wet bar, and poured out the cognac.

"We also know that Armas most likely knew his killer."

"I see," Slobodan said, relieved that he had his back to the detective. He wanted to know how they had arrived at this but hesitated to ask. Or should I display more curiosity?

"Or at the very least did not feel threatened by the killer."

"How do you know this?"

Slobodan turned around and at the same time drank some of the cognac so he would not betray his agitation.

"I can't tell you that," Lindell said. "Another thing, you gave me a list of people that Armas knew. It was strikingly short. Have you thought of any other names?"

"No, his circle of acquaintances was small."

"But large enough to include a killer."

Whore, he thought, I should throw her out. He started to ponder how best he could punish her, convinced as he was that every person had a weak point.

"Perhaps you have this in common—an acquaintance or someone you at least know, who is prepared to hurt you or those close to you."

Lindell did not reply. Serves you right, you damn bitch, he thought and downed the last of his cognac.

"One must feel somewhat vulnerable in your profession," he added and set the glass down sharply, pleased with the turn their conversation had taken.

"It is your business to satisfy peoples' appetites in pleasant surroundings," Lindell said and let her gaze wander to his belly, "and that is an honorable occupation." Now she stared him straight in the eye, "It is my business, however, to put them on a rather restricted diet in a more spartan environment."

"From what I understand, the food served in our prisons is excellent."

"The menu is limited," Lindell said, "and most likely tiresome in the long run."

Slobodan smiled tauntingly.

"And no cognac is served there," she added.

He watched her march off across the parking lot. Their conversation had been brought to an end by her cell phone, and she quickly left, thanking him for their chat.

He hated her. No one could treat Slobodan Andersson in that way.

✦

Thirty

Lindell was worried. She had allowed herself to engage in a ridiculous war of words with Slobodan Andersson. It was amateurish and stupid. It worried her because it revealed the extent of her desperation. Armas did not want to take shape. He slid behind a curtain that consisted of an unknown background and such a strict and unimaginative life as to appear almost indecipherable.

To understand the victim was many times the prerequisite for understanding the perpetrator. No one had known Armas fully, she was convinced of this, not even Slobodan.

Who knows me? she thought as she took the walking path along the railway. The intense heat of the past few days had been replaced with large clouds that threatened from all sides. Will there be thunder? No one knows my fear of lightning, she thought, no one except Edvard.

The telephone call from Haver that had prompted her to leave Slobodan Andersson was about the forensic investigation. Some fifty meters from the clearing that they believed to be the scene of the crime, the technicians had found tire marks from a car. The ground was dry and therefore the tracks were unclear, but it was apparent that someone had opened the barbed-wire gate, after following a old path down to the river, and had subsequently parked. The car had been hidden behind a thicket of alders and underbrush.

Lindell went straight to Ola Haver's office. He had barricaded himself behind piles of papers, his hair on end as it always was when Haver sat lost in deep thought.

"The hardworking Constable Ola Haver," Lindell said lightly, relieved to escape her own thoughts after the meeting with the restaurant owner.

Haver grinned. Their relationship had only continued to improve after a romantic snag a few years ago. Nothing remained of their earlier attraction. Both of them realized now that it had never been a real infatuation, that what they had felt was simply a result of Lindell's disappointment over her and Edvard's relationship and Haver's frustration with a marriage that appeared to be idling.

"That Morgansson is a sharp bastard," Haver said, "but you must already know that. I missed the marks but he's a real pathfinder, quiet as the devil but tracks like an Indian."

"What do they look like?"

Haver took out several photographs, but they did not say much to Lindell: the faint impression of what could possibly be traces of a car tire.

"That isn't much," she said, disappointed.

"Don't say that," Haver replied. "We'll be able to match it to a tire brand, determine how wide the vehicle is, and from there perhaps even identify a specific make and model. It's already clear that this is a small, narrow car."

"Why does someone camp?" she started, unsure of where the discussion would lead. "Well, if one is a guest in town and doesn't want to be visible at a hotel. How do you get to Uppsala? In your own car?"

"Doubtful," Haver inserted, aware of where she wanted to go. "Why risk being seen in your own car?"

"A rental," Lindell said.

"A person who camps is probably no Richie Rich," Haver said. "I mean—"

"If this was an isolated task, to kill Armas, then why the need to camp? He could have gone into town, done the deed, and disappeared."

"Maybe he had to spy him out first," Haver said, "and needed a few days. Or the mission is more complicated than that."

The back-and-forth between Haver and Lindell led to the topic of motive and there they had nothing, even if they could speculate.

"Slobodan became noticeably upset when I brought up the homosexual angle," Lindell said after a while. "Maybe we should pursue that."

"A triangle drama, you mean?"

"I don't know," Lindell said and shrugged.

They stopped talking, well aware of the fact that it was rarely useful to spin on for too long. Over the years they had developed this style of conducting brief discussions that could later be revisited in more detail.

"Let's see what the technicians uncover," Lindell concluded. "Have you heard anything from Berglund?"

"Not a word. Are you worried?"

"Not really," Lindell said. "But we need him."

Haver moved the computer mouse and the computer switched to another humming sound before it turned off.

"There was one more thing," Haver said as Lindell was getting ready to leave.

"Oh?" Lindell said, pausing at the door.

"It was Fälth, the technician, who discovered it."

"What?" Lindell said, tired of his evasiveness but also irritated at herself for her impatience.

"He noticed part of a branch on the ground, it was close to the tent, and he thought it looked a bit strange. It had been torn off a larger branch at a height of three meters above the ground."

"How do you tear down a branch that high?" Lindell asked, and watched Haver revel in smugness.

"A bullet," he said. "And we were damned lucky to find it in a tree trunk."

"You mean a bullet was fired at the campground?"

Haver nodded.

"Nine millimeters. Fälth dug it out."

Lindell stared at her colleague.

"I think Armas was armed, fired a shot, missed, and got his throat cut as punishment," Haver said.

"Only now? Shouldn't they have spotted this branch before?"

"One might have thought so," Haver said laconically.

"That makes this a completely different investigation," Lindell said. "But it could equally well have been the perp who fired the shot?"

"Morgansson doesn't think so. Look at this and you'll see," Haver said and reached for a notepad.

Lindell took a couple of steps closer, increasingly agitated by her colleague's attitude.

"This is what we think happened. Armas was standing here, facing the tree where they found the bullet, he fired, had his throat slashed, and fell backward. The bloodstains corroborate this."

"There was no trace of gunpowder on his hands," Lindell said.

"He was found in the water," Haver replied.

His smug expression had waned and he looked at Lindell with his former look of mutual understanding.

"Armas had no gun license," Lindell said.

"How many gangsters do?"

"We have nothing on him."

"He was a shady character, I am certain of it. This was an armed conflict with the owner of the tent."

"Slobodan Andersson," Lindell said thoughtfully, registering the fact that Haver was smiling almost imperceptibly.

"Should we put him under surveillance?"

"No sense," Lindell said. "If he is involved in any funny business, he'll be lying low right now. Armas was going to Spain, packed, exchanged money, was ready to leave, and the question is, was the meeting down by the river planned all along, or was it something that just happened?"

"Do we believe it really was a vacation trip, with a few Spanish restaurants planned in on the side, as Slobodan claimed?"

"That's impossible to verify," Lindell said.

She walked toward the door, but then turned again.

"Have you ever worked with Barbro Liljendahl?"

"Not really, we worked together a little before I started at violent crimes," Haver said. "At the time she was a bit, what should I say, fussy. Why do you ask?"

"She's in charge of a case of a stabbing in Sävja and had some idea that there was a connection to Armas since both crimes were knife-related. Do you happen to know anything about Konrad Rosenberg?"

Haver shook his head, closed a folder, and pushed the papers on his desk together.

"I don't either. We need a Berglund for that," Lindell said and went to her office, logged onto her computer, and looked up Konrad Rosenberg.

It was as if she and Haver were involved in two different investigations. Maybe his surprise song-and-dance number was a kind of protest at her way of leading the investigation?

She smiled to herself as Rosenberg's history slowly printed out. A bullet in a tree was indisputably progress. Before she turned to Rosenberg, she dialed Fälth's number and felt incredibly generous as she praised the technician for his fine work.

"One needs a Smålander for detail work," she said. Smålanders were known for their attention to detail, and Lindell wondered if he picked up the compliment.

✦

Thirty-One

A well-functioning restaurant kitchen is a strange creature, as sensitive as a mollusk, it reacts in self-defense with lightning rapidity at the smallest external interruption. Anyone who disturbs this vulnerable and sophisticated organism experiences this.

"We don't have time for this shit," Donald snarled.

Gunnar Björk pulled back quickly in order not to be in the way.

"This is a workplace, not a social club," the chef continued.

Feo smiled, blinked at the union representative, and sat down on a stool with deliberation.

"And on top of everything this is the worst possible time," Donald went on, unusually expressive, though without explaining why.

"What do you say, Eva?" Feo asked.

"I belong to a different union," she said tentatively, uncertain of the atmosphere in the kitchen.

Gunnar Björk summoned up his nerve, encouraged by her words.

"Then we'll arrange a transfer for you to Hotel and Restaurant," he said and immediately started to dig in his briefcase.

"I will never join," Donald said.

"Why not?"

Donald stopped short, turned to Feo, and bored his eyes into him.

"I hate all organizations, all collective pressure where everyone has to sing the same damn song in the same damn choir."

"You can sing whatever you like," the union rep said.

"You know what, if you want to agitate, then go do it in your spare time and not here!"

"But you agitate on the job," Feo objected, and tried to catch Johnny's gaze. He was standing right in the line of fire with a bunch of leeks in his hand.

Donald twirled around and gave Feo a hard look.

"Stop it! Get back to work."

Johnny started to cut the leeks. The sound of the knife against the cutting board softened the effect of Donald's wrath somewhat.

"I'll come back at a different time," Gunnar Björk said in a conciliatory tone.

Donald returned to preparing the meat.

"This land is free, isn't it?" Feo said.

Donald shook his head and sighed heavily.

Johnny put the cut leeks into a bowl. Eva was standing in the doorway to the dining room.

"I'll go help Tessie," she said.

Feo stared at Donald for a minute before he also left.

Johnny took out more leeks. He loved leek rings and could go on chopping them forever.

"Lovely," he muttered to himself. For the first time since coming to Dakar he experienced something of what he had been looking for: the joy of working a sharp knife on a chopping block. He was rested and sober. Two meters away, Donald started to whistle, as if his earlier irritation was already forgotten. The aroma of raw beef mingled with the pungent smell of onion. The fish broth was already starting to bubble and hiss and Donald reached out to turn down the gas flame.

"Ten leeks are enough, don't you think?"

"That's fine for now," Donald said.

Johnny felt his coworker's gaze like a radiator in his back.

"Do you know a chef called Per-Olof, nicknamed 'Perro'?"

"The one who left for the States?" Donald asked.

Johnny nodded.

"Sure, we worked together at Gondolen for a year."

"He's good," Johnny said. "He trained me at Muskot in Helsingborg."

"Then you know Sigge Lång?"

"That was before my time," Johnny said, "but I know who he is. He went to Copenhagen."

"Didn't he become head chef at some fish restaurant?"

The conversation went back and forth, about restaurants and cooks, owners and head chefs, while Donald prepared duck breast, veal, and lamb and Johnny laid out ingredients for the garnish, took out the butter, kept an eye on bread in the oven, and tidied up.

Dakar's kitchen had been hit hard by Armas's murder, and both of the cooks felt the need for casual chatter. Not because Armas had been particularly well-liked but because of the turbulence his death had caused. The police had questioned everyone, asked Donald to check the kitchen knives and make sure that none were missing. Donald tried to explain that every chef owned their own knives, and that it would never occur to them to contaminate them with human blood.

"And the rest are so worthless that we basically never touch them," he explained further and refused to entertain the idea that anyone at Dakar was a murderer.

Feo returned to the kitchen.

"The cops are coming here again," he said. "They are going to talk to Tessie and Eva."

"Damn it, we have a job to do!" Donald exclaimed.

"As do they," Johnny said calmly.

The police had searched every corner and taken a bag of papers from the small desk squeezed in behind the counter. The desk was Donald's territory and it had upset him, though he had not said anything. He knew they would pay no attention to his objections anyway. Instead, the chef's wrath had gone out over the rest of them and above all Johnny. It was as if Donald connected the murder with the arrival of the new cook.

Donald hated change and irritating elements that disturbed the balance of the kitchen. He did not grieve for Armas as such but for the work peace that had been lost.

Naturally there had been wild speculation about the motive of the murder. Feo had launched a theory that it was Slobodan who had taken out his companion. His coworkers listened in fascination as he embroidered a story that contained almost everything: black money, trade in prostitutes from the Baltic states, and Armas's and Slobodan's murky past.

"The past caught up with Armas," he said and waved the fillet knife in illustration.

The one to whom the police had shown the most attention was Gonzo, but nothing spoke for the fact that he had been involved, even if the alibi that he presented for the day of the murder was flimsy. It was his day off, he had slept until eleven and gone into town at around two o'clock. He could prove that he had been to the Saluhallen markets by way of a receipt from the cheese vendor that had 14:33 printed on it. In addition, the sales clerk could remember Gonzo's purchase. He had bought some Stilton.

It was after this that his account became less substantial. He had wandered around downtown, ducking briefly into Bergström's clock store in order to look at a watch, but no one there could recall seeing him. Then he had gone to Alhambra and talked to Slobodan, returned home at around four o'clock, and then stayed in until shortly before nine when he had a beer at Svensson's.

He stubbornly claimed that he had resigned, even though everyone knew that he had been fired by Armas. But Gonzo's version of the events could of course be worth as much as Armas's .

Eva returned to the kitchen after the police had left. She had been off for two days and wanted to know what had happened. Tessie was not particularly communicative and only gave monosyllabic answers to Eva's questions.

"Tessie is still in shock," Feo said. "I think she was the only one who liked Armas. In a way they were similar to each other, though Armas was more ruthless. Tessie has a heart."

"What do the police say?"

"To us? Nothing. And Slobban has hardly shown his face. He came down once and then he went on about how everything would go on as normal. He is holed up at Alhambra."

"He's scared," Donald said, unexpectedly.

"How do you know that? Has he said anything?"

"No, but you can tell. Armas meant more to him than you realize."

Donald expressed himself as if he knew more than the others but did not find it worth his while to try to explain it.

When it came to the kitchen and the food he was number one and no one questioned it, but Donald often adopted his superior attitude in other areas. When they discussed politics he mostly gave jabs at Feo.

Feo was eager to re-create a good feeling in the kitchen and therefore he overlooked the arrogant tone.

"It must have been a quick one to slit the throat of someone like Armas," he said. "Armas was no one you toyed with."

"Maybe it happened in bed," Donald said.

"What?"

"You didn't know, did you? Armas was a fag."

"I don't believe it," Feo said.

"Talk with Nicko at the local video store," Donald said nonchalantly. "Once Armas came in and checked out twenty homo-films at one time. That's serious business."

"No, I don't believe it," Pirjo exclaimed.

Everyone looked at the kitchen assistant, who immediately became beet red.

"I see," Feo said, grinning, "you don't believe it. Maybe he came on to you?"

Pirjo turned away.

"Don't pay any attention to us," Donald said.

It was not the first time he defended the shy Pirjo, who found it so difficult to express what she wanted or thought. But now she turned back again.

"You're speaking ill of the dead," she said vehemently. "When Armas was still alive you said nothing, least of all to his face. Am I right?"

Feo nodded. Donald looked at her with curiosity.

"You are right," he said, "we are cowards. Everyone who works in a kitchen is a coward, you should learn that. If someone has balls, he'll take his knives and leave, that's how it is. Such a chef is unhappy."

"More unhappy than the coward?" Feo asked.

"Yes," Donald said.

"Is that why you don't want to join the union?" Johnny hazarded, though he regretted it as soon as he said it.

"As if that is any of your business. No, that isn't why, and you should have been able to figure it out."

Johnny got it. With Donald's work ethic and with the quality of the dishes he presented, there was a negligible chance that he would be badly treated by his employer. Not even if he joined the union. He was too valuable.

Their hands did not rest while they gabbed. They prepared sauce bases, sliced meat, took some things out, wrapped others in plastic, and continued their preparations. Only Eva stood passively. She lingered in the kitchen. There was still a quarter of an hour to go before her shift officially began. She wanted to absorb as much as possible of the new world that was opening to her.

The atmosphere here was completely different from the post office. Perhaps it was the stress that created the raw tone that dominated. There was an urgency to her former job as well, but it was as if the warmth of the stoves, the clatter of china and silverware, the steam from pots and pans, the sudden sizzle of meat, and the waitstaff's shouted orders . . . everything created a never-ending restlessness.

"Can you help me, Eva?"

Johnny was busy stocking the refrigerator.

"How are the boys?" he asked softly.

"They're fine," Eva said and looked up.

He held her gaze.

"Patrik has started to talk," she went on, "but he is still grounded."

She looked at her reflection in the mirror that the roll of aluminum foil attached to the wall provided and where her face appeared cracked in a thousand wrinkles, before she tore off a sheet and handed it to Johnny.

"What do the cops say?"

"Let's talk later, okay?"

Johnny nodded.

"Thanks for the help," he said and Eva sensed that the thirty seconds she had helped him were as important for Johnny as for herself.

"Let's get a cup of coffee," she said. "I mean some day before we start work."

He nodded and glanced at the others.

"Then you can start your own chapter of the union," said Donald, who had his back to them. He then turned his head and gave them a look of amusement.

"Only if you join us," Eva said, and swept out of the kitchen.

It was ten o'clock when Eva got home. Her legs were tired and her headache did not want to go away, but she felt satisfied and sent Tessie a mental note of gratitude. She had let Eva go home early. It was as if no one was being so precise anymore, and she had also been understanding when Eva withdrew to call home.

Patrik had answered every time, irritation in his voice, but he turned out to be sitting up waiting for her in the kitchen when she got home.

Hugo was in his room. She heard the sound effects from his computer game. She opened the door a little wider and said hello. His tense back and the concentration in his face testified to a crucial moment in one of these games he spent most of his time on.

She went to the bathroom and got herself some pain relievers.

"Hi, have you had anything to eat?"

Patrik nodded and Eva followed his gaze to the kitchen counter. They had even loaded their dishes in the dishwasher and wiped the counters.

She laughed and put her hand through his hair.

"Was it fun?"

"There were a lot of people," Eva said. "But they let me go early. When the dinner guests start to get finished it's mostly drinks and such, and I'm not so good at that yet. The bartender has promised to show me some things. I can't even tell all the different kinds of beer apart yet."

"What did they say about that guy who was murdered?"

"No one knows anything, there's just a lot of talk."

"Was he a good guy?"

Eva shrugged.

"I met him twice and he said all of five words. What about you, what have you been up to?"

"Nothing," Patrik said.

"Do you want some tea?"

She started to get things out, while Patrik put water on to boil.

"I don't think Hugo will want any," he said.

When they sat down at the table, Patrik started to talk. Eva realized that he must have spent the evening thinking about it and even how to formulate his beginning.

"Zero is actually not stupid, you know? He is easy to deceive, that's his biggest problem. He wants to be king but doesn't know what to do."

Eva figured out that by "king" Patrik meant "liked."

"Has he been in touch with you?"

Patrik nodded and took a sip of his tea. Eva waited.

"What are you doing?" Hugo called out suddenly.

"None of your business," Patrik yelled.

"Patrik!"

"He's so annoying."

"What did Zero say?"

"He's hiding."

Eva wondered where a fifteen-year-old boy could hide.

"He doesn't dare go home. His brothers will beat him up."

"Has he been in touch with his mother?"

"He called but she cried the whole time."

"What did he say to you?"

Patrik looked up. After a couple of seconds' hesitation he told her that Zero had been selling drugs in Sävja for the past couple of months. There was a man who had turned up and given him the drugs to sell to his friends.

"You wouldn't believe what he makes. It can be a couple thousand. He's planning to go to Turkey and rescue his father," Patrik said.

"What really happened that evening?"

"That man came by with more drugs but Zero didn't want to keep going. He was scared, but he didn't say that. He started to pull some racist crap instead. The man made trouble and Zero punched him."

"What about you? What did you do?"

Eva forced herself to remain calm. The least slip of the tongue or sign of being upset could result in Patrik clamming up.

"Helped Zero out," he mumbled. "Then we took off."

"That was when you came home bleeding?"

Patrik nodded. Eva could see that he was close to tears and felt an enormous gratitude in the fact that he was sitting there across from her, that he was talking, and that he could cry.

"And later, the next evening?"

"Another man came. We were up at the school, just hanging and talking. Then the other man came and started to talk. At first I thought it was a cop."

"He was the one who was stabbed?"

"He started it!"

Eva nodded.

"Whose knife was it?"

"Zero's."

"Do you have a knife?" she asked, wishing she hadn't the moment she saw Patrik's expression.

The sound from the computer had stopped and Eva was convinced Hugo was listening.

"Forget it," she said. "Go on."

"He started in on Zero, said something about how he owed him money and stuff about, you know, what happens to people who don't pay their debts. He was pretty scary."

"What did Zero do?"

"Nothing! He was scared shitless, I could tell. Then the man wanted Zero to go with him to his car but he didn't want to, he started to run. The guy caught up with him and pulled him down on the ground. The whole thing went so fast. Zero shook him off and then took out the knife. And then he was just lying there, the guy."

"And this is what you told the police?"

Patrik nodded.

“Why didn’t you tell them this from the beginning?”

“I wanted to talk to Zero first,” Patrik said, and now his eyes were shiny with tears.

Eva stretched out her hand and put it on his arm.

“I’m glad you told me. I’m proud of you, you know that?”

After a couple of minutes of silence, Patrik stood up, took his teacup and put it on the counter.

“Helen called,” he said. “She wanted you to get back to her.”

Eva glanced at the wall clock.

“I’ll do it tomorrow,” she said.

“She said you could call late. She sounded really worked up. She has some stuff she’s doing, I didn’t get what it was.”

Eva took the handheld phone with her into the bedroom and dialed Helen’s number.

✦

Thirty-Two

It is like California, but much smaller, Manuel thought. Even so he was pleased with his new location. The landscape constantly awakened memories of his brothers and their time in Anaheim, but he liked this place better than the last one and not only because of the connection with Armas.

Here his gaze did not get snared in brambles and stones. When he climbed up the steep ravine he could look out over wide swathes of good earth, and that had a calming effect.

He recognized the strawberry plants and they were still bearing fruit. The first morning he had been awakened by a tractor and the sound of voices. The evening before, he had wandered down the rows of plants and concluded that there were not many berries left and he was surprised that they still took the trouble to harvest them.

He had picked a few strawberries and put them in his mouth, but this reminded him too much of Angel and Patricio for him to really be able to enjoy the sweetness. How he longed for his brothers! This feeling tore at his heart like a furious animal. It had only gotten worse since he arrived in Sweden.

Slashing that gringo's throat had not helped, if he had even imagined it would. The first night after he killed Armas and dragged him down to the river, in the hope that he would sink or float away, he had suffered hellish nightmares and woken innumerable times, alternatingly in a cold sweat and feverishly hot. He fell to his knees outside the tent and prayed to San Isidro for forgiveness, *ben ládxido zhhn,* to make his little heart bigger.

In the darkness of the night he thought he could see a beautiful woman with waist-length hair and copper-colored skin. She disappeared in the direction of the river with a taunting laugh. It was *matelacihua* and he chanted his prayers more intensely. The bad air surrounded him, constricted his chest, and threatened to suffocate him. He was afraid of losing consciousness only to wake up many miles away.

He knew that his crime was enormous. He had taken on the role of God. This was unforgivable.

The next day he had gone back to the river and discovered that the body was gone. It was as if part of his guilt had washed away with the water. He relaxed, turned his face up to the heavens, and spoke to Angel.

Now, some days later and in a new spot next to the same river, his guilt pricked him like tiny mosquitoes, but not more than he could wave away. He had done the right thing. It had been an act pleasing in the eyes of God to kill a *bhni guí'a.* The world was the better for it, and Manuel was convinced that Armas's soul was now subjected to the torments of Hell.

What were the alternatives? he debated with himself. Should he have allowed himself to be killed like a dog? But the knife—why did he carry it in his pocket, if not to use it? Hadn't he unconsciously prepared himself to kill when he took it out of the bag and slipped it into his pocket? Had he sensed Armas's intentions as they drove to the river?

If he went to the police he would join Patricio in jail, he knew this. To be thrown in jail was nothing foreign to Manuel and his family. Zapotecs had been persecuted in all ages in any manner of ways, and many were holed up in Oaxaca prisons. Eleven *campesinos* from a neighboring village had been taken away four months ago and subsequently imprisoned or killed. No one had heard from them again.

But these cases were grounded in defending their land and forests, in matters of autonomy and justice. Manuel had admittedly killed in self-defense, but he did not think anyone would believe him.

He lay in the river ravine in the shadow of fir trees that reminded him of cypresses. A couple of predatory birds hovered in the sky, just as in the valley at home. Would he ever see his village again?

He got to his feet quickly, in one movement, just like a startled animal, but it was only a lone man walking along the riverbank, a fishing pole in one hand and a bucket in the other. Manuel had seen him the day before. The man's tall, gaunt body was topped by a small head with a face so wrinkled that Manuel was reminded of the old woman in his village who gathered bunches of *epazote* that she sold for fifty centavos apiece.

Did he sell the fish, or was it done only for enjoyment? Manuel knew so little about Sweden, about the people who lived in this country. He had read a little in a guidebook in a store in Mexico City, that was all.

He knew that there were many different types of Swedes but didn't really care. His role here was not the eager curiosity of the tourist nor the systematic investigation of the ethnographer.

The fisherman disappeared behind a bend in the path and Manuel left his secluded spot. Ever since he had set fire to the short man's house he had felt a growing anxiety. There were so many. He had aimed for Armas and the fat one, but in encountering the short one his task had suddenly increased. Although the short one had not been actively involved in the recruitment of Angel and Patricio, he was a link in the chain, and apparently an important one. He may even have been the brains behind the whole operation, and perhaps Armas and the fat one had simply been his errand boys?

The anxiety also stemmed from something Patricio had said to him in prison: "We could have said no." That was true. Manuel had said no, and had warned his brothers against going to Oaxaca, where they were going to stay in a hotel and receive new clothing. They could have spoken up, continued to cultivate their corn, which others now harvested.

But they had chosen to say yes. How far did their responsibility extend?

Manuel drew a deep breath, locked the tent with the little padlock, and then strolled up to the parking lot. He looked around before wandering out into the open. Some twenty cars were parked in the lot. His rental car did not stand out, it blended in with the others, but he felt like an exotic creature as he carefully made his way to it.

The parking lot was located at the edge of an arts and crafts village that appeared to have a steady stream of visitors. The place was ideal. He knew that no one would pay any attention to the car, even if it stayed there overnight. It could belong to one of the workers from the strawberry fields.

That morning he had bathed in the river, scrubbing himself thoroughly, and relished it despite the cold temperature. He had swum back and forth, caressed by waterlilies and reeds, and thereafter dried in the sunshine back on shore.

He was a short, wiry man and there were those who misjudged his slight build. But he knew his own strength. Like all Zapotecs, schooled in farm labor, he was capable of working long and hard. He could carry a hundred kilos on his shoulders, clear the land with his hoe or machete for hours without tiring, take a break, eat some beans and *posol* only to resume his work, walk for miles up and down through valleys and over mountain passes.

He was the kind of man Mexico relied on, trusted. He would support himself, his family, and also take part and help add to other peoples' riches and excess. He had erected all churches and monuments, put in roads along steep mountain ridges, cultivated corn, beans, and coffee, so why could he not be allowed to rest for a few minutes at an unfamiliar river, stretch out and let the sun dry his limbs?

Nonetheless his anxiety was there and he sensed its source: he had lost his ability to rest, to feel happy for the moment, to take pleasure in the small things and nurse his hope for the future. It was the "man from the mountain" who had taken from him these attributes so necessary for a Zapotec.

He despised himself, aware that his *ládxi*—his heart and soul—were lost. He had become exactly like them.

When he reached his car, he tried to shake off the sombre mood of the morning, because it made his movements plodding and his thoughts dull. He needed all the sharpness he could muster. This foreign country was placing great demands on him, there were no resting places here, whether in time or space.

After a glance at the map he started the car, turned onto the main road, crossed a bridge, and drove toward Uppsala. The landscape was varied, with fields of wheat, newly harvested with the golden brown stubble that reached toward the horizon, and gracious mounds, shaped like women's breasts, where the grazing cattle, fat and healthy, looked up unconcerned as he passed. His mood immediately improved.

On the horizon he could see the cathedral with the towers pointing up into the clear blue sky. Up in that sea of air, thousands of black birds were struggling in billowing formations against the blustery southeasterly wind. They, like Manuel, were on their way into town.

Right before he entered Uppsala from the north, he stopped and checked the map for the best way to "K. Rosenberg," the name that he had seen on the short man's door.

He parked the car outside a small mall, crossed the street, and took the final stretch to the building on foot.

✦

Thirty-Three

Since his childhood, Konrad Rosenberg always woke early. His inner clock started to ring as early as six. He didn't like it, had never liked it, but it was the inheritance from Karl-Åke Rosenberg making itself felt. His father had gotten up at five every morning and started fussing, making coffee and rustling the newspapers. Since Konrad was the youngest, he slept in a pull-out sofa in the kitchen, so he had no choice but to be woken up.

The power of habit is great, and so even this morning he woke up early. It was half past five when he opened his eyes. He had to pee, and he had a pounding headache. He lay in bed a while longer and tried to fall back to sleep, then realized it was hopeless. At exactly six o'clock he got up and went to the bathroom.

The night before he had boozed it up, as thoroughly as in the good old days, but with the difference that this time he had drunk completely alone. This had perhaps contributed to the amount of alcohol he had managed to consume.

It was an unaccustomed feeling, almost solemn, to pour the first drink and raise his glass by himself. After the third one there was no solemnity left, only determined drinking. After the fourth one, Konrad started a long, embittered monolog about the "fat devil-chef" who believed he could lord it over Konrad Rosenberg.

Konrad had received a letter, not by ordinary mail but stuck in his mailbox. It was printed by machine and lacked a signature, but the content convinced Konrad of the identity of the writer. He assumed that Slobodan had hired someone to deliver the letter. He was simply too scared to show himself in Tunabackar.

Slobodan wrote that they could have absolutely no contact, no telephone calls, and could not allow themselves to be seen together. Slobodan instructed Konrad to stay at home: "only go to the store and then straight home," he wrote, as if Konrad were a child. He was not to place himself in "risky situations," not to spend his evenings out, not to "get in touch with any of our shared associates" or engage in anything that could awaken the interest of "persons unknown to us who we do not wish to know better," which Konrad assumed meant the police.

At first he thought it felt ridiculous and was actually tempted to defy the instructions and call Slobodan, but realized it was wiser to keep a low profile until the whole thing had died down. The fire was a real blow, but not a complete catastrophe. Konrad trusted completely in the fact that his brother would not say a word about Konrad using the house. His brother simply wanted to get the insurance money.

He turned on the radio but turned it off immediately. Normally he would have gone down to the newsstand and checked the program for the week's harness-racing results, maybe gone downtown and frittered away a few hours. He considered calling Åke to see if he had heard anything more about the fire, but then concluded it would only make him nervous.

It was a little after eleven when the doorbell rang. Konrad jumped as if he had been struck in the back with a whip. He tiptoed over to the door and listened, at a complete loss as to who it could be.

His old drinking buddies, who were liable to turn up at any hours, had not shown themselves for months and no one else ever came to see him.

He put his ear to the door and thought he heard panting but decided it was his imagination. No one could breathe so loudly, but when he opened the mail slot with extreme care he heard the hissing sound more clearly.

The doorbell rang again. Konrad felt the sweat start to trickle down his back. His curiosity won out and he straightened his back.

"Who is it?" he called out.

"Mr. Rosenberg, something has happened to your car," he heard a high-pitched voice say from the other side of the door.

He opened the door and there was an older man who Konrad thought lived in the building next door.

"Excuse me for disturbing you, but I saw—"

"My car?"

"Yes, isn't it your Mercedes on the street? Someone has vandalized it."

"Vandalized?" Konrad echoed stupidly, before slipping his shoes on.

As he ran down the stairs, leaving the asthmatic man behind, it struck him that it could be a trap and so he slowed down. But concern for his Merc drove him to a run.

Someone had pulled a sharp object along the full length of the car, from the hood all the way to the brake lights. Konrad stared at the almost completely level scratch, and when he circled the car he saw that the other side had suffered identical damage.

The neighbor arrived out of breath and explained that he discovered the whole thing when he came back from the store.

Konrad stood as if paralyzed, could not even manage a curse. His car, his Mercedes, vandalized by a couple of young hooligans.

"It's terrible what they get up to these days," the neighbor said. "They can't even leave a beautiful car alone."

Suddenly it struck Konrad that perhaps it was not the work of hooligans. He looked around. "That bastard is laughing somewhere," he thought, and asked the neighbor if he had noticed anything suspicious on his way to the store. Yet another neighbor came up to them and in some way Konrad felt honored by the attention. He recalled that the first neighbor had referred to him as "Mr. Rosenberg." Also, it felt good to have company, even if their average combined age was high.

"Call the police," the neighbor said. "Even if they don't do anything, you have to report it. I remember when someone drove into my Amazon, it was parked in the lot of Lagerquist's hardware store. What I went through. There were papers to fill out, reports to file."

Konrad listened with half an ear. The word *police* made him nervous and then increasingly infuriated.

"I wonder what it costs to have it repainted," one neighbor speculated and Konrad's anger increased further.

"I'm going up to make a call," he said and left the two men on the sidewalk.

He sensed that this was not a normal prank, but a calling card left by an unknown man who was apparently capable of anything. As he walked slowly up the stairs his anger diminished and instead his anxiety grew. What kind of forces were at work? That Armas was murdered could be explained. Konrad and Slobodan had discussed various possible motives, but to burn down a house and above all to damage a car . . . it was so illogical that it was frightening.

✦

Thirty-Four

There are moments in the career of a police officer when the red carpet is rolled out. That was how Barbro Liljendahl felt. Its length testified to a row of unforeseen experiences and discoveries, but also consisted of routine matters, as well as large amounts of work—hours, days, and weeks of labor—but that must be the reward, she thought.

Ever since the stabbing incident in Sävja she had had the feeling that the case involved a number of hidden connections. One thread had loosened and now she could start the unraveling process.

After hanging up the phone she sat lost in thought for a long time. What occupied her mind, and that which demanded a great deal of skill and finesse, was the fact that the young boy Zero had demanded that he not be accused of stabbing Sidström.

Otherwise he would not talk. Barbro Liljendahl knew she had to tread carefully. If he were to be charged with the deed and convicted—something of which one could not be sure—then the end of the thread would break off after only one revolution. The ball of thread would remain almost intact.

Sidström would never admit to knowing Zero from before, he would have no reason to try to seek any kind of justice and would prefer silence. As long as Zero, who had sliced open his abdomen, kept quiet, Sidström would be satisfied. He would heal, maybe receive some compensation from the Crime Victims Fund, and return to his work, while Zero, if he were convicted, would meet a decidedly bleaker fate.

Barbro Liljendahl had seen enough of youth crime to realize that he would most likely reappear in future cases. The boy could be saved, but only if he could avoid the charges. Then it would hopefully serve as a useful lesson and for her part Barbro Liljendahl would be free to keep unraveling.

She decided to look up Ann Lindell. One reason was the fact that they had discussed the case when they bumped into each other at the hospital. But it was also with a measure of calculation that she got in touch with her colleague.

Barbro Liljendahl worked in the intelligence unit, often together with Harry Andersson. He was a decent enough policeman, but could, on and off, be a real pain. In a deliberate way, he went about diminishing her efforts, often accompanied by an obnoxiously macho comment that was perhaps intended to be funny but always sounded offensive. He laughed away her protests and told her she was oversensitive.

She wanted to leave intelligence and join violent crimes. Lindell could perhaps put in a good word for her. Barbro liked what she had seen of Lindell. She already knew Beatrice Andersson from the Police Academy, and finally, Barbro had heard that Ottosson, the chief in violent crimes was a timid and kindly soul.

"It's a stab in the dark," Lindell said when Barbro completed her account. Barbro smiled at the unintended pun.

"If we can make this self-defense," Lindell went on, "then perhaps the DA can approach the whole thing from a different perspective. Fritzén is reasonable, but the new one—you know, the one with the earrings—I don't know, she seems so . . . what should I say . . . rigid."

"I know you have a lot going on with the Fyris river murder, but should we question Sidström together? You could make a case for it by saying that there may be a connection."

"It's weak," Lindell said.

"I know, but I feel sorry for the guy somehow," Barbro said. "His whole family is insane. If he is charged, they will make his life a living Hell. They'll say he's shaming the entire family. And his father is already in prison in Turkey."

Lindell reflected for a moment.

"You know how things end up for a guy like Zero," Barbro Liljendahl added.

"Okay," Lindell said finally, "but I have to talk to Ottosson first. Have you worked through the list of Sidström's acquaintances?"

"Yes, I've talked to some of them. Three of them are doing time."

"There was a name I reacted to and that is Rosenberg, have you questioned him?"

"No, he and three, four others are left," Barbro Liljendahl said.

"Okay, let's go to Akademiska and listen to what our punctured friend has to say."

Lindell didn't really know why she went along with all of this. She shouldn't have done so and Ottosson had his reservations, but in a childish way he was flattered that she wanted his blessings.

She sensed that this had to do with Berglund. His comment about Rosenberg being in the money was the kind of information she heard almost daily, and if you listened to all loose chatter then every single investigation would grind to a halt.

Was she doing this to impress him? So she would later be able to say, Thanks for the tip, it led to . . . or was it Ola Haver's superior remarks in the lunchroom?

Regardless of the reason, she entered the surgical wing accompanied by Liljendahl with a certain amount of anticipation. She was also curious to see how her colleague handled the situation.

Sidström was sitting slouched over in a chair. His head was leaning forward, his chin against his chest, his arms draped over the armrests and the emaciated, very sinewy hands twitched almost imperceptibly.

"I wonder what he's dreaming about?" Lindell whispered.

He looked considerably older than his forty-two years. Lindell guessed at a long history of drug abuse behind the grayish cast of the skin, and she was convinced his arms and perhaps his legs were covered in scars from hypodermic needles.

According to Liljendahl he had been drug-free for a year, and Lindell wondered how he had reacted to the anesthesia and painkillers he must have received at the hospital. His last charges were three years back in time: burglary.

"Olle," Liljendahl said.

The man reacted by jerking his head, but he did not wake up. Liljendahl shook his shoulder gently and Lindell felt an involuntary distaste, bordering on revulsion, at her colleague's touch but also at the watery eyes that opened.

"What the hell?"

"Time to wake up," Liljendahl said.

The man looked around in confusion, discovered who his visitors were, and quickly sat up in the chair.

"Fucking hell," he said emphatically, and grimaced.

There was more to come once Liljendahl, after having introduced Ann Lindell, took out a small pocket tape recorder, recorded the facts of the questioning session, and proceeded with her first question about how much cocaine he had sold recently.

"What the fuck are you talking about? Turn that damn thing off."

Liljendahl smiled. Lindell went and stood over by the window, diagonally behind Sidström.

"We don't have a lot of time," Liljendahl said and Lindell couldn't help smile, "and we would appreciate a little cooperation."

"What the hell are you talking about?"

"We know that you sell cocaine, we also know a great deal about your activities in general."

"I am not telling you shit, or your—"

"There are others who talk," Liljendahl said tiredly, and Lindell guessed how she was planning to approach the whole thing.

"Konrad Rosenberg, is that name familiar to you?"

It was Lindell who took the chance, and the man flinched, grimaced again, then turned his body, and stared at her in terror. Lindell saw that her guess had hit the mark and she exchanged glances with Liljendahl.

"You can start talking now," Lindell said and almost heard his body deflate. His facial features changed in one stroke and displayed all the signs of extreme fatigue and despondency. He shook his head lightly and audibly drew in all the mucus in the sinus cavities in his skull.

Sometimes it is almost too easy, Lindell thought, and leaned against the windowsill.

In the cafeteria half an hour later, when they were reviewing their session, Liljendahl was so excited that Lindell had to laugh.

"You did that well," she said.

"Thanks for the help," Liljendahl said. "That was so perfect!"

"What's your partner going to say?"

Liljendahl's expression fell immediately and Lindell was sorry she hadn't given her happiness a few more minutes.

"He'll be upset," Liljendahl said. "But I don't give a damn. If you only knew how sick and tired I am of his comments."

Lindell nodded.

"Should we go look up Rosenberg right away?"

"It's probably best for me to step down at this point," Lindell said. "I mean, if Harry gets upset about something like this then it won't be better if we just keep going. We don't actually have that much on Rosenberg right now. Sidström did not expressly say that it was Rosenberg who was the supplier, only that they were in contact."

"But you saw how he reacted," Liljendahl said. "His body language spoke volumes."

Lindell hated having to step down, but there was a chance this was going to go too far. If she followed along to Konrad Rosenberg and it took off from there, she would be drawn deeply into an investigation that, strictly speaking, she didn't have anything to do with.

"You tackle Rosenberg on your own and then get in touch with me," she said, and the disappointment in Liljendahl's face was unmistakable.

They drove back to the police station in silence, but before they parted ways they agreed to meet the following day.

"I need the perspective of an experienced colleague," Liljendahl said and Lindell found this both flattering and irritating. She guessed that there was something behind the appreciative words. Maybe, she thought, her motivation was as simple as just wanting to piss off Harry Andersson.

✦

Thirty-Five

Eva Willman chuckled to herself. In front of her on the table lay at least one hundred flyers. She already regretted having promised Helen to circulate them. The text was too aggressive in Eva's opinion, too stark and bordering on schmaltz. Eva had little patience for the sentimental while Helen liked to lay it on thick.

"But this is about our children," Helen said, when Eva objected to one of the phrases.

"But this one, Helen," Eva said and read aloud: " '. . . drug dealers are like predators who destroy our children, luring them into the marsh.' "

"So?" Helen said. "If some bastard came here and threw our kids in the Stordammen to drown them we would stop him, wouldn't we?"

Stordammen was a lake with a swampy shoreline, encircled by a belt of reeds, located in the woods just south of the residential area.

"We haven't fully come to terms with what is happening," Helen went on. "These are our children they have targeted. One should line them up against a wall, these damn pushers—no, that would be too kind—one should—"

"You are not allowed to say that at the meeting," Eva interrupted.

Helen smiled.

"Do you think I'm completely crazy? I am going to be exceedingly calm and dignified. You can talk instead, if you like."

There was a note of both derision and indignation in Helen's voice.

Helen had booked the old post office. That turned out to be a good choice because it was centrally located and, above all, everyone knew where it was. A good friend of hers had printed up the flyers at work. Helen had also organized coffee and cake through the congregation and invited the police to talk about drugs.

Eva had suggested they invite some politicians but Helen had dismissed the idea with a snort.

"We're going to have to tackle this ourselves," she said. "If those clowns took their jobs seriously, surely the schools wouldn't be the way they are. Soon there will only be one school counselor per district. And there should be a community center worthy of the name, at the very least."

Helen continued to list the things she thought the politicians should do. Nothing came as news, and the more Helen talked the more tired Eva felt.

Eva started in her own courtyard, walking from building to building and taping the yellow flyers to the doors. Then she continued on through the area, down toward the ICA grocery store and the pizzeria.

She met several people she knew outside the store. She was slightly ashamed of the flyers with their silly phrases, but everytime she received some encouragment she felt more comfortable.

"I'm glad someone is doing something sensible for once," said a mother she recognized from the soccer practices.

Maybe we could post a large advertisement outside the store, she thought, and went inside to talk to the manager, returning with something close to a promise.

She knew that the rumor would quickly spread in Sävja and Bergsbrunna that Patrik and Hugo's mother was running around with flyers like some kind of Jehovah's Witness, and she wondered what her boys would say. They would be embarrassed, Eva felt sure about that. But, emboldened by the praise, she went by the nursery school on the way home, went in and talked to some of the staff, and was allowed to post flyers there as well.

Eva called Helen as soon as she got home.

"Wonderful," she said. "It's perfect that the flyers are yellow. And another thing, I got Mossa's mother to translate it into Arabic. She's going to print it out. Do you think we need it in Kurdish? What does that boy in fifth grade speak? Is it Iranian?"

"Yes, Ali's family is from Teheran."

"If we don't get all the *svartskallar* to attend, it won't work. Then it will be like in France."

Eva did not protest her choice of words—*svartskallar* was a derogatory word for immigrants—and did not ask what Helen knew about France. She had probably seen a documentary on television.

Eva promised to speak to the Iranian family, who had a boy in the fifth grade, and they finished the call. She sank exhausted into the sofa. On the floor in front of her was the magazine she had been reading the other night. She picked it up and leafed through to the article about the yacht off the coast of South America, and she realized that she had never swum in anything saltier than the brackish Baltic seawater, had never taken in a really salty gulp of water.

She tried to imagine heat and sandy beach. Tropical warmth and fine, white grains under bare feet, and she smiled to herself. She knew it was only a dream and that she would never be able to afford to travel farther than the Canary Islands, if even that. For the past two years she had saved four thousand six hundred kronor in a special account. Last fall there had been almost seven thousand, but before Christmas she had been forced to withdraw several thousand.

Her only hope was a Triss lottery win. Together with Helen, she bought a ticket every week, but so far the yield had been thin, some fifty kronor and, once, a thousand kronor. They had celebrated with a bottle of wine.

She wanted to travel with Patrik and Hugo. It felt urgent because soon they would be too old to want to accompany her. It pained her that she could not offer them more of the good life. They heard about classmates who traveled both on winter and summer vacations, and once the usually so loyal Hugo had let it slip out that it was unfair that they could not go farther than to Värmland.

But now the outlook was somewhat better. Donald had mentioned something about needing more staff in the kitchen, someone who managed the dishes. Right now it was the waitstaff that had to take care of loading the dishwasher and supplying the bar with glasses, but in view of the fact that the number of guests was increasing and that Eva was unused to the work, it was stressful. Perhaps she would be able to work a few extra nights a month and put away a little money?

She was due at work soon. She smiled, happened to think about Donald and his resistance to the union. Maybe she should put Helen on him.

Despite her reservations about her friend's antidrug campaign, she felt strengthened. You could say what you wanted about Helen, and there were many who did, but she had a fantastic ability to make things happen, even if Eva was not getting her hopes up about the meeting at the old post office. There would most likely not be the turnout that Helen expected. To relocate a garbage room in your own courtyard was entirely different from altering county politics and fighting drugs.

✦

Thirty-Six

Barbro Liljendahl parked on the street and the first thing she noticed was the Mercedes. Lindell had told her about Konrad Rosenberg's car purchase. She also saw the scrape along the side that almost looked like a racing stripe.

Therefore she was not all too surprised by Rosenberg's opening remark when she introduced herself as from the police.

"I'm grateful that you could come down here so quickly. You saw the car, didn't you?"

"Someone else will have to take care of that," Liljendahl said. "We have something else to talk about."

The air in his apartment was smoky and stale, but it was surprisingly neat. They sat down in the kitchen. Konrad Rosenberg had a veteran criminal's gaze. He pretended to be relaxed but avoided looking her in the eye.

"Maybe we should talk a little about the Mercedes, after all," Liljendahl said.

Konrad looked up and she noticed a glint of hope in his worn face. For a moment she could identify with him.

"It must be some kids," he said and lit a cigarette.

"May I ask how you can afford such an expensive car?"

"I won on a race in Solvalla. And I've only ever driven junk cars before so I thought . . ."

"How much did you win?"

"A couple of hundred thousand," Konrad said and coughed at same time, as if the amount caught in his throat.

"Do you gamble on a regular basis?"

"Every week. I am the best client at the gambling station, and sometimes I go down to Solvalla and sometimes up to Gävle. Do you bet on horses?"

Liljendahl shook her head and smiled at Rosenberg.

"Are you acquainted with Olle Sidström?"

Here Rosenberg displayed great finesse. He took a final drag of his cigarette and then carefully extinguished it in the overflowing ashtray.

"Yes, he's come out with me a few times, but that was more in the old days. He gets so overbearing when he wins. You need to be discreet when you play."

"Right now he's not doing any gambling," Liljendahl said. "He's in the hospital."

"Oh?"

"Stabbed."

Now Rosenberg's defenses crumbled. Liljendahl watched as his wall came tumbling down, how his jaw slackened and how terror established its grip on him.

Attack, Liljendahl thought, nonetheless she held back and allowed time for Rosenberg's bewilderment to take hold before she told him about Sidström's condition. She described in detail what his chest looked like, the way his fear had manifested itself, and what an urgent need he had to talk to the police.

"What does this have to do with me?" Rosenberg tossed out and lit yet another cigarette. Liljendahl, who had encountered this question many times, smiled, but said nothing.

"If he says that I owe him money then he's bluffing" was Rosenberg's next tack. "He's always been full of shit."

"I am not here as an advocate for Sidström," Liljendahl said. "I am investigating an attempted homicide and drug trafficking. I thought that, as an old addict, you would maybe have something to tell me."

Rosenberg shook his head.

"I am a law-abiding citizen," he said.

Liljendahl could not repress a look of merriment.

"And you have nothing to add," she said.

"No, nothing."

Before Barbro Liljendahl left Tunabackar she stopped by the magazine store on Torbjörns Square and confirmed that Rosenberg was a heavy gambler and spent "a thousand or so" on horse bets and lottery tickets.

According to the manager, Rosenberg did "fairly well" and won small to "decent" amounts from time to time.

Liljendahl realized that she had to uncover something concrete in order to break Sidström and possibly confirm a link to Rosenberg. She felt very strongly that Rosenberg was hiding something. The nervousness he had displayed was not the usual stress all criminals showed in their confrontation with law enforcement. She had managed to unsettle him and it would be a good idea to pay another visit to Rosenberg in a day or two, keep the pressure on and maybe get him to make a mistake. He would never start to talk of his own accord. Only new information would bring this about, and lead to him selling information in order to save his own skin.

She also knew that the weak link in this chain was Zero. He was the one who had to start talking.

✦

Thirty-Seven

Lorenzo was not happy, but the people around him did not usually notice a difference, since he was trained to maintain his composure. Olaf González was nonetheless experienced enough to take heed of Lorenzo's right hand nervously pulling through his hair, smoothing it back.

"Who?" he asked, and Gonzo wished he had an answer.

"There are a couple of possibilities," he began gingerly, "either someone in the business that Armas went too far with, or someone from his past has turned up."

When Gonzo found out that Armas had been murdered, his initial reaction had been to leave town. He was convinced that it was Lorenzo who was behind it, and since he was the only one who knew about Armas's relationship with Lorenzo, he felt he was in a vulnerable position. Perhaps Lorenzo wanted to silence him in order to cover his tracks.

"That much I have figured out on my own," Lorenzo said. "But since you worked closely with Armas, I would have expected you to have picked something up, for god's sake."

Lorenzo seldom cursed or raised his voice. They were sitting at Pub 19, each with a beer in front of him. It was half past six and there were only a few other people in the room. A couple of students were standing at the bar and a group of women, whom Gonzo assumed all worked together, had claimed two tables at the window looking out onto Svartbäcksgatan. One of the women looked up and stared at them.

Gonzo chose not to answer. Whatever he said, it would most likely rub Lorenzo the wrong way. Gonzo wanted to stay on his good side. That was his only chance. Since he had been fired from Dakar there was no possibility of working for another restaurant in town—Slobodan would see to that—and so Lorenzo was his only hope.

Damn it, he thought, why did I have to go poking my nose in other peoples' business? The first time Lorenzo contacted him, he assumed that it was about work, that Lorenzo was fishing for information and was looking to establish contacts in the restaurant business. That was at least how he made it seem, that he was thinking of establishing himself in the city and needed "points of entry."

Gonzo was flattered and saw before him the chance of advancement, and the very thought of walking into Slobodan's office and tossing the keys on the table made him willingly tell everything he knew about Dakar and Alhambra. He did not feel disloyal because Armas and Slobodan had always treated him like shit. And then that Tessie bitch came along who thought she owned the place and could order him around like a house slave. What did she know about waitressing? He had worked his ass off for fifteen years while Tessie had taken it easy at some burger joint in Boston.

He had realized too late that Lorenzo was aiming higher than that. He wanted to break Armas and in this way weaken Slobodan and perhaps take over his restaurants. But there was also something more that Lorenzo was after. Gonzo had never managed to put his finger on what that was. This feeling had grown stronger during the past week. Lorenzo's anxiety could not be explained in any other way. There was more at stake than two restaurants in Uppsala.

"What do the cops say?"

"They said nothing to me," Gonzo said and recalled how the police had peppered him with questions about his disagreement with Armas and why he had quit Dakar. "They thought I had something to do with his murder."

"And do you?"

Lorenzo smiled as he posed the question.

"Fuck you!" Gonzo exclaimed, and one of the youths at the bar turned his head to stare with curiosity at the duo tucked away in the corner.

Gonzo took a large gulp of beer. He kept his eyes closed as he drank but felt Lorenzo's gaze. When he opened his eyes again he decided to tell him what he knew.

"I passed a package on to Armas," Gonzo said, "but that turned out to be a mistake. He double-crossed me."

"Stolen goods."

Lorenzo nodded, posed no further questions, sipped some beer and smiled again.

"If you wish to join us when we sail, you will have to step on board soon," he said.

"And what is the cargo?"

"To join the crew, one does not have to know the nature of the cargo," Lorenzo said.

He stood up, pulled out a hundred kronor note, and tossed it on the table.

"Multiply that with a thousand," he said cryptically, and left the pub.

Gonzo signaled to the bartender that he wanted another beer, mostly to quell the temptation to stand up and follow Lorenzo. He stared at the bill and mentally added three zeros.

The beer was placed in front of him and at the same moment he saw an image from his childhood. A clothing line was suspended between two trees for his mother to hang the family's laundry. His father's colorful shirts were next to his own T-shirts and underwear, a red dress, and some sheets.

"How's it going?"

Gonzo looked up bewildered.

"It's fine," he said.

"You're leaving Dakar, I hear," the bartender said.

Gonzo nodded, but the image of laundry was fixed in his mind. The clothes billowed gently in the breeze. It was the height of summer and Gonzo was standing in the open window on the second floor. For a moment he thought he could smell the laundry detergent.

The bartender looked at him devoid of expression, and then left the table. Gonzo drank some more beer and wondered why he was seeing laundry. He had not been back to Norway for several years. Was this vision a sign that he should leave Uppsala and go home? The house was still there and his mother was probably still hanging the laundry in the same place.

Gonzo finished his beer, stood up from the table, and walked briskly through the pub, suddenly extremely irritated at the women who were growing increasingly raucous. It was as if their laughter was aimed at him.

What the hell do those bitches know about Uppsala, he thought and glared at one of them as he negotiated his way through the narrow spaces between tables and chairs. She met his gaze defiantly as if she sensed his thoughts and wanted to express her resistance and disdain.

Once out on the sidewalk he could not decide which way to go. His own will had left him. He felt there was trouble brewing, a kind that was considerably worse than losing his job. An inner voice told him to go home, pool his assets, and book a ticket to Oslo. Maybe he could start over there, find a job and put Uppsala behind him forever. Another voice urged him to take revenge, even if Armas was no longer reachable. Slobodan was still there.

An old man was pushing a walker along on the other side of the street. A plastic bag hung from the handle. The old man was making his way forward with the utmost of effort. But still he smiled. Gonzo shook his head and turned left toward downtown.

✦

Thirty-Eight

There was nothing attractive about the courtyard behind Dakar. There was a rusted Opel in one corner, three green garbage containers in the other, and a worn old bicycle in a deteriorating bike rack.

The asphalt was uneven and cracked and had undergone various rounds of repair. Even the weeds that stuck out of the cracks looked miserable and wilted in the still air. There was a strong smell of garbage, but this did not affect Manuel. He hardly noticed it. His whole attention was fixed on the red-painted door that bore the restaurant's name in white.

He had been standing there for half an hour. Initially he had approached the door purposefully but then stopped himself, his finger poised on the doorbell. He had lowered his arm, drawn back, and sat down on the bike rack. In this state of indecision, he experienced peace for the first time in this foreign land. Maybe it was precisely the smell of garbage and the baking sun that made him lean up against the wall and smile. He could easily recall and identify the smell as well as the warmth from his earlier life. There was comfort in this passive state of waiting. How many times had he not experienced this in California? The waiting for work, for someone to drive up in their pickup, roll down the window, and size him up without a word, along with the other men, evaluating their physical strength and stamina.

He wished that he could roll himself a cigarette and maybe share a beer with someone. When he closed his eyes he thought he could hear the quiet talk of the other men. Brief stories of villages and families that he had never heard of, but that nonetheless appeared as vivid as old acquaintances, about bosses you had to watch out for, slave drivers and racists, and about women, living and imagined. The men were never as bold, and at the same time as bare, in their longing and grief as when they were waiting for work.

And the hope that these men kept alive as they spoke. It was as if the silence threatened to burst their already frozen hearts.

Even then Manuel knew that it was all in vain. None of their dreams were going to come true, yet he allowed himself to be influenced by their delusionary hopes and plans for the future. He rarely participated in the discussions but he allowed the muffled voices to keep even his hope alive. Maybe it was the same for them? Manuel believed that even behind the most innocent and naive compatriot, there was a realist. They all took part in an enormous game of pretend that included millions of impoverished job seekers. They allowed themselves to be duped in the same way that they, for a few moments, let themselves be tempted by the tricks of the jesters and verbose fantasies of the fiesta.

Was it this that Angel and Patricio had no longer been able to bear? Manuel wanted to think so, that it was not pure foolishness that drove them to associate with drug smugglers, that they were not deluded but fully conscious of what they were doing. They did not let the quiet chatter soothe them any longer. They knew that there was no future for a miserable and poor *campesino* who was waiting for work and happiness. They could not stand this farce, and decided instead to snatch a part of the fortune that the fat man's drug trade created.

Angel used to ask why the white men were rich and why the Indians lived worse than dogs. Manuel's talk about five hundred years of oppression and extortion did not impress him.

"But there are more of us," he would object. "Why do we accept the white man taking the best for himself?"

Manuel knew that all Angel dreamed of was a woman to share his life. Where and under what circumstances did not matter. His brother had an uncomplicated attitude to life; he wanted to love and be loved. Manuel had always imagined Angel as the father of countless offspring, small chubby Zapotec children in a village like all the others.

Why should he talk politics when he couldn't understand it? Why ponder the injustices of life when all he wanted was a woman's embrace?

Almost an hour had gone by when a man suddenly appeared in the courtyard. It was only as he approached the red door that he noticed Manuel. He jumped but then smiled and said something that Manuel did not understand.

Manuel nodded and asked in English if he worked at Dakar.

"Are you Spanish?" the man asked.

"Venezuela," Manuel answered.

"A friend of Chávez," the man said, in a strange kind of Spanish.

"*No,*" Manuel replied.

"Your president, I mean. Forget it," he added, when he saw Manuel's look of incomprehension. "My name is Feo and sure, I work here."

"Are you from Spain?"

"Portugal," Feo said.

Manuel stared at him. Feo took out a set of keys.

"Are you waiting for someone?"

Manuel shook his head. "I'm looking for work," he said.

Feo put a key in the lock but did not turn it. Manuel felt the tense feeling from California, and got to his feet.

"At Dakar? Do you have any experience?"

"I can work," Manuel said hastily. "I am used to everything. I can work hard and long."

Feo studied him. Manuel stood with hanging arms, met his gaze, and thought of Angel. He decided to go to Frankfurt to see where his brother had met his death. Perhaps there were some stones on the railway tracks with dried blood? Perhaps someone had seen him run?

"You'll have to speak to the owner," the Portuguese man said. "He isn't here, but come in and wait. You look like you could use a Coke."

He unlocked the door and let Manuel go in first, locked the door behind him and Manuel was struck by how cool everything was. There was a faint smell of cleaning solution and food.

Feo put a hand on his shoulder.

"You look like you could use a Coke," he repeated.

Manuel looked around him as if he were expecting to be ambushed at any second. Feo brought him out to the bar, took out a Coca-Cola, and held it out with a smile.

There was a clatter of pots from the kitchen and a radio playing Bruce Springsteen. Manuel was thirsty but did not manage to swallow more than a mouthful.

"Come along and meet the chef," Feo said.

Manuel accompanied Feo to the kitchen. As Feo was introducing him, Manuel wondered why he was being treated so kindly. He watched the Portuguese and heard him explain in Swedish why the stranger was here. Donald gave him a cursory glance and nod but then immediately turned back to his work. In front of him lay herb-stuffed lamb roulade that he was slicing into portions, then weighing and stacking them in a plastic container. Manuel drew in the smell.

"You speak English?" Donald asked.

Manuel nodded.

"Damn, you speak English with an Indian accent," Feo said and thumped Donald in the back.

"Do you have a work permit?"

"No," said Manuel.

"Then it will be difficult. Slobban, the guy who owns this place, is pretty particular about things like that."

"No problems," Feo said.

"You are from Venezuela?" Donald continued. "Where did you learn English?"

"I have worked in California."

"*Grapes of Wrath*," Donald said in Swedish, and smiled unexpectedly.

He finished slicing the lamb.

"A novel" was his reply to Feo's quizzical look, and then switched back to English again. "I'll talk to Slobban because we do need a dishwasher. If you have worked in the States then it will be like a vacation to wash dishes at Dakar."

Manuel listened in fascination to the chef. His English really was funny.

"But I think we can arrange a couple of hours every evening," Donald explained. "Do you think it smells good?"

"Yes, very," Manuel said.

✦

Thirty-Nine

"We've found something," Allan Fredriksson said, but was not overwhelmingly enthusiastic as he stepped into Ann Lindell's office.

She waited for an elaboration that did not come. Allan looks worn out, she thought, as he sat down in the visitor's chair. The gray hairs were more numerous and the circles under his eyes were more marked.

"What is it?"

"The tattoo," Fredriksson said. "Armas went to a place that is on Salagatan. There are four tattoo salons in town. I checked three of them earlier, but this guy was closed and on vacation."

"And he remembered Armas?"

"Very much so. He remembered the tattoo and the scar on his back as well."

"What scar?"

Fredriksson gave Lindell a look of surprise.

"Then you haven't read up on it well enough. Armas had a scar below one of the shoulder blades, perhaps from a knife."

Lindell felt her cheeks grow hot. She had missed that.

"Right," she said. "Now I remember. He went there to get the tattoo?"

"He wanted to get a second tattoo, on his other arm. The one that we found the remains of was already there."

"But he never got another one," Lindell observed. "Did Armas say anything about the one he already had?"

"Not more than that he thought it was fitting. The tattoo artist looked it up online. It was a depiction of a Mexican god with a name with too many letters."

Fredriksson laid a paper on her desk. It was a copy of the tattoo. It represented an animal—or was it a person?—who appeared to be dancing. Feathers hung from its back.

"Thought it was fitting," Lindell mused, studying the figure. "And this is a Mexican god? We'll have to check with Slobodan Andersson. We know they both went overseas a couple of years ago. Didn't the tax authorities say something about that? Maybe they were in Mexico."

Fredriksson stood up with a sigh.

"How is it, Allan?"

"I must have caught Berglund's bug," he sighed. "Can you take Mexico?"

Lindell nodded.

"Thanks for your help," she yelled after Fredriksson as he walked back down the corridor.

What was it that he had found so fitting? A dancing figure from Mexico. "Quetzalcóatl," Fredriksson had written on the piece of paper. What did it mean to Armas and what could it tell them now? It meant something to the killer, that much was clear. Lindell knew absolutely nothing about Mexico, except for the fact that its capital city was a disaster for asthmatics—here she was dealing with a mythological figure that she could not pronounce the name of and that did not tell her anything.

Why, she kept asking herself as she scrutinized the copy of the tattoo design. Why remove a tattoo depicting a Mexican god?

She reached for the phone to call Slobodan Andersson, but changed her mind. Better to go down to Dakar, she thought, and instead she called Görel, her friend who often babysat Erik.

"You want to go out for dinner?"

"What do you think?" Görel replied.

"We're going sleuthing," Lindell said.

"It's about time."

"Do you think Margot can watch Erik?"

"My sister is always up for that sort of thing," Görel said. "I'll call her right away."

They decided to meet at the main square at seven o'clock.

"Sleuthing" was the last thing Görel said as she put the phone down.

A series of calls followed. The first went to Schönell, who had gone through Armas's video collection. He had scanned around one hundred films but had not discovered anything particularly noteworthy. They were mostly action and war movies.

"Was there anything about Mexico?" Lindell asked.

"A Mexican film, you mean?"

"I don't actually know what I mean."

"Something in that vein, I think, I was mostly checking for porn, but I can look through the covers and see if there is anything related to Mexico," Schönell said.

"I'd appreciate it," Lindell said and hung up.

Her next call went to Barbro Liljendahl. She was in Järlåsa tracking down a suspected fence but had only found chantarelles.

"Loads of them, right next to the road. There are patches of yellow. I'll have to get Janne and come back here tonight. He loves mushrooms."

"Great," Lindell said, but she was irritated by her colleague's enthusiasm and the information that there was a Janne. She found her out-of-breath and agitated voice disconcerting, almost repellant.

"I just wanted to hear about Rosenberg," she resumed.

"He was furious about his Mercedes. Someone has amused himself by scraping the paint job. He claimed that it was gambling wins that had paid for the car."

"And the contact with Sidström?"

"They were just friends he said, but he was clearly shaken when I told him that his friend had been stabbed and admitted to Akademiska."

"What's your hunch?" Lindell asked.

"Drugs," Liljendahl said. "There is something here. I think it would pay to put Rosenberg under surveillance."

"Good luck," Lindell said, convinced that there would not be enough resources for that and happy that her colleague did not appear to want to draw her further into the stabbing incident in Sävja.

"One more thing," Liljendahl said. "Rosenberg smoked like a chimney and the matchbox he used was from Dakar. Isn't that the restaurant where Armas worked?"

"Yes," Lindell said.

"I was wondering if you should circulate a snapshot of Rosenberg among the restaurant staff."

Lindell heard how pleased Liljendahl sounded and realized she had held back the information in order to drop it in like this as if in passing.

"Maybe," Lindell said.

She was on the verge of saying something laudatory, but refrained.

They ended the conversation and Lindell took out her pad of paper and started to draw circles and arrows.

In the large circle she wrote "Dakar" and lines extended from it in all directions with names of places and people who had figured in the investigation thus far. She stared at her attempt to create an oversight before adding "Mexico?" in the left-hand corner and drawing a line to "Armas."

Then she called Ola Haver and told him about the tattoo and the matchbox at Rosenberg's and asked him to retrieve all the files on the old drug user, as well as print out a photo.

She leaned back, slipped her shoes off, put her feet up on the desk, and whistled several bars of a song by Simon and Garfunkel off-key.

✦

Forty

Eva Willman spotted him from a distance. He was unmistakable: the broad back, the swollen neck, and the bald spot on the back of his head. Slobodan proceeded along the sidewalk like a bull, with head lowered and shoulders hunched, forcing the pedestrians he encountered to step aside.

He's going to die of a heart attack, Eva thought, and rested her feet on the pedals, slowly rolling forward, passing the restaurant owner who did not notice her, and then speeding up again. She cycled up to the Old Square at high speed, then took a rest.

The ride from Sävja had done her good. She checked her watch and saw that she had beat her personal best. Slobodan approached on the other side of the street and Eva turned to the river, leaned over the railing, and stared down into the water where she could see the outline of a bicycle among the stones at the bottom.

Watching the current made her dizzy and she lifted her head, looked up at the sky, and smiled to herself. Despite the problems with Patrik she felt happy. I am worth it, she thought. Just biking the eight or nine kilometers into town imbued her with a feeling of strength. She usually looked down at her thighs as she pedaled across the Ultunagärdet, registering how her muscles tensed under the fabric of her pants, count to twenty pushes on the pedals before she looked up.

Sometimes she closed her eyes for a few moments, allowed the wind to caress her face, and listen to the high-pitched whine of the tires on the asphalt.

She had discovered that it was the same people who biked to the city every day. She had already started to nod in recognition to some. An older man in a helmet and bicycle bags had even shouted something to her when they met at Little Ultuna. She did not hear what he said but noted his friendly gaze.

The restaurant owner was past her now, continuing along the sidewalk, past the bathhouse and the old library. She wondered where he was headed. Despite his large frame he managed to maintain a fast pace.

Eva stared after him and thought she saw him turn to the right, up Linnégatan. She was still a little afraid of him. He was nothing like anyone she had ever encountered before.

In general the people in the restaurant business were foreign to her, tougher and more outspoken than she was used to. She knew she would get used to it but missed the intimacy of her last workplace. Feo was the only one she had connected with at all. She couldn't really get a handle on Johnny, with his rapid shifts in mood and sad expression. Feo had told her that he had just ended a relationship with a woman and had more or less fled his hometown of Jönköping.

"He needs to cook," Feo had said. "He needs us, he needs a little warmth from the stove, then it will pass."

Everything passes with time, she thought, and got back on her bike. Already the minimal downward slope from the bridge to East Ågatan made her forget about Johnny's long face. She had the impulse to stick her legs out to either side as she had done as a young girl in the steep parts of the gravel roads outside Flatåsen, and coast the whole way to Dakar, even though it was five hundred meters away, and partly uphill.

A stranger was sitting in the kitchen. Eva did not like the look of him. He reminded her of a gangster she had seen in an American movie that she and Helen had rented on videocassette. He looked up and glanced at her briefly. There was nothing to focus on in his expressionless eyes.

"Hello," she said, and gave Feo a little shove.

"This is Manuel, but I call him Mano," Feo said. "*La mano,* the hand, who will help us with the dishes."

"Okay," Eva said and nodded to the newcomer.

"You'll have to speak Spanish or English. He's from Venezuela."

"Venezuela," she said.

She thought of the article about sailing in the Caribbean and took a closer look at him. He also emanated a sense of sorrow. Not an outwardly lamented sorrow but a tightly compacted, almost cramplike, grief. The clenched hands resting in his lap and the watchful eyes gave the impression of a man who, at the least sign of concern or danger, would jump up and run out of the kitchen.

Eva suddenly felt ill at ease. What was he doing at Dakar? Was he an old friend of Feo's?

"If Slobban agrees, that is," Feo added.

Donald came in from the bar at that moment, a bottle of mineral water in his hand.

"I can hire him," he said, "and that lying poodle can go fuck himself. We need more people, damn it, we're drowning."

"You have the job," Feo said in Spanish, gave a triumphant smile, winked at Eva and shrugged.

Manuel stood up.

"Where should I work?"

"There," Donald suddenly said in Spanish, and pointed. "Feo will show you how it works. Learn it now and then come back at half past six. Understand?"

Manuel nodded.

"So you speak Spanish," Feo said. "I didn't know."

"I've worked in Majorca," Donald answered.

Feo and Manuel went over to the dishwashing station. Eva looked at them. It was clear that Feo liked his role as adviser. The newcomer received the information attentively but without a word, nodding and then repeating mechanically what Feo said.

"He'll do fine," Feo said when he returned to the kitchen area.

Slobodan Andersson wiped the sweat from his forehead.

"Damn, it's hot," he breathed.

No one had seen or heard him come in. He had simply materialized in the kitchen. He had entered Dakar through the staff entrance, the same way Manuel had left the restaurant some moments earlier.

Donald informed him that he had hired a dishwasher who would be able to jump in for a couple of hours every evening.

"It won't work, otherwise. Tessie and Eva can't run around like antelopes between the dining room and the dishes and the rest of us don't have time, just so you know."

Surprisingly, his boss had no objections.

"Yes, yes, I'm sure it will be fine," he said, and fingered a stack of plates. "Have the cops been here?"

"They're clean," Donald said.

Slobodan looked up, opened his mouth to say something, but changed his mind and removed his hand from the china.

"If the cops return I want to be informed immediately," he said.

"Have you heard anything new?" Feo asked.

"They make me damn nervous, those pigs," Slobodan lashed out. "Why the hell can't they leave me in peace!"

He stalked out of the kitchen and they heard him yell at Måns in the bar, who was often the one who bore the brunt of his temper.

Everyone was surprised at Slobodan's lack of interest in the kitchen situation. Even if it had been Armas who made the final decision when it came to new hires, Slobodan had always wanted to have his say. But now it seemed that their boss did not have the curiosity or stamina to summon sufficient interest.

✦

Forty-One

Lindell had chosen a black dress and a cropped white jacket.

"Let the sleuthing begin," Görel said, when they met up on the main square.

Lindell had picked up Erik at day care and driven him directly to Görel's sister's house, where Erik was going to spend the night. Then she had driven home to change.

The rain came without warning. It poured down and splashed over the streets.

"Where did the clouds come from?" Görel said, perplexed.

Ann Lindell stared at the sky. They had taken shelter in a doorway on Svartbäcksgatan.

The shower stopped as abruptly as it had started. Uncertain as to whether they could trust in the powers above, they half-ran down the street.

As they drew closer to Dakar, and the sun peeked out from between the clouds, they slowed down and adopted a leisurely pace.

Lindell had said nothing to Görel about her reasons for the visit, but she was sure that her friend understood that there were hidden motives for Lindell's generous proposition.

"I'm paying, just so you know," Lindell repeated as they entered the restaurant.

"Sure," Görel said. "I have no problem with that."

The dining room was half full. A waitress approached them as soon as they came in and showed them to a table by the window. Lindell looked around.

"The sleuthing starts right away," Görel observed.

At the very back of the room, partly concealed by a pillar, there was a man who immediately attracted Lindell's interest. She let her gaze brush past him and then she pulled the menu that the waitress had provided toward her.

"I'm having lamb," Görel said without prompting. "I have it so rarely."

Lindell studied the menu and tried to recall where she had seen the man before. She knew that she had encountered him in the world of law enforcement but could not place the face.

"What are you going to have?"

"I don't know," Lindell said, not feeling particularly hungry. "Fish . . . maybe the Zander."

The waitress returned and took their drink orders. Lindell kept herself to light beer, while Görel asked for a glass of white wine. She immediately took a long sip.

Lindell leaned forward. The man had leaned back and was now almost completely blocked by the pillar. Suddenly she got it. He was a fellow criminal investigator from Västerås: Axel Lindman, and they had met at a function at the Police Academy some six months or so ago.

"Have you zeroed in on someone?" Görel inquired, having noted Lindell's distractedness.

"No, it's just a colleague who tried to pick me up at a workshop."

"You mean the guy in the dark blue suit and yellow tie, the one drinking red wine?" Görel asked.

Lindell gave Görel a quizzical look.

"He looks nice enough. He came on to you? And you froze up like an ice queen, of course. Is he married?" Görel watched the man discreetly, as she sipped a little more wine.

"I don't think so."

"Then there's nothing to hold you back, is there?"

"He's not my type." Lindell did not like the turn their conversation had taken.

"Cheers," she said and raised her glass.

Görel drank more wine, found that she had finished her glass, but continued unabashedly.

"And what exactly is your type? Don't say Edvard, because I'll throw up. Can't you stop thinking about that country bumpkin once and for all?"

She had raised her voice and the couple at the next table looked up with interest.

"He's lumbering around on Gräsö Island with a ninety-year-old crone," Görel said, raising her glass as a signal to their waitress to bring another before she went on. "He is and always will be a boring old fart. It was amusing and charming several years ago, but you are living here and now. There are loads of great men, including that cutie over there for starters, but you're clinging to the memory of a socially handicapped bumpkin. It's pathetic!"

Lindell's first reaction was one of anger, but then she felt something more akin to embarrassment, which she tried to conceal when she saw her friend's look of satisfaction. Her intended protest sputtered out as the waitress returned at that moment and placed a new glass of wine in front of Görel.

"I'll have one as well," Lindell said.

"Aren't I right?" Görel picked up again after the waitress had gone. "It's sick that you still feel guilty that you had Erik. If I'm going to be completely honest, I felt sorry for you at first, but now I don't know. You are good-looking and personable—no, don't start contradicting me—you have a job, a completely wonderful son, and you must be in good shape financially because you never splurge on anything. What are you waiting for? For Edvard to come riding in on his white steed? He never will."

"He wanted to take me to Thailand a couple of years ago," Lindell said.

"But then he picked someone else, didn't he?"

Lindell received her wine. The evening was not progressing as she had planned. She was at Dakar in order to establish a better sense of the restaurant and thereby of Slobodan Andersson, but now she was sitting here holding back the tears.

"It's easy for you to talk," she said. "You have everything you want. You've never been a single mom."

"Erik is no barrier to meeting someone, when are you going to get that through your head? Hundreds of thousands of people are single parents and they meet new partners."

Lindell looked around the room. More and more guests arrived and the bar area was crowded. She studied the backs of the men by the counter. They were standing there like a herd of animals at the watering hole, shoulder to shoulder, talking, laughing, and drinking.

"I got together with Charles," she said.

"And left, after a while," Görel said.

She's going to have to control her drinking, Lindell thought. She decided to try to steer the conversation to something else. If Görel were provoked, she would become increasingly aggressive, and Lindell could only guess at what kind of truths would start flying out of Görel's mouth if she really got going. Lindell knew she meant well and that there was a great deal of truth to what she said, but at the same time she felt unjustly attacked.

"I'm here for professional reasons," Lindell said quietly.

"Don't you think I realize that?"

At that moment the restaurant owner stepped into the establishment. He walked with rapid steps to the bar, taking advantage of a temporary opening in the herd in front of the bar, and sat down. The short, stocky legs dangled from the bar stool. The bartender immediately placed a beer in front of him.

He sat with his back to Lindell and Görel. The latter gently turned her body and glanced toward the bar.

"Is that him?"

Lindell nodded and watched as Slobodan Andersson let his gaze wander around the room. Suddenly his gaze fixed on a booth near the Västerås detective's table. There were two men sitting there. One was Konrad Rosenberg, whose snapshot she carried in her purse and had briefly sighted in a questioning room several years ago. The other man was unknown, and sat with his back partly toward her. She estimated his age at around fifty. He had dark hair and was well dressed, especially in comparison to his dinner companion.

The men were intent in conversation and Lindell did not think they had noticed Slobodan, who quickly slid off his bar stool and left the room. His beer was left on the bar.

Lindell's gaze followed him as he left. Görel sat with the glass of wine in her hand, watching the events.

"He left," she commented unnecessarily. "Should we follow him?"

Lindell chuckled and shook her head. She wondered who Konrad Rosenberg's companion was. Apparently they had a great deal to discuss.

"I have to go to the ladies' room," she said and stood up.

In order to get there she had to pass the booth with Rosenberg and the unknown, as well as her colleague's table. She noticed his quick glance as she approached and how he subsequently stared down at the table. When she was a couple of meters away, he looked up and raised his hand as if he was engaged in a discussion.

"No, no, I don't know her," he said in a loud voice, and looked at Lindell for a second with complete indifference and emphatically shook his head, before he looked back at his dinner companion, a woman of around thirty-five.

Lindell swept past the table and into the bathrooms, convinced that her colleague had not wanted her to make herself known. Her immediate reaction was one of surprise, before she pieced it together. She felt certain that Axel Lindman had recognized her but had not wanted to establish any contact. There could only be one reason: he was on a case. Because surely it couldn't be the case that her colleague was afraid that she would embarrass him in front of his lady friend? No, Lindell decided that Axel Lindman must be undercover.

Was it Rosenberg who was the object of interest? Or the dark-haired man? Or perhaps someone completely different? Slobodan? For a second, she considered getting in touch with the crimes call center, having them call Västerås and see why Lindman was in Uppsala, but then she quickly realized that this information could not be produced by a simple phone call.

On her way back from the ladies' room she ignored him and instead focused on Rosenberg's partner, whom she could now see from the front. He was leaning forward and saying something to Rosenberg, and Lindell picked up a streak of irritation beneath his well-polished exterior. Her intuition told her that the unknown man was very agitated and exerting a great deal of control in order not to show it.

For a while they ate in silence. The fish fillet was done to a turn, the slightly sweet pepper sauce and the carefully sauteed rice, which Lindell at first thought was a fish stick, complemented the fish perfectly. There was much one could say about Slobodan Andersson, but the food at his restaurant was first class.

She drank a dry white wine from the Loire with her fish. It had been recommended by the waitress, and she could easily have ordered another glass if it hadn't been for the difficulties that would create for her in maintaining her concentration.

She was having trouble focusing on Görel's chatter, which jumped from her work to world politics with increasingly abrupt transitions.

Rosenberg and the unknown man continued their intense discussion. Axel Lindman and his companion had proceded to coffee. Lindell imagined that underneath his relaxed look, her colleague was attentive to every word and slightest shift in atmosphere at the neighboring table, and she thought she could percieve the network of tension that stretched out into the dining room where three of the tables had become invisibly connected.

Slobodan's hasty retreat was clearly connected to the presence of the two men. How should this be interpreted? Lindell believed he had not wanted to be seen by them. She pondered his motives, but there were too many unknown factors for her to understand why. Perhaps Axel Lindman was sitting on the answer.

"Let's get the check," she said and Görel looked astonished.

"Aren't we ordering dessert?"

"I'm too full," said Lindell, "and also too tired."

"Are you in a bad mood?"

"No, of course not."

She didn't understand why she felt such reluctance to tell Görel that she wanted to leave Dakar shortly after Lindman and if possible find a way to talk to him. Curiosity at what he was doing in Uppsala and Dakar distracted her from listening to Görel.

She waved the waitress over, ordered two espressos, and asked for the check at the same time. She felt mean and unfair as she did so, knowing she had to ask Görel to drive home alone while she established contact with Lindman. Their conversation could wait until the following day, but she had the feeling that something was going on. She wanted to get answers to her questions this evening.

"I'm sorry if I've hurt your feelings," Görel said. "I know I talk too much."

"Don't worry," Lindell said, but knew it wasn't true. She had been wounded by Görel's presumptuous comments. Of course she should meet a man. Many evenings when she sat alone, she longed for the man of her life to walk in and settle in beside her on the couch. But who was Görel to come with her meddling opinions? She herself lived with her great love, and she should know better. You only met a man like Edvard once in your life. That he was a "socially handicapped bumpkin" didn't matter. What did Görel, or anyone else, know about what he had meant to her? She could still almost recall the physical sensation of his hands on her body. He is a good man, she thought, and was suddenly very sad, a sorrow that quickly turned to anger when Görel made an attempt to pick up the check. Lindell grabbed it and took out her card.

"I'm paying," she said curtly, and avoided her friend's gaze.

They left Dakar in silence. It was only a little after nine. Lindman and his companion had left half a minute before. He had passed Lindell's table without glancing at her.

Lindell saw them strolling up the street toward the main square. She was struck with doubts about her hasty exit. Would it have been better to linger at the restaurant and concentrate on Rosenberg? Then she would also not have had to rid herself of Görel in the rude way she was now forced to act.

"I think it's best that we go our own way from here. I'm going to catch up with my colleague," she said, and pointed at the man, "and it will just lead to talking a lot of shop and there's no point . . ."

Görel didn't listen any further. She twirled around on the spot and left Lindell.

Axel Lindman was looking at Lindell with amusement. His companion, who had simply introduced herself as Elin, was noticeably less amused at having to accept this third wheel. Maybe she had been nursing other ideas about the continuation of the evening that did not include sitting in a burger joint with a juice box in front of her.

"You seem like you're on the go," Lindman said. "What were you doing at Dakar?"

Lindell looked around. There were almost no other people sitting in the section where they were.

"I was scouting it out," Lindell said. "The owner's business partner was murdered recently. How about yourself?"

"We're on an assignment from our Stockholm colleagues," said Elin from Västerås, and made it sound as if they had been sent from the Vatican.

"It concerns a man called Lorenzo Wader," Lindman said. "Does the name sound familiar?"

"Was he the one who was sitting opposite Konrad Rosenberg?"

"We don't know Rosenberg," Elin said.

"Then we complement each other," Lindell joked, as Elin deliberately and with feigned lack of interest picked apart the straw.

Axel Lindman told her that Lorenzo Wader figured in an extensive investigation that spanned the jurisdiction of several authorities from Stockholm to Västmanland. Money laundering, art theft, fencing, and many other activities. The Stockholm crime unit had had their eye on Wader for the past six months and it was likely that he would recognize the Stockholmers. That's why they had turned to Västerås.

Why not Uppsala? Lindell wondered, but thought of the answer almost immediately.

"He's been staying at the Hotel Linné for the past four weeks," Lindman continued. "Calls himself a businessman and lives fairly luxuriously. He seems—"

"Who is Konrad Rosenberg?" Elin interrupted.

"Excuse me, I didn't catch your last name," Lindell said.

"Bröndeman," she said, and Lindell thought she caught a twitch of Lindman's lips.

Lindell told them about Rosenberg. The Västerås duo listened without interrupting.

"Cocaine," Lindman said when she finished. "Our Lorenzo is a man of many talents."

"We only have a suspicion of crime when it comes to Rosenberg and even less when it comes to Wader," Lindell said, "but it certainly looks interesting."

She wished that Lindman would elaborate on the background but sensed resistence from Elin Bröndeman.

"Who's in charge of the investigation in Stockholm?" Lindell asked, in the hopes that it was someone she knew.

"Eyvind Svensson," Lindman said with a laugh.

He looked around the establishment and then fixed his gaze on Lindell, as if he wanted to bring the discussion of their Uppsala assignment to an end.

"Apart from this, how is everything?"

Axel Lindman had a roguish glint in his eye as if he had resumed the innocent flirtation from the police workshop.

"Everything is fine," Lindell said absently, suddenly thinking of Görel, how she had left without a word.

Then Görel's words about Edvard came back. "A socially handicapped bumpkin" and a "boring old fart" was what she had called him. What right did she have to speak about him that way? It was as if her assessments washed over onto Ann herself. The criticism had hit her harder than she wanted to admit, or that she had shown. Of course she had described Edvard in similar terms, but he was so much more. What did Görel know about that? Nothing!

She got up from the table, thanked them politely, and left her bewildered colleagues sitting at the table. All that remained was a box of orange juice.

✦

Forty-Two

The waitress gave him a coffee refill. Lorenzo Wader smiled at her and praised the food, while he scrutinized the man on the other side of the table. Rosenberg was aware that he was being evaluated and felt as if he were on the edge of a cliff.

"Yes, it was very good," Rosenberg told the waitress, as if he wanted to avoid Lorenzo's gaze. "Are you new here?"

"I started a week ago. I'm still getting used to it."

"You are doing a fine job," Lorenzo extolled. "Slobodan has a real ability to find good staff," he went on generously.

As she left the table he nodded and repeated how delicious the dinner had been. Rosenberg could not figure him out. One second he looked dangerously ferocious, only to be smiling the next.

"What I don't understand," Lorenzo said, "is how Armas could deliver the goods in such a secure fashion. I have trouble imagining him running around town and handing it out himself."

Against his better judgment, Rosenberg had let slip that Armas dealt with the cocaine, perhaps through a muted need to be of service, to shine as brightly as Lorenzo, who already appeared to know how everything hung together.

"Some people are prepared to do whatever it takes to make a buck," Rosenberg said.

"Are you?"

The question came quickly and demanded an equally rapid answer.

"It depends," Rosenberg said, and heard as he said it what a lame answer it was. "If the risks are small and the rewards are good enough," he added.

"There is always the danger that one ends up with a knife in one's back," Lorenzo said and sipped the coffee.

Konrad took an overly large gulp of his drink, and started to cough.

"Give me some names," Lorenzo said, unaffected by the coughing fit, and put up a hand when Rosenberg made an attempt to protest. "I know that you have been in the industry and I don't care about that, but if we are going to be friends then you have to help me."

Rosenberg cursed his decision to accept Lorenzo's invitation to dinner, and that he had chosen Dakar as their meeting place did not make things better. Not to be friends with Lorenzo would mean trouble, he realized, and the alternatingly jovial and satanic Stockholmer was a considerably greater threat than Slobodan. Was it Lorenzo who had had Armas killed? This thought struck him with full force as he stared at Lorenzo's slender hands and ring-laden fingers.

"There is a guy," he said finally. "Still wet behind the ears, but very eager. He wants to make money to save his father, he says."

"Is he in jail?"

"In Turkey or something," Rosenberg said, feeling relieved that he could talk about someone other than himself. "He sells to friends and is very diligent."

"Does he use it himself?"

Rosenberg shook his head.

"What is his name?"

"He is called Zero."

Lorenzo smiled.

"Now we are starting to get somewhere," he said and waved the waitress over. "I think we will have cognac."

✦

Forty-Three

The lid of the dishwasher started to vibrate. Manuel leaned back, regarded the shiny machine, and heard the water rush into it. After the first hour's initial confusion at everything new, he worked with increasing satisfaction and pleasure. The heat in the dishwashing station did not bother him, quite the opposite. Nor all the dishes that were brought over to him. The towers of plates and all the glasses took his thoughts away from drugs and Patricio and Armas.

In addition, he liked the other staff members. Above all, the Portuguese cook, but also Eva, the waitress, who was also the one he had the most contact with. She knew no Spanish but could make herself understood in broken English.

Manuel had been told that she was also new at Dakar. She had a way of looking at him that made him bewildered. She looked him straight in the eye, with curiosity and a smile on her lips. She asked about Venezuela, what the country looked like, the clothes, climate, and how the food tasted. She wanted to know everything, the questions seemed never to end and she showed such interest that he could not ignore her.

For a moment, he was tempted to tell her the truth, that he was a Mexican. He did not really want to lie to her, the first person in Sweden who he had real contact with and who showed this bold interest. Instead, in order to speak truthfully, he created the country anew, added his experiences from the mountains to the north of Oaxaca and applied them to Venezuela. He described the peasant farmers' lives and found that Eva liked it, those slight details about how the coffee was dried on the roof and who fired up the stove in the mornings.

Manuel had felt no guilt in this, for he believed that the people in Venezuela and Mexico lived basically under the same conditions. He realized that the driving force behind the waitress's inquiries was a longing for something else, and in this intense conversation they could join in mutual enthusiasm for a land that in reality was two. Eva made him speak and experience longing, and he looked forward to their brief meetings when she came flying in with more dishes.

Once he had looked out into the restaurant and received a shock. The fat one was sitting at the bar with a beer. He had his attention directed at the bartender and did not notice Manuel, who quickly ducked back inside.

Once he was back at the dishwashing station the old hate, which that had temporarily fallen away in his conversation with Eva, rose up. When Feo came over to see how things were going, Manuel asked what the fat one's name was and how often he usually came to Dakar.

"You don't have to be afraid," Feo said, "we have talked to him and he knows that you have been hired."

"Is he nice?"

Feo laughed heartily.

"You don't need to be afraid," he repeated.

Manuel was not afraid but he was unsure of what he should do. He had looked for a job at Dakar on impulse. He had come here in order to see what the place looked like and perhaps catch sight of the fat one. Now he found himself in the lion's den.

There was an advantage in working at a restaurant: he could eat his fill. During his first days in Sweden he had not indulged in more than bread and canned corn and it was only now, in the presence of so much food, that he realized how hungry he had been.

He spent the remainder of the evening trying to figure out what he should do. One way out would be to destroy the drugs that he had stolen from the house, say good-bye to Patricio, and fly back home. That was the easiest solution, but he knew he would never attain any peace if he went back with his tail between his legs. The thought of his brother behind bars, while those who had masterminded the drug smuggling would still be free, was unbearable. He wanted to make things easier for Patricio, that was his duty as an older brother. But how should he proceed? To extract ten thousand dollars from Slobodan Andersson in exchange for his silence was perhaps not an impossibility, but it felt inadequate. Manuel did not want to see Slobodan Andersson dead, it was more than enough to have Armas's blood on his hands. But he wanted to punish him in some way.

He dreamed every night about how he dragged the dead man to the water, how the shirt tore and revealed the tattoo. That had been the worst part, removing Quetzalcóatl from the gringo's upper arm. A white man could not be allowed to bear such a symbol. That was how he had felt at the time, in his bitterness and confusion. But he regretted it now. What right had he had to mutilate a dead man?

He picked up cutlery, plates, and glasses, rinsed and cleaned with something approaching work satisfaction. He did not do it to win approval. It was the warmth and the movements in themselves that motivated him and lifted his mood. Something that Feo also contributed to when he came out to him. They exchanged a few words and joked a little.

He listened to the talk between the coworkers without understanding a word, and saw how Tessie, the gringa, and the new waitress submitted orders. There were clattering noises from the kitchen, warm steam rose from the pots and pans, and the clouds that wafted into the wash station brought with it the smell of fish, garlic, and other things that made his mouth water. Particularly enticing was the sound of meat hitting the pan. For a few moments Manuel forgot why he was in Sweden and he even hummed a song he had heard Lila Downs sing in the square in Oaxaca.

At eleven o'clock the steady stream of dishes and silverware started to wane and he was able to relax somewhat. Eva and Tessie served the last of their desserts and the cooks started putting things away and cleaning up. Feo called out to him and asked if he was tired, but Manuel felt as if he could have worked all night.

Eva came out with a tray of glasses. She looked at him as if she was wondering if he could take more questions about his homeland. That was at least how he interpreted her appraising glance and hesitant smile, and when he nodded kindly to her she went and stood next to him and helped to load the dishwasher.

"Do you come from a small village?" she started, and Manuel nodded.

"How could you afford to come here?"

"I saved," Manuel answered, suddenly on his guard.

"I'm also saving," Eva said, "but I never get anywhere. There is never enough money. I dream of traveling but I have never left Sweden. Well, once my grandfather and I walked into Norway."

"Norway is another country?"

"Yes, it borders on Sweden."

"Were you looking for work?"

"No," Eva laughed, "we were picking berries and grandfather got it into his head that we should visit Norway. I remember how tired I became."

"Were there no police there? At the border, I mean."

"Police?"

"You can't simply walk into another country?"

"Yes, you can. The border between Sweden and Norway is almost completely open," Eva explained. "You can come and go as you like."

She told him about the close contact people on either side of the border had always had. She told him her grandfather's more or less accurate stories about heroic deeds during the Second World War, how Norwegian resistance fighters had been smuggled over the border in each direction. Manuel listened, fascinated.

"Everyone helped out. Almost everyone voted for the communists and hated the Nazis, so it wasn't hard to find volunteers."

Eva smiled to herself.

"Do you miss it?" Manuel asked.

"Yes, sometimes. But it's a two-sided thing, as it was for my grandfather, sort of. When he was home in the district of Värmland he was a completely different person. He was happy, talkative, and laughed a lot.

It even happened that he mixed in Finnish words. In Uppsala he was always grumpy."

"He also missed the place," Manuel stated.

She smiled and Manuel recognized it as a smile that concealed something else.

"Maybe I should visit you," Eva went on suddenly. "I mean, your family, not that I want to stay for free but it is always good to know someone . . ."

She stopped and Manuel saw a blush spread across her cheeks. He placed several plates in the dishwasher and saw out of the corner of his eye how she closed her eyes and brushed her forehead with the back of her hand.

"Are you tired?"

"Yes, it is starting to get late," she said.

"It would be nice to have a visitor," Manuel said.

He could be generous, he thought, especially as he sensed that such a visit would never take place. But then it struck him that he was very far from his homeland. Why wouldn't Eva also be able to cross the Atlantic.

He halted his movements, inadvertently shifting a tray of glasses in toward the wall and studied her more closely. At first she did not notice that he was looking at her, but when she was done putting glasses into the dishwasher and had closed the door she saw that he had stopped working.

"What is it?"

"Nothing," Manuel said, but he did not take his eyes off her face even though he realized that she thought this close scrutiny was, if not disconcerting, then at least somewhat unorthodox.

"It would be good if you came to my country. The tourists who come to Mexico are different from you. They walk across the plazas, into the churches, and sit in the outdoor cafes without really seeing us. If you only knew how we felt—"

"Mexico? You said Venezuela."

"I was lying," Manuel said and only now did he avert his gaze. "Don't ask me why and don't tell anyone."

"No, why should I," Eva said simply, "and I'm just as happy to go to Mexico."

He joined in her laughter and thought that it was the first time he laughed in Sweden. Manuel felt how his joy, bolstered by Feo's humming from the kitchen and the warmth of the dishwasher filled him and gave him several seconds of optimism. It was as if the release from his lie reconciled him to the events of the past few days. It did not even occurr to him that Eva could betray him, and it was perhaps this trust in another human being that allowed him to simply exist and speak freely for a moment, as he was when he was home with his own kind.

He began talking about California, about the work of harvesting, about the barracks that he and his brothers had lived in, about the sun that at first made them sweaty and tired, then agitated and bad-tempered. He told her about the water faucet in the yard that some days only yielded a few drops, while the crops were irrigated with large water canons that wandered the fields like primeval animals.

He took Eva to Orange County, because he could tell that she enjoyed the details. She also followed the trio of brothers back to Oaxaca. He described the village as if it were a paradise, he found himself beautifying it and corrected himself by describing the poverty, the bad roads, and how divided the villagers were.

Eva sat on a stool with her hands clasped in her lap and listened.

Occasionally she asked a couple of questions, otherwise she sat quietly for long periods of time and watched him. A quarter of an hour went by. When the roar of the dishwasher came to an end and was supplanted with a ticking sound, Manuel also grew silent.

"It is my country," he concluded his tale, and felt as if it had been accurate, but also knew how much had been left out. He felt uplifted and appreciated the fact that she had listened with genuine interest. Even so, the emptiness and upheaval that he had felt ever since he heard of Angel's death in Germany and the imprisonment of Patricio returned at the same moment that Eva stood up and said she should get back to work.

She left the kitchen and Manuel watched as the door to the dining room swung back and forth until it reached a point where it was definitively closed.

The next moment, Slobodan Andersson stepped into the room.

✦

Forty-Four

"Who are you?"

Slobodan Andersson stared at Manuel, who unconsciously raised the blue dish rack that he was holding in his hands.

It was as if the proprietor was unable to take his eyes off the new hand in the dishwashing area. Manuel was forced to look down, he turned and pushed the tray on the shelf above the counter.

"Where do you come from?"

Manuel looked quizzically at the fat man, who then repeated the question in English.

"America," Manuel answered, and at the same time felt an unexpected euphoria. Perhaps it was the evening's conversation with Eva, or the fact that Slobodan Andersson was drunk that raised his spirits, after the initial shock and terror at encountering the fat one so unexpectedly had subsided.

Slobodan Andersson sat down on the stool by the door to the dining room. His upper body swayed and an almost desperate level of exhaustion was visible in his face.

"America is a big country," he slurred. "There are . . . I have been to Las Vegas, what a fucking city."

Manuel observed him and was treated to a lengthy account of Slobodan's experiences in the United States before he abruptly stopped, raised his heavy head, and looked at Manuel.

"I don't trust anyone," he said with vehemence. "All they want to do is put one over on you. You're lucky you only have to worry about the dishes."

Manuel smiled and started putting wineglasses in a rack, happy to have something to do with his hands.

"I have a friend who was murdered, you have probably heard about it. We had known each other for twenty years, at least . . . twenty long, fucking years . . . and then the bastard goes and gets himself murdered. Is that right? We were like brothers. . . . Do you have a brother?"

Manuel nodded.

"Then you know. A brother is everything. Brothers don't let each other down."

"He let you down?"

Slobodan Andersson trained his glassy eyes on Manuel and for several seconds the latter forgot himself, felt sorry for the man before him. In his pitiable eyes he could read the man's great sorrow and all the human misery he knew so well.

He picked up a knife from the container of silverware. A piece of meat still clung to it. He would be able to drive this knife into that fat body and then leave Dakar. Then all accounts would be paid and settled.

"I don't know," Slobodan said, his gaze on the knife.

Manuel tossed the knife back in the basket, turned his back on Slobodan, and opened the dishwasher, which disgorged a cloud of steam.

"The uncertainty is the worst thing," he said and lifted out a tray of glasses.

"I started with nothing," Slobodan resumed and held up his palms as if to illustrate his starting point. "Just like you. I slaved like an animal, so afraid I almost wet myself. I have struggled, built something, and I don't want some bastard to come and take everything. Do you know what I mean? There has to be some justice. I have received nothing for free! Work, work, work, all day long, all year. And what is the thanks? The authorities chase you, they want taxes to fatten themselves up, so they can sit on their big behinds and pick their nails. It has to be clean as a laboratory, otherwise they close you down. The union hounds you, as if you were made of money. And regulations for everything, damn it! I sure as hell didn't get overtime or vacation compensation. I was happy I had a job."

Slobodan steadied himself by putting his arm on the counter and rising to his feet before he went on.

"I'm creating jobs, damn it! Do you know how many people I have trained, given a life? Yes, that's how it is, I've provided them with a life, all the people who don't have the balls to fix something for themselves."

He slapped the counter with his hand as if to underscore his words.

"I make people happy. They come here to eat and drink and forget for a moment that we live in a society of thieves. I am a generous person, but now there is no place for this. Everyone wants a piece, without making an effort."

He fell silent as suddenly as he had started his outburst and sank down on the stool. He studied his hands, the cuticles and knuckles.

"Ungrateful," he whispered in Swedish.

Manuel was not sure if he should take this opportunity to reveal his identity and the fact that he was here to claim Patricio's money, but he decided to wait. A new idea had formed in his mind, one that had the potential to yield considerably more.

He did not want to kill Slobodan, only take his money and then crush him. The pathetic man on the stool could very well be allowed to suffer in torment several more days.

"I am done now," Manuel said and pushed in the final tray.

He wanted to speak to Feo before he left Dakar. He longed for the peace and quiet of his tent, but perhaps there was something else he should do before he left. He peered out into the bar. Feo sat at the counter, leaning over a beer. Måns said something that made Feo smile and look around the dining room.

Manuel felt a pang of envy at the Portuguese. His smile was genuine. His tender talk of his wife and child was without artifice. He was happy in his work, prepared his food in laughter and with an economy of movement as if he were allied with fortune.

Slobodan coughed behind his back and Manuel turned around. The fat one was staring into space. His head drooped and there was a glint of saliva at the corner of his mouth.

Manuel again felt a kind of sympathy for the man and for a moment, forgetful of the context, he had the impulse to help Slobodan Andersson to his feet, to console him and see to it that he made it home.

Then the door to the dining room was thrown open and Tessie entered, glancing at Slobodan who had slumped on the stool. She laughed.

"Are you the babysitter?" she asked with an American accent that took Manuel back to California.

"Wake up," she said and shook Slobodan's shoulder, without taking any further notice of the dishwasher. "It is time to go home. I'm calling a cab."

The proprietor shook his head.

"I can't . . ."

"Of course you can," Tessie said, and Manuel understood, even though she was speaking Swedish.

"There's someone out there," Slobodan slurred.

"What are you talking about? Are you supposed to meet someone?"

Slobodan tried to stand up but fell back onto the stool. Tessie sighed.

"Damn, I'm tired," she muttered in English. "It's bad enough that I have to wait on the customers, let alone play mom to this lump."

"He thinks you should be grateful that you have a job," Manuel said.

Tessie stared at him.

"Grateful! I should be grateful? Are you on drugs?"

She flounced out of the kitchen, exasperated and disgusted. Slobodan looked up.

"They're out to get me," he groaned, before the heavy body jerked and the vomit projected straight out from his mouth. He stared at the floor in astonishment, with the slack jaw of a drunkard.

Manuel walked out into the bar and gave Feo a sign that he should come out into the kitchen. The Portuguese smiled at him, slid off the bar stool, and rounded the counter.

"What is it?"

"It's the fat one."

The stench was indescribable. Slobodan had fallen asleep with his head against the wall. They cleaned it up together. Feo sprayed water onto the floor while Manuel mopped it up with rags.

"I have never seen him so drunk," Feo said, and for once he looked worried.

"He talked about someone being after him," Manuel said.

"I have heard him talk about that," Feo said, turning the water off and looking at the sleeping man. "He thinks the person who killed Armas is after him."

"Who would want to kill both of them?"

Manuel's tension was like a cramp in his stomach.

"Armas should have been here," Feo said, as if he hadn't heard the question. "He would have picked him up by his arms and carried him home. Can you help me? He can't stay here."

One hour later they had lugged Slobodan into his apartment. The first cab had refused to take them, and they had to call for a bigger cab that was able to fit Slobodan in the luggage area.

Manuel and Feo then dragged the half unconscious proprietor up to his apartment and onto his bed.

They stood for a while and watched the shapeless body that flinched from time to time as if from a cramp. His breathing was heavy and wheezy and Slobodan muttered something in his sleep.

"Can you stay with him for a while?" Feo asked.

Manuel nodded and looked around the bedroom.

After Feo had left, Manuel walked from room to room in amazement. It was the largest residence he had ever set foot in. Five rooms and a kitchen for one person. Everything was so light. The furniture, textiles, wallpaper, and polished wood floors virtually lit up the dark August night.

"Maria," he mumbled, pulling his hand across the beautiful surface of the dining room table.

He took out a can of beer from the refrigerator, but only had one sip before he set it down. He opened cupboard after cupboard and viewed the multitude of glass and china. Who can afford this, he thought. And who can use it all? In the drawers, there were knives and gleaming utensils that had, for him, an unknown purpose. He picked up a knife whose extremely slender blade appeared to exclude it from all normal use, and weighed it in his hand but then tossed it back and closed the drawer with a bang.

He returned to the bedroom. One of Slobodan's hands hung over the edge of the bed and Manuel picked it up and laid it across his stomach. Slobodan muttered something in his sleep.

The feeling of being an intruder grew stronger. What was he doing in the apartment? He looked at the man who now appeared to have settled in and was snoring heavily.

A freight train went by outside the window and Manuel walked over to the window. The coupled sections jerked and squeaked, and the mild thumping of the wheels against the track was soothing. He counted the cars, container after container, tank after tank; it seemed they were never going to end.

Once he had read a book about a man who was traveling through the United States on a freight train. Occasionally he worked temporarily on a farm or at a gas station, but mostly he wandered restlessly from state to state, looking for a woman he had once known and loved. Manuel did not remembered how the book ended—if the man reached his goal—but something of the anxiety and feeling of being an outsider that had plagued the rambler now gripped Manuel.

The clanging signals stopped, the bars at the nearby crossing were slowly raised, and Manuel stared at the disappearing lights of the last car until they were completely gone.

Slobodan suddenly snuffled. His heavyset body twisted as if in pain and he let out a sob. A rivulet of vomit ran down his cheek. Slobodan pulled his hand across his mouth in his sleep and muttered something.

It occurred to Manuel how easy it would be for him to end Slobodan's life. The feeling had been in the back of his head ever since Feo had left him alone with the fat one. How easy it would be. Armas and Slobodan gone, their debts paid. But to what purpose? Would Angel come back to life or Patricio get out of prison because Slobodan died?

He turned his head and looked at the man in the bed. The fat one had appeared like a *bhni guí'a,* a man from the mountain, filled with promises and green bills, thundering and powerful. Now he lay there like a helpless colossus. Manuel would easily be able to suffocate him with a pillow and then disappear for good. No one would suspect foul play, everyone would believe that Slobodan had suffered a drunkard's violent but natural death.

He recalled the story of Ehud. When Manuel and his brothers were small, their father would read aloud from the Bible in the evenings. He had reached all the way to the book of Daniel until his worsening sight put an end to all reading.

It was perhaps the fact that Ehud, like Manuel, was left-handed that had fixed the story in his mind. Edud murdered a king in secret. Manuel tried in vain to think of the king's name. The king, who came from the land of Moab, was enormously fat. Ehud had been assigned the task of murdering the king and had thrust his sword into him. The sword sank to its hilt in the voluminous belly. Ehud fled, and managed to escape. The people rose up and freed themselves from their oppressors.

Am I Ehud, he asked himself. Is it right to kill another person?

Manuel weighed Slobodan's life. Carried on a silent dialogue with death or, rather, himself, the man he could be, the man he was in actuality. This was how he experienced those hours in Slobodan Andersson's darkened apartment. It was as if he were reasoning with an inner being who spoke to him, advised and admonished him, sometimes querulously and somewhat snobbishly. But mostly reasonably and calmly, soothingly, like a good friend, the only true friend who loyally accompanied him through life.

When this voice fell silent, so too did Manuel, and therefore he pursued the dialogue, even though it became increasingly disjointed due to his exhaustion and his longing for a life far from poverty and death.

He sat down in an armchair, stared into the darkness, and allowed his thoughts to wander freely. He may have fallen asleep, dreamed about the village and his mother, Maria, his friends and the scent of rain. Slobodan snuffled occasionally, flailed his limbs, and shouted something with such desperation in his voice that for a moment he appeared quite human.

He was like a shapeless mound of flesh and bones as he lay there, a shadow figure who dominated the room with his snoring and other sounds. There was a stench of sweat and vomit, but that did not bother Manuel. What he did find distracting, however, were the human sounds. Perhaps there were memories from another time stored in his unconscious that made him reflective and filled with melancholy? Was it memories of his father, as he turned in his sleep and muttered something inaudible? Perhaps it was memories from the barracks at McArthur's farm in Idaho where he had worked one summer erecting fences and clearing fields? There, seven men were crowded into a few square meters. The odors emanating from their bodies and the pressing restlessness as they slept in heat and congestion forced Manuel to leave the barrack and sleep on the veranda, where he was safe from the rain but not the mosquitoes that flew in from the marshlands to the south. Even out there he could hear the sounds of the men who he both hated and loved as he lay close to the stars, with the bloodsucking fiends buzzing around his head.

He is a person, Manuel thought, and felt acute consternation. He would have preferred not to admit there was any human aspects in Slobodan Andersson, the man of the mountain who sold and bought souls. A man whose only goal was to enrich himself, cost what it may. It had cost Angel his life and Patricio his freedom.

But if? Then Manuel was back at the beginning: his brothers' own responsibility.

"If," he said aloud.

If. If they had not followed the enticements of a *bhni guí'a*? If they had been men, if they had been true Mexicans?

He stood up and walked over to the bed, leaned over the sleeper.

"Are you a human being?"

The pale cheeks in the fleshy face trembled as Slobodan turned over. His eyelids twitched and he whimpered like a dog.

Exhaustion drove Manuel back to the armchair. It was starting to get light outside and the shadows of the room went from black to gray. Manuel closed his eyes and immediately fell asleep.

He dreamed he was a happy man. The woman he loved, and to whom he had promised to return as soon as he could, was walking by his side. Sometimes the image changed and they were lying together somewhere outside, but not so far that they could not hear the barking dogs and the occasional shout of a villager. Manuel felt an unprecedented sense of strength, it was as if his physical powers had been amplified and he knew that they would soon meet. It filled him with a feeling of hope that he had not experienced for a long time.

He reached for Gabriella and when she crept up into his lap he woke with a start, sat up, and did not know at first where he was.

"Who the hell are you?"

Slobodan Andersson's voice had nothing of the authority or acerbity for which he was both feared and hated. In fact, he appeared frightened and confused.

Manuel, who had not understood what he had said, got up out of the chair.

"How are you feeling now?" he asked in English.

Slobodan stared at Manuel, then looked around the room before he once again stared at the Mexican without comprehension. Then he seemed to recollect something from the previous day and night.

"You are the dishwasher," he observed.

"I am the dishwasher."

"Have you made any coffee?"

Manuel shook his head.

"Then do it. I need to clear my head."

Slobodan Andersson swung his legs over the side of the bed, made a face, and rubbed his hands over his head. He muttered something and drew in the snot in his nose.

Manuel sat down again. He took hold of the idea that had been slumbering and growing unexpressed since his visit to the summer-house.

"I come bearing a message," he said.

Slobodan looked up.

"I come bearing a message from my brother."

"What the hell are you talking about. What brother?"

"Angel."

The astonishment momentarily made Slobodan look human, until he realized who Manuel was.

"You are the brother who was not so enthusiastic, is that right? The one who stayed behind? What kind of message?"

"That which Angel was not able to deliver," Manuel said and stood up again. Slobodan was five meters away.

"The German cops didn't take it?"

Manuel shook his head, not sure if Slobodan would buy the lie. He did not know what had appeared in the papers or what Slobodan knew about where the drugs had gone.

"But it will cost you," he went on.

"I have never received anything for free in my entire life," Slobodan said, and smiled.

He appeared unaffected. The hangover he most likely had felt as he woke up appeared to be gone.

"But I don't buy something that already belongs to me," he added.

"Well, then," Manuel said. "There are other buyers."

"Did you try with Armas first?"

"I don't know who that is," Manuel said and Slobodan stared at him for a long time before he spoke.

"How is Patricio? Is he well?"

"I am going to visit him tomorrow."

Manuel did not like the situation. There was a veiled threat behind Slobodan's questions, the same tactic that Armas had used to try and shake him up.

"How long have you been in Sweden?"

"Not long."

"I can reimburse you for your costs."

"Fifty thousand dollars," Manuel said and tried to keep his voice level.

Slobodan chuckled. Manuel watched him without moving a muscle, hoping the fat one would not realize how nervous he was. He had been taking a chance when he threw out that figure, but now he saw in Slobodan's reaction that fifty thousand dollars was in the ballpark.

The thought of offering Slobodan the chance to buy back his own stash of drugs had come as an inspiration, and now seemed like sheer genius. He imagined the possibilities; now his brother could get a more comfortable life in prison.

Slobodan stared thoughtfully at Manuel for a few seconds before he stood up and left the room. Manuel heard the sound of liquid pouring into the toilet bowl and how the fat one splashed water, snorted, and talked loudly to himself. Finally there was some rinsing and a short laugh.

When the restaurant owner returned he looked decidedly more alert. The thin hair had been water combed back over his head and several drops of water glittered on his cheek.

He glanced quickly at the double bed, the sheets lay wrinkled and bunched up at its foot, so he shook his head and sat down in the other armchair.

"So, let's do business," he said and smiled broadly.

Manuel longed for his tent by the river. He was tired and stiff and feared what was to come. Did he have enough power to stand up to Slobodan Andersson?

"Fifty thousand," he said and knew in the moment what he should do. Patricio would get money and Slobodan would be punished without Manuel having to exert any extra effort.

"Why should I trust you?"

"You trusted my brothers."

"How much do you have?"

Manuel measured with his hands.

"Two kilos, maybe more, I don't know."

"If it is Angel's package it is around two kilos," Slobodan said. "And you are charging fifty thousand dollars? Do you understand what that means?"

Manuel shook his head.

"It is worth perhaps a million Swedish kronor. I can make five hundred kronor per gram. So far I have paid out one hundred thousand dollars and with your fifty thousand that comes to more than one million kronor. I get the money back and that is good, but I deserve a small profit," he went on in a conciliatory tone, "I could perhaps scrape together twenty-five thousand. That is a fortune to you."

Manuel calculated feverishly in his mind but there were too many numbers.

"My family has suffered a great deal," he said.

They negotiated a little longer and finally agreed that Manuel would get forty thousand. Manuel was sweating, while Slobodan appeared to be enjoying himself. He got to his feet with some effort, walked over to Manuel, and stretched out his hands as a sign that they were in agreement. Manuel hesitated for a second before shaking the hand of the man of the mountain.

Have I sold my soul now, he asked himself.

As Manuel stepped out onto the street below Slobodan Andersson's apartment, he stumbled momentarily as if he had been struck, steadied himself by pressing his back up against the wall and brought his hands over his face. A woman who was walking by stared at his with undisguised curiosity and distaste.

"Filthy scum!" she hissed.

It was a little after nine o'clock. Manuel walked in the direction of Dakar where his car was parked, completely wrung out and empty inside.

✦

Forty-Five

Detective Inspector Erik Schönell was deathly tired of American action films. Luckily, he only needed to watch a few seconds of the start of each film, fast-forwarding to check out a couple scenes further on, before he could eject the videotape from the player. The problem was that there were one hundred and twenty-two movies in Armas's video library.

Now he was done and he had found nothing notable in the collection. There was definitely no Mexican connection, if you didn't count the murder of a Mexican family that occurred in one of the films.

The porn flick that had been found on the top of Armas's television was the only jarring element. Schönell had earlier watched several minutes of it and thought it was most likely shot somewhere in the Mediterranean region, perhaps Spain. The plot was very simple: a party of four golf players with athletic builds suddenly realized they were gay and devoted several days to traditional swinging and putting, with intermittent bouts of intense copulation in the sand traps and on the fairways. The dialogue was thin and scanty. The sex scenes were mechanical and without finesse. It was, in other words, a traditional porn flick.

"A hole by any other word," Schönell, who was an avid golfer himself, muttered, and inserted the tape into the player.

He leaned back in his chair but then stood up and closed the door, adjusted the volume and sat back down again. On his initial viewing he had seen something that in a vague way awakened his interest. There was something in the film that nagged at him but he was unable to put his finger on it. Given that Lindell believed the videotapes could have an implication for the investigation—she had not elaborated on her interest in the Mexico angle—Schönell was determined to do a thorough job. No one would be able to claim that he had been sloppy. Most of all he did not want this Lindell at violent crimes to be able to find fault with him.

The movie went on. Schönell checked the time and wished he had gotten himself a cup of coffee and a sweet. When one of the golf players inserted a club handle into the backside of his opponent, Schönell sighed heavily.

The camera focused on the penetrated man. Sweat ran down his face and several fine pieces of gravel had stuck to his forehead. He rolled his eyes and pretended to be enjoying himself, though surely no one found pleasure in a five iron back there, Schönell thought. Then Schönell stiffened, fumbled for the remote control, played back the same scene and paused the picture at the moment when the man in the bunker turned his upper body and looked back at his partner.

Schönell reached for the phone and dialed Lindell's number. She promised to come by at once. Erik Schönell whistled smugly. I should have asked her to bring me a cup of coffee, he thought, and studied the picture on the screen.

There was a knock on the door several minutes later. Schönell opened and pointed at the television without a word. The satisfaction in seeing Lindell's chin fall, and her hand rise up at the frozen image was worth all the time spent watching bad movies with Bruce Willis and Sandra Bullock.

"Holy shit!" Lindell exclaimed.

"Isn't it great?" Schönell said.

"Good work."

This was exactly what Schönell wanted to hear.

"It took awhile," he said, "but I had the feeling there was something here."

Then he discarded his indifferent attitude and eagerly explained how many hours he had spent watching the videos, and how something about the porn film had nagged at him, and how he had watched it over and over again until he finally spotted the likeness.

Lindell laughed and added a comment about his doggedness to her earlier praise.

"Let's call Otto. Do you have any coffee in here?"

"I'll get it," Schönell said and rushed out into the corridor.

Schönell's office quickly became crowded. Whether it was the promise of seeing something awesome or Lindell's enthusiasm that had lured their colleagues was of no importance to Schönell, who basked in the glory. People came and went and the speculation went into overdrive.

"I bet it's a case of blackmail," Fredriksson said, and that appeared to be the theory that found the most support.

Lindell did not say much, but studied the image with extreme care, seeing in the man's eyes a desire to please but also the opposite, a kind of defiance. She estimated his age at between twenty and twenty-five. He had brown eyes and a wide forehead. But what clinched it was the small mouth and the cruel angle of the thin lips.

The man could have been Armas's twin. Lindell was willing to bet good money on his being the son of the murdered man. The question of which direction this find was going to take the investigation was already being discussed, even though his identity had not been confirmed.

"This video may have nothing at all to do with the case," Sammy Nilsson threw out.

Ottosson shook his head.

"It has a connection to Armas, and therefore to the case," he said. "It has some sort of bearing on the crime. Well done, Schönell!" he added, cast a final glance on the television screen, and left the room.

Before Lindell returned to her office, she delegated the tasks that the new find presented. She asked Schönell to arrange for copies of a number of pictures of the actor. Beatrice Andersson, who had been looking at the image with distaste for a few seconds, only to turn away, received the task of identifying the company that had produced the video and determine if they were in any way cooperative.

Bea took a look at the cover and read the information in fine print.

"It was produced in California. I'm more than happy to go there," she said.

Ann Lindell was too restless to return to what she had been doing earlier in the day, and ended up standing in front of the window trying to put together a picture of what had happened. If the man in the video really was Armas's son, then that presented a complication. But it could also further the investigation. Was this blackmail? Had someone discovered that Armas's son was a porn actor and tried to use this to press him for money? What did Slobodan know? He had claimed that Armas had no relatives. Was this a lie or did he simply not know about Armas's son?

Slow down, she thought, he hasn't been identified yet. But that was an objection with little practical value. She had made up her mind: this was Armas's son. The prints that they had secured on the videotape belonged to the blackmailer, she also decided.

She walked over to the phone, located Slobodan Andersson's number, and called him up. For the first time the restaurant owner sounded relaxed, even suggesting that he could stop by the police station if that was more convenient for Lindell.

"What is this about?"

"I have some thoughts that I wanted to test out on you," Lindell said, trying to reciprocate his friendliness, even if she sensed an element of calculation in his unusually mild tone.

They agreed that Slobodan would report to the police station reception area in one hour. During that time Lindell planned to read a report on Quetzalcóatl that Fryklund, a new recruit, had assembled.

It turned out that the report plunged her into a description of Indian mythology that she had trouble following. There were too many unpronounceable names and, in addition, the information was periodically squeezed out by her memory of the frozen image on the television screen. But she managed to pick up enough to understand that Quetzalcóatl was a powerful god in Aztec culture. The recruit had also included half a dozen different illustrations that all depicted a figure with a frightening face and feathers. Some depicted a dancing figure.

Attached was also a list of tattoo artists who had identified this god as one of their more popular designs. The first name on the list was a Sammy Ramírez from Guadalajara, Mexico, complete with address and telephone number, who used the exact design that Armas had had tattooed onto his arm.

Lindell reached for the phone in order to dial the number, when it occurred to her that there must be a significant time difference between Mexico and Sweden. What time could it be in Guadalajara? She did not know and decided to take a chance.

"Sammy," a man answered in a groggy voice, followed by something in Spanish that Lindell did not understand.

Lindell introduced herself and apologized for the fact that she was probably calling at an inappropriate hour. Sammy groaned but did not hang up, something that encouraged Lindell to continue in her labored English.

The tattoo artist listened attentively to her story, that she was calling in regards to a serious crime and that they were looking for a white man who may have once have been Sammy's client. She described Armas as best she could. While Lindell was zealously talking it struck her that this was like looking for a needle in a haystack, and she concluded her monologue with this metaphor.

"And I am the needle," Sammy Ramírez said, and Lindell heard a low, delighted chuckle. Sammy then told her that he could very well recall the tall man from Sweden. They had come into contact about two or three years ago. Armas had come to his studio and leafed through the folders with the different designs until he fell for the Quetzalcóatl. Why it had been this design Sammy could not remember, perhaps because he himself was drawn to mythological symbols and had spoken very warmly in favor of the Aztec god.

"Did he say anything about why he was in Mexico?"

"Not as far as I can remember. One reason I remember him so well is that he did not say very much."

"Was anyone with him?"

"Yes, a fat man who stank of sweat. He came several times and watched but mostly seemed irritated."

"Where is Guadalajara?"

"Western Mexico. About the same longitude as Mexico City but more west, toward the Pacific Ocean."

"What do people do there?"

Sammy Ramírez laughed.

"What do you do in Sweden?"

"What I mean is, why was he there?"

"I think he was traveling through, came from the north, perhaps from the States, on his way south. I don't know. As I said, he did not say very much."

"Was he sensitive to the pain? I imagine it must hurt."

"No, it does not hurt very much, and from what I can remember he did not complain."

"Did he say that he was Swedish?"

"I assume so, you are calling from Sweden."

"Do you have a fax machine? Could you look at a picture and tell me if it is the same man."

Ramírez gave her a fax number and they ended the call.

Ann Lindell was having heart palpitations. The last hour had brought some breakthroughs. First the video, and now this. Then the question would be how far this could take them, but she felt as if the mystery of Armas was starting to crumble, the cracks were becoming wider and more visible.

She called Fryklund and praised his thesis on the Mexican gods.

"But it was fun," he said, audibly surprised at Lindell's overwhelming praise, and she wished in silence that more of them could say the same about their work.

Then she faxed a photograph of Armas to Guadalajara. Three minutes later she received an answer from Sammy Ramírez: the man in the picture was the same person he had tattooed.

Just as Ann Lindell had started to think about food there was a call from reception, informing her she had a visitor. Lindell peeked at the time. He was punctual. It was exactly one hour since she had spoken with Slobodan Andersson.

On her way down she met the police chief and nodded slightly, but hurried into the elevator before he could come up with some cheery comment. She was not fond of him, and even less so since rumors had started that Liselotte Rask in the public relations department was going to be taking on very different work in the building.

Sammy Nilsson had jokingly claimed that Rask was going to be appointed responsible for the meditation room in the basement. This was a room that very few, if anyone, ever visited and which served as a constant source of conversation. Someone had suggested that the master would be able to conduct gender awareness and relaxation exercises there.

Slobodan Andersson was standing in front of the fish tank in the foyer, watching the fish. Lindell slowed her pace and took stock of him. Had he lost weight? He looked slimmer, if one could apply that adjective to a man she appraised to be around one hundred and thirty kilos.

She walked up to him and perceived none of his earlier irritation. Lindell led him quickly and without speaking to her office. He looked around attentively, his breathing labored.

"Welcome," she said and offered him the visitor's chair, which gave protesting creaks when he sat down.

She went directly on the offensive, eschewing polite phrases and social chitchat.

"I want you to tell me about Armas's son," she said, taking a chance.

Slobodan looked taken aback.

"What son?"

"Come on, Slobodan! You knew each other for many years."

He denied having any knowledge of a son. Lindell believed him. Not because of the look of foolishness on his face, but more because of the hint of hurt in his expression. It was obvious how unpleasant he found this, not because he had to conceal anything but because Armas had kept him in the dark and not told him about his child.

Lindell became unsure for a moment. Perhaps the man in the video was not a son at all, it could as well be a nephew or some other relative, but now she could not back down in front of Slobodan.

"Let's drop this," she said lightly. "We can talk about Mexico instead."

Slobodan was caught off-guard. The generously proportioned body trembled and he tried to smile but failed miserably. His gaze shifted between her and the door, as if he was considering running out of the room.

"Why that?"

"The tattoo Armas had means something, doesn't it? You were with him in Guadalajara. And that's in Mexico."

Lindell had to concentrate to pronounce the words correctly. Slobodan said nothing, so she carried on.

"That's why we need to talk about Mexico. Why did Armas choose a Mexican god and what could it mean to the person who killed him?"

"I have no idea. How would I . . ."

"You have to focus," Lindell interrupted him. "What connection did the two of you have to Mexico?"

"Okay, we were there," Slobodan said compliantly, "but that doesn't mean anything. It's possible that Armas got a tattoo there, I can't really remember. We partied some and I was probably not . . ."

He fell silent. Lindell studied the sweaty man in front of her as if he were a new apparition, someone who had slipped into her office and whose identity she was trying to figure out.

"What were you doing in Mexico?" she said, breaking the silence that for Slobodan, Lindell assumed, must have felt like a decade.

He suddenly became enthusiastic and leaned forward.

"We had some cash flow problems, you have probably already established this. We were maintaining a low profile, I admit this freely, but we kept our side of the bargain. The tax authorities received their due, didn't they? And when times are tough you try to live cheaply and Mexico is affordable. You can find a hotel room for ten dollars. No luxuries, but you can survive."

"But then you came back?"

Slobodan nodded. His breathing was labored after his speech.

"And kept your side of the bargain. But the question is where the money came from. Did you find bagfulls of dollars in Mexico?"

"You don't know how all this hangs together, I take it. I am an experienced restauranteur and there are those who are willing to invest a sum. I have good friends who were willing to pony up."

"In Mexico?"

"No, in Denmark and Malmö. And then we won at a casino in Acapulco. Armas put in quite a bit as well. I believe he received an inheritance or something."

"Okay, so you suddenly got some money and returned, we'll leave it at that for now. Could something have happened in Mexico that later led to Armas's death? Did you meet anyone who since then may have had a reason to hold a grudge against Armas?"

"Who would that be?"

"That's what I'm asking you," Lindell said.

Slobodan shook his head.

"Are you threatened?"

He looked up as if he had had a new insight.

Slobodan Andersson left a stench of sweat in his wake. Lindell stood up and opened the window, at the same time helping a bumblebee find its way to freedom. She could not understand how it had gotten in. The bumblebee made a couple of circles outside the window before it set off and disappeared. To the east, Lindell observed.

She stood there at the window. She had not yet exhausted all of the details the new view from her window afforded. She followed pedestrians and cars below, discovered buildings and rooftops, looked out over the cityscape and recalled with some nostalgia the view from her old office in the former police building on Salagatan. Not because it was more beautiful, in fact it had been mostly of concrete, but she associated the view with old cases and perhaps even with Edvard and Gräsö. That was where they had met, not for the very first time, because that had been at a crime scene where Edvard was the one who had discovered the body, but later. She remembered his first visit and the impression he had made, so different from other men she had met.

She erased him again and let her gaze travel across the Uppsala roofs.

Other people created things, roofs and building fronts, for example, while she herself gathered information and testimony, ruminated over the origins of the frustration and violence she encountered in her work. There were no easy answers, that was the only conclusion she had drawn.

Sometimes she chastised herself with the fact that she thought too much, that she made things difficult for herself. Didn't these thoughts block effective investigative work? No, that isn't true, she countered, quite the opposite: our thoughts are too limited. Many times she had heard other people speak out, it could be at day care or on the radio, and she thought: we should bring that into our work, we need this knowledge.

Insufficient staff and lack of time was the noose from which they hung. A noose that was slowly strangling Lindell and her coworkers. With enough personnel—and not necessarily police officers—they would be able to solve most crimes, and above all help prevent them from occurring in the first place.

It could have been so different. Everyone knew it, few spoke about it and hardly anyone fought for a better system. Habit had become the modus operandi.

She left the window, sat down at her desk, and called Ottosson to report on her talk with Slobodan. After that, she called Beatrice, who had managed to reach the company that had produced the films but had not been able to get in touch with anyone who was able or wanted to talk about the people involved. She promised to continue her investigations.

"Mexico," Lindell mumbled, after having hung up the receiver.

What did the tattoo mean, and above all, its removal? The motive must have been personal, she thought again. What had Armas, and maybe also Slobodan, done in Mexico that could arouse such feelings? Was there love involved? She had the thought that perhaps Armas had ducked out of a relationship, made a woman pregnant and then left. Revenge took the form of an angry relative who had looked him up in order to deliver justice, perhaps get him to pay compensation. In this light, the feathered snake could act as a symbol.

The question was if the murderer had known that Armas had the tattoo, or if it had been discovered by accident. In the first case Armas must have known the killer, or perhaps the betrayed woman had been able to describe the tattoo in order to establish a way to identity Armas.

Ann Lindell turned and twisted the questions. Her conclusion in all cases was that Slobodan knew more than he was telling. She was convinced that he knew more than he was letting on. She was convinced that he was aware of the tattoo's history, where and in what context it had been acquired. His sweat-drenched face and apparent restlessness corroborated this.

But where was the connection between the video and the tattoo? The porn film had been produced in California, but had it been shot there? Was it Mexico? Schönell had guessed the Mediterranean, but the landscape featured in the film—golf courses and beaches—could surely be found as well in Mexico. Wasn't Acapulco, which Slobodan had talked of, a tourist resort on the coast?

If it was Armas's son who was penetrated with the golf club and Armas felt it was embarrassing, which was likely, given the homophobia that Slobodan and others had recounted, what more had Mexico to do with this other than as a possible location for the shoot?

Had Armas and his son bumped into each other in Acapulco?

There were too many questions. Lindell felt a need to discuss it with someone, but first she wanted to let all the new information sink in.

Forty-Six

Sören Sköld had been a truck driver for eleven years, the past four of which he had been at Enquist's timber and construction materials. The truck he drove was a two-year-old Scania. He was pleased both with it and with his job. Wilhelm Enquist himself, closer to eighty years old but still active in the firm, was the one who gave Sören his daily deliveries and doled out good advice as if it was fantastic news.

I know, the driver would think with exasperation, I know everything about today and tomorrow's deliveries, but he let Enquist talk, tossed his bag into the cab before he circled the truck, and inspected the straps on the tarp.

"Well, off you go," Enquist said.

The old man is getting confused, Sören thought, which was mean-spirited because Enquist had not shown evidence of any age-related problems other than worsening hearing.

First, he made a trip to a small company south of the city where he delivered a pallet of ready-made fence sections. Thereafter there were doors and insulation to a house construction project and in the same area an order of mortar, nails, and panel clips to a builder Sören recognized from elementary school in Hallstavik. The builder offered him coffee, but Sören said no as he suspected his school friend wanted to dredge up childhood memories. He blamed it on the fact that he was already behind schedule, and drove off in the direction of the Norrtälje prison.

At the entrance to the road to Vätö there was a stationary dark-blue Saab so poorly placed that it blocked the entire intersection. Sören waited a couple of seconds before he honked. He could see two men in the front seat. One of them got out and approached the truck. His face lacked expression, neither irritation nor an apologetic smile since they were blocking traffic. Sören sighed. He hoped they didn't want help with their car, he thought, and lowered the window. Before Sören had a chance to react, the man opened the door and stepped up on the foot ledge. His breath smelled of garlic.

"We're taking over," he said.

There was nothing threatening about him, he actually looked very relaxed. But he had a black gun in his hand.

After that Sören could only recall fragments of what happened. The psychologist he spoke to the following day said it was a natural reaction. What he could remember was that he was suddenly sitting in the passenger seat, and that the garlic-stinking intruder put the truck in gear and drove away. The Saab was gone. The road to the prison was unblocked. Then Sköld's cell phone rang.

"Don't answer it," the new driver said, and only then did the situation sink in for Sören. The truck had been highjacked.

The Scania was expected and was let in through the gate without fuss. If any of the prison staff asked him why there were two drivers, Sören Sköld had been instructed to say that the new driver was being trained.

The truck pulled up to the carpentry area. Then everything happened very fast. The door to the wood shop opened, Agne Salme came out and jumped into the forklift in order to drive it around to the back of the truck. Out of the corner of his eye he saw Sören Sköld, whom he knew well, and an unknown man walking toward him.

Agne Salme stepped out of the truck, put his hand up in greeting but stiffened when he saw the gun in the stranger's hand. At the same time three men came running from the mini–golf course that was right next to the large open area in front of pavilions two and three.

Agne knew Jussi Björnsson, Stefan Brügger, and José Franco very well. They were all long-timers.

"Let's take it nice and easy," the man with the gun said. "Loosen the tarp!"

Sören Sköld automatically obeyed without protesting or saying a word. Agne Salme followed the instructions for a hostage situation and remained completely passive in order not to worsen the situation unnecessarily.

When the golf trio passed Patricio Alavez, who was weeding the strip between the metal fence and the sports field, José Franco slowed down and shouted something to Alavez. Salme saw how the Mexican stared at the truck, hesitantly lowered his basket, stared at Franco who had run on, and then he set off after him.

Jussi Björnsson immediately received a gun from his partner. Brügger, who was the most nervous of them all, went and stood very close to Agne Salme.

"I'm leaving now, you damn slavedriver. Do you understand? Now you'll have to put your damn shelves together yourself."

Agne Salme nodded. He was too smart to make any comments. The German had worked in the carpentry area before and Salme knew the unpredictable killer from Rostock too well.

"Fuck you," José Franco said—he had been doing nine years for attempted homicide, arson, and resisting arrest. He kneed Salme in the groin.

"Stop it! Get in, damn it! Are you coming?"

The highjacker looked at Patricio, who was standing completely passive.

"*Venga!*" Franco shouted from the back of the truck.

Patricio jumped up and thereafter Agne Salme was forced to his feet.

The alarm had been triggered when security had seen the three golfers leaving the sport area. About one minute later the truck left the prison grounds. Law enforcement was notified, but the situation looked anything but good. There was a traffic accident on the approach to Spillersboda, and a patrol car was at the scene. In Gräddö, a house had caught on fire, which required attention from both the fire department and the police. Several minutes later a dispatch was received about gunfire between Finsta and Rimbo. A truck and two cars had been shot at from a wooded hillside. No one was hurt but all available patrol units were directed to the spot.

Police officers Sune Bark and Kristian Andersson were located north of Norrtälje, on their way back from Grisslehamn, where they had been questioning a retired man about a series of burglaries in the area, when they received word of the gunfire. They were ordered to proceed directly to Finsta.

A quarter of an hour later they received a counterorder: they were to drive straight to the Norrtälje prison facility.

Bark was a recent graduate of the Police Academy and the most serious event he had encountered to date was a violent drunk on the ferry to Blidö. This incident had occurred off-duty, but he had felt compelled to intervene and had done so with great aplomb. The neutralizing of the drunk man had been facilitated by the fact that the latter was seventy-seven years old and basically unconscious by the time he was brought under control. Bark had received praise for his efforts.

Andersson had spent more than twenty years on the force, most of the time in a radio patrol car, and thus had seen and heard considerably more. He had been called out on a number of incidents, escape attempts and even successful escapes. This time the situation was grave, he realized as they received more information from central dispatch, and he made an effort to repeatedly impress this fact on his partner.

"We have hostages to consider," he said, "and we are faced with an armed opponent who is probably capable of anything."

In the next moment he swore at a driver who apparently hadn't noticed the patrol car's flashing lights and sirens. Andersson swerved expertly and drove on the wrong side of a highway divider in order to advance more quickly.

They spotted the Scania at a parking lot approximately one kilometer from the prison. Kristian Andersson braked, turned off his siren, and passed the truck slowly but could not see a person inside. One hundred meters on he made a U-turn while Bark contacted central dispatch.

They knew that when an inmate facing a long incarceration escaped, he was usually nervous. Inmates serving ten years who saw a chance to escape were not afraid to use any means when in a tight situation. But after two or three days on the run, hunted by police and with their faces in every newspaper, hungry, thirsty, and cold, they tended to become more cooperative. So the initial phase of an escape was often the most critical.

Kristian Andersson instructed Bark to remain in the car and stay in touch with the team at headquarters, which had hastily been assembled, then he stepped out of the car and took out his weapon.

The tarp on the back of the truck fluttered. A red Amazon drove up at slow speed. The driver, an older man, stared at him and swerved in the direction of the ditch for a moment before he regained control of the car.

"Make sure to close the road to traffic!" Andersson shouted, before he carefully approached the truck. He kept to the side of the road, came to a bus shelter and stayed there for several seconds. Nothing was happening at the truck.

He jumped a low fence into a private garden, crossed a raspberry patch where the occasionally berry could still be seen, stepped into the adjacent lot and came increasingly closer to the truck.

Partly obscured by a bush, he stared through an open door into the empty cab. A shoe lay on the asphalt. The truck was abandoned. The inmates and their rescuer had fled. Kristian Andersson looked around and discovered two faces in the window of a house some fifteen meters back on the lot. He instinctively fell down on one knee and raised his gun.

Kristian Andersson let out a curse. The thorns of a gooseberry bush scraped his hands and for a moment he was transported to the garden of his childhood home at the foot of Kinnekulle hill. Harvest time. Currents, gooseberries, and raspberries. White plastic bins and buckets, insects and thorns.

The couple in the window were staring intently at him as if they were waiting for him to act. He could make out the woman's gray hair, and the dark frames of her glasses made her look like an owl. They probably had nothing to do with the escape. They were simply afraid.

Andersson rose up and ran doubled-over up to the door of the house and felt the handle. It was unlocked. He entered and called out that they should remain calm and move away from the window.

"Have you seen anything?" he shouted and walked into the hall. The woman appeared. She looked much younger than his initial impression, perhaps around forty-five.

"They jumped into a car," she said.

"What kind of a car?"

"A van," the man said, who had now joined them in the hall.

"Color and make?"

"Blue," the man said. "Maybe American. What is going on? Has there been a burglary?"

Kristian Andersson left the house and the couple's questions and ran back to the patrol car. Sune Bark was talking agitatedly into the dispatch. Andersson grabbed the microphone from him.

✦

Forty-Seven

The fugitives abandoned their blue van at the edge of a forest just west of Norrtälje. Two cars were waiting for them there: a Volvo that looked to be in bad shape, and a newer Audi. Björnsson and Brügger jumped into the Audi, while José Franco got into the Volvo. Everything was done very quickly. The high jacker left them without a word and disappeared into the forest on foot. Sören Sköld and Agne Salme had been left tied up in the van, eyes and mouths bound and gagged.

"Come on!" José cried out to Patricio Alavez, who just stared bewildered at the events rapidly unfolding among the trees. He, like the other inmates, had removed his prison clothes during the trip and been able to choose pants, T-shirts, and shirts from a large bin. Patricio had selected a pair of blue jeans and a white T-shirt.

"Where are you going?"

"Jump in!"

The Audi had already left. Patricio gestured to the van and opened his mouth to say something when José Franco engaged first gear and the Volvo started rolling away. Patricio ran after it, José slowed down, leaned across the passenger seat, and opened the door.

After a minute or so they were driving on a gravel road. Patricio sat without saying anything. After several minutes, José chuckled.

"Freedom," he said and looked at Patricio. "Put on your seat belt."

They journeyed along small roads. José was quiet. Patricio had not yet recovered. One minute he was weeding behind high walls and had steeled himself for doing so for the next eight years, and then he was sitting in a nice car, passing farms and grazing cows, and feeling the wind through the open window.

He was amazed that so few words had been exchanged during the escape. Jussi Björnsson had said nothing during the quick trip in the van and while they changed clothes, while Stefan Brügger had said all of ten words. And now José was mum.

Patricio liked it. That they hadn't screamed and mouthed off, hugged each other, grown overconfident and nonchalant in their movements—all this indicated that the escape had been serious and well-planned. The quick changes of vehicles also bore this out.

He realized there was no point in asking where the highjacker, who had dived into the underbrush, had gone or who he was. Perhaps there was a car waiting for him on the other side of the wooded area? Where Björnsson and Brügger were headed in their Audi, Patricio couldn't even imagine. He did not know Sweden. So far he had only seen customs, the holding cell, and prison.

"Where are you going?" José asked unexpectedly.

"I don't know," Patricio answered. "I don't know anything."

"I'm driving north," José said.

Patricio had heard that there were mountains in the northern part of the country. It was said to be beautiful there, or so the prison minister had said when he had described Sweden.

"Uppsala, where is that?"

"You're going to Uppsala? I don't think that's a good idea," José said. "It's full of cops."

"Where are you going?"

"North," José said, and even though he tried to look impassive, Patricio could sense the faint smile of satisfaction in his thin face—a face that appeared almost emaciated, as he had also managed to shave his beard off during his brief trip in the van.

"I want to go to Uppsala," Patricio said.

"Do you know anyone there?"

"Maybe."

"I would like to help you, since we are countrymen. But I cannot go there, you understand that, don't you? It's crawling with pigs. But I can tell you what you should do. I have some money, check the glove compartment."

Patricio was touched by his thoughtfulness. He had the impression that José was genuine when he said he wanted to help. He opened the glove compartment and saw a brown envelope.

"Open it," José told him.

Patricio did as he was told and saw a wad of bills.

"There should be twenty thousand kronor," José said. "Take five."

Patricio protested but accepted in the end. He knew the money would come in handy.

José slowed and pulled into a church parking lot, took a map out of the door pocket, unfolded it, and showed Patricio where they were, and traced the way they were going to proceed through Uppland.

"I can let you off in Tierp. From there you can take the bus or train to Uppsala. You can speak a little Swedish, can't you?"

José thought for a moment and then explained to Patricio what he could do: board the train as calmly as possible, buy a ticket from the conductor, simply say "Uppsala" and nod if the conductor asked any questions, as this was likely to be as to whether or not it was a one-way trip.

In Uppsala he should get off the train, buy a map, and mingle with people downtown, not check into a hotel, buy food in a large grocery store and thereafter try to find some place where he could spend the night.

"Buy a blanket or sleeping bag. If anyone asks where you come from, tell them you are a Spanish tourist. Okay?"

Patricio nodded.

"You can't get in touch with your friend right away, understand? The cops might be keeping an eye out."

"I don't think so," Patricio said, who only now started to think about his brother, who had told him he was going to Uppsala to look up the tall one and the fat one. Where was Manuel?

"You won't change your mind?"

"No," Patricio said, but he wasn't convinced it had been right to escape from prison.

"If you get caught then never tell them how we did it, that you came with me in this car, and where I let you off."

"I'll keep quiet," Patricio said.

José gave a chuckle. Patricio looked at him and smiled. It felt good to hear a laugh in freedom, to have found a friend.

"We live a while longer," José said.

Dark clouds were pulling in from the south as Patricio stepped off the Upp-train at the central station in Uppsala. The rain came down with an almost tropical force and for several moments he stood absolutely still and let himself be struck by the strong, hammering drops before he ran over the platform, crossed the tracks, and hurried into the station.

There was a convivial atmosphere in there, with laughter and a cacophony of voices. A damp heat rose from the travelers' clothes and a metallic voice issued from the loudspeakers. People poured effortlessly through the station like lava streams down a mountainside, curving around groups of stationary people, continuing on out the doors that reluctantly slid open and let in the smell of rain and car exhaust.

Patricio stopped for a moment, shivered from the dampness that had soaked through the T-shirt, listened and was amazed at this throng of colors, voices, and movements. Then he followed one of the streams and ended up on some stairs by a small square. A patrol car was parked on the street.

"Manuel, where are you?" he muttered and looked around. To the left there was a parking lot and beyond that, a bus terminal. To the right there was a disorganized army of a thousand bikes. It was in this direction that most people walked and Patricio followed the river of people in toward the city center. The rain had stopped as quickly as it had started. The clouds in the sky were torn apart, a pale sun peeked out and spread a warm, indolent light over Uppsala.

Patricio was gradually overcoming his shock at having escaped the prison and no longer being imprisoned by closed doors and walls topped with barbed wire. Nothing prevented him from walking in any direction he chose. He could sit on a park bench, rest for fifteen minutes, an hour, or half a day, and then saunter on to wherever he wished.

Nonetheless it still seemed as if others determined his steps. During his walk he became a helpless victim of other peoples' desires and directions and found himself standing outside a hamburger joint. He walked in, and once he had satisfied his thirst and hunger, he tried to come to his own decision.

His brother was somewhere in this city, but at his visit to the prison he had not mentioned where he was planning to stay. Patricio could not imagine him checking into a hotel, but he must have spent his nights somewhere. He could not simply sleep outside as they did in Mexico, resting on a *petate* and rolled up in a blanket.

And where should he himself spend the night? He sank down onto a bench, suddenly exhausted. The scent of coffee from an outdoor cafe brought back memories of the village. Should he call Gerardo back in the village so he could get word to his mother? No, she would be beside herself with worry. He could see Maria, the shriveled body that had become more stooped over the years, the abundant hair gathered into two braids running down her back, and her busy hands. What was she doing now? His longing for Mexico and the village caused him to let out a sob. A youngish woman walking by glanced at him. The child walking at her side—with apparent reluctance, a boy of perhaps five or six—stopped short and stared wide-eyed at Patricio, but the woman pulled him along.

Patricio stood up. The wet T-shirt was still cold. The pants he had put on in the van were too short and the large shoes from prison looked clumsy. He looked around and spotted a clothing store nearby. He could spend some of the money José had given him on some new duds.

He came back out onto the street sixteen hundred kronor poorer. He had not realized how expensive it was going to be, but he had not wanted to protest or haggle at the register. Now he was wearing yet another pair of blue jeans, a red T-shirt, and a short jacket. In the bag he had an extra T-shirt, a pair of underpants, and three pairs of socks.

He put on the sunglasses and cap that he had bought and immediately felt better. He looked down at his shoes, but decided that they would have to do for now.

The sales clerk had been friendly and had not seemed surprised that Patricio only knew a few words of Swedish. On the street he saw many dark-hued people and realized that Swedes were used to foreigners.

He walked toward the central square that he had seen earlier. It was an old habit. In the village and even in Oaxaca, the *zócalon,* the square, was the meeting place where you strolled around, sat on a bench, bumped into people you knew and exchanged a few words. He was hoping that Manuel would think along similar lines and find his way to the square. What else was he to do in a strange city?

He heard music coming from a pedestrian zone, and he paused. A group of musicians were giving a concert. He immediately saw that they were South Americans. He had encountered similar groups of usually Peruvians and Bolivians in California. He gave them some of the change he had received from the clothing store and lingered there. During a pause in the music he mustered some courage and walked up to one of the men.

"Hi, *companero,* do you know where the restaurant Dakar is?" he asked in Spanish.

The flute player gave him an interested look. Patricio almost regretted asking. What did he know about Dakar, perhaps it was an infamous hangout for bad people.

"It's not far from here," the musician said and pointed with his flute. "Take the first street to the right and then you will see Dakar about fifty meters away."

"You play well," Patricio said.

The man nodded curtly as if he did not care for compliments.

"Where do come from?"

"California," Patricio said.

There was nothing unfriendly about the man, but his expression what somewhat sullen and forbidding. Patricio had the feeling he was on his guard.

He walked in the direction the man had pointed at. The tension in his body made him want to run, but he controlled himself and tried to match the rhythm of those around him on the street, without looking back.

He turned to the right and saw the restaurant sign at once. It had the name of the place and three blinking stars in red and green. I've finally arrived, he thought, and had the unpleasant feeling of having been on this sidewalk, looking at this sign before.

The next thought that struck him was just as unpleasant. If I had not gone along with the fat one's talk of innocent letters that needed transporting to Europe, or rather, if I had admitted to myself what I deep down believed about the package, where would I have been then? Who would I have been? Who am I today?

His life was wasted. He had, against his better judgment, allowed himself to be tricked, had been seduced by the power of money and dreams of a better life. What he and his family had gained was not a fortune but dishonor. Why not complete this thread by walking into Dakar and killing the fat one and the tall one? For his own part, nothing could get worse. They would not judge him back in the village, perhaps they would even hail him as a hero. They would see this as the appropriate punishment for a *bhni guí'a.* Angel would be doubly revenged and no more Zapotecs would be tricked, at least not by these two.

If we kill everyone who sucks our blood and throws us on the dirt pile when we are used up, then will it be a better world? The Zapotecs would benefit from it. No one would be forced to go to *el norte,* the villages could live and no corn would be dumped on the market in Talea.

Patricio's thoughts were not new, they had emerged in prison, but now for the first time they appeared possible to realize. For the first time he would be able to make a contribution to his country and his village. To demonstrate in Oaxaca that to be subdued by police dogs, batons, and water canons did not lead anywhere.

The white ones always won. Again and again they triumphed. For five hundred years they had always picked the longest straw. Now he, Patricio Alavez, Zapotec, would easily defeat two white men. Angel would be revenged and Miguel would not have died in vain.

Patricio grew as he stood outside on the sidewalk. He looked down at his new clothes and realized it was his fighting gear. He would not have to feel ashamed. Even a Zapotec could look sharp.

Afterward the police could take him, throw him back into jail, perhaps kill him. It wouldn't matter. He would no longer be dishonored.

✦

Forty-Eight

The tent flapped in the wind. Home, Manuel thought, and sat down in his favorite spot on the riverbank with a stone shaped like a back rest. From there he had a view of the river and the opposite bank where the well-fed cattle grazed. But now he shut his eyes and tried to squeeze everything to do with Sweden out his mind. He sat like this for several minutes before getting up and scouring the landscape. The sun was in the southwest and its light was reflected in quick-moving glints in the river water. Downstream some birds chattered anxiously. Manuel lifted his gaze. A hawk was circling up in the sky.

He made his way up the riverbank on stiff legs, but neither the billowing fields nor the pencil-straight lines of the strawberry plants could give him peace. He only felt bewildered by the fact that there were so many realities. All over the world, people were standing at the edges of fields, by deserts and lakes, in front of homes and graves. Or else they were resting in bed or on a sleep mat, alone, or with their beloved by their side. Many were on their way somewhere, restless or full of anticipation.

Everywhere there were people with dreams and beating hearts. Manuel looked down at his hands as if they could tell him who he was and where his rightful place was.

Miguel's death, the violent force of the bullets that struck his body, his children at the window. Angel's sprint across the railway tracks in Frankfurt, his mother's sad eyes and her body worn and aching from a lifetime of work, the scent and beauty of the fields and crops, words of love exchanged in the dark with Gabriella—everything was mixed together in a burning anguish.

Give us a land to live in, he thought, a land where we can toil and love in peace. Why do you have to come to us with your manipulated seeds, your pesticides that give us panting lungs and burning wounds, your agreements that no one can understand until it is too late, fierce police dogs, armed thugs in souped-up jeeps, your drugs and your newspapers and radio stations that only lie? Why can we not till the earth in peace? Is that too much to ask?

Manuel did not understand the world. Everything was racing, as if life were a flock of horses stung by a gadfly, setting off at a furious pace.

"Patricio!" he shouted across the Uppsala plains, overcome with terror.

He looked around as if looking for his brother, but the only person he saw was a lone worker with a pesticide applicator who walked between the rows of plants and gave them their dose of poison.

The man, who may have heard his cry, looked up and waved his free hand in greeting. Manuel waved back.

A thunderclap from the sky interrupted his thoughts. A fighter jet appeared as if from nowhere, zoomed over at low altitude, banked, and disappeared. It was over in a couple of seconds. The man with the pesticide applicator and Manuel stared at the horizon and thereafter at each other. Manuel thought he could see the man laugh and how he made a gesture with his hand before he returned to his work. Maybe he's happy that something broke the monotony, Manuel thought, even if it was a war machine that created the diversion.

He stumbled down the slope to his tent, pulled over his bag of clothes, undressed, and carefully stepped into the river. Last time he had slipped in the slick mud and fallen headlong into the reeds and cut his arm. The water was cool and the stiff and cold stems of the lily pads brushed against his limbs.

The water did him good. He swam several strokes, turned onto his back and let his head sink, and saw the sky above the water line as if in a kaleidoscopic shimmer. For a moment he had the sudden impulse to allow his body to sink to the muddy bottom. A burst of anxiety made him shoot up out of the water and quickly swim back to the edge.

He combed and shaved with care, pulled on clean pants and a T-shirt with a design by José Guadalupe Posada on the chest: a man on a horse riding across a field of grinning skulls.

From his hiding place under a low bushy juniper growing in the middle of a hawthorne thicket, he pulled out the sports bag he had stolen from the summer house, unzipped it, and checked to make sure the cocaine was still there.

At the sight of the packets wrapped up in plastic and tape, he felt a pang of grief at his brothers' ignorant greed, but also triumph at having been able to cheat Slobodan Andersson.

As he left his tent he carefully looked around, as if it was his last time by the river. He let his gaze wander back and forth. A gray heron made a low, swooping dive over the water, some small fish rippled the surface of the water, perhaps chased by something bigger. He watched how the cattle on the other side lazily helped themselves to grass and shook their heads in order to ward off their buzzing tormentors. The cows looked dully at Manuel before resuming their chewing.

Again the image of Miguel's death rose up in his mind. It was the thought of the children who from the window became witnesses to the execution of their father that plagued Manuel the most. One of them was also physically marked for life as she had been hit by a ricocheting bullet and received an ugly scar on one cheek.

Had the villagers actually done anything to protect their neighbor and friend? They observed passively as the murderers came to the village and asked for directions to Miguel's house. Surely no one could have been unaware of their intentions? The villagers made their way up through the alleys to Miguel's house without speaking, and arrived in time to see him being dragged out. He who had started the association and unselfishly had made himself a target for threats and harassment was shot in front of their eyes without anyone lifting a finger. In fact, they betrayed him even in death by giving in to idle chatter and leaving the association in dribs and drabs.

Why did no one offer any resistance? Why did I do nothing? Their shared indecision and cowardice had haunted him ever since Miguel's murder, but now his self-contempt grew so intense he started to shake.

There was only one cure: do the right thing. Standing there before the foreign field, he made the sign of the cross and promised himself that if he ever returned to his village he would honor Miguel's memory. What form this would take, he was not sure.

Manuel drove in the direction of Uppsala in order to meet Slobodan Andersson. The latter had described how to get there: take a left at the roundabout where the freeway to Stockholm began. It was the same road as when he had followed Slobodan and the short one. After a hundred meters he should turn right onto a parking lot.

He had left in plenty of time, found the roundabout without any difficulty, but drove straight on the road without turning into the parking lot. After a couple of hundred meters he reached the turnoff to a golf course. There he turned and stepped out of the car. He wanted to reach the agreed-upon meeting place from behind so that Slobodan would not see his car and in that way be able to track him down.

He sat down behind some bushes and waited. Twenty minutes left.

He felt a niggling unease. Not because of the transaction with the fat one—it was open area and Slobodan could not do anything—but because he doubted the very reasoning behind his plan.

At exactly two o'clock Slobodan Andersson pulled into the parking lot. Like Armas, he drove a BMW. He turned off the engine but did not get out of the car. He looked around. He took a call on his cell phone that he terminated almost immediately. Manuel waited behind the bushes. Slobodan writhed uncomfortably in the car and Manuel watched as he strained to look back toward town and check out all the cars heading east from the roundabout.

Manuel stood up from the ditch. Slobodan had his attention aimed in the opposite direction and did not observe him. Manuel snuck over and tapped on the window. Slobodan threw open the car door.

"Hell, you scared me!"

"Do you have the money?" Manuel asked.

Slobododan glared at him.

"Where do you have the goods?"

"I want the money in my hands first, then you will—"

"Where is your car?"

"I walked here," Manuel said. "We have to hurry now."

"Walked? Give me the goods."

"I want to see the money first."

Slobodan looked around, then picked up a dark plastic bag from the passenger seat and held it out. Manuel opened the bag and there were the bills. One-hundred-dollar notes. Four hundred of them.

"Forty thousand?"

"Of course," Slobodan snapped, his brow wet with perspiration.

Manuel left the bag and went to get the sports bag with the cocaine. When he returned to the car, Slobodan was talking on the phone.

"Stop talking!" Manuel said.

Slobodan smiled tauntingly, but turned off the phone. Manuel handed him the bag, Slobodan checked the contents and held out the plastic bag with the money, shut the car door without a word, and drove away. Manuel ran back, jumped into his car, and quickly drove onto the highway. He caught sight of Slobodan's car on the E-4. As Manuel approached the roundabout he saw Slobodan's brake lights come on. He had hit a red light. Manuel chuckled smugly.

Slobodan drove at great speed north on the E-4 until he suddenly turned off toward town. Manuel was afraid of losing him, but he did not want to stay too close. Luck smiled on him again and he was just able to pass the intersection before the lights turned red.

The fat one crisscrossed through town and finally ended up by the river, where he parked the car and got out. Manuel, who was forced to stop several times for pedestrians saw him cross the street with the bag in his hand. Manuel took a empty parking space.

Slobodan disappeared down an alley and Manuel hurried to keep up. If he was going to have a chance to punish the fat one he could not lose him now. Slobodan walked quickly at first but then slowed the pace and Manuel sensed that the rapid clip had worn him down.

After several minutes he entered a restaurant. The sign said Alhambra. Manuel recognized the name as being the same restaurant that Feo had mentioned.

After ten minutes Slonodan was back on the street again, minus the bag. How dumb can a *gringo* be? Manuel thought and watched Slobodan blend into the crowd.

Manuel breathed freely. He felt how hungry he was. The tension surrounding the delivering of the drugs and following the fat one had suppressed all needs.

A little way down the pedestrian zone there was a group of musicians and Manuel walked over to them. He thought about the men he and his brothers had joined forces with in crossing the border, and how after their successful crossing they had sung a few songs and shown them the typical dance steps of their region. It would probably be a long time before he would have the pleasure of a *huapango,* he thought, and left the musicians in order not to be overwhelmed with longing for his country.

He walked toward Dakar. It was the irony of fate that the only stable point he had in Uppsala belonged to Slobodan Andersson. At Dakar there was the Portuguese, and above all Eva, the waitress who was so curious about his country and culture. She listened and asked him a never-ending stream of questions, everything in an astonishingly strange English, in which her limited vocabulary forced her to take long pauses before she managed to communicate what she wanted.

She had also not cared about his lie. For her it didn't matter if he came from Mexico or Venezuela. It made him even more willing to talk to her. She gave him the freedom to be himself.

On top of all this, she was the first white woman who had spoken to him as an equal. He had met many *gringas* in the United States, but they had seen him as a dirty *chicano* whom they could exploit for underpaid labor but never treat as a human.

She is also beautiful, he thought, not without a pang of guilt, because ever since the message of Angel's death and Patricio's incarceration had reached him he had had increasing difficulties caring about Gabriella in the village. Love and future plans faded away. He became irritable and listless. How could he talk of personal happiness as his family was breaking apart? Did he love her? He no longer knew.

He walked to Dakar in a rare mixture of depression and excitement. This time he banged on the back door. The chef who smoked in the dishwashing area and looked like a bulldog opened the door.

"Well, well, look who's back," he said and looked at him with a smile that Manuel could not evaluate.

"I need to work," he muttered. "Is there anything for me to do?"

Unconsciously he adopted the subordinate tone he had learned in California.

"There are no dishes, but it's been a while since the dressing room was cleaned.

Manuel was supplied with cleaning solution, rags, a bucket, and a mop. He decided to do a thorough job. Not in order to please anyone but because he needed to do something well, something that made a difference, for quite egotistical reasons. He needed to disappear into work. The past week had shaken him. He would never again be the Manuel Alavez he had been. Everything that he said in the future would contain a measure of untruth, or so he felt. Only work was honest.

He kept polishing, wiping down lockers and benches, scrubbing the floors frenetically, and taking the light fixtures down in order to pick all the dead flies out of the glass globes.

He had just finished and sat down on a bench when Eva walked in.

"What a difference!" she exclaimed. "And how good it smells."

Manuel stood up at once. Eva pulled off her coat and hung it in her locker. He could not help looking at her breasts. Her look of amusement confirmed that he had been caught.

"I'll go," he said.

She smiled even more broadly and patted him on his blushing cheek. His confusion only increased before this fearless woman. Why was she laughing? Was she offering herself to him?

"Are you married?"

Manuel shook his head. Eva took her black work skirt from the locker, brushed away some dust, and reached for the white blouse on its hanger. Manuel forced himself not to look at her clothes.

"It should be . . ." she started, but couldn't find the right word in

English, and simply made a gesture with her hand. He understood that she meant the blouse was wrinkled.

"See you soon," he said and left the dressing room. He wished he could iron her blouse, simply to touch it. He wanted to do something for her, more than just scrub the dressing room. He wanted to make her happy.

He walked over to the dishwashing area. A man in a white hat had just put down a load of pots, dishes, and utensils, nodded to Manuel, but did not say anything. Manuel guessed it was Johnny, the one who had started recently and that Feo had told him about. Manuel took on the dishes, happy that there was something to do.

Eva emerged from the dressing room in her work clothes. She looked in on him, running her hand along her blouse and laughing, before she continued out to the dining room.

Whore, Manuel thought, but took it back immediately. Eva was not a whore. She was a fine woman. The fact that she was divorced was not her fault, he was sure of it. She lived for her children and for her dreams, so much he had understood. Behind her interest in Mexico there was a longing, a desire to experience something new, if only in her thoughts. It occurred to him that perhaps she was interested in him. The day before she had asked him about his village and daily life there, and today she had asked if he was married. Why would a woman ask that?

He scraped an oval dish clean but his movements became slower and slower until his hands grew completely still. He stared unseeing into the tiled wall in front of him and tried to imagine Eva in Mexico. It both worked, and it didn't. A white woman was changed when she came to Mexico and his village, just as a Zapotec became another when he left the mountains and encountered white society. Would she speak to him there as she did here in Sweden? Would she retain her laughter and curiosity or become frightened by all the poverty?

It was only when he heard Feo's voice from the bar that he started scrubbing again.

Feo must have entered through the street entrance and Manuel knew it had to be past five o'clock. Perhaps Feo was off today and only dropping by for a visit? Just as he had looked forward to speaking with Eva, he wanted to talk a little with Feo.

The dishes were done and he arranged all the pots along the counter so they could air dry, but then grabbed a dish towel and dried them. No one would be able to say he did not do his job.

Despite the clatter from the dishwasher and the pots, Feo's voice could be heard clearly. Manuel went out into the kitchen and gently cracked the door to the dining room, an area he had only caught sight of before.

Now he worked up the courage to go out there. The dining room was considerably larger than he had thought. Eva was in the process of setting tables at the far end of the room. She smiled and waved with a napkin. He walked on. Feo was standing at the bar. He was talking to someone behind the counter whom Manuel was unable to see.

It struck him that he liked it at Dakar. Imagine if . . . Yes, he could work here, become good friends with Feo and get to know Eva properly, perhaps visit her home and meet her two children. They could travel to Mexico together and then he could show her everything beautiful and satisfy her curiosity.

But it was a dream, Manuel realized this the moment a couple of customers entered the restaurant and he quickly retreated to the kitchen.

Everything was a dream. Angel was dead, Patricio was in jail, and he himself had buried thousands of dollars under a bush by a river. The fat one was smuggling drugs and new brothers would be lured into his trap if Manuel did not do something about it.

He could not remain a dishwasher at Dakar. He would never become friends with the others. Eva would be only a memory. He must see his brother and punish Slobodan Andersson. Everything else was only dreams.

Manuel heard thundering laughter from the kitchen. He peered over the shelves and saw Feo, dressed in a suit and tie, with a pleased but also embarrassed expression.

The person laughing was Donald, and the reason, Manuel gathered as soon as he came out into the kitchen, was the suit. Feo took a turn around the room as if on a catwalk.

"Where are you going?" Manuel asked.

"Dinner with my wife and her parents," Feo said, and now he looked purely embarrassed.

"You look elegant," Manuel said.

Feo nodded, but did not appear convinced. Donald walked over to him and pinched his cheek. When he removed his hand, there was a red mark.

Donald said something in Swedish and it sounded neither superior nor mean-spirited—Manuel identified an almost tender tone, and Feo assumed something of his usual carefree manner.

"Yes, he looks good as a gentleman," Manuel added.

Donald glanced at Manuel.

"We are all gentlemen here," he said harshly, and then directed all his attention at the stove.

Feo smiled uncertainly, Pirjo looked down at the floor, and Johnny stared at the chef's broad back.

Then Pirjo did something that filled the entire kitchen with a feeling no one could quite identify. She walked up to Donald and put her arm around his shoulders, stretched on tiptoe, leaned forward, and gave him a kiss on the cheek.

✦

Forty-Nine

Lorenzo Wader did not own a cell phone. In his assessment, only amateurs spent their time constantly chattering into their telephones. How many had been felled by the charting, by police and prosecutors, of their incoming and outgoing cell phone calls? Why make it so easy?

So when Konrad Rosenberg asked him for his telephone number, he laughed heartily.

"If you want to reach me, you will have to look me up," he said.

"But if Zero wants to call?"

"Zero is not to call me, nor is anyone else for that matter."

Konrad Rosenberg nodded.

"But if you don't have a telephone, then you can—"

"You will speak to Zero," Lorenzo interrupted. "I would like to speak to him at half past eight tonight. Tell him to go to the Fyris movie theater on Saint Olofsgatan, stand and look at the movie posters there, and then walk up the hill and into the graveyard."

"And then?"

"That is all he needs to know," Lorenzo Wader pronounced.

He was starting to tire of the nervous Konrad, who was also overly curious. But he could nonetheless be of use. Lorenzo had a strategy to never let anyone else in on the whole picture. It had been his tactic for many years, and it worked beautifully. Thanks to his caution, Lorenzo had never been prosecuted in court, had never even had charges filed against him.

Konrad's task was to create contacts with useful idiots who could be put to work in the field. Lorenzo needed street runners and he had no qualms about helping himself to some of Slobodan Andersson's "staff."

Konrad had dismissed Lorenzo's theory that it was Slobodan who was behind Armas's murder, but Lorenzo did not consider it impossible. Armas had been a tough nut and had not cracked, despite his obvious fear that the world would find out about his unknown son's sexual orientation and activities. Lorenzo had approached Armas through shared acquaintances, but in the absence of any reaction Lorenzo simply got in direct contact with him himself in order to suggest working together, something that Armas had appeared to consider but ultimately rejected.

The following day he had had Gonzo deliver a package to Armas with a videotape. There was no accompanying letter, no greeting or anything that could be traced back to the original sender, but Lorenzo was convinced that Armas was intelligent enough to connect Lorenzo's offer of cooperation with the indirect threat that the videotape signified.

Gonzo was completely ignorant of what he had delivered but was the one who had to take the blow. Armas had reacted vehemently and fired the waiter on the spot.

This did not trouble Lorenzo in the least, and moreover capitalized on the lust for revenge that the waiter expressed. Lorenzo had lost a source close to Slobodan and Armas. On the other hand he had won a messenger and foot soldier who was not held back by any false loyalties.

✦

Fifty

The police had distributed an advisory to the public after Armas's murder, asking the public to notify them if anyone had seen a blue BMW. It was a relatively exclusive car, and an uncommon model, so Lindell was surprised that no one had called in.

But after a week, Algot Andersson, a retired hardware store owner, called the police and was put through to Ann Lindell.

All summer he had been busy renovating an old schooner that he had hauled up out of the water off the Fyris river, and he had seen something that might "be of interest to the police."

A little way down from his work area, something had suddenly turned up. A blue tarp, pulled over something that he at first believed to be a boat. He knew the family that used that space, knew they were on a long sail trip and that they would not be back until the end of September.

Therefore, the tarp had caused him some consternation from the outset, and he had speculated about what the Gardenståhls had allowed to be erected in their space.

After a week, his curiosity had won over his desire not to be nosy, and when he had checked under the tarp, he had found a car.

"There's something not right about it," Algot Andersson said. "I thought I had better call in."

"You did the right thing," Lindell said, convinced that they had finally located Armas's car.

Andersson had not made a note of the license plate number, but both the color and make corresponded.

The boat club dock was on the Fyris river, close to the southern industrial area and the area upstream from it where Armas had been found bobbing among the reeds.

"I'm still here and can check the license plate for you," Algot Andersson offered. "Hang on!"

Lindell heard static on the line and imagined the man approaching the car with agile steps. She imagined him looking like an older version of Berglund.

"Hello," he said, and quickly recited the number.

"I could kiss you," she said.

She called Ryde at forensics, but it was Charles Morgansson who picked up.

"Eskil had to go to a funeral today," he explained.

Lindell told him about the car find and the technician promised to go down to the Fyris river right away. Lindell, who had been planning to go down there herself but who definitely did not want to bump into her ex-lover, informed him that he would be working with Ola Haver.

"How is everything?" Morgansson asked.

She knew he didn't mean work, but she still chose to tell him about the situation of the case. Morgansson took the hint and did not ask further questions.

Lindell called Haver, who was pleased to have a reason to leave the building. Thereafter she read Beatrice's summary of Armas's life. It had been lying on her desk for a day or so, but now she pulled herself together and read through the brief report.

Armas's background was murky, to say the least. He was probably born to Armenian parents in Paris, but there was also information that suggested Trieste, Italy, as his birthplace.

He had claimed to have been born in 1951. He had come to Sweden eighteen years ago and immediately found work at the shipbuilding company Kockums in Malmö. In France he had apparently trained as a welder. After six months at the shipyard, he most likely left the country, but returned in 1970 and was hired at Club Malibu in Helsingborg.

Beatrice had put in a great deal of effort in tracing his career, but there were many gaps and questions. He was convicted of assault in the mid-seventies and was sentenced to eight months in prison. It was a matter of a fight in a nightclub. It was the only occasion on which he was seriously in trouble with the law.

After serving his sentence he again disappeared from view only to reemerge many years later when he moved to Uppsala at the same time as Slobodan Andersson.

His income the past several years had been even but not excessive. The most recent information indicated a taxable income of just two hundred thousand. He had been cited by the tax authority thirteen times, but all notations were in regards to small sums. Fourteen parking tickets and a speeding fine were also registered.

Lindell sighed. In spite of Bea's efforts there was nothing to go on. Not a word of any son. No information that was useful in their current situation. Nothing.

Irritably, she tossed the report aside, took out her notebook, and flipped through her notes from the past few days but had no new ideas. And she knew why: her thoughts were at the Fyris river and Armas's car. She should be there.

Given a lack of anything else to do, she called Barbro Liljendahl, who answered on the first signal.

"Great! I had been thinking of calling you. I've checked out Rosenberg. He is a regular at Dakar."

This was not news to Lindell, who had seen him there in the company of Lorenzo Wader.

"How did you find out?"

"I talked to Måns Fredriksson. He works in the bar and is the son of my sister's neighbor. I was over at my sister's having a cup of coffee. She has a patio and the neighbor was sitting out on her patio with her son. We started to talk and I don't know how it came up but we started talking about the Armas murder and then Måns told us that he worked at Dakar."

Lindell chuckled. This is how it is, she thought, the harvest of fate.

"Måns said that Rosenberg and Slobodan Andersson know each

other. Rosenberg tends to hang at the bar and talk a lot of nonsense. Måns doesn't like him, I could tell."

"How did you manage to get on to Rosenberg?"

"It was easy," Liljendahl said, but did not reveal how she had done it.

"How is Rosenberg? What does he talk about?"

"Deals. He wants to give the impression that he is a successful businessman. Likes to brag. Always leaves a big tip, but in a way that draws attention to it."

"Has the bartender seen Rosenberg and Slobodan together?"

"Definitely," Barbro Liljendahl said. "They not only know each other, they are friends. At least that is Måns's impression."

"What did he say about your curiosity, I mean, how did you explain your interest?" Lindell asked; she had the feeling that her colleague was using Armas's murder—a case that was not on her desk—as a way to get Rosenberg. Maybe also to show off.

"I lay very low," Barbro Liljendahl said, most likely sensitive to the unspoken critique.

The hell you did, Lindell thought, but was nonetheless grateful for the information. That Konrad Rosenberg was no choirboy had already been established, but a connection between him and Slobodan Andersson was candy.

"Can there be drugs involved?"

"Why is someone like Slobodan tight with someone like Rosenberg? Drugs is the only thing he knows," Liljendahl said.

Lindell took her words as a kind of redemption. The Armas investigation had never really gathered momentum, no self-evident motives had been uncovered, the background investigation was idling, no crucial witnesses had been heard from, and the questioning that had been undertaken had not really provided any breakthroughs. The only elements of interest thus far were the removal of the tattoo and the video.

Now Liljendahl's words provided them with a background against which they could proceed. Drugs could be a motive to the murder. The tattoo was a piece of the puzzle, and probably also the video, but Lindell did not understand how they all hung together.

After the phone call, Lindell pulled out her notebook again, drew new circles and arrows, and tried to create a believable chain of events.

The telephone rang. She saw that it was Haver and answered.

"Clean as a whistle," he said. "There was not a single thing in the car that gives us an idea. We'll have to see if the technicians find anything. It seems Armas was packed and ready for Spain. Two small suitcases and a shoulder bag in the trunk. As far as I can tell they haven't been touched. That speaks against robbery."

Lindell heard voices in the background.

"Are you still at the marina?"

"Yes, but I'm leaving as soon as we've arranged for transportation. We'll have to examine the car in the garage."

"No traces outside the car?"

"Morgansson is looking into that right now, but it's gravel so the prospects are minimal."

They ended the call and Lindell continued to scribble in her notebook. Why was the car located so far from the murder scene? Did the killer drive it there? Or had they met there and gone to Lugnet together in the killer's car? No, she reasoned, it was covered with a tarp. The killer had done everything not to connect it to the scene of the murder, where he had most likely camped, with the car. He wanted as much time as possible to go by before we found it. Lindell decided that the perp must have driven the car there after the murder and had then made his way back to the tent. Maybe he had an accomplice who had given him a ride back? So far everything had indicated a lone killer, but she could not completely rule out an accomplice.

Should she bring in Rosenberg? He was most likely the weakest link. He associated with Slobodan and was familiar with Lorenzo Wader, which was interesting for their colleagues in both Stockholm and Västerås.

She was interrupted in her train of thought by Ottosson. He stepped into her office after a short knock on the door.

"I have bad news," he said. "Berglund isn't doing so well."

Lindell saw his hesitation. She wanted everything to be fine with Berglund, and did not want to hear anything else.

"He has a brain tumor."

"No!" Lindell exclaimed. "That's not true!"

"They've done one of those scans," Ottosson said, and proceeded with an account of what he knew.

He kept speaking somewhat disjointedly because the alternative was silence. Lindell listened, and the tears started to run down her cheeks. She mechanically wiped them away. Ottosson finished.

"What happens now?"

"He has an operation on Monday," Ottosson said.

"Have you talked to him? How is he taking it?"

Ottosson nodded.

"You know how he is. He said to say hello."

The thoughts surrounding the case, which for several minutes had filled her with optimism and a desire to act, suddenly appeared meaningless. Berglund was her favorite, her mentor, and her walking encyclopedia regarding policework and a general knowledge of Uppsala. Everything would seem meaningless if Berglund was no longer part of their unit.

"Berglund," Lindell mumbled, and the tears started to flow again.

"We'll have to hope for the best," Ottosson said.

She saw that he wanted to say something comforting, as he was always prepared to do, but a brain tumor was a disease of such gravity that not even Ottosson could find words of encouragement.

Once Ottosson had left Lindell's office, with some reluctance, she remained at her desk, reflective but distracted from all policework. The whole time she saw Berglund before her, his cunning smile, his laughter and the eagerness he could display when he saw interest and understanding in the person he was talking to. She caught herself already regarding him as dead and buried.

It took an hour before she got anything done. She called Beatrice and asked if she could bring in Konrad Rosenberg the following morning.

Haver returned shortly after three. Lindell let him talk, lacking the energy to jump in and tell him about Berglund. He would find out in due course. She remembered a conversation from the lunchroom recently when Berglund had talked about "Sture with the hat" and Rosenberg. Haver's tone then had been superior, bordering on condescension.

Finally, he left to go down to the garage and join the technicians in examining Armas's car, and Lindell was happy to be left alone.

Her peace did not last long, however. Sammy Nilsson walked in without knocking and she was on the verge of blasting him for his annoying habit, but then immediately noticed from his expression that he had something important to tell her.

"An escape from the Norrtälje prison this morning," he started, in his usual abbreviated way. "Four men got out, with armed threats and hostage-taking."

Lindell stared at him. A break-out in Norrtälje only indirectly involved law enforcement in Uppsala, and was above all a matter for the patrol units and criminal information service.

"One of the guys is of interest," Nilsson went on. "He's Mexican."

Lindell became attentive.

"His name is Patricio Alavez and he was sentenced for illegal trafficking, that is to say, drugs."

"Cocaine?"

"Yes," Sammy Nilsson said smugly.

What a day, Lindell thought. Absolutely nothing one week, and then the information starts to rain down on us.

"I heard Johansson, you know that lug of a guy from Storvreta, talk about it down at the communications headquarters. When he said Mexico, my ears perked up."

"Any traces? Is the hostage—"

"As if swallowed up by the earth. There is some information on a car, most likely an Audi, that drove through Kårsta at high speed, but it hasn't yielded anything so far."

"Mexico," Lindell said. "We're going to have to take this fucking nice and easy."

Sammy Nilsson looked at her, at first with surprise, then amusement. Lindell cursed very infrequently.

"I am calm," he said. "I'm fucking calm."

Like Lindell, he sensed that they were closing in. She continued her line of reasoning, but without really turning to Sammy. It became a monologue where she was trying to connect all the threads. Connections between the stabbing of Sidström in Sävja, cocaine, and Rosenberg. Nilsson could not clearly see the connections between these events and Slobodan Andersson and Dakar, and he interrupted her. Lindell looked somewhat taken aback, but then told him about Barbro Liljendahl's case and speculations.

"That's a lot of arrows," he said.

He had seen her open notebook on the desk.

"I've asked Bea to bring in Rosenberg tomorrow morning, but the question is if we shouldn't do it right away. And we have to get in touch with Västerås and Stockholm."

"Why?"

Lindell realized that she hadn't told him about her visit to Dakar, and she suddenly felt very embarrassed, but Sammy Nilsson simply waved away her explanations about having had too much to do.

"I'll go with Bea to track down Rosenberg," Sammy said. "You take on the Stockholm colleagues who are working on this jewel, what's his name? Lorenzo? Otto will have to check to see if there is more news on the escape. I looked in on him just now but he was just staring into space like some zombie."

Lindell knew why, but did not want to say anything to Sammy Nilsson and take the edge off his enthusiasm.

"Sounds like a plan," she simply said, and reached for the phone. "I'll call Bea back."

✦

Fifty-One

Zero nurtured a dream of moving back to Kurdistan, the land that his father had described so many times. There were those who said that Kurdistan was only a dream, which made Zero laughed. When he was in the seventh grade, the teacher had said that this land did not exist. That made Zero angry. That was the time when Zero put up his hand and asked when they were going to read about Kurdistan. After all, they had to study all the other countries, rivers, and mountain ranges.

"How can a land that exists not exist?" he had asked the teacher.

"I'm afraid that I don't understand the question. We have to keep to . . ."

Maybe the teacher was convinced that Zero, who otherwise never raised his hand, was trying to mess with him, to cause trouble and confusion.

Zero stood up from his seat and walked out. Zero's father was at home, reading. Zero asked him if the country existed. His father lowered the paper and looked at him.

"In here," he said and thumped his chest, "Kurdistan is in here. If God wills it, we will move there and build a home. If we can only follow our hearts, I will drive a bus in Kurdistan."

He drove a bus in Sweden, most often route 13.

"That is my lucky number," he said, and laughed.

He could not understand the Swedes, a superstitious and unmodern people, and their fear of numbers. He loved buses, and liked to drive route 13.

Zero was afraid. It was a feeling he had more often now. Mostly he was afraid his father would not make it back from Turkey. At night he dreamed that he rescued his father from prison. He would drive a bus up close to the prison wall, on which his father and his friends had climbed, and then they jumped down into the seats on the bus. When it was full, Zero drove the sixty or so Kurds to freedom. His father sat up at the very front and told him how to drive, pointing to the right and to the left, but never with irritation. His father glowed with pride and he turned to his friends, pointed to the driver, and said that it was his son who was driving. Not his oldest son, admittedly, but his bravest.

When Zero awoke he was happy at first, but then he grew afraid.

The fear he felt as he stood in front of the Fyris movie theater was of a different order. Ever since the incident with the drug dealer outside the

Sävja school, Zero had moved around with great caution, had not attended school, had hidden himself from his brothers, and had only spoken to his mother on the phone and to Patrik in the community gardens.

That the man with the Mercedes found him, terrified him. The car had come gliding up, stopped, and waited for Zero, who was on his way to buy some food at the local grocery.

He understood that they must have great power. Not even his family knew where he was holed up. Was it Patrik who had squealed? Zero did not think so. It was most likely Roger who had been indiscreet. He drank alcohol and took pills every day and was in constant need of money. Zero did not like him, but was allowed to stay in his apartment in Gottsunda in return for running some errands. Maybe he had sold Zero's location so he could get more alcohol and pills?

The man in the Mercedes said that everything would be all right, that the old debts were no longer an issue, and that he was forgiven. All they wanted was for him to meet with an important person and apologize.

He had never been to the Fyris movie theater before, did not even know that it existed, and he did not understand the point of the movies that they were advertising.

As arranged, Zero stood outside the movie theater for a while before continuing on up the hill. Up ahead he could see tall trees and he knew he was supposed to go to the graveyard.

He hesitated at the entrance. The graveyard lay before him in complete darkness. There was a strong wind that was causing the trees to toss back and forth as if they were worried about what was going to happen.

He slipped in through a space in the fence. Gravel crunched underfoot. A sudden crack brought him to a halt, but it was only a branch that had broken off and was bouncing down through the canopy before landing on a grave.

Zero walked on. Nothing had been said about who he was to meet or what was going to happen, but he was convinced he was being watched. He rued his decision. He did not like walking among the dead. There was another crack overhead and Zero was convinced he was going to be struck in the head with a branch or be crushed by a falling tree.

Then he saw someone, partly obscured by gravestones, walking toward him. He stopped a couple of meters from Zero, who could not tell what he looked like except that he was a large man wearing a dark coat and with a hat pulled low over his eyes.

"Zero?"

"Yes, that's me."

"It's good that you came."

The stranger's soft voice in the strong wind forced Zero to walk closer, but the man put up his hand and drew back behind a bush.

"This is for enough," he said. "We can speak like this."

"Who are you?"

"That doesn't matter. I only want to ask you to do something."

No, Zero thought, I don't want you to ask me to do something. But he had no time to protest before the man spoke again. He had a different voice from Sidström, deeper and more firm.

"I want you to go to the police and tell them what has happened."

"Are you a cop?"

The man let out a laugh.

"I want you to go to the police and tell them who is selling drugs in this town."

"But that's me!"

"Who is behind it?"

"I don't know that."

"But I do," said the man, and Zero saw his teeth glimmer momentarily in the light.

"They will kill me."

"No, they won't. You will not have to appear in public."

Zero did not know what he meant.

"No one will have to know that it was you," the man clarified.

Zero stared into the darkness and tried to get a sense of what the man looked like. He was no *svartskalle,* he spoke like a Swede, almost like a teacher.

"I don't want to," he said.

"I think you do. You don't want to hide any longer, do you? You only want to put this episode behind you."

Zero tried to say something, but the man gestured with his hand and continued.

"I know what you are thinking. You are wondering how much you will get for your trouble. Shall we say five thousand kronor. Cash. Now."

"I'll get five thousand?"

"Yes, and another five thousand when everything is done."

Zero was speechless. It was a dizzying sum. For ten thousand he could go to Turkey and visit his father. Maybe there would be enough money to buy him out of prison?

"What should I do?"

"Easy. You will go to the police and ask for someone who works with drugs, understand? Tell them that you have repented, and that you were pulled into the drug business against your will. You did not want to sell drugs. You were threatened. And now you want to talk."

The man told Zero what he should tell the police. He went over this several times and asked Zero to repeat what he had said.

"But I'll go to jail," Zero objected.

"No," the man said. "You are too young. The police won't care about you. They want to catch the real bad guys. Understand?"

Zero nodded. He thought it was like in a movie. The police would be pleased and forget about him. And he would get ten thousand.

"I understand," he said, and at that moment a new branch broke off and fell through the trees.

✦

Fifty-Two

"K. Rosenberg" it said in ivory letters on the noticeboard in the A-stairwell. Four flights of stairs, Sammy Nilsson observed.

He shot Beatrice a humorous look.

"Can you make it?"

Bea made a face and started to walk. Damn, they're sensitive, he thought and followed.

The assignment of bringing someone in for questioning was routine for both of them, but even so the tension mounted at each floor they passed. Sammy Nilsson absently read the names on the doors they walked by: Andersson, Liiw, Uhlberg, Forsberg, Burman.

Bea stopped on the third floor and turned around.

"Will he resist?"

"I doubt it," Sammy Nilsson said, but automatically checked with the weapon holster under his jacket with his hand. "Our Konrad is not known to be violent."

They walked on up, taking a breather for a couple of seconds before Bea rang the doorbell. They listened at the door but heard nothing that indicated Rosenberg was home. Bea rang the doorbell a second time as Sammy Nilsson peered through the mail slot.

An hour later, after Sammy had called Lindell and the district attorney, the chairman of the condo association, arrived. He carefully examined their police identification before he put a key in the lock and opened the door.

Konrad Rosenberg was sitting in the only armchair in the living room, a dark red monster of a chair with a nubby, worn cover. Sammy Nilsson thought he looked pleased, perhaps it was the angles of his mouth that created this impression.

On the floor below his arm was a syringe.

"Well, I'll be damned," said the chairman, who had snuck in behind the police.

"Get out!" Bea snapped, and he obeyed immediately.

Ann Lindell was on her way to the day care when she was informed that Konrad Rosenberg was dead. She felt no grief, of course—she didn't even know Rosenberg, and what she knew of him was hearsay. Nonetheless she shed a few tears because it was Berglund she immediately started to think about when Sammy Nilsson called and told her about the depressing scene in the shabby apartment in Tunabackar.

Rosenberg was in some way intimately connected to her colleague. Perhaps it was only the fact that Berglund so recently had talked about how the former drug addict appeared to have come into money, but perhaps it was deeper than this. Earlier in the day she had intended to call Berglund and ask how he was doing, but had lacked the courage. Then when Sammy delivered the news of Rosenberg's death, she was overtaken with the enormity of grief, though not for Rosenberg—for how many people in depressing circumstances hadn't she seen, and how much misery and death had she not had to deal with? No, it was the suddenness of death that rattled her.

It looked like an overdose, Sammy had said, but had added that nothing was certain. Lindell agreed. Nothing was more certain than death, and she increased her speed, performing an insane maneuver in order to get there faster.

The first thing she saw in the day care playground was Erik, who was kicking his way along on a tricycle. A couple of other children were nearby. Ann Lindell recited their names to herself: Gustav, Lisen, Carlos, and Benjamin.

Erik was wearing only a T-shirt. I hope he doesn't catch a cold, she thought. But he was like that, it didn't matter what you put on him, jackets and sweaters ended up being pulled off.

She walked up, lifted him off the tricycle, and took him into her arms.

"We're going home," she said.

✦

Fifty-Three

"No signs of forced entry in the apartment, no drugs other than a couple of grams in a bag on the table in the living room, no outer injuries on Rosenberg, probable cause of death an overdose of what we believe to be cocaine," Sammy Nilsson summed up his report.

Allan Fredriksson pinched the bridge of his nose. Ottosson helped himself to a cookie. Bea stood leaning against the wall. Barbro Liljendahl was the only one who looked even moderately fresh. It was a little past eight in the evening.

God, how he munches, Sammy Nilsson thought, and watched Ottosson put yet another cookie in his mouth, followed by a sip of coffee.

"I see," Ottosson said and stared longingly at the plate of cookies, but apparently realized that three were more than enough and sank back into the chair with a sigh. "He was a longtime addict," he went on, "and that speaks both for and against an overdose. He should have known better."

Barbro Liljendahl coughed.

"Yes," Ottosson said and nodded at her. "You met with him recently, what do you have to say?"

"I don't think he took the needle willingly," she said.

She had been called in by Ottosson and was now participating in a case review with the violent crimes unit for the first time.

"He seemed completely free of drugs when we met last. Granted, he still had some of the drug addicts' mannerisms, but if I were to guess I don't think he was an active user. This is also the picture I got when I went around with questions. One detail that may be of interest is that Rosenberg never used to do cocaine. He kept to amphetamines. This may of course be a contributing factor in the overdose. He may simply have been unused to cocaine."

"Maybe he had a relapse?" Nilsson said, and his eyes lit up momentarily. "He was feeling under pressure; then it's easy to turn to something comforting, like when we pour ourselves a drink."

Bea sighed.

"Well, what do you do? Eat a carrot?"

"Lay off!"

Ottosson broke in before Sammy had time to reply. "We know that Rosenberg had contact with Slobodan. Barbro has established this and Ann has made similar observations, among others noting the fact that Konrad was a customer at Dakar. Barbro's investigation also indicates that he was aquainted with Sidström. He was stabbed in a drug-related context. Why haven't we yet nabbed the perpetrator, that young man from Sävja?"

"He's gone into hiding," Barbro Liljendahl said. "There's information indicating that he has been seen in Gottsunda, but it hasn't been verified yet. Apparently he's scared. I have questioned his friend, Patrik Willman, and he claims that Zero is terrified of his brothers, perhaps also that a friend of Sidström will take revenge. The funny thing in this context is that Willman's mother is a waitress at Dakar."

"Now that's interesting," Sammy Nilsson said.

"Eva Willman appears to be a reasonable woman," Liljendahl went on, "and I don't think she has anything to do with drugs. She's simply happy to have a job."

"A coincidence, in other words," Ottosson said, but looked doubtful.

"Who would want to see Rosenberg dead?"

Bea's question hovered in the air. Ottosson reached for another cookie. Sammy Nilsson scratched his head and yawned. Barbro Liljendahl hesitated, but when no one else spoke she tossed out her theory that it was Dakar's owner, Slobodan Andersson, who had had his henchman Rosenberg murdered, that the latter had potentially been involved in the murder of Armas and that the overdose had perhaps been an act of revenge, or alternatively, a way of silencing a compromising witness to drug dealings.

"Too bad Ann isn't here," Ottosson said when Liljendahl had finished. She went bright red and mumbled something about these simply being ideas.

"As good as anything else," Ottosson said, "But we will have to wait until forensics is done with the apartment and Rosenberg's car. What is the situation with the immediate family? Have they been notified?"

Bea nodded.

"Good," Ottosson said. "Then we continued tomorrow morning, but if you can, Barbro, I would like you and Sammy to drop in on that Turkish boy in Sävja tonight, if that is possible."

"What does that mean?" Sammy said, obviously displeased at the prospect of putting in even more overtime.

"Check out his family and and try to draw out those leads that he has been spotted in Gottsunda."

"It works for me," Barbro Liljendahl said.

"Wonderful," Ottosson said and smiled broadly at her.

"I have to call home," Sammy said and stood with a grimace, but before he had left the room Ottosson's cell phone rang.

Ottosson answered, listened for several seconds, then raised his hand to stop Sammy.

"Okey-dokey," Ottosson said and ended the call.

Everyone looked expectantly at the chief. He was clearly enjoying the situation.

"Give it up," Sammy said, but he couldn't help smiling at Ottosson's boyish expression.

"Speak of the devil," he said.

"Who?"

"Our young man from Sävja," Ottosson said. "You don't have to drive out to the suburbs, the suburbs are coming to us. Babsan and Sammy will take our friend who is waiting anxiously down below."

Sammy called Zero's mother, who only understood the word *police* and, sobbing, handed the phone over to her oldest son, Dogan.

Twenty minutes later Dogan was standing outside the entrance of the police station, ringing the after-hours buzzer, was let in and accompanied by a uniformed officer to the room where both of the police officers and Zero were waiting.

When Dogan caught sight of his brother, he let out a flood of curses. Or that was what Sammy Nilsson guessed the gist was. He put a hand on Dogan's arm and told him to control himself, then pulled out a chair and asked him to sit.

"It was good that you came, Dogan. Your brother wants to help us," Sammy Nilsson said, "and we are grateful for this. He came here of his own free will. You can be proud of Zero."

"*Kar,*" his brother growled, but sat down.

"I regret everything," Zero said. "I want to confess."

Sammy Nilsson turned on the tape recorder and Zero spoke without ceasing for ten minutes. When he finished, they all sat quietly for a moment. Dogan was staring at his brother. Barbro looked touched, while Sammy Nilsson put his hand on Zero's shoulder.

"That was great, man," he said, before turning to Dogan. "If I hear a single word about you making trouble for Zero, then you and your brothers will have problems. Understand?"

Dogan looked Sammy Nilsson in the eye and nodded.

"Have you personally met Slobodan Andersson?" he asked Zero. The latter appeared completely drained and had let his head hang.

Sammy Nilsson turned to Liljendahl.

"Could you get a coupe of sodas?"

She nodded and left the room.

"Okay, Zero, Slobodan Andersson. He's the one we're interested in."

"I don't know," Zero said quietly. "I have never met him. But all of this is his doing."

"Who has talked about Slobodan?"

Zero shook his head.

"But how do you know his name?"

"I just heard it."

"What did you hear?"

"You know . . . stuff."

"Damn it, Zero!" his brother exclaimed.

"I don't know," Zero repeated, "but that old guy . . ."

Liljendahl returned with a six-pack of Fantas. Sammy Nilsson opened two and gave Zero and Dogan each a can.

"Who was talking?" Sammy Nilsson resumed. "Was it the guy you stabbed at the school?"

Zero shook his head.

"If you want us to believe you, you're going to have to tell us."

Zero nodded.

"Are you scared?"

"I don't want to go to jail!"

"We can probably arrange it so no one has to know you were the one who tipped us off," Sammy Nilsson said and glanced at Liljendahl, "but you won't get away with the stabbing. However, you're a juvenile, you aren't old enough," he added for clarification, "to go to jail. I promise."

"It was Konrad," Zero said suddenly.

"Konrad Rosenberg?"

"Yes," Zero mumbled.

"Where did you meet him?"

"Downtown."

"Why did Konrad talk to you about Slobodan Andersson?"

Zero stared at Sammy Nilsson uncomprehendingly.

"That Slobodan was boss," he prompted.

"He probably wanted to show off," Zero said. "Impress me that he knew people with money."

And even though Sammy Nilsson tried to tease out more information, Zero couldn't or wouldn't be more concrete. After a while, Barbro Liljendahl changed the topic.

"I wanted to ask you something," she said. "Why did you start selling cocaine?"

"I wanted to rescue my father."

"Idiot," Dogan said angrily, but in his eyes Sammy Nilsson also glimpsed something other than just anger. There was sadness and desperation.

"He's in prison?"

Zero nodded.

"What do you do, Dogan? Do you have a job?"

"I'm training to become a bus driver," he said.

"That's great," Sammy Nilsson said.

"Our dad is a bus driver," Zero said.

The session ended just after ten in the evening. Before the brothers were allowed to leave the station, Sammy Nilsson drew the older brother aside.

"Dogan, you probably remember what I said. Zero is a sensitive boy. He loves his father and probably you too. Be a brother to him now. Help him! Your father is gone, you have to shoulder the responsibility. Don't say anything to him tonight. Don't scold, don't do anything more than make him a cup of tea, or whatever you normally drink. Have tea together when you get home. Just you and him."

Dogan said nothing but nodded. His dark eyes glittered momentarily.

"My mother makes the tea," he said after a compact moment of silence.

Sammy Nilsson smiled.

"You'll be fine," he said and held his hand out.

"Thanks for the Fanta," Dogan said, but he did not shake the officer's hand.

"Dogan," Sammy said, "what does *kar* mean? That thing you said to your brother."

"Donkey," Dogan said, and smiled for the first time.

✦

Fifty-Four

It was early evening, dusk was falling over Uppsala. Thousands of black birds circled above the rooftops. The streets were becoming empty.

There was still life and movement, though, outside Dakar. Patricio Alavez had been standing behind a tree for the past several hours. Earlier in the day he had kept a lookout over the restaurant, but he had not seen a single person come or go. Finally, he had summoned his courage and gone up to the front door and seen that the restaurant only opened at five o'clock. He realized that a Mexican, even one who was well dressed and sober, would attract attention in the long run if he stood in the same spot for several hours at a time, so instead of hanging around the restaurant, Patricio found a park where he tried to get some sleep. But the excitement associated with the escape had not yet worn off, and he had trouble being able to relax.

Now he was hungry, tired, and anxious. He was worried that the fat one or tall one would not even turn up. He could of course walk into the restaurant and ask, but was worried about being recognized. Yet what would they do? Call the police?

In a way, he regretted having escaped, but everything happened so fast and he had not had time to think. The prison routine had been safe. Now he was a fugitive without friends, with Swedish money in his pocket but without the means to stay out of trouble in the long run. He would most likely receive a severe sentence for his escape, but that did not scare him. Eight or fifteen years in prison did not matter.

To him, his life had ended when he left the village and Oaxaca to fly to Europe. Many times he had cursed himself for his naïveté. How could he have believed that a gringo would help a Mexican get rich? Manuel used to say that it was the earth that was important, that to leave the earth was to leave one's family and one's origin.

What does it mean to be rich, he asked himself while he studied the people who went in and out of the door to Dakar, but he found no answer. He knew what having no wealth meant. What kind of life would it be to remain in a condemned village where almost everyone was getting poorer and poorer? Why did the young ones flee to Oaxaca, Mexico City, and the United States?

Not even Manuel made much noise about this. After Miguel's assassination, he had been as if paralyzed for several weeks and had then undertaken a frenetic project to clear new ground for coffee bushes, and that on a mountain side that was so steep that no one had ever tried it before.

Manuel went there every morning and came back absolutely exhausted late at night. Nothing of the joy of new planting was in his eyes. Shredded by the thorns, his ripped hands, steaming with sweat, he sat on the roof for a while before he rinsed himself off under the tap in the yard.

He lost weight and after a month or so developed a cough that never seemed to go away. Was this the kind of life he wanted them to have? Working day after day on an ill-fated project. Even if they now managed to plant hundreds of bushes on a *milpa* that no one else wanted to cultivate, what did this prove? And then, what happened when the buyers lowered the price of the beans or when coffee flooded in from somewhere else? Because this was how it had always been. Every advance was blocked with setbacks. There were always new directives from the government or the governor. Always new agreements that were barely explained to the villagers but were guaranteed to make them poorer and their lives more difficult.

Patricio abandoned his bench and his caution and paced back and forth on the sidewalk. A growing number of customers were leaving

Dakar and he sensed they were about to close. He could make out a bar through the window and there were still many customers crowded around it. He himself longed for a glass of mescal, to feel the stinging heat in his mouth and throat. In order not to tempt himself more, he hurried back behind the bushes and trees.

Suddenly he spotted a familiar figure. Patricio stepped back out of the shadows in order to see better. Surely it was the fat one who was waddling up the street? A man was walking next to him. He said something that made Slobodan Andersson laugh. Could it be the tall one? No, the man by Slobodan's side was too young.

He laughs, Patricio thought bitterly. Rage shot up like bile into his throat and he had to control himself not to burst out of his hiding place and run across the street. He could have killed the fat one with his bare hands. He needed no weapon, his wrath was enough. Leave him lying there like roadkill, and Angel would be revenged at last.

The men arrived at Dakar, stopped, and discussed something. Slobodan looked even fatter than when Patricio had met him in Mexico. He can afford to eat well, the Mexican thought with hatred.

Suddenly, Patricio felt that it was God's will that he escape from prison, and this made him happy for a brief moment. The escape had made it possible for him to take revenge.

Slobodan opened the door to Dakar, exchanged a few words with his companion, then entered the restaurant. Patricio took a couple of steps back as the other man passed on the opposite side of the street.

This opportunity had been lost, but the next time perhaps Slobodan would be alone. Then all he had to do was wait him out.

Slobodan Andersson nodded at Måns, looked around in the dining room, greeted some acquaintances, and, against his will, came to think of Lorenzo Wader. I hope he doesn't drop by, Slobodan thought, and wondered if he should ask his bartender if he had seen the unpleasant gangster, for gangster was what Slobodan was convinced he was. But he said nothing to Måns, who poured a grappa and set it in front of him.

"How is Ms. Post Office doing?"

"Fine," Måns said. "She's doing a good job. I think Tessie is pleased. It's a step up from Gonzo, at least."

"Don't remind me," Slobodan said and raised the glass to his mouth.

In view of last night he shouldn't have anything to drink, but the force of habit was strong. He could let himself have one glass.

"The dishwasher is a gem," Måns said. "The waitstaff have much more time now."

"What?! Is that bastard still here?"

Måns looked at Slobodan in astonishment.

"Yes, that's good, isn't it?" Måns said, clearly taken aback at this reaction.

"That little shit is out of here," Slobodan said and got up with unexpected haste, went around the bar, and opened the door to the kitchen.

"Is the Mexican still here?"

Donald gave him a quick and angry look.

"Venezuela," he said.

"What? That dishwasher, is he still here?"

Donald gestured at the dishwashing area with his head and sighed.

Slobodan walked out there with only a single thought in his head, to grab that blackmailer by the scruff of his neck and throw him out, but was greeted with a smiling Manuel.

"*Hola,*" he said.

He was standing at the far end of the dishwashing station. He had a knife in his hand. Slobodan slowed down and steadied himself against the dishwashing machine.

"What the hell are you doing here?" he shouted in English. "Get out!"

"Take it easy," Manuel said, his smile only getting wider. "We have some things in common. Have you forgotten? I am happy here, and I am useful."

Slobodan stared at the Mexican. That insolent devil was laughing at him! He recalled the old conflict so many years ago in Malmö. That time *he* was the one who had been holding the knife.

"Leave!" he screamed.

"I will work a couple of more days," Manuel said calmly. "Then I'll go. But by then maybe you have disappeared."

Slobodan stared, astounded at him. Not a trace of yesterday's meekness remained. Was it the knife that made the difference? Was he so damned impudent that he was threatening him?

"What are you talking about? What do you mean 'disappeared'?"

"You are sitting on a fortune; it must be tempting to see other places," Manuel said with a smile.

Slobodan turned on his heel, pushed open the doors to the dining room, and left. He walked right up to the bar and told Måns to pour him a large Bowmore.

"Has be been fired?" Måns asked, and Slobodan could sense the criticism behind the innocent question.

"That's none of your damn business."

Måns made a face, reached for the whiskey bottle, and poured Slobodan a glass.

"He's still here, in other words," Måns said, grinning.

By the time the glass was half-empty, Slobodan had managed to calm himself somewhat. It was really not worth getting upset about. The Mexican had a need to assert himself and feel good about himself for once. Slobodan decided to forget about him. He had said he would leave in a couple of days. Never again would he use any of those tortilla guys. In future he would stick to Spaniards.

The reason for his clemency, and he freely admitted this to himself, was that the man's unusual generosity in delivering the unexpected load of cocaine had solved many problems. After the fateful fire at Konrad's house he had suddenly found himself without any goods, unable to distribute what he had promised, and that was devastating. The clients would sour and find new channels.

So certainly he was justified in celebrating with a glass or two. He wondered how Manuel had managed to get a hold of the drugs in Germany. He was probably not as innocent as he had made himself out to be. He had probably been with Angel on his journey up through Europe, and then when the brother died, he had simply taken over. They are alike, Slobodan thought smugly, hold up a couple of dollars and they come running.

He waved his chubby hand and Måns poured him a beer.

"Is this going to be a repeat performance?" he asked, but Slobodan did not have time to answer before the bartender had turned his back.

Johnny and Donald were busy picking up in the kitchen, rinsing the floor, and cleaning the stovetops. Tessie and Eva were clearing the tables in the dining room while at the same time being attentive to the remaining guests. A party of six that had eaten their way through appetizers, main courses, and desserts had asked for coffee and cognac, and Eva guessed that they would be sitting around for a while. Apart from them, the room was getting empty. A young couple Eva had served paid and left. They had left a tip of one hundred kronor. A hundred kronor, she thought. I can't have been so bad. She placed the small tray with the money on the counter with a certain measure of pride. Måns entered the amount, tucked the hundred kronor note in a large partition where the tips were kept, and turned to her and smiled.

"Did you notice that they were newly in love?"

Eva nodded. She had felt old when she looked at them, even though there was probably no more than ten years between her and the couple. She had felt a tinge of envy when she had seen how he placed his hand over hers, how they had joked and bantered with each other, sometimes lowering their voices and whispering what Eva imagined to be words of love.

Tessie called out to her, interrupting her thoughts. Together they moved a couple of tables and set out new tablecloths.

It had been a good evening. She had gotten past her worst nervousness and was no longer as embarrassed about asking Tessie for advice.

Eva cleaned some glasses. She noticed that Slobodan was watching her. He was sitting at the bar with a glass in front of him. Eva had heard from Tessie about last night's events, how the proprietor had drunk himself into a stupor, thrown up in the kitchen, and how Feo and Manuel had had to help him home.

In a way Eva thought it was good. He had shown a weakness. Maybe the violent drunken episode was an expression of grief at Armas's death. Eva glanced at him. He really did look worried, and she hoped he would have the sense to stop drinking in time.

A couple of newspapers lay scattered on a table. She had started to fold them up when her gaze fell on a headline. The word *extra* was printed in bold letters, then "New escape—hostage drama," and below this a picture of the four men. Astonished, she read the short article, flipped to page five where there was a slightly more detailed report but still not as much as one would have assumed in the case of a dramatic escape in which someone had been taken hostage. She realized it must have been added just before going to press, and that they had not managed to include more than the main points.

She leafed her way back to the photographs again. The similarity was striking. And the last name was the same. It could not be a coincidence. She carefully folded up the paper and took it with her, walked into the kitchen, nodded at Johnny, crammed the paper into the trash, hesitating a couple of seconds as if to check if she were frightened before walking out into the dishwashing area.

Manuel was just pushing the dishwasher closed. He turned his head and Eva studied his face again but without seeing any fear or doubt.

"Eva," he said and laughed as if she had made a funny and unexpected face.

"Manuel," she said, and searched for the right words in English before she continued. She wanted to be precise.

"Have you lied to me about why you are here? You said you wanted to work and earn some money."

He stopped and the look he gave her confirmed her suspicions.

"Do you have a relative who is in prison?"

Manuel searched for something to steady himself, found the counter, cast a nervous glance at the door before he slowly moved himself along the counter and sat on a stool.

"Have you talked to Slobodan?"

Eva shook her head.

"No, but is it true, then?"

Manuel nodded.

"My brother Patricio is in prison," he whispered. "How did you find out?"

This reassured Eva somewhat. Apparently Manuel did not know about the escape.

"Why is he in prison?"

Manuel was silent for a long time while he debated with himself. Then he told her the story of how his brothers had been tempted to become drug runners, how one of them had died in Germany, and how the other had been caught in Swedish customs.

Eva felt immediately that she did not want to be pulled into anything. Patrik's problems were enough. She caught a glimpse of Johnny's chef's hat and heard Donald say something that was drowned out by the roar of the dishwasher. She did not want to hear more. She thought about her sons and her fear became anger.

"Drugs," she spit with such disgust in her voice that Manuel lifted his head and looked sadly at her.

"You are my friend," he said.

"Never!"

"Let me explain," Manuel said, as if speaking for his life. "I did not want to lie to you. I came to Sweden to visit my brother and to help him. I don't like drugs. It costs us our lives."

He assured her of his innocence. Became agitated and loquacious. I don't want this, Eva thought. I want to work and have a decent life. She did not even want to have a meeting about drugs and youth. She did not want to hear Helen's complaints and rants, nothing about drugs, she did not want Manuel's sad eyes.

"Go now," she said, and turned her back.

"I dreamed that you came to Mexico," Manuel said. "That you wanted to see my country . . ."

Eva paused for a tenth of a second, but then opened the hinged doors to the dining room and left.

Manuel stood as if turned to stone. Eva, his friend, had told him to leave. When Slobodan had said he should leave Dakar for good he had not cared. He had returned for Eva's sake. He did not need to do more dishes, he did not need to make money, and he had no desire to see the fat one anymore. Tomorrow the fat one would be gone from the restaurant, perhaps for good.

He washed dishes at Dakar because he liked Eva and wanted to see her. He pulled off his apron and laid it like a shroud over the dishwasher. He hesitated in the dressing room. Should he leave without saying good-bye to the others? No, he should let it be, it was best simply to leave.

He kicked off the rough shoes he had borrowed, put on his sandals and jacket, and went out into the night. A rustling sound came from the garbage cans outside the door. Strangely enough, it made him feel better. They still have to put up with the rats, he thought ungenerously, but immediately felt guilty. It was Feo, Tessie, and Eva who brought out the trash. It was not Slobodan who ran the risk of being bitten.

He walked slowly across the yard. Now the fat one got what he wanted after all, he thought, and walked up the alley to the street where Dakar had its entrance. Suddenly he saw movement in some bushes. He stopped and tried to see what it was that had set the branches in motion.

The old terror from Oaxaca returned. The police was his first thought, but he dismissed it just as fast. Why would they be hiding behind some bushes?

He came out onto the street and looked toward the restaurant entrance. The fat one was standing there. Manuel thought he saw him sway. At the same time he saw in the corner of his eye how a shadow slipped away from the bushes on the other side of the street. Manuel automatically crouched down behind a parked car. The shadow figure was pressed against the wall, then took several careful steps. Manuel thought there was something familiar about the figure. He glanced at Dakar and saw how Slobodan slowly started walking down the street. A taxi passed and Slobodan turned his head and raised his hand awkwardly, as if he was thinking of flagging it down. He is drunk again, Manuel thought.

The shadow on the other side of the street had now speeded up and when it passed a shop window Manuel received the shock of his life. Patricio! It was Patricio who was half-running on the sidewalk. Manuel could not believe his eyes, it could not be Patricio. The clothes looked unfamiliar, the cap was pulled down over his face, but the carriage was his brother's, the long gait and the swinging of his arms. That was how Patricio would make his way through the mountains, half-running, leaving everything behind. But it could not be him. Patricio was in prison. His mind was playing games with him.

Slobodan had now stopped and was trying in vain to bend down in order to tie his laces. He cursed and continued.

The shadow figure on the other side of the street was now only some twenty meters from Slobodan. Manuel became convinced that the shadow was following the fat one.

"*Hermanito,*" he shouted, but not too loudly, afraid that the fat one would hear him.

The man on the other side of the street froze.

"Here," Manuel shouted, now convinced that it really was Patricio, and held his hand up over the top of the car.

The man on the other side of the street turned his head and Manuel staggered when he saw his brother's face.

Patricio looked just as shocked. He stared at Manuel for a couple of seconds before he ran across the street and they fell into each other's arms.

Patricio pulled back from Manuel.

"The fat one is over there," he said and pointed.

"I know."

"I'm going to kill him," Patricio said.

"No, it's wrong," Manuel said harshly, and at the same time wiped the tears from his cheeks. "We won't get Angel back."

"Don't butt in!"

Manuel put his arms around Patricio's shoulders.

"Did you escape from prison?"

Patricio nodded while his gaze followed the fat one, who was now drawing out of sight and finally turned a corner.

"He's gone," Manuel said.

Patricio's entire stance changed after Slobodan Andersson disappeared. He collapsed into a heap, sobbing.

"Patricio," Manuel said with so much love in his voice that the city around them no longer existed, no cocaine and no prison walls, no death and no reprimands stood in the way of the happiness the brothers felt.

This state of unity lasted until Manuel asked the question.

"Why?"

Patricio looked down.

"It just happened," he said. "There were some others . . ."

"There are always these others," Manuel growled, but the flare of anger subsided when he saw his brother's crushed expression.

"We can't stand here," he said and pulled Patricio with him into the shadows.

Patricio started to say something but Manuel put up his hand and shushed him. What should we do, he wondered. His previous plans were no good now. He had to remove Patricio from the streets, hide him, and figure out a way to . . . yes, what?

"Wait here," he told his brother, "don't go anywhere. I'll get the car."

"What car?"

"I've rented a car."

He left and half-ran down the street. A patrol car came gliding along. Manuel jumped over a low fence and landed in a thicket. The patrol car drove on. Eva has called the cops, he thought, getting up and running to the car that he had parked on the street on the next block.

He had been chased by the police once before. That was when he and a dozen other Indian activists had left the headquarters of Consejo Inídgena Popular de Oaxaca to take the bus and join the demonstrations in Oaxaca's central square. The police were waiting behind the school by Carretera Nacionàl and threw themselves over the group. Manuel managed to climb the school wall and through the schoolyard to the other side of the neighborhood. In the background he heard sirens and the barking of police dogs. Manuel ran for his life. Two policemen came after him, one tired after only a couple of hundred meters, the other Manuel managed to shake next to the soccer field by crawling into a shed. Manuel heard the policeman's heavy panting, and he fingered his machete. If the dogs came at least he had this.

Manuel spent the whole night there before he dared leave his hiding place. When he came down to the square the following day the demonstration had been dispersed and only a torn poster bore witness to the small-farmers' monthlong protest.

Now there were no police in sight and no sound of dogs. He swung out onto the street from his parking spot and made a U-turn. As he passed Dakar, some customers were stepping onto the street. They were noisy, laughing, and sauntered away. It was a good sign and Manuel grew calm. If the police were inside Dakar, the guests would probably have stayed inside from curiosity.

He rolled slowly to the place where he had left Patricio.

✦

Fifty-Five

Manuel was awakened by bird song, or rather, a violent screeching outside the tent. After a second or so, when he became conscious of the previous evening's events, he threw back the blanket and sat up. Patricio was gone. They had fallen asleep next to each other, like they used to when they slept in the mountains, and in the darkness Patricio had asked Manuel to tell him about the village.

Manuel crawled out of the tent and looked around before he crawled up the slope. From the top he anxiously scanned the riverbank area. He worried that Patricio had run away yet again, but then he saw him. His brother was sitting some hundred meters downstream, up close to the river. Perhaps he even had his legs and feet in the water.

Manuel walked over to him slowly, following the edge of the field, plucking a couple of grass stalks and trying to figure out what time it was. The sun was still low in the sky.

Patricio turned when Manuel came down the riverbank with running steps. They smiled at each other.

"It was worth the escape just for this moment," Patricio said. "Now I could go back to prison."

Manuel sat down at his brother's side.

"You are going home," he said.

"How can I do that?" Patricio asked after a while.

Manuel told him what he had been thinking. Patricio was speechless.

"It won't work," he said when Manuel had finished explaining his plan. "The police will take me."

"Maybe," Manuel said, "but it is worth a try."

"What about you?"

"I'll manage," Manuel said, but did not sound completely convinced. "You have to get home."

"But that costs money."

"That I have," Manuel said. "I have a lot of money."

Patricio did not ask where his brother had acquired these funds. Maybe his time in prison had taught him not to be too curious.

While the sun rose and slowly moved across the sky they went through all the details and what could go wrong. Manuel was surprised that Patricio was being so compliant. He raised no objections as he usually did. Instead he listened and repeated what Manuel said.

"Should we take a dip?"

"The river is full of plants," Patricio said.

"I know a good place."

While they undressed, Manuel teased Patricio about his potbelly. He only laughed, patted his stomach, and jumped in the water. They splashed and played like children, spraying each other and diving in the muddy water.

If only Angel were with us, Manuel thought suddenly, and was overcome with the grieving thoughts that had dominated his mind the past six months. But he did not want to ruin Patricio's joy, and therefore he said nothing.

What if his plan to get Patricio out of the country failed? His brother still deserved whatever few moments of freedom he could snatch. He knew that their nighttime talks in the tent and their swim in this foreign river would forever appear among of the happiest moments in their lives. One day, if they got to be together in the future, they would think back on this day and remember it with gratitude.

Nothing could be allowed to muddy this brief moment of shared joy.

When they had put their clothes back on, Manuel took the bag out of the hiding place and showed Patricio the money. He said nothing, asked nothing, but Manuel felt obliged to tell him how he had come to be in possession of such a fortune. If Patricio had his own views or was critical of his brother's actions, he did not say it, simply fingered the bunched bills a little absently.

Manuel put the money back in its place. Patricio appeared lost in thought. It was as if the sight of all the dollars depressed him. Perhaps the bills reminded him of Angel?

After a couple of hours Manuel decided to go up to the arts and crafts village for provisions. He had seen a small cafe there. If only they could get a little bread, they would be fine. They could take water from the river.

They had agreed to stay by the river until the police reinforcements in connection with the escape had thinned out some. The likelihood was that the highways around Uppsala had roadblocks.

If Eva had called the police and told them about Manuel, they would also be looking out for him and his plan would fail. But he did not think Eva had said anything, even though she had reacted so harshly and unsympathetically. That reaction was harder to bear than if she had gone to the police. But Manuel knew he only had himself to blame. He had lied to her, and she felt betrayed. He tried not to think of her, but it was difficult. There was something about the woman that was incredibly attractive to him. Was it her generosity and openness? Maybe it was only that he had been flattered by her eager questions about his life, or else it was simply that he was dazzled by her breasts under the form-fitting blouse, her smile, and blond hair?

In the tent, he had dreamed that they bathed together in the river. Now he had to stop dreaming. Eva was a memory.

He bought sandwiches and soda at the cafe. He did not think anyone paid attention to him. The parking lot was full of cars and groups of tourists and young families wandered between the cottages. Manuel saw a man painting something that Manuel imagined was going to be a large toy. He stopped and watched the craftsman slowly brush yellow paint onto the broad planks and realized it was going to be a small house. He was amazed that one would put so much effort into a pretend house.

The painter looked up and gave Manuel a hasty but friendly glance. Manuel felt irritated and realized that envy was the source. Everything looked so harmonious, everyone appeared well-nourished and well-dressed. There were no poor people selling trinkets or begging. The craftspeople appeared carefree and pleased with their work. Everything was so different from Mexico.

Back in the village children played with scraps. If they in fact had any spare time to play, they had to make their own toys. No one built special houses for them.

Manuel continued on, passing trees laden with apples and families who had spread blankets in the grass. They ate and drank. Some of them were playing a game with wooden sticks that they swung through the air in order to strike down the wooden sticks of their opponent.

A young couple was walking in front of him. The man had his hand on one of the woman's buttocks. They stopped and kissed. Manuel walked past them and tried to avoid staring at them.

When he got back to the tent, Patricio was sleeping. Manuel sat down on the side of the bank. He thought about Gabriella in the village and from there it was not a great leap to Eva. His brother snored and turned. Some birds flew up from the water.

The sight of the man's hand on the woman's buttock had excited him. He thought of Eva. It was as if his thoughts automatically returned to her.

Manuel stretched out in the grass and was asleep within a couple of minutes.

✦

Fifty-Six

The morning started with an unusually short case review. Ann Lindell had taken Erik to Görel's so that she could drop him off at day care. Görel had not commented on their dinner, had in fact not been particularly communicative.

While her colleagues were filing in—some cheerful, others reticent and glum with fatigue—Lindell tried to repress her friend's coldness. Once this case was over and Lindell could gather her thoughts, they could have a talk and sort out this misunderstanding. Everything later, that was how she experienced her life. The fault lay with her, she had combined her work with her personal life and it was clear that Görel had felt pushed aside. Lindell decided to call and apologize.

Fredriksson, Sammy Nilsson, Beatrice, Barbro Liljendahl, Ottosson, and a handful of other police officers were present, among them three men from the drug unit and two superior officers from patrol. The head of the criminal information service, Morenius, accompanied by district attorney Fritzén, came sauntering in when everyone else was already seated.

Ottosson began the meeting and briefly sketched an outline of the situation. The circumstances regarding Konrad Rosenberg's abrupt end had created a flurry of speculations, and Ottosson emphasized very strongly that they were not interested in Rosenberg even though his case involved drugs and sudden death.

Their focus was on Slobodan Andersson, his potential involvement in the cocaine wave that had washed over the city, and the question of how Armas's murder could be plugged into this context.

"Mexico," Lindell said when the lecture was over.

"I've been reading up on this," Sammy Nilsson said. "Everyone is still at large. The hostages are, as you know, unharmed. They were left bound in a locked car that was found around eleven o'clock last night.

A guy who has a logging harvester was bringing some diesel up and he discovered the abandoned van. He is planning to start harvesting timber in the area. But as I said, there is not a trace of this gang of four. The whole thing seems professionally planned and executed."

"I saw Bodström on TV last night," Fredriksson said. "He could hardly contain himself."

Sammy Nilsson cast an angry glance at him before he went on. He hated to be interrupted.

"One of the four is Mexican. His name is Patricio Alavez and he was serving an eight-year sentence for drug smuggling. A bungled job at Arlanda. It seems like the drugs are now finding other ways to enter the country, isn't that true, Olsson?"

"Smaller airports and the Öresund bridge appear to be more popular these days," the drug detective answered drily.

"Alavez is a peaceful man, according to Norrtälje," Sammy Nilsson said. "It is most likely that he did not partake in the preparations. Apparently he was roped in during the excitement. But how can we really know? It may have been an act. During the investigation and trial he refused to say on whose behalf he had traveled to Sweden. According to his ticket he was traveling from Bilbao, and two days before that had come directly from Mexico. He may have contacts outside prison who are willing to help him, especially in view of the fact that he did not rat on anyone."

"Both Slobodan and Armas were in Mexico two years ago," Lindell interrupted.

"You mean that they recruited this peaceful Mexican at that time?" Morenius asked.

"It's possible," Lindell said. "We've determined that Slobodan returned with money. The drug trade is as good a guess as a lottery win."

"We'll go into Dakar, Alhambra, and his apartment at the same time," Ottosson said and glanced at the district attorney, who did not appear to be fully awake yet and did not appear to have any comments.

"We believe Slobodan Andersson is currently at home. The lights were on in his apartment at half past eleven last night. The guys from surveillance thought they saw Andersson in the window, but we cannot be sure, and we also do not know if he is alone. No one has left the apartment, at any rate."

Ann Lindell was looking forward to the raid. The look on the face of the arrogant restauranteur alone would be worth it. This time they had a little more to show for themselves, in part about Mexico, but also surrounding Slobodan's connections with Rosenberg. He had some explaining to do and simpy the knowledge that they were going through his apartment and his two restaurants with a fine-toothed comb would make him extra nervous. He was shaken, Lindell was sure about that. Behind the self-assured mask, there was genuine concern.

At exactly eight o'clock—Sammy Nilsson read the time from his thirty-year-old Certina—Slobodan Andersson's apartment was pierced by the ringing of his doorbell.

The sound of coughing and dragging footsteps approaching the front door were heard from inside.

"Who is it?"

"Sammy Nilsson from the police."

A new cough and thereafter the rustle of a chain and then the door opened several inches.

"Good morning," Sammy Nilsson said and gave Slobodan Andersson a wide grin.

"What do you want? It's the middle of the night, damn it!"

"Open up and I'll explain."

Slobodan Andersson sighed, opened the door, and started at the sight of five officers standing in the hallway.

Fifteen minutes later he left the apartment in the company of Sammy Nilsson and Barbro Liljendahl.

The first thing Slobodan Andersson was asked to do at the police station was to have his fingerprints taken. He did this without protest but then refused to utter a word until his lawyer arrived.

During this time the police embarked on their search of his apartment and the two restaurants. They had collected the keys to Alhambra and Dakar from a groggy Oskar Hammer, the head chef at Alhambra, who for the past few years had been waiting for exactly this, that one day the police would be standing outside his door. A technician was dispatched to each restaurant. The head of forensics, the semiretired Eskil Ryde, took care of the apartment.

The canine unit consisting of officer Sven Knorring and the Jessica the Labrador went through the apartment first but found nothing. Not a single indication of drugs anywhere.

At Dakar, an expectant Ann Lindell followed Jessica's sniffing at tables and chairs, through the kitchen, cold storage, and staff areas.

"Clinically clean," Knorring summed up.

Lindell was about to ask if the dog was one hundred percent reliable but stopped herself at the last second. They decided to walk to Alhambra. Downtown stores were opening, people were starting to fill the streets, and those who recognized Ann Lindell—and they were quite a few after the last murder investigation and the blaze that had almost cost her her life—followed her stroll with the accompanying canine unit with interest.

Alhambra was lit up. Charles Morgansson came to meet them and took on the role of maître d'.

"Have you made a reservation?" he inquired politely, and scratched Jessica's ear. But the dog paid no attention to the technician, pulling on her leash, straining to go in deeper.

Lindell noticed a change in the officer's expression as well. It was as if he and the dog were one. Jessica whimpered pleadingly and Sven Knorring nodded to Lindell and let the dog go. She immediately took off through the dining room.

Knorring followed. Morgansson and Lindell followed them with their eyes. There was total silence. Only the click of the Labrador's claws against the lacquered wood floor could be heard.

The lawyer Simone Motander-Banks was a vision. Sammy Nilsson could not help staring at the woman who swept into the questioning chamber as if it were a cocktail party. She was dressed in a tight skirt, a light-colored jacket, and high heels. A wide gold bracelet dangled on one wrist. She smiled tightly, ignored the foolishly staring Sammy Nilsson and the bewildered Barbro Liljendahl and turned to the restaurant owner.

"You have definitely lost weight," she said. "It suits you."

"Simone," Slobodan Andersson said, "wonderful to see you."

For a few moments he appeared to have regained his self-assurance, stood up and kissed her on the cheek. Sammy Nilsson observed that Slobodan Andersson for a moment studied her remarkable earring. He then suavely engaged the lawyer in conversation, completely ignoring the two detectives.

"I'm glad you were able to come down on such short notice," Sammy Nilsson said, taking advantage of a pause in the bright chatter.

The lawyer had all of the characteristics Sammy Nilsson found hardest to bear: arrogance and pretentiousness, complemented by a disdain for the police, as if they were a lower order of beings engaged in a filthy profession which they practiced with a halfhearted sloppiness. He had heard one of the city's more renowned attorneys refer to the police as "farm hands."

The lawyer and Slobodan sat down. Simone was cool, with crossed legs and her hands demurely clasped in her lap, the restaurant owner sweaty, heavy, and somewhat out of breath.

"Well, now," Sammy Nilsson began, after first recording the particulars of the questioning session on the tape recorder, "we have some things to sort out here. First Mexico. What were you and Armas doing there?"

"Vacation," Slobodan answered quickly.

"No acquaintances there? No deals? Business connections?"

"No."

"You have spoken with my colleague Ann Lindell about this."

"Exactly," Slobodan Andersson replied, then added, "I don't know why we have to go on about Mexico. Are there laws against going there?"

"Of course not. Perhaps I or one of my colleagues will be fortunate enough to have reason to go there. We simply want to get to the bottom of why Armas got his tattoo. We now know where it happened. We also know that you were present. The tattoo artist, Sammy Ramiréz, remembers you very well. But why did the symbol that Armas chose for his tattoo come to play a role at his death?"

"I don't know what you are talking about."

"We believe that the person who slit your partner's throat had a motive that was grounded in Mexico. Therefore the tattoo played a role."

Slobodan Andersson stared at the policeman, astonished.

"Quetzalcóatl," Sammy Nilsson read with some effort after first consulting his notes, "was apparently meaningful, and not only for Armas."

"What are you talking about?" Slobodan asked.

"The killer removed the tattoo from Armas's arm. He skinned your friend."

Slobodan Andersson's jaw literally dropped and in his eyes there was only confusion and doubt.

"Skinned," he repeated foolishly.

"That's why we need you to talk about Mexico."

"Would you like something to drink?" Simone Motander-Banks asked, and at the same time shot both of the detectives an exasperated glance.

Slobodan shook his head.

"I don't know anything about the tattoo," he said hoarsely.

Barbro Liljendahl rose, left the room, and returned quickly with a pitcher of water and some glasses.

Sammy Nilsson poured a glass and placed it in front of Slobodan before he continued.

"Talk about Patricio Alavez. Was he the one you met in Mexico?"

Slobodan's hand, which had just grabbed hold of the glass, shook and he spilled water onto the table.

"Oops," Sammy Nilsson said cheerfully.

"I would like to know on what grounds you are subjecting my client to this attack," the lawyer said.

"I'm happy to oblige," Sammy Nilsson said and leaned forward. "We have good reason to believe that your client has smuggled cocaine into this country to the estimated value of at least three million. Does that count as reason enough?"

The demolishing of Slobodan Andersson's line of defense continued. Sammy Nilsson continued to systematically counter each attempt at explanation and denial. When Slobodan was asked about his contact with Konrad Rosenberg he at first denied all knowledge of him, but was then forced to concede that he had a faint memory of a guest named Rosenberg.

"Your friend Konrad is also dead," Sammy Nilsson announced brutally. "Cocaine became his death."

At this point Simone Motander-Banks interrupted the proceedings for a private consultation with her client. Both of the detectives left the room.

"Yes," Sammy Nilsson said, and sat down in a chair in the little lounge outside the questioning room, but got to his feet almost at once.

"Can we pin Armas's murder on him as well?" Barbro Liljendahl wondered.

"I doubt it," Sammy said. "He has a good alibi. At least twenty people had confirmed that he was at Alhambra all evening."

"He could have hired someone."

"It's possible, but I don't think he wanted Armas dead. Ann doesn't think so either. But we'll put him away on the drug charge. I'm one hundred percent certain that his prints are on that bag."

They resumed the session. The detectives had anticipated a counterattack from the lawyer, but she was surprisingly passive when Sammy Nilsson turned the tape recorder back on.

"Alhambra," he began. "Isn't it careless to keep so much cocaine there? We found a bag in your office that—"

"I don't know anything about a bag!"

"We have secured a number of prints and it is only a matter of time before we can establish if yours are among them," Sammy Nilsson said calmly.

"I've been set up!" Slobodan Andersson exclaimed. "It's a trap. Don't you get it? That briefcase was given to me by—"

"By whom?"

"I don't know," Slobodan Andersson muttered.

"You can do better than that," Barbro Liljendahl said.

He lifted his head and stared at her as if she were an alien. In his eyes, she read that the coming retreat would not be orderly, that everything that followed would in fact be panic, lies, and condemnation. The police held all the trump cards.

Slobodan Andersson's enormous body appeared to have lost all control and sunk down on the chair. He muttered something that no one present was able to catch.

✦

Fifty-Seven

Ever since Eva Willman woke up at six o'clock that morning she had wondered if she should contact the police.

The escape from the Norrtälje prison had been allotted a great deal of space in the paper. She had read every line with an increasing sense of anxiety and indecision. She stared at the photograph of Manuel's brother. They were very alike.

Where are they now, she wondered, and recalled Manuel's awkwardness about all things Swedish. He had displayed a sweeping lack of knowledge about the country and Uppsala.

She believed him when he had pleaded ignorance about his brother's escape. Perhaps not last night—then there had only been room for surprise and bitterness at his duplicity—but now in hindsight, as she recalled his assurances and above all his expression, she was prepared to take him at his word.

What had he said as she left the dishwashing area? That he had believed she had wanted to visit his country. She pushed the paper away and tried to imagine herself in Mexico. She had toyed with this thought, of course. And it was not only from curiosity about another country or the fact that she had recently read an article about the Caribbean. It was also Manuel the man. After her initial assessment, when she had pegged him as a movie villain, she had gradually adjusted her impression. He was perhaps not exactly handsome, but he possessed a strength that appealed to her.

She was drawn to fit, wiry men. She did not like couch potatoes with jutting stomachs and poor posture, she might as well admit it.

She had noticed how he studied her in secret. These had not been unpleasant looks, as opposed to Johnny in the kitchen who stared at her with a mixture of disdain and lust. Blushing, she thought about how she had put in a little extra effort to make herself look good before yesterday's shift, and the look he had given her in the changing room had been exhilarating, in a somewhat bewildering way.

She was not in love with this lying Mexican, but it was as if her new job also involved a new relationship to life and the future. She was not stuck. She could develop. She could make money and have the opportunity to travel, as she had dreamed of for so long. She could meet a man to flirt with and perhaps love. Love in a new way, not like with Jörgen. Dakar promised this. Even the new, trendy hairstyle that had been more or less forced on her, but that she had immediately liked, was a confirmation of all this.

It was in this context that Manuel had entered Dakar as a messenger of the fact that the world was bigger than just Uppsala. However many articles she read, and however many travel programs she watched on television, a living person was a much more effective catalyst for dreams.

Eva had met people from foreign countries before—taking a walk through Sävja was enough for that—but Manuel's stories about Mexico and his village vibrated with a love and a longing that Eva absorbed with all her senses. She could not put her finger on what it was exactly, but he had intensified her longing.

Now he was gone for good. She felt it as a betrayal, as if she had been double-crossed at the start of a budding and promising romance.

Hugo stumbled groggily into the kitchen. Eva stood up and quickly put breakfast on the table. She smiled at the sound of Patrik in the bathroom.

"How are you doing?"

Hugo grunted something and shouted at Patrik to hurry up.

When they were done with breakfast—it took five minutes because both of the boys had slept in—and they had hurried off to school, the telephone rang. Eva glanced at the wall clock. It was shortly after nine.

She lifted the receiver and heard Feo's agitated voice. He told her he had been called by Donald, who in turn had a received a call from Oskar Hammer at Alhambra. Oskar had told Donald about the visit from the police and that he had been forced to hand over all keys. Dakar, Alhambra, and Slobodan's apartment were being searched. The police had not wanted to tell him what it was all about, but Hammer had guessed that it was a matter of suspected tax fraud.

When Donald had rushed down to Dakar, he had been stopped by a police officer who stood at the entrance like a bouncer. Donald had managed to catch sight of a dog inside.

"It must be drugs," Feo said. "The tax authorities don't bring a dog."

"Do they think Manuel . . . ?"

"No, why would they be interested in him? An illegal worker is not enough for them to hit Alhambra and Slobodan at home. It must be something else. Damn it!"

Eva knew Feo was thinking of his job, and it struck her that the same went for her. If the police closed Dakar she would be unemployed again.

"Did Donald say anything else?" she asked.

"He tried to talk to the police, but they were cold as fish so he went home. We'll have to see."

"Are you going down there?"

"I'm supposed to work today," Feo said despondently.

When she had hung up she just sat at the kitchen table. It was too much. First the revelation about Manuel and his drug brother who had escaped, and now this.

Eva stood up with a sigh, took out the telephone book from a kitchen drawer, found the number of the police, dialed the numbers, and found herself speaking with a recorded, mechanical voice that urged her to make a selection from one of the available options. After a couple of seconds she slammed the receiver down onto the table and the call was disconnected.

✦

Fifty-Eight

Manuel woke up with a start. The sun was high and beamed down from a clear blue sky. A sudden shadow in his face had awakened him, and when he opened his eyes a man was standing there. Manuel sprang to his feet, the man jumped back and uttered something that caused Patricio to awaken and sit up.

The man said something they did not understand. Manuel exhaled. It was the fisherman, the one who usually walked by with a fishing rod over his shoulder.

Manuel made a calming gesture to Patricio.

"Not understand," Manuel said in English.

The fisherman laughed but kept speaking in Swedish. Then he bent over, pretended to pick something up from the ground, and brought his hand to his mouth while he had a wide smile on his face.

Manuel stared at him without comprehension, but when the man pointed over the edge of the bank in the direction of the fields, he realized the fisherman meant the strawberries. Manuel nodded eagerly.

The man pulled his hand over his brow, made a face that was supposed to indicate pain, and then put a hand on his back.

Patricio regarded the whole pantomime with amazement.

"What does he want?" Patricio asked.

"He thinks we work with strawberries."

The man entertained the brothers for several more minutes with charades about how poor the fishing was and how good the sun felt.

Then he took his leave and went downstream. Manuel thought he looked happy as he walked.

"He's fishing," Patricio said and watched the slow-moving water flowing by.

He got up and went to the water's edge. Manuel watched him as he sat in a crouch and wet his hand in the water, before he turned his head and met his brother's gaze.

"Do you remember when we stood by the Rio Grande?"

Manuel nodded. How could he forget?

"We were foreigners there, too. We had to be on guard even with the friendly people. What if that fisherman was simply pretending?"

"I don't think so," Manuel said.

"Like Hamilton, the broccoli farmer who bought beer and gave us food," Patricio said. "We thought he wished us well, but then he called the cops and withheld our wages."

"I remember," Manuel said, "but there is no sense in worrying about this now."

He understood his brother, but was also irritated at his doubts.

"You are free!" Manuel said, and threw his arms wide, as if he could scrub away all the doubt with a single stroke.

"Am I?"

Patricio turned back to the river and stared into the water.

"We have to stay here a few days until the police calm down," Manuel said, "but you have to believe it will work out."

Patricio said nothing. Manuel came to think of Eva. What was she thinking about him? That he was a liar, of course, but she probably also thought he was a drug dealer. He would so have liked to have her as a friend, and it hurt him that she did not think well of him. It felt both unfair and unnecessary. He should have trusted her and talked about why he traveled to Sweden. Then they might perhaps still have been friends.

He had understood that she had been attracted by the thought of traveling to Mexico. It had not simply been an innocent joke between them. In her eyes he had seen a longing and a spark that was lit. She had considered the possibility, but now all that was gone.

Manuel cursed himself for having disappointed her and he wondered if the wound could be healed.

Patricio interrupted his thoughts by standing up and helping himself to a sandwich and soda. He ate and drank in silence.

"Is it edible?" Manuel asked.

"I've had worse," Patricio replied, smiling.

Manuel laughed with relief when he realized that his brother was making an effort to bridge the discord and the tense atmosphere.

"I'm also going to have some," he said, taking out the wrapped sandwich and sitting down next to his brother.

"This afternoon I'll get us some fried chicken," he continued.

At that moment a helicopter approached at a low altitude. It swept in from the north and flew over the river a hundred or so meters from the place where the brothers were sitting.

Taken by compete surprise as they were, they did not even manage to react until the helicopter had vanished from view.

"The police," Patricio whispered.

Manuel did not know what to believe.

"Maybe it's the military," he said, and told him that he believed there was an air force base on the other side of the river.

"They're looking for me," Patricio said, and stood up.

"I can swim across and check," Manuel offered. "Maybe it was something routine and nothing to do with us."

He checked the bushes where he had hidden the money. Patricio noticed his gaze.

"If you cross the river, I'll put the tent away. Even if they are not looking for us we are clearly visible from the air."

Patricio was right. Their tent must stand out like a torch from up above. He undressed, swam across the river, climbed up on the other side, and in the distance he could just make out the helicopter that had landed. He was unable to determine if it was a police helicopter, but he could not spot any activity on the airstrip.

Twenty minutes later they were on their way. They followed the Fyris river to the southwest. Manuel had seen a forest in the area. There they should be able to find a more secluded spot. The car could remain parked near the arts and crafts village for now.

After a trek of a couple of kilometers, the river turned directly south toward Uppsala. The brothers crawled up the bank and discussed what they should do. Before them lay a field and beyond that the woods rose up thickly.

They took a chance and crossed the field, arrived at a highway that they crossed, avoided a couple of houses, finally reached the shielding curtain of trees and followed an almost invisible path into the woods. Wine-red mushrooms peeked out between the heavy branches on either side of the path.

"It is like a cathedral," Patricio said and stopped, stroking the sticky fir with his hands. "How beautiful it would be if—"

"Let's push on."

Manuel was irritated. He was in a way, however, grateful for the short break—his brother had not shown any fatigue despite their quick march, while he himself was panting.

"They're hunting us," Patricio said.

"As if I didn't know that," Manuel said.

"If we were free I would—"

"What?"

"I don't know," Patricio said hesitantly. "Do you go to mass?"

"Why wouldn't I do that?" Manuel asked, perplexed.

He continued on deeper into the woods. Patricio lumbered on behind him. After a short while they reached a house.

"It looks abandoned," Patricio said.

There was no movement either outside or in the windows, and no smoke rose from the chimney. An old tree, still green and covered in apples, was lying straight across the gravel path that led from the gate up to the house. The sight of the giant that had been struck down in the midst of its fruitful phase depressed Manuel. The top of the tree was partly torn to pieces. Manuel walked up and studied the jagged wounds where the branches had been torn from the trunk. The wood was light but with a core of murky brown rot that Manuel was easily able to crumble between his fingers.

"Who lives here in the woods?" he asked and looked around.

There was a small field behind a low stone wall. It was not in use and small trees were growing in a tangled sea of high herbs and grass. The red-painted wooden wall glowed with a warm and welcoming light in the afternoon sun and some yellow flowers that Manuel recognized from his homeland waved by the high stone foundation.

He walked up to the door and tried the door handle. It was locked.

"Manuel, come!"

Patricio was standing in the doorway of a smaller building, waving for his brother.

"We can sleep in here," Patricio said when Manuel had caught up.

The shed consisted of one small room. Firewood was piled up to the ceiling along one wall. On the other side there was an old metal frame bed. A mattress was rolled up against one end of the bed. Patricio undid the string holding the mattress together and it unrolled over the bed frame. He chuckled.

"The bed is made," he said and threw himself down.

They carried in their few belongings and installed themselves. Manuel hid the bag of money behind the stack of firewood. It felt unpleasant to force oneself into a stranger's house, but on the other hand it had been open and they were not causing any damage. The most important thing was that they were no longer visible from the air if any more helicopters appeared.

Patricio stretched out on the bed with his hands under his head. Manuel sat down on a rickety wooden chair.

"What if we were to tell our whole story," Patricio said after a long period of silence.

Manuel looked quizzically at him. He was too exhausted to think. This fatigue was of a different order from at home. In the mountains he could wander for hours, even carrying a load, without tiring.

"I don't think Swedes know what it is like in Mexico," Patricio said.

"That is not so strange. How many people in our village know what it is like here? And how would you make this happen? Are you going to be on TV?"

Patricio shut his eyes. A spider walked across his closely cropped hair. Manuel studied his face. I have to get him home again, he thought, bending forward and brushing the spider away. Patricio smiled, but he did not open his eyes. After a minute or so he slept heavily.

If we could tell our whole story, Manuel thought, where would we begin? How many would listen? Maybe Eva, but how many others?

He got up from his seat and walked as quietly as possible back out into the yard. He walked up to the main house, forcing his way through some bushes to a window, and peered inside. It was a kitchen. There was a wood-burning fireplace with a white-washed hood. A table and four chairs was the only furniture. On the table was a yellowed newspaper and a pair of glasses.

When he left the window and walked back over the flower bed he felt a familiar scent. He sniffed the air, looked down, and received a shock when he realized what it was that was giving off the aromatic smells.

He had stepped on a Ruta, or rue. He recognized the mild yellow-green leaves so well.

Will I die here? he wondered, swiftly making the sign of the cross and backing slowly away from the house. When he lifted his gaze from the flower bed he thought he could see Miguel's children in the windows. He wanted to leave the house and run away but controlled himself.

It struck him that maybe the poor people in this country also planted Ruta outside their houses. The rich men took pills when they had an ache, while the poor prepared an infusion of herbs or a poultice of healing leaves. It was a poor man's house they had broken into. That immediately felt better. A rich man would be beside himself. A poor man would understand. That was how it was in the village. The poor were the most generous, but on the other hand they did not have much to give.

Manuel had the idea that they should help clear up a little in the yard. He thought he had seen a saw leaning up against the wall in the shed. They could saw the fallen tree into firewood. That could be done in the wink of an eye.

He went inside where Patricio was still sleeping. He had curled up and turned to the wall. Manuel pulled the blanket out of the bag, crawled in beside his brother, and pulled it tightly around them both.

✦

Fifty-Nine

Very rarely or perhaps never before had Ann Lindell experienced such a veritable storm of information. It started with new leads from the Norrtälje prison, which was shifting the focus of the Armas investigation. Patricio Alavez, who was serving a sentence for attempted drug smuggling, had received a visit from his brother, Manuel Alavez, several days earlier. Lindell immediately tried to flesh out the details on this new player in the game. Faxes were coming in and e-mails were popping up with information that was making her more and more convinced: this brother was of great interest.

She asked Fryklund, the new recruit who had turned out to be a pearl, to look into how and when Manuel Alavez had arrived in Sweden. After half an hour, Fryklund called her back.

He had arrived on a flight directly from Mexico City to Arlanda, and from there he had rented a car, an almost new Opel Zafir. The Mexican had paid the whole rental fee in cash. The car was due to be returned in four days, the same day that his return flight to Mexico had been booked.

Before she finished the call, she gave Fryklund an additional task: to request all available information on the Alavez brothers from the Mexicn authorities. Some of this had probably been done in connection with the investigation of Patricio Alavez, but now there was also his brother. Had he been accused of any crimes in Mexico?

Then Lindell called Morgansson at forensics, gave him the number to the company that had rented out the Opel and asked him to see if the tire marks collected from the scene at Lugnet could have come from the rental car.

"It'll be a matter of what brand of tires they use," Morgansson said.

A superfluous comment, Lindell thought, who was increasingly irritated when her colleagues pointed out something obvious.

"Is there DNA from Lugnet?" she went on.

"Sure," Morgansson said.

"Run it against Patricio Alavez, the one who escaped from Norrtälje."

"Aye aye, Captain," he said.

Lindell did not feel like a general commanding her troups from a field telephone, but she did not take Morgansson's comment as an implied criticism. She knew he liked it when there was action.

"This thing is starting to crack," she said, in an attempt to adopt a more relaxed attitude, and perhaps it was also an unconscious attempt to show her appreciation of her colleague's work.

"It looks good," Morgansson agreed. "If the Alavez brothers are hanging out together, we'll get them."

"Anything more on Rosenberg?"

"No, not really. The apartment was completely free of narcotics, apart from the cocaine on the table. He kept his place surprisingly clean. We have secured three sets of prints apart from his own."

"Slobodan's?"

"No, he wasn't one of them."

They hung up, and Lindell felt relieved. It was the first time they had been able to speak naturally with each other without their failed relationship looming in the background.

"We'll get them," she repeated the technician's words out loud to herself.

She tried to visualize the two hunted men. Was there an accomplice hiding them? The Norrtälje colleagues had reviewed footage from the prison's security cameras and had, just like the prison staff, drawn the conclusion that Patricio's escape was a spontaneous occurrence. The staff had also confirmed that the Mexican had not had any particular contact with the other three escapees. They were housed in separate quarters and had never worked together.

If it had been an unplanned escape on Alavez's part, then it was not clear that he could reasonably have expected to be taken in by friends outside the prison walls. But no one really knew anything about whatever network he might have. Alavez had remained silent through the entire court process and had not revealed a single detail of his smuggling attempt. He was perhaps not entirely welcome if he unexpectedly turned up at an associate's house on the outside, but his loyalty should nonetheless give him bonus points.

Was there actually anything that spoke in favor of the brothers even being in Uppsala? Yes, Lindell decided, because if there was a connection between the fugitive, Slobodan Andersson, and Armas then it would be reasonable for Alavez to find his way to the city. And the connection existed, she was sure of it. The tattoo, and above all its removal, as well as the fact that cocaine had been both Alavez's and Slobodan's "business area," backed this up. Had Patricio Alavez tried to contact Slobodan Andersson?

Sammy Nilsson hurried past Lindell's open door. She called out to him and he stuck his head in.

"We're going to put out an APB on an Opel Zafir," she said and held out a piece of paper. "Can you do it? And another thing: where would you go if you had a tent and a fugitive brother?"

Sammy Nilsson took the information on the rental car and then sat down.

"Did you hear about Berglund?" Sammy asked.

Lindell nodded.

"It's too fucking depressing," he went on. "There are so many dumbasses running around healthy as can be, while someone like Berglund gets hit."

"There is no justice," Lindell said. "We already knew that."

She waited a couple of seconds before she picked up the thread about the Alavez brothers again.

"Where would you pitch your tent?"

Sammy stared back at her for a second before he looked down at his notes. Lindell knew he wanted to talk more about their colleague and his brain tumor.

"Not in a camping area, that's for sure," Sammy said. "Is this a guy from the country or the city?"

"No idea," Lindell replied. "What do you mean?"

"If he's from some kind of city gang or drug cartel then he wouldn't camp out. Too rustic. That type would check into a hotel."

"We've checked them all," Lindell said.

"Assumed name?"

"Possible, but if it really was brother Manuel who camped by Lugnet then that would seem to indicate a particular style. The question is just where he went after Lugnet."

"Most likely close to the city," Sammy Nilsson said. He stood up and walked over to the map of Uppland that Lindell had on the wall.

"Okay," he resumed, "if you've killed someone south of the city then you probably don't just set up camp on the opposite side of the river."

"But what about local knowledge?"

"What would you do yourself?" Sammy Nilsson asked.

"Buy a map and try to figure out a good area."

"What is good?"

"Far away from people."

"But still fairly close to a road, wouldn't you say?" Sammy Nilsson said, his back to Lindell, studying the map.

He moved his finger from the southern parts of the city north, tracing the E4 motorway with his index finger.

"Månkarbo," he said suddenly and turned around, "that's where I would swing up to the northwest."

"Månkarbo?"

Sammy Nilsson nodded.

"You'll have to do the rest of the orienting on your own," he said with a grin.

Once he had left the room, Lindell went up to the map and located the small hamlet some twenty or thirty kilometers north of Uppsala.

She had a vague memory of Månkarbo as a small town with a painfully low speed limit, a couple of stores, and a gas station.

She went to Ottosson.

"A cement foundry," he said, "and a mission house in the middle of the village. Why do you ask?"

"Just a guess by Sammy that the Alavez brothers may have gone north, and then he named Månkarbo of all places."

"The foundry has been closed since God knows when, but the missionaries are probably still active. Do you think they're camping?"

"Yes, or alternatively, that they are hiding out at some drug associate's."

"Do you think the brother was involved in the break out?"

"I do, actually," Lindell said. "The visit in prison was perhaps a last instruction on how the escape was going to be executed. That Patricio Alavez playacted for the cameras has no significance. Maybe he had some last-minute hesitation because the escape was not proceeding as he had been instructed."

"The hostage?"

"According to Norrtälje he was a peaceful sort and he may have objected to the amount of force that the taking of a hostage involves."

"The Norrtälje police say that they spread out. At least two cars were left in the woods where they dumped the van. But why would any of them want to get to Uppsala? If they now—"

The telephone interrupted his train of thought. He lifted the receiver and listened for a minute, hummed in response a couple of times, thanked the speaker for the information and hung up.

"Björnsson and Brügger were apprehended one hour ago in Stockholm. The idiots tried to rob a post office. How stupid can you be? The Västerort police are going to get in touch right away if and when they uncover anything of interest."

"Brilliant," Lindell underscored. "Two down."

"And our Mexican friends and the Spaniard remain," Ottosson said cheerfully.

Police questioning of Slobodan Andersson was resumed after lunch. Lindell went down to listen. She recalled their exchange of ideas about the food served in jails and prisons. Now he would get to test it for himself, and the prospect filled her with great joy.

Sammy Nilsson and Barbro Liljendahl handled the continued sessions. Lindell entered the room while Simone Motander-Banks was launching into a lecture on the violation of rights by law enforcement. Everyone, including the apprehended man, was staring at her with dull eyes. Slobodan did not indicate with any change of expression that he had registered Lindell's arrival.

Once the lawyer was finished, Sammy Nilsson nodded kindly. He did not comment on the criticism but instead turned on the tape recorder with a sardonic grin and recorded the particulars of the session.

This time they were focused on Slobodan's circle of acquaintances. They started with Konrad Rosenberg, where the answers given were the same as earlier in the day: they had no association, he only knew Rosenberg as a customer and he had no idea why or how he had died.

Barbro Liljendahl dropped this topic and Sammy took over. He again tried to review Slobodan's Mexican adventures but even here nothing new emerged. When Sammy Nilsson broached the topic of Lorenzo Wader, Slobodan straightened his back. For Lindell it was obvious that the predictable answers from his side concealed an increasing concern and perhaps also astonishment. It was as if Slobodan Andersson was gradually starting to realize that the police were in possession of unexpected information, and that he himself was only a pawn in a game that he had believed he controlled.

"Wader and I have chatted two or three times. He is in the habit of coming to the restaurant, having a beer and a bite to eat. Why do you ask about him? I know nothing."

"We have information indicating that he associated with Konrad Rosenberg," Sammy Nilsson said.

The restaurateur stared at him.

"I know nothing about that," he said, tension causing his voice to crack.

"What about Olaf González then?"

"What about him?"

"He works at—" Nilsson began.

"Not anymore!"

"Not only that, he has disappeared. Would you happen to know where he has gone?"

Slobodan shook his head.

"Is that a no?"

"No!"

"Your former waiter has also been in contact with Lorenzo Wader," Sammy went on. "They have been seen together both at the hotel Linné and at Pub 19. It's remarkable how observant waitstaff can be."

"The swine," Slobodan Andersson let slip.

"Why did he get fired?" Sammy asked.

"It was some tiff with Armas. I don't know. I can't keep my eye on everything," Slobodan said grimly.

"No, that is very apparent," Sammy Nilsson said.

At one point in the session, Slobodan Andersson lifted his heavy head and gave Lindell a hateful look. She smiled back.

Slobodan Andersson made a swift and almost imperceptible gesture with his finger over his throat.

"Can you tell me more about the man who gave you the bag," Sammy Nilsson said.

Slobodan Andersson shook his head.

"I don't believe my client has anything to add on this topic," the lawyer said.

The session was brought to an end, but before Slobodan was led back to his cell, Ann Lindell asked him what he thought of the food.

Sammy stared at her. Lindell gave her sunniest smile. Slobodan muttered something and lumbered after the jail guard.

✦

Sixty

Oskar Hammer from Alhambra, Donald from Dakar, and Svante Winbladh from Ehrlings accounting firm concluded their hastily arranged meeting with the decision to keep the restaurants going—starting up again the day after tomorrow—even though their owner was being held in custody.

The news that cocaine was involved had dropped like a bomb. None of the three would have guessed that their boss and taskmaster had devoted himself to the smuggling and selling of narcotics. Svante Winbladh was the one who was the most distraught.

"It is completely inexcusable that we should have to be pulled into something like this," he exclaimed. "It is bad for our reputation as serious—"

"Calm down," Oskar Hammer interrupted. "You're clean, aren't you?"

The accountant gave him an antagonistic look.

"I don't think you fully understand the impact," he said and got to his feet.

"Yes, I do," Oskar Hammer said. "This is about our jobs. Donald, can you call around to all the Dakar staff?"

Donald nodded. He had not said much during the meeting, had only aired his exasperation with the fact that there would probably be new rounds of questioning with all the employees.

His immediate thought had been to quit, but he had decided to stay and see how the whole thing played out. He knew that Hammer was planning to take over Alhambra, and he himself had toyed with the idea of buying out Dakar and running the restaurant on his own.

Hammer and Donald left the accounting firm and returned to their respective restaurants. They had been promised the reservation books so that they could call the customers who had booked tables for that evening.

The forensic investigation continued at Dakar. Donald exchanged a few words with a criminal investigator he knew from before and found out that the cocaine that had been seized at Alhambra had been worth around three million kronor on the street.

"But what do you hope to find here?"

"Something," the officer said. "We don't know what."

"But no drugs here, or what?"

Donald would have taken it as a personal insult if they had found cocaine on "his" premises.

"I can't comment on that."

Donald left the restaurant and walked the short way home in order to start his calls. This was a job he most of all wanted to avoid.

He started with Feo, who in turn promised to call Eva. Thereafter he dialed Johnny's number.

Eva Willman's first emotion was anger, followed by shame. She was working for a man who sold drugs. Incredible. How would she be able to tell Helen? Her friend was spending a great deal of her spare time right now trying to convince the neighbors to attend the meeting about drugs in the area. Eva would not be able to go. It would be too shameful.

Her joy at having a job was blown away. Feo had said that everything would continue as before, but Eva had her doubts. How would the customers react? Who would want to eat at the trafficking center for a cocaine ring?

And what would Patrik and Hugo say?

She sat anesthetized at the kitchen table and recalled the joy she had felt earlier; the bike ride to the city and back, how she already felt more fit, the feeling of putting on the black skirt and the neat blouse, her new appearance that the hairstyle and her more conscious application of makeup gave her, the appreciation of the diners, that she had been given one hundred kronor by the young lovers, the talk with her coworkers, the incipient friendship with Tessie. Yes, everything that had happened at Dakar since the first nervous beginning had promised a different and better life.

And then Manuel. Why had she been so excited about him? Was it because he looked at her with both appreciation and a kind of respect behind the controlled desire? For surely his gazes and gestures indicated lust. When they had been talking and laughing in the dishwashing area she had surprised herself in thinking: touch me! And it was as if her thoughts had unconsciously influenced Manuel. He became both shy and eager at the same time. The heat of the dishwasher made his dark skin bloom and the sweat that gleamed at his hairline made her want to brush his wild bangs aside and cool his brow with her hand.

Shame on me, she thought. I wanted him. Not enough that I worked for a drug lord, I desired a drug pusher who may have been involved in smuggling and who has a felon for a brother.

A brother who had been featured in the headlines of every newspaper. Eva was surprised that no one else at Dakar had reacted to the pictures of Manuel's brother. Maybe they had been too upset about Slobodan's arrest to reflect on the obvious resemblance between the Alavez brothers.

Eva stood up and walked to the bedroom to make her bed but ended up standing with the bedspread in her hand. Now she was back to her earlier life, with passivity and anxiety for the future. Feo's words that she could always find other waitressing gigs, if Dakar did end up closing, did not comfort her. That brief period of time at Dakar that was all she had to show for herself, how impressive was that?

A butterfly fluttered outside the window but disappeared as quickly as it had appeared. Eva dropped the bedspread and sank down on the bed.

The dream was over so fast, she thought.

✦

Sixty-One

The Alavez brothers had been holed up in the shed for three days. They had not seen a single person. Sometimes they heard the muted roar of traffic and the cracking sound that they believed came from a weapon, a series of rhythmic salvos, and which they later realized must come from military training exercises.

In the evening of the first day, Manuel had walked back to the arts and crafts village. He had watched the parking lot for several hours before he had dared venture out. Now the car was parked in a tumbledown garage on the property.

On the morning of the second day, Manuel had raised a ladder against the side of the main house, climbed up and managed to open a window. In the kitchen they had found crackers, a box of canned food, and a packet of raisins. They brought up water from the well, and in an earth cellar they found some dusty jars of jam with the year 1998 written on the label.

They were used to meager diets and did not really want for anything. The lack of anything to do was worse. Patricio became anxious and irritable. Manuel had joked with him that he should be used to lying around on a cot, but Patricio had just muttered in reply.

Manuel had wondered if he should tell him about Armas's death. It was only on the second day, when they were talking about the fat one and the tall one, that Manuel was struck by the fact that his brother knew nothing. In an unconscious way Manuel had simply assumed that Patricio knew what had happened by the river. He decided to say nothing.

Manuel had sawed the apple tree and piled the wood against the wall of the shed. Patricio had helped gather up the sticks that were left over.

The rest of the time was filled with passive waiting.

Now it was one day before Manuel's flight to Mexico was due to leave. They talked about how they should proceed and decided to go together to Arlanda. Patricio would use Manuel's passport and ticket in order to leave the country. Patricio had increasingly started to doubt the plan and raised objections.

"How are you going to get home?"

"We've already talked about that," Manuel said grumpily. "I'm not wanted for anything. They can't charge me with anything. I'll go to the Mexican embassy and get a new passport. I can say that I was drunk and lost both the passport and the ticket and that I missed going to the airport. They can't punish me for that."

"But if—"

"Stop it! Don't you want to go home?"

Manuel had grown tired of Patricio's nagging pessimism and got up from the bench outside the shed.

"I'm going into town tonight," he said abruptly.

Patricio looked up.

"Is that why you are so worried?"

"I'm not worried," Manuel snapped.

"What are you going to do there? We have everything."

"I have to . . ."

Manuel left his brother without listening to the rest and walked up toward the edge of the woods, then he stopped halfway, returned to the shed and walked in. Patricio heard him bustle about inside.

A little while later Manuel emerged with a bag and a towel over his shoulder, walked over to the clothesline where his change of clothes were hanging, and pulled down a pair of pants and a T-shirt.

When Manuel started pumping up water and filling the washbasin, Patricio laughed.

"You want to look clean and nice," he observed.

Manuel looked up angrily, but when he saw Patricio's expression he couldn't help let out a chuckle.

May this go well, he thought. I want to see him happy in Mexico. He took off his clothes and soaped up his whole body. The sun sank behind the trees and he shivered. Patricio came over, filled a bucket of water, and poured it over Manuel.

"Now you will do," he said.

While the Alavez brothers were hiding in the forest outside Uppsala, the police continued their efforts to locate them as well as the other fugitive from Norrtälje, José Franco, who was still at large.

The questioning of the two failed bank robbers, Brügger and Björnsson, had not yielded anything. They claimed they had no idea where the other two had gone. Björnsson had maintained that the Mexican, whose name he could not even remember, or so he said, had not been involved in planning the escape.

The police in Norrtälje, and the National Crime Division, who had immediately become involved, were working with the theory that Franco and Alavez had joined forces and were perhaps still together. They had systematically worked through the Spaniard's network of contacts and most recent known addresses and haunts, without results. José Franco appeared to have been swallowed up by the earth.

A tip from a Tierp resident who claimed to have seen Patricio Alavez get on the train to Uppsala was deemed to be not very credible. In part because the witness was clearly intoxicated, not only when he called the police, but he had also, as he himself put it, been somewhat "in his cups" at the time he claimed to have noticed the Mexican on the platform in Tierp.

This tip never reached the Uppsala police.

The sessions with Slobodan Andersson stalled. He kept stubbornly to the story that he had received the bag from a stranger who had asked him to look after it for a day. The stranger was then going to pick it up from the restaurant.

More difficult for the restauranteur was the fact that the police had found Konrad Rosenberg's fingerprints on the plastic surrounding the cocaine packets. When Slobodan Andersson was asked to explain how this happened, he stopped talking for good.

Even his haughty lawyer looked stricken. Sammy Nilsson noted with satisfaction how impossible the situation was for Slobodan Andersson and how the lawyer gradually abandoned her somewhat intimate attitude toward him. When he subsequently held his tongue throughout the next attempted round of questioning she openly showed her irritation.

Information on the brothers Alavez came back from Mexico with unexpected speed. Neither of them was known to the narcotics division. The elder of the two, Manuel, had been arrested for "disturbance of the peace" charges but had been freed after five days. What this actually meant was not spelled out in the e-mail from Comisario Adolfo Sanchez at the Policía Criminal in Oaxaca.

A group with representatives from both the Norrtälje and Uppsala authorities had been formed. The Uppsala team included Inge Werner from the criminal information service, Sammy Nilsson from violent crimes, and Jan-Erik Rundgren from narcotics.

They were trying to connect the murder of Armas, the cocaine seized at Alhambra, and the escape from the Norrtälje prison. They had met twice in Uppsala but had not experienced much progress. Now the updates were conducted by telephone and mail.

Ann Lindell had conferred with her colleague Lindman from Västerås and discussed the arguments in favor of bringing in Lorenzo Wader for questioning. There were reasons for this. He had been observed at Dakar together with Konrad Rosenberg and together with

Olaf González at Pub 19. The waitstaff at both Dakar and Alhambra had also seen how Slobodan Andersson had conversed on several occasions with someone whom they knew as "Lorenzo."

But Lindman was hesitant and resisted. Maybe a meeting would make Wader clam up. Lindman's view was that Wader was not to be disturbed and that the investigation that he and the tax authorities in Stockholm had been pursuing for six months could be jeopardized.

Ann Lindell discussed the matter with Ottosson, who said that Lorenzo Wader should definitely be brought in. However, when Lindell and Ola Haver sought him out at Hotel Linné, they learned that he had checked out the day before.

When Lindell relayed this information to Lindman, he chuckled into the phone.

"He's as slippery as an eel," Lindman said with evident satisfaction, a reaction that so irritated Lindell that she immediately flagged Lorenzo Wader in the register as significant to a current narcotics and murder investigation.

Together with Sammy Nilsson and Beatrice Andersson, Lindell tried to evaluate the situation in the three intertwined cases—Armas, Konrad, and Slobodan—and thereafter decide how to proceed.

Armas's murder was still unsolved, but in all likelihood they knew who the perpetrator was: Manuel Alavez. Whether he had acted in self-defense or not could not yet be determined.

Nothing had emerged that contradicted the idea that Konrad Rosenberg had overdosed. His connection to the cocaine cache and Zero's claim that Konrad Rosenberg was a drug distributor clearly made him interesting, but they could get no further.

Sidström, who had now been discharged from the Akademiska Hospital, had acknowledged the connection to Rosenberg and admitted that he himself had "bought some" cocaine, though mainly for his own consumption but also that he had "sold some that was left over."

Slobodan Andersson was caught. He was awaiting sentencing on charges of drug possession and would presumably disappear from the restaurant world for many years to come—of this all three detectives were certain. There was the bag with two sets of fingerprints, Konrad's and Slobodan's. The only thing that could be considered unusual was the fact that they had found a number of dried leaves in the bag, which Allan Fredriksson had identified as hawthorne.

Slobodan's silence and unwillingness to cooperate, however, had meant that the case opened and closed with him. Konrad was dead and could not add anything.

There was nothing to indicate that the staff at either Dakar or Alhambra were involved or knew about their boss's hobby. The only uncertain card was González. He had moved out of his apartment, a rented studio in Luthagen, and disappeared without a trace. This did not have to mean anything untoward. He had been fired and perhaps decided the best course of action was to leave town. One of the chefs at Dakar had said something about González talking about going back to Norway. Lindell put Fryklund on it.

"We only have one hope," Lindell said, "and that is that Manuel Alavez tries to leave the country on his booked flight tomorrow."

"How likely is that?" Ola Haver asked. "Then he must be incredibly stupid."

"Let's hope so," Lindell said with a shrug.

"How the hell can two Mexicans lie so low?" Sammy Nilsson asked. "Someone must be helping them."

"They're hanging in Månkarbo," Lindell said with a tired grin.

✦

Sixty-Two

The inner yard was even darker than Manuel remembered. He looked around. Two windows in the level above Dakar were lit. Apart from this the entire courtyard was dark and he realized that the light on the wall, that earlier had blinked on and off, had now gone out for good.

The wind had picked up and paper and other garbage was lifted up in tight whirls by the strong breeze.

He moved with the utmost caution, staying away from the rectangles of light that the illuminated windows created in the yard, crept over to the bike rack, and then to the garbage containers outside Dakar's staff entrance. The stench was overpowering. A mixture of rotten fish and sour milk that made him hold his nose as he crouched down behind one of the containers.

After a while he grew used to the smell and was able to relax. He leaned against the wall in a pose reminiscent of all the hours he had sat waiting for work.

Suddenly one of the rectangles of light in the yard went out, and the lamp in the front hall of the entrance next to Dakar went on. Through the windows of the stairwell Manuel could see a man walk down the stairs and step out into the yard. Whistling, he unlocked a bike and left.

The stairwell went dark and Manuel's heart rate slowly went back to normal.

He tried not to think about the fat one even if it bothered him that he had not been able to trip him up completely. Maybe he could get in touch with the police anonymously? During the days in the shed he had thought out various alternatives but dismissed them all. He could not risk Patricio's flight out of the country with unnecessary maneuvers and contacts.

The fat one was perhaps on the other side of the door, several meters away, within reach, and yet not. It didn't matter, because Manuel had decided never again to use force. It was a ridiculous decision, he realized this, for if he ever returned to Mexico the violence would be there as a reality. If he in the future participated in a demonstration or a protest in the main square, then it would be under threat from batons and firearms. If he was attacked, would he then not defend himself, strike back? He did not know. Maybe the time of demonstrations was over now.

He had to wait for an hour until the door to Dakar opened. It was Feo. Manuel heard this from the curses that the Portuguese used when he lifted the lid of the garbage container. The lid shut with a bang and Feo closed the door behind him. Everything became quiet again.

Perhaps another thirty minutes went by. The door opened again. Manuel was struck with fear when he heard Eva's voice. She yelled something into the kitchen, and he thought he heard Feo reply.

The door banged shut and Manuel heard Eva's steps in the gravel. He looked out from behind the container. She was alone. He stood up slowly.

"Eva," he whispered softly.

She froze in the middle of unlocking her bike.

"It's me, Manuel."

She turned slowly. He could tell she had trouble seeing him and so he stepped out further, while tilting his head up toward the illuminated window.

"You?"

Manuel nodded.

"What are you doing here?"

"I wanted to talk to you."

She shook her head but didn't say anything. He took this as encouragement.

"I'll be going home soon and I wanted to say good-bye."

"Why . . ." she started energetically, then fell silent as if her voice had been carried off by the wind, or as if she could not find the right words in English.

"You think I'm lying, but I'm not," Manuel assured her and took another couple of steps forward.

"Stay where you are! Where is your brother?"

Manuel shook his head.

"This is not about him. This is about us. I don't want to leave Sweden without saying it."

"What is it you want to say?"

Eva's voice was hoarse. He could hardly hear what she said.

"That I wish, that I want . . . for you to visit my country."

He took some quick steps up to her, grabbed something from his pocket, and held it out.

"What is it?"

"A present."

She accepted the rolled-up sock.

"I have nothing else," Manuel said, "but it's clean."

Without a word she pushed the sock into her pocket and bent down to unlock the bike. Manuel wanted to say so much but he did not know how to proceed. He was afraid she would run away, curse him, or start to scream at the top of her lungs.

"He tricked my brothers, you know that. So I set up a trap for him. I wanted to see him in prison, but now I can't do it anymore. I have to make sure that my brother gets home."

"He is in jail," Eva said.

"No, he ran away," Manuel said, confused. "But now I should go. Tessie or someone else might come."

Eva stared down into the ground.

"But how will you get home?"

"My brother will fly home on my passport and my ticket," Manuel explained. "Then I will see what I do."

Eva stared at him.

"Don't you get it? The police are looking for you, too."

"Have you spoken with the police?"

"I haven't said anything, but they know you are in Sweden. The papers have claimed that you belong to a Mexican drug cartel and that you came to Sweden to . . . Arlanda will be full of police."

"Full of police?" he repeated.

Eva nodded.

"I have to go," he said.

"Armas. Did you . . . ?"

"He tried to shoot me," Manuel said. "I defended myself. Believe me! I am not an evil person."

The whites of her eyes glowed in the dark as she studied him. Manuel felt that she was trying to decide what she should believe.

"You do have to go now," she said finally.

"In the sock there is a note with my address. The phone number of a neighbor. He is nice and speaks a little English."

Eva laughed unexpectedly.

"The neighbor is nice," she repeated.

Manuel reached out his hand and nudged her cheek. She flinched but did not pull away. Manuel leaned over and briefly kissed her on the mouth before he left. She thought he resembled a cat as he slunk out of the yard.

Manuel had parked the car behind a Dumpster in the alley. He was trembling with emotion and had trouble getting the key in the ignition. He hastily drew in air through his nose in order to experience her scent one last time.

He nonetheless drove calmly onto the street, past Dakar and out of the city. He found his way easily. He had studied the map all afternoon and memorized the route. Traffic was sparse and after several minutes he was out on highway 272, heading north.

Despite what Eva had said about the police, he was relieved. He had managed to make his way to Dakar and back. He had been lucky that Eva was working and above all he was overjoyed that she had spoken with him.

It was almost midnight when he got back to the house in the forest. He drove the car into the garage. A thin sliver of light could be seen under the door to the shed.

Patricio was sitting in bed. A candle was perched on a stool. He looked ghostlike in the flickering light.

"Did it go well?"

Manuel nodded and pulled the door shut behind him.

"Are you hungry?"

"No," Manuel said, although in reality his belly was screaming for food.

He sat down on a chair in the middle of the room. It was only now, that he was looking at his brother, that he fully took in the significance of what Eva had said. Up to this point he had been preoccupied with his thoughts of her.

"We have to find another way to leave Sweden," he said. "You can't use my ticket. The police will take you right away if you try."

Patricio stared quizzically at him.

"Who told you this?"

"Eva," Manuel said curtly and then sighed deeply.

As the sound of her name, his despair welled out. He suddenly saw their predicament in a different light. It was as if someone from above was looking down at their primitive dwelling, surrounded by the darkness of the night, and the deep forest, the flickering light on the stool, and Patricio and himself as two figures who were trying in vain to escape a nightmare. He saw two strangers, two Zapotecs, in enemy territory, who, like soldiers cut off from their command, found themselves in an impossible situation. Now nothing remained but capitulation or a desperate breakout attempt.

Manuel's energy and creativity were at an end.

"I'm sorry," he sighed.

Patricio stood up and pulled a slip of paper from his pocket, much like an illusionist setting up for a magic trick.

"Here is a telephone number," Patricio said and held out the slip of paper.

"What do you mean?"

"José gave it to me, the Spaniard who was part of the escape. If I ran into big problems I should call this number. The one who answers is also a Spaniard. But it should only be in case of big problems. He said the number was secure. I should just call. Don't we have big problems now?"

Manuel stared at Patricio and then at the wrinkled note.

"We should call a another crook?" he asked.

"You have another fifty?"

Manuel got up and turned his back on his brother. The painstakingly stacked firewood on the opposite wall reminded him of the open hearth at home in the village and how his mother would insert the sticks and get the fire going. How she silently kneaded and baked a stack of tortillas that she wrapped in a cloth, took out the chili, and boiled water for coffee. It was almost as if he could hear the crackling in the wood and how Gerardo's cock impatiently crowed again and again. Manuel used to joke with his neighbor that the cock had taken after its master both in temperament and productiveness. Never did their poverty appear as extreme as these early mornings when their night-stiff bodies shook with cold. Never was the warmth as welcome, and the togetherness as strong, as when they approached the fire, mumbling to each other as they drank their coffee and greeted a new day.

"We'll call," Manuel said abruptly. "There is a telephone in the house."

✦

Sixty-Three

It was a northerly wind and it gave Eva a boost across the fields. In spite of this, she wished she had taken the bus. It had driven past her by Lilla Ultuna. Seeing Manuel had frightened her. Not because she was afraid of him but because she had been reminded that there was a dark side to Uppsala, where murder and drugs were everyday things.

She biked with a frenzy that meant she was over the fields in a matter of minutes and arrived, damp with sweat, at Kuggebro, where she was forced to reduce her speed somewhat. Then the trip went uphill, at first a tough slope up past Vilan and then a decidedly steeper one the last stretch before she home.

She had called home at ten o'clock. Hugo had answered. Eva had asked to speak to Patrik to make sure that he was home as well. Now she only had one thought in her mind: to see them both in bed.

She was greeted by a thermos of tea on the kitchen table, a plate of crackers, and a note that Hugo had written wishing her good night.

They were asleep. Patrik lay on his back snoring a little, while Hugo was turned on his stomach, arms outstretched.

Eva returned to the kitchen, draped her jacket on a chair, drank a cup of tea, and munched on a cracker. The encounter with Manuel had stirred up her mind. Her feelings had gone from surprise to anger and from there to sadness. His touch on her cheek and brief kiss had paralyzed her.

She remembered his present, took the sock from her pocket and shook out the contents. It was a hard roll of bills wrapped in a wrinkled note.

She unfurled a bill, one hundred dollars, and then quickly counted the rest. There were fifty one-hundred-dollar notes. She did not know exactly how much a dollar was worth, but realized she had been given tens of thousands of kronor.

She stared at the note with Manuel's home address and the neighbor's telephone number. The nice neighbor.

Before Eva went to bed she counted the money one last time, tucked the bills into an old envelope from the social insurance administration, and hid it in the very back of the utility closet.

Even though she was completely exhausted she couldn't sleep.

"Manuel," she ventured in a whisper into the darkness. In a way she now regretted having warned him. If he had gone to Arlanda and been arrested by the police he would have received a trial and perhaps been found not guilty of the murder accusation. It wasn't inconceivable that Armas . . . Of course, his brother would wind up back in prison, but Manuel would . . . If he were found to have committed voluntary manslaughter or whatever it was called.

"Stop it," she said out loud, tormented by her own loose thoughts, threads that she could not manage to bind together into a satisfying conclusion. She both wanted and did not want him to get caught. The horrifying thing was that she understood him so well. He had lost one brother and the other had received a long prison sentence. Of course Manuel was trying to get him out of the country. How would she have reacted if Hugo or Patrik were in jail in Mexico? Wouldn't she have done everything in her power to free them, regardless of what they were accused?

After having tried and failed at all the old tricks to conjure sleep, Eva got up and went out to the kitchen. The clock on the wall read half past two. She took out milk and heated a cup in the microwave. Her eyes were constantly drawn to the utility closet. Never before in her life had she had so much cash. She would be able to go wherever she wanted. It would make Helen so curious and not a little envious. But could she keep the money? Where had he got hold of five thousand dollars?

She drank the last of the milk, which had cooled down, got up and walked over to the calendar on the wall. When did the kids have their fall break? It was around All Saints, but was it the week before or the week after? Her gaze went to December. They were off for three weeks then. Wouldn't it say in the paper how much a dollar was worth?

She quickly leafed through both sections of *Upsala Nya Tidning* and finally found a whole page of stock and currency exchange and other numbers she had never paid any attention to. Over seven kronor for one dollar, and she had five thousand! Thirty-five thousand kronor in the utility closet.

She pushed the paper away and sat back down. What if the police caught Manuel and he told them that he had given her money?

"No way," she said, as if to convince herself of the unlikelihood of this.

"What are you doing?"

Eva twirled around in the chair. A groggy Hugo was standing in the hall.

"I couldn't sleep," Eva said. "Go pee and go back to bed."

"Was it fun at work?"

"It was great," Eva said, knowing the question concealed a considerable concern. The children had heard and read about what had happened. Maybe Zero had filled them in.

"Go back to bed. I'm going to take a painkiller and do the same."

Hugo turned back toward his room and gave her a final glance.

"Thanks for the tea and your nice note," Eva said.

He smiled a little and then closed the door behind him.

Sixty-Four

He called himself Ramon, but they did not think this was his real name. It didn't matter. There was no question that he was Spanish, nor that he was a real professional.

During the night, Patricio and Manuel had made their way to the small town of Märsta, with the help of Manuel's map. They had taken a small road that snaked through the darkened landscape, encountered at most ten cars, and once they reached Märsta they parked outside the grocery store that Ramon had picked as their meeting place. They had waited for half an hour until the Spaniard turned up.

He had taken them to a basement room in an apartment building.

"If you get caught, we expect you not to say a single word about our meeting."

He did not explain who the "we" referred to. Perhaps he meant José Franco.

"Of course," Patricio said.

"I hear you can keep quiet," Ramon said and smiled.

"How is José?"

"Very good," Ramon said and his smile widened. "He sends his greetings."

"Send our greetings back and thank him for all his help," Patricio said.

Despite the early hour—it was not even six yet—Ramon appeared energetic and focused. He took out some photographic equipment, a couple of lamps, and a screen. He took a dozen photographs each of Manuel and Patricio. The whole thing was over in minutes.

Manuel held out the agree-upon sum without a word. Ramon licked one thumb, then quickly flipped through the pile of bills and stretched out his hand for a handshake.

"Who will we be?"

"Two Chileans. I have a lot of those passports."

"When and how will we get them?"

"One of you drives to Rotebro and leaves the car there, that is not so far away. I can show you the road. Take the train back here. Someone waits here until I turn up. That will be tonight."

"But taking the train seems dangerous," Manuel said. "Someone might recognize—"

"We'll take care of that," Ramon said and left them for a moment.

They heard him looking around for something in the next room, and when he returned, he smilingly held up a wig.

"This is how you become a blond," the Spaniard grinned. "This and the glasses will be good. Which one of you is going to Rotebro?"

"That would be me," Manuel said.

Beside himself with fatigue and confused by Ramon's precise instructions, Manuel tried to memorize everything. He felt a teary gratitude for the help they received. He had never imagined how quickly it would go.

"I don't know how we can thank you," he said.

Ramon slapped his hand across the pocket where he had tucked the money.

"Now let's get moving," he said. "On with the wig!"

The last thing Ramon did was to show them how they could make coffee, and where bread, butter, and soda was stored.

The last thing he said before he and Manuel left the basement was a warning not to call anyone, not to leave the basement, and not to drink any alcohol.

When Manuel returned to the basement, Patricio was sleeping on a mattress in the inner of the two rooms. He woke up but immediately fell asleep again. Manuel opened a bottle of soda and drank greedily. He had been thirsty ever since the night before.

What is Eva doing now, he wondered sadly but immediately chastized himself. Why should he think of her? The important thing was to leave Sweden. Wasting thought on anything else was idiotic. He looked at Patricio who was muttering something in his sleep.

Manuel lay down on the floor and stretched out his exhausted body. We should shave, was the last thing he thought before he fell asleep.

✦

Sixty-Five

It was five o'clock in the morning when Sammy Nilsson and Ola Haver stepped into the Arlanda police headquarters. The combination of morning fatigue with the tension that had mounted the previous day meant that neither one of them was particularly talkative during the short ride to the airport.

Now they were greeted by a shamelessly alert colleague. He introduced himself as Åke Holmdahl. Sammy Nilsson had a vague memory of having seen him before. Maybe they had been at school at the same time?

"Hi there, Nilsson. So you're still around."

"Got no choice."

"I see that the daily special is one or two Mexican delicacies. This should be a real pleasure. And your name is Haver? *Gud som haver barnen kär,*" Holmdahl quoted the well-known psalm "God who holds the children dear." "But you must have heard that one before? Okay, let me tell you a little bit about how we've planned things out. We have people outside and in the hall, next to Avis as well as the check-in. Two officers have been stationed by the gate and two canine units are on call. All personnel have been briefed and instructed not to act until further orders. Maybe you saw them on the way in?"

Sammy Nilsson shook his head.

"Fantastic!" Holmdahl snorted. "But maybe you saw a car pulled over with engine troubles? That's Olofsson. That's usually his role. He will report to us if an Opel Zafira goes by. We have a couple of more cars in motion."

Ola Haver nodded.

"Our Norrtälje colleagues are also in place. It's their man, after all. If Alavez, number one or two, turn up we'll nab him."

Sammy Nilsson's mood was gradually improving. It was as if his colleague's enthusiasm and confidence were catching.

"Is there any coffee?" he asked.

"Are you kidding?" Holmdahl said, and Sammy Nilsson realized that even he had teenage children.

"Come with me and we'll get you some. Have you had breakfast?"

Holmdahl led Nilsson and Haver to a small kitchen.

"The plane leaves at a quarter past eight, isn't that right?" Ola Haver asked.

"BA to London and then on to Mexico City."

Ola Haver gave a big yawn.

"I wish I had a ticket," he said.

At half past nine they concluded their failure. Manuel Alavez had neither returned the rental car nor checked in for the flight to London.

Åke Holmdahl was muted. Sammy Nilsson and Ola Haver were grumpy. They felt duped.

"We should have known," Haver said. "He wouldn't have been this stupid."

"We'll have to try something else," Holmdahl said.

Sammy Nilsson suddenly remembered where he had seen him. The Arlanda colleague had worked in the patrol division at Uppsala for a brief period of time.

Both of the Uppsala detectives took the motorway north. They had already called a disappointed Ann Lindell and told her they had come up with nothing.

When they were just passed the exit to Knivsta, Lindell called back.

Sammy Nilsson answered and then pulled over by the side of the road, looked around and started to back up to the exit.

"What are you doing?" Haver said perplexed.

"We missed him," Sammy Nilsson said. "I'll bet you anything that Alavez was at Arlanda, but somehow he spotted our welcoming committee. The rental car has turned up in Rotebro."

He reached the Knivsta exit, turned down, went under the E4, then drove up onto the motorway again, this time in a southerly direction.

They arrived just after Tomas Ahlinder from forensics in Uppsala. The Opel was neatly parked not far from the commuter train station. Next to the car was a policeman in uniform and a man in civilian dress, whom Haver and Nilsson assumed was a colleague.

The latter, who said his name was Persson, turned out to be the one who had noticed the car. He lived in Rotebro and every day he took the commuter train to his office in Kungsholmen, in Stockholm.

"Sometimes my brain works," he said with a laugh. "I happened to see the APB yesterday. I remember thinking that it was an unusual make for a rental car. And then today I catch sight of a Zafira with a somewhat odd license plate number."

Sammy Nilsson looked at the plates, on which three letters formed the word *RAR*.

"What do you say, Ahlinder?"

"I'll do an initial search and then we'll tow it to Uppsala. If that's all right," he added.

"No problem for me," the uniformed policeman said. "We're just happy to be rid of it. Are there drugs in the car?"

Sammy Nilsson nodded. He circled the car and looked in through the windows but saw nothing of interest.

"When was it left here?" he asked.

"Late last night or this morning, if I have to guess," Persson said. "I walked by here around seven o'clock last night and I don't think it was here then."

"Okay," Nilsson said. "We'll ask around. It's possible someone saw something."

He nodded at the small grocery store directly across the street.

"I'll start there," he said. "Ola, can you take the kiosk over there?"

One hour later, Nilsson and Haver decided to head back. A tow truck had already loaded up the Opel onto the flatbed for transport to Uppsala.

The door-to-door efforts in the neighborhood had already yielded results. It was the manager of the small grocery who, shortly before seven that morning, had observed a light-haired man next to the car. He had noticed that the man was wearing sunglasses even though it was not a sunny morning. As the grocer was setting up an advertisement on the sidewalk, he had seen the man walk toward the commuter train station.

That was all.

"Light-haired," Sammy Nilsson said as they overtook the towtruck on the motorway. "Can it have been an accomplice?"

"If he had something to do with the car," Ola Haver said. "We don't know if he was the one who parked it there."

"It's thin," Sammy Nilsson agreed. "But if the car really was left there early in the morning then it could work. Alavez parks the car, because he doesn't want the car to be sighted near Arlanda, gets himself to the airport somehow, sees something that makes him suspicious, and skips the flight."

"It doesn't add up," Haver objected.

"What?"

"It just doesn't add up," Haver maintained, without explaining what he meant.

"No, I know," Sammy Nilsson said with resignation.

When they reached the police station there was a certain commotion in the division. Fredriksson and Bea were in Ottosson's office.

"Has something happened?" Sammy asked, reading the excitement in their eyes.

"A guy who claims to be Armas's son has just turned up," Ottosson said. "Lindell is talking to him right now."

"Did he seek us out of his own accord?" Haver asked.

"Is he blond?" Sammy wondered.

"No, he has a shaved head, and he came here on his own," Ottosson replied.

"What did he say?"

"That he wanted to talk to someone who was investigating the murder of his father."

"Does he speak Swedish?"

"English," Ottosson said. "We'll have to wait for Lindell's report."

Sammy Nilsson told him about the Opel in Rotebro and how little they had managed to find out. Maybe, just maybe, a blond man with sunglasses could be tied to the car.

"An accomplice," Fredriksson said and Sammy sighed heavily.

Lindell came back ten minutes later. She shook her head as soon as she saw her colleagues gathered in the lunchroom.

"I need something strong," she said and sat down.

"What did he say?"

Lindell told them that Armas's son was thirty-two years old and named Anthony Wild. He was born in England. His mother was English, and missing for many years. Her son thought she was living in

Southeast Asia. Armas and Anthony had never lived under the same roof. Armas left when the mother was pregnant, but they had intermittent contact. The last time was about a year ago. Anthony had been in Sweden once before. That was over twenty years ago when he had visited his father who lived in Copenhagen. They had taken the ferry across to Malmö for the day.

"Did you ask about the video?" Fredriksson interrupted.

Lindell smiled. Yes, Anthony had been an "actor" for several years. He admitted to having participated in porn films and did not seem particularly embarrassed about it. In fact, he had bragged that he was one of the more successful ones in the business.

"What does he want?" Ottosson asked.

"To claim his inheritance, I'd say, even if he did also seem genuinely griefstruck. He returned several times to the question of how Armas had died. And then he wanted to talk to Slobodan. They had never met but Anthony knew that Armas and Slobodan had worked together for many years. Maybe he thought Armas owned part of the restaurants, what do I know?"

"Has he been to Mexico?"

Lindell felt as if she was at a press conference, where the questions came from all directions. This time it was Bea.

"Several times. He said that if you live in southern California you often travel down to what he called 'Basha.'"

"Ba-ha," Haver corrected.

"Ba-ha," Lindell repeated in an exaggerated way, and then went on. "Wild had never been to Guadalajara or our friend the tattoo artist, and he did not know that Armas and Slobodan had been to Mexico."

"How did he find out Armas was dead?"

"Through the film company. We made several inquiries with them and then we mentioned Armas's death in order to create more urgency for them to give us a name."

"Is he trustworthy?" Ottosson asked.

"He appeared honest to me. A little flaky, maybe. Not a wholesome person, as you would put it, Otto, but . . ."

"He's an actor," Sammy Nilsson reminded them.

"Does it make your mouth water?" Fredriksson asked.

Everyone looked at him in astonishment. It was a Sammy-comment that he had made and nothing that one would expect of someone normally so rigid about moral topics, and predictably enough he blushed deeply at his own spontaneous remark.

"Sure," Sammy said, "with a delicious morsel like that around, of course I get a little peckish."

Everyone laughed except Bea.

They continued to talk for a while longer. Naturally they would question Anthony Wild several more times. He was planning to remain in town for at least a week in order to go through Armas's apartment and take care of the legal aspects of the inheritance. He was also going to visit Dakar and Alhambra to see the places where his father had worked. In addition, he had requested to visit the scene where his father had been killed.

They did not know if he would obtain permission to meet Slobodan, but Ottosson could not see any obstacles. There was a legitimate and reasonable interest on the part of the son to speak with the murdered father's best friend, even if the latter was being held under arrest for a drug crime.

Ann Lindell withdrew to her office. The conversation with Armas's son had at first made her hopeful and then increasingly disappointed. Anthony Wild's tactfully formulated and yet clearly stated critical comment about the murderer still remaining at large had struck her with unexpected force. All technical evidence, DNA, fingerprints, and tire marks were there. They had skillfully unraveled the question of the tattoo's removal and clarified the Mexican connection. With the Mexican's existence revealed, and now also documented on the Norrtälje prison's videotape, she had assumed that Manuel Alavez would quickly be caught.

He had all the odds against him, and yet he was still at large. It contradicted all logic. Manuel Alavez was a statistical abnormality, a relationship that was strengthened when Patricio Alavez escaped and most likely joined forces with his brother.

Lindell had difficulties evaluating the find of the car in Rotebro. It was natural to dump the car that Alavez most likely understood was hot, but how were they getting around now? Assuming they even had any plans, what were they? To leave the country? But how and when? Patricio had no passport and both brothers were wanted in all of Europe.

Her chain of thought was interrupted by a knock on the door.

"Yes!" she called out, more loudly and harshly than she had intended.

Ottosson opened the door a crack.

"The operation was a success," he said.

It took a while until she realized he meant Berglund.

"Come in!"

Ottosson stepped inside, sat down, and told her that Berglund's brain tumor had turned out to be benign and easy to remove. Berglund's wife had called from the hospital.

"Thank God!" Lindell exclaimed. "Finally some good news."

"Yes, isn't it?" Ottosson said, who had grown teary by his own words.

✦

Sixty-Six

Manuel and Patricio were awakened by a thud and they sat up at the same moment, as if synchronized.

"What was it?"

"I don't know," Manuel said.

Outside the narrow window just under the ceiling, they heard shouting and angry voices. Manuel got up.

"It's the police," Patricio cried.

"Keep quiet!"

Manuel fetched the only chair in the room and placed it under the window that was covered with a black piece of fabric. He climbed up and started to pick away at the tape at the edge of the cloth.

"No," Patricio said, terrified, "they'll shoot you."

"I have to see what it is," Manuel said, lifting a corner and trying to peer through the dusty glass.

"I see some legs," he whispered.

"Are they in uniform?"

"Don't think so."

At that moment the window was struck by a projectile and the glass shattered. Manuel instinctively dived onto the floor. Tear gas was his first thought. The voices outside died down. A piece of glass that had caught on the fabric trembled before it fell to the floor with a clinking sound.

Patricio and Manuel stared bewitched at the window. The cloth fluttered in a sudden breeze.

What were they waiting for? Manuel wondered. No gas was spreading in the basement, the voices outside were quiet and no sounds were heard from the other side of the door.

Manuel pulled over his bag and took out the pistol he had taken from Armas's lifeless hand. Patricio stared at the weapon.

"You're armed?"

"Keep quiet," Manuel barked.

Suddenly they heard a laugh and someone screamed in a high voice. Manuel climbed back up on the chair and moved the fabric aside.

"They will shoot you," Patricio repeated.

A soccer ball was wedged in the window frame. Manuel quickly refastened the tape, slipped rather than climbed down from the chair, and collapsed on the mattress.

"A soccer ball," Patricio said and burst into hysterical laughter.

"Quiet! We have to be quiet."

Patricio stared at his brother who had stood up and was leaning over him.

"Where did you get the gun?"

"That doesn't matter," Manuel said, but then told him what had happened, how he had been forced to kill the tall one and afterward had taken his weapon.

Patricio stared sorrowfully at his brother. Manuel avoided his gaze.

"So the tall one is dead," Patricio said flatly at the end.

Manuel nodded.

The silence and inactivity was complete until they heard a key turn in the lock and Ramon swiftly snuck in and closed the door behind him.

"Hello, my Chilean friends," he said in greeting. "What has happened? You look a little somber."

"A soccer ball hit the window so the glass shattered," Manuel explained. "We thought it was the police."

Ramon grinned.

"It scared you?"

"Guess," Manuel said, surprised at how lightly the Spaniard was taking it.

"We'll have to fix it later," Ramon said and took two passports out of his coat pocket. "Right now we're in a hurry. You are going on a flight."

"Fly?"

Ramon told them what he had planned. Twenty minutes to ten this same evening there was a plane to London.

"The airport is a little south of Stockholm and you can buy the tickets there. If there are no seats you will have to wait until tomorrow morning. Then you can sleep in the forest."

"But why London?" Patricio asked.

"You have to get out of the country as soon as possible. From London it will be easy for you to keep traveling."

"Okay," Manuel said.

For him the most important thing was to leave the basement.

"I have brought two small suitcases for you to pack your belongings. Wash up quickly. It's important that you look tidy. I will drive you there. That will cost a little. Do you have money?"

"How much will it cost?"

"Three thousand dollars."

Manuel nodded.

"Is it so far?" Patricio asked.

Ramon laughed.

"No, but it is your only option. We have to pass Stockholm. You will have to sit in a closed van. It is the van of a paint company. Understood?"

Manuel and Patricio looked at their new passports. Abel and Carlos Morales were the names that would get them out of Sweden.

Manuel was a little unhappy that Ramon was charging so much to drive them to the airport but said nothing. He knew what the answer would be.

They arrived at the airport a little before eight. Ramon dropped them off at the parking lot and gave the brothers final instructions on how they should act. Manuel took out his gun and handed it to Ramon without a word. The latter smiled a little and surprised the brothers by immediately taking out the ammunition, carefully cleaning off the weapon, and then disappeared for a minute or so into a nearby patch of woods.

"I'm dropping you off here," he said when he returned. "With a little luck you will be fine."

He looked at them almost tenderly and gave them each an unexpected hug good-bye, then jumped into the van and left the area.

The airport was much smaller than they had imagined. It basically consisted of a hangarlike building with a cafe and a departure lounge that looked more like a bus terminal.

At his brother's question if they should split up and buy tickets separately, Manuel simply shook his head. He felt as if he were incapable of speaking.

The flight with a departure time of 21:40 to London was fully booked, they were told at the ticket counter in the terminal. The woman behind the counter saw their disappointment and tried to comfort them with the fact that there was a flight the following morning. Could they wait until then?

"Our brother in England is sick," Manuel said. "There is no possibility that we can make it on this flight?"

"No, I'm sorry. It's full, but there are three seats left on the early flight tomorrow morning."

The brothers looked at each other. Manuel felt as if luck was deserting them. They had managed to get this far but no further. So close. He looked at the young woman behind the counter. Her eyes were so blue.

"We'll take two tickets," he said finally.

✦

Sixty-Seven

The first thing Ann Lindell did when she reached the police station at shortly after eight in the morning was to check if any tips had come in during the evening and night. The police had set up a special telephone number that the public could call with observations related to the escape of and search for the Alavez brothers.

Twenty-eight calls had been received, of which three could be considered of interest. The first one that Lindell decided to follow up on had come in from an older couple, reporting a breaking and entering of their holiday cottage in Börje. The burglar was believed to have spent the night in their shed and had stolen some food items but had otherwise not caused any damage. The remarkable thing was that the burglar had chopped up a fallen apple tree and even taken the trouble to stack the wood. At first the man thought it was a nephew who had taken the trouble to do this. The nephew would often help the couple with practical tasks that they themselves could not or did not have the strength to do, but the nephew had known nothing about this when his uncle called.

Lindell decided that Ola Haver and a technician should go to Börje and perform an initial examination.

The second tip came from a woman who claimed to have seen "a dark-skinned man of suspicious appearance" behave strangely outside her home. Lindell looked up her address, checked the time and called up the woman.

"Admittedly I am an old woman, but I am not blind."

"I'm sure you aren't," Lindell said.

"He was all sweaty. At first I thought it was one of those who messes about."

"What do you mean?"

"They scurry back and forth."

Her voice was sharp as a saw blade. Lindell smiled to herself.

"The strange thing was he made the sign of the cross. One reads so much about religious fanatics. Do you know how old I am?"

"No," Lindell said.

"Eighty-nine this fall. On Sibylla-day."

"I wouldn't have believed it."

"No, I can't believe it myself. My husband says I am like an antelope. He is a retired forester and knows such things."

"I believe it," Lindell said, "but if we go back to the man that you saw. Why are you calling now, several days after you saw him?"

"I saw it in the paper. He looked like the one in the picture. The one you are looking for. I told Carl-Ragnar I had to call."

"That was excellent," Lindell said. "Could we possibly come by with some photographs for you to look at?"

"You will do as you like. I am home until noon. Then I have to go to the hospital."

"Nothing serious, I hope," Lindell said and immediately cursed her amateurishness.

After the conversation, which had continued for several minutes with talk about the woman's many female friends who were doing poorly, she dialed first Bea's number then changed her mind and called Sammy Nilsson instead. She gave him the delicate task of compiling a collection of pictures and visiting a charming lady who lived in Slobodan Andersson's neighborhood.

The third tip had come in that morning regarding an observation made in the vicinity of the Fyris river. A man with the unusual surname Koort from Bälinge had seen two men camping not far from Ulva mill north of Uppsala. They were foreigners and according to the notes that had been made, the man had thought they worked in the nearby strawberry fields. But when he had bumped into the farmer yesterday by the river and mentioned the two men, the farmer had denied that any of his employees were camping.

Lindell dialed the number. Mrs. Koort answered. Istvan Koort had left to go fishing.

"He will be back for lunch, hopefully without fish," his wife sighed.

"Does he have a cell phone?"

"Not when he's fishing."

"Where was he going?"

"He tends to stay around Ulva."

Lindell asked her to call as soon as he returned home.

After the three calls, Lindell felt more confident that the Alavez brothers would soon be located and arrested. The likelihood that they would manage to remain hidden in the long run were small. She checked the time. Five to nine. Time for a first cup of coffee.

At 06:43, three minutes delayed, Ryan Air flight FR51 took off from Skavsta airport outside Nyköping. Abel and Carlos Morales were on board. The check-in had gone smoothly. A brief glance in their passports, some phrases in English, and a wish that they have a good trip. That was all.

Then they had gone aboard and taken their seats without saying a single word to each other. From the window, Manuel had watched the contours of the city recede into the distance. It was his last glimpse of Sweden before he leaned back and closed his eyes.

At 07:57 local time, the plane prepared for landing at Standsted airport, north of London. Manuel drank the last of his coffee and checked his watch. A couple of minutes to nine.

✦

Epilogue

The landscape resembled a brown-green weave in which the cultivated fields were patterns in a warp consisting of the sharp mountain ridges. After a moment he grew dizzy from staring out the window and closed his eyes.

The ripple of voices of expectant travelers rose the same speed as the plane sank through the layers of air. He opened his eyes and looked around. As far as he could tell, he was the only white man in the cabin.

He folded his tray table. It had been a long trip but he would soon be at its end. If he had understood the details correctly there were buses that went up into the mountains. If not, he would have to rent a car and maybe someone to guide him. He had a generous travel kitty.

The mountains looked ominous. How could people live this way? Was it really possible to grow anything in this broken terrain?

He saw the plane's shadow on the ground. It looked like a hawk darting forward. The shadow grew clearer. They would be landing shortly.

His mission was simple. The only thing that worried him was the possibility of catching a stomach bug. He hated suffering from uncontrolled diarrhea.

Gerardo's only son, Enrico, came rushing down the alley under the Alavez family's house. Manuel and Patricio were on the roof. They had carried up sacks of coffee in order to spread the beans to dry. They saw him come running, out of breath.

"A gringo," he got out.

Manuel leaned over the fence that surrounded the roof terrace.

"What are you saying?"

"A gringo came on the bus. He is asking for you."

Manuel stared at the boy.

"For us?"

Enrico nodded avidly.

"What does he look like?"

"Like a gringo."

Manuel turned to his brother. Patricio stood frozen, an empty bag in his hand.

"Pack our things," Manuel said, running down the steps. He took a firm hold of the boy's shoulders and looked him in the eye.

"Tell me everything!"

"That is everything!"

Enrico stared at his neighbor who had never before been threatening or violent. Manuel let go of the boy and Enrico shook himself, as if he wanted to rid himself of the remaining pain from his bony shoulders.

"Follow me!"

Manuel set off down the alley, the boy at his heels. They ran along a drainage ditch, turned down toward the village center, and took the stairs. There they were forced to slow down. The stone steps were damp and slippery. They heard panting chimes from the little bell of the church.

Manuel peered out from behind the dilapidated house where the recently deceased logger Oscar Meija had made the best plows in the village. He was partly concealed by a set of stacked *yebágo*. Then he spotted the gringo. It was a tall man. A leather suitcase stood at his feet. It resembled a fallen animal. He was talking to Felix, the village idiot, the boy who never grew big or sensible. A flock of children stood nearby. The exhaust from the bus that the man had come on still hovered like a dark cloud over the square outside the veranda of the town house where the local officials of the PRI were drinking as usual.

Felix pointed first here then there, and laughed wholeheartedly. Manuel knew the gringo would get no help there. Felix pulled on the man's arm. The stranger shook him off but turned his body to see where the boy was pointing. He looked up toward the school where the faded portraits of the heroes of the revolution hung in a row, and then he turned around completely.

Manuel staggered back. The man from the mountains had returned! The man whom he had killed by slashing his throat, and then heaved into the water far away in Sweden now stood here in the flesh.

"What is it?" Enrico whimpered.

"*Bhni guí'a,*" Manuel whispered, turning around and stumbling on a pile of lumber. He got back on his feet and ran away as if he had seen an evil spirit.

Enrico remained behind uncertainly, but when he saw the gringo reach for his luggage he followed Manuel, who had now climbed to the top of the stairs and disappeared behind the bushes.

The dead return, the dead return, Manuel recited silently to himself as he ran. The tall one had not only returned, he also looked younger and healthier than when Manuel had met him in Sweden.

When Manuel stormed into the house, Patricio had packed two bags of clothes. Maria stood beside him, pulling on his shirt. She repeatedly asked them what had happened. Patricio freed himself from his mother and took a machete down from the wall without a word.

"We have to flee," Manuel said vehemently and yet controlled, as if his face had congealed into an unchanging death mask.

He grabbed his own machete and a small ax. Patricio and his mother looked fearfully at him. They had never seen him so distraught.

He went up to his mother, gave her a hug and a kiss on the cheek, took hold of one of the bags and ran out.

"We will be back," Patricio said, hugged her and left.

She followed them out into the yard where Manuel was anxiously looking into the alley. The neighbor's boy stood waiting by the gate.

"Where will you go?" the mother asked with such despair in her voice that the brothers paused for a moment.

Manuel shot Patricio a glance before he replied.

"*El norte,*" he said.